The Jaguar Legacy

Maureen Fisher

Lachesis
Publishing
www.lachesispublishing.com

Published Internationally by Lachesis Publishing
1787 Cartier Court, RR 1,
Kingston, Nova Scotia, B0P 1R0

National Library of Canada Cataloguing in Publication Data

A catalogue record for this book is available from the National Library of Canada.

ISBN 1-897370-04-0
Also available in multiple eBook formats from
www.lachesispublishing.com
ISBN 1-897370-05-9

Credit: Giovanna Lagana, editor

Dearest Cindy,

One of the biggest
inspirations in my life,
you helped me find myself,
a dear friend.

love
Maureen Fisher

Still crackling with nervous energy, Charley jumped to her feet and paced the temple. She craved movement, to touch and be touched, to re-affirm that she was still alive, safe and unhurt. To prove that life was worth living.

She needed Kincaid.

"I see you found the boots."

Charley whipped her head around at the deep, familiar voice, and blinked once. Kincaid looked different today, but she couldn't put a finger on the disparity. Then she got it. He was wearing black jeans and a black work shirt instead of his customary aloha shirt. He looked harder, more dangerous and wickedly sexy.

Her heart jackhammered in her chest as she took a step towards him. "Kincaid. Come with me." She grabbed a fistful of shirt and led him to the side of the temple where rubble performed the task of hiding them from prying eyes.

"What's this all about?" he asked, his eyes widening in surprised disbelief.

Instead of answering, she stepped forward until her body brushed against his, then threaded her fingers through his hair in unspoken invitation. He was warm and solid – a perfect antidote to the feeling of flat futility that had enveloped her since her near brush with death. A shudder of sexual delight coursed through her veins. "Kiss me, Kincaid. Hold me." Hungrily, she raised her lips, allowing a primitive mating urge to sweep her rational qualms away.

He made an inarticulate groan before drawing a finger down her neck, sending licks of flame flickering along her quivering nerves. Catching her chin in his fingers, he slanted a hot, hungry kiss on her lips. His tongue entered her mouth – firm and velvety and demanding. He was fully aroused already, taut and hard.

The cold, twisted knot deep inside her started to thaw. Ragged breathing caught in her throat. Flinging common sense to the wind, she ground her hips against his with a desperation she hadn't known she possessed and reached down to rub his erection through the fabric. Liquid fire smouldered and coiled inside her belly. If she didn't find her release soon, she'd go out of her mind.

"I need you." She gasped between ragged breaths.

"Oh, sweet Jesus. Slow down, Charley. If you do that, there'll be no turning back."

In reply, she captured his lips with her own in a frenzy of need and desire, and gave herself up to the raging inferno that consumed her. Wordlessly, she unbuttoned her blouse and brought his hand to her breast.

He kissed her neck and delved lower. She could swear he muttered: "*Mhuirnin*."

"More," she panted and arched her back, allowing her head to fall backwards and exposing her throat and breasts to his questing lips. A wave of primal heat tightened her body. Through filmy lace, he captured her nipple between his teeth and tugged. Dimly, she heard her soft, throaty whimpers turn into urgent entreaties. An unbearable pressure built between her thighs and she tugged his shirt loose then raked her fingers down his back, aching to feel the touch of flesh against flesh.

Dazed and throbbing, lost in the searing blaze of sensation, she tugged his shirt out of his jeans. Why did they make the damned fasteners so difficult to undo?

DEDICATION

To my husband, Jiri, whose collaboration made this book possible.

With saintly patience, he helped develop the plot, read every word (countless times), provided insight into the mysteries of the masculine mindset, held my hand, gave me confidence when things got tough, fed me chocolate, and applauded my efforts during the entire process.

ACKNOWLEDGEMENTS

Au author never writes a book in isolation. For that reason, I offer my thanks and appreciation to all of those who helped me in this endeavour: to Shirley King, energy healer, who helped me decide what I wanted to be when I grew up; to Kathryn Smith, who taught the 5-day seminar on Writing a Novel, which jump-started my book; to Andrew Roddick, who gave me the inside scoop on life on an archaeological dig; to my great writing group, Alex Anderson, Cora Von Hampeln, Dawn Lamarche, and Erika Bertram, for their off-the-wall ideas and thorough critique; to Tammy Beals, who taught me about deep third person point of view; to Peggy Rasmussen and Keira Morgan for fun brainstorming sessions and laughter; to Sandra Hickey, my critique partner; to LeeAnn Lessard, my publicist, who is teaching me the ropes about the business; to Carole Spencer, publisher, who took a chance on a beginning writer; to Giovanna Lagana, my brilliant editor, who acted as my cheering section throughout the entire editorial process and helped me double the suspense of my book.

The Jaguar Legacy

Prologue

Wracked with chills and nausea, the high priest lay on the stone floor of the sacred space, curled into a foetal ball. Fire flickered in the stone-ringed pit, its feeble flames barely dispelling the inky darkness.

His agony was more than the familiar price of a drug-fuelled trance. Communion with his bestial god had already shown him far more than he had ever expected, ever dreamed of, ever dreaded. Death approached, padding towards him through the jungle on sure, silent feet, just like the Master of Darkness, the Jaguar God he worshipped. A worm of apprehension writhed in his belly. His end would be violent and bloody. And it would be soon. Too soon.

Shuddering, he dragged himself to a sitting position and added fuel to the glowing embers. He had not yet finished with those flames – the same flames that had disclosed his death. Crouching shadows retreated, banished by the sudden flare of brilliance. "This time, I shall harness your power to serve my purposes," he whispered on a long, slow breath. "This time, you shall disclose the identity of my successor before all is lost."

He chewed another peyote button and swallowed the pulp. Bile pooled in his mouth, leaving a bitter aftertaste, but the drug transported him deeper into his trance. Something inside expanded, and once again, dark energy surged into his body. He stared into the fire, knowing the flames would provide the answers he sought, if only he could ignore the encroaching darkness that waited to pounce. He stiffened his spine. "Show me the answers I need," he commanded, satisfied with the renewed note of authority in his voice.

In response, the flames parted to disclose the image of a woman.

He studied her face, dismayed by a jolt of recognition. Sparked by the irony of his successor's identity, a bubble of mirthless laughter escaped his lips. Even though this woman possessed the raw talent he sought, he had never once considered contacting her.

Flames flared in a shower of sparks that drew his attention to a flicker of movement in the heart of the fire. He leaned in closer. A second form emerged from the flames, dancing and shimmering, coalescing into a dark shape that dwarfed the woman.

The priest's heartbeat thundered in his ears. "Who are you, and what do you want?" he whispered in a hoarse voice, his mouth so dry he could hardly move his lips.

The mysterious figure expanded, its outline rippling and shifting, wavering and solidifying. At last, the movement ceased. A feline face hovered, motionless, above the woman's head. The phantom jaguar opened its mouth in a silent snarl.

As if stirred by an invisible hand, a bright burst of flames shot up amidst billows of acrid smoke, concealing both figures. When the air cleared, a pair of jaguars now writhed and twisted in a sinuous struggle within the pyre before fire consumed them both.

An overwhelming queasiness coiled in the priest's gut. This would be no ordinary rivalry. The challenger would try to destroy the legacy of dark powers bestowed on the priests, handed down from master to acolyte for over two millennia.

His trivial death no longer mattered. Before the darkness claimed him, he must summon his chosen successor to his side to prepare her for the battle ahead – the battle for supremacy.

Mesmerized, he stared into the fire, which danced in the low breeze carrying the heartbreaking fragrance of the Mexican jungle into the cavern. The flames would act as a conduit to the woman. She would hear and obey his summons, drawn by the potent lure of unlimited power.

Chapter 1

The searing heat felt like a sauna on overdrive.

This may not have been my most brilliant idea.

Charley Underhill's arms windmilled to fend off squadrons of bloodthirsty insects swarming her head with ravenous persistence. She now failed to see the wisdom of the impetuous decision that had seemed so brilliant after one martini, hold the olive, and three glasses of Pinot Grigio. While mulling over her troubled life in the smoky nightclub called *El Patio Grande*, barging into Dr. Kincaid's archaeological field camp to sniff out the scoop of the decade had seemed like a brilliant solution to her problems – almost as if someone or, more accurately, *something*, had taken control of her thoughts and actions. Now, broiling under a white-hot sun with only an arrogant fellow passenger for company, her optimism faltered.

"Ouch! Dammit." She squashed the sparrow-sized mosquito. Shading her eyes and swallowing hard around the lump in her throat, she peered into the distance. The six-seater floatplane – her only link with civilization – had dwindled into faded blue infinity. When the last engine-throb died away, she sighed once and scanned the shore, searching for signs of human habitation.

Scalding heat burned through her thin-soled sneakers and mosquitoes continued their relentless attack. An impenetrable wall of sweetgum trees and cypresses furred the shores of the Mexican lagoon. Where were the buildings, the roads, *the people*? Hell, where was Dr. Kincaid's welcoming committee? Someone must have heard the infernal whirring of the plane.

She cleared her throat. "Hello-o-o," she yodelled in her most ladylike tone.

Only the insolent whine of insects broke the silence.

Louder, more assertive, she tried again. "Anybody home?"

A mocking echo boomed back. "*Home ... home ... home.*"

Charley rolled her eyes, sucked in a lungful of air, and bellowed: "Is everybody in this hell-hole deaf?"

Thankfully, nobody replied. Her unfortunate tendency to babble her innermost thoughts before her brain kicked into censorship mode often landed her in hot water.

"Dumb, dumb, dumb," she muttered. An edgy display of temper would only compound her elusive quarry's displeasure. There was no doubt in Charley's mind that Dr. Alistair Kincaid would be angry enough to kick some serious butt when he found an eager investigative journalist, uninvited and panting for a story, camped on his doorstep.

She mouthed the headline etched on her brain: "*Secret of Ancient Curse Revealed.*"

A frosty feminine voice intruded on Charley's musings. "I wouldn't hold my breath waiting for a rescue team if I were you."

Charley whirled around to face her haughty fellow passenger, who had draped herself with a piece of designer luggage. Exotic Ice Queen had sauntered into the floatplane terminal and sweet-talked a ride, all the time ignoring Charley while she flirted with the pilot to wheedle an immediate departure.

Charley stared at her companion's knowing little smile with mild irritation. "What are you talking about? Of course someone will come."

Ice Queen checked her watch. "The plane landed almost an hour early, so don't count on a welcoming committee. The crew is probably taking a siesta."

The superior tone set Charley on edge. "I can wait."

"Suit yourself. After I touch up my makeup, I'm heading out to the dig. That's where Alistair is sure to be."

Alistair? Exactly how well did Exotic Ice Queen know Dr. Kincaid? Charley feigned disinterest with a dismissive shrug. "You can't possibly know that."

Exotic Ice Queen cast a sharp glance in Charley's

direction and drawled: "Alistair and I go back a long time. I happen to know he loves to be alone with his artefacts, especially when the rest of his team is taking a siesta. Do whatever you want, but just make sure you don't follow me."

Seething inwardly, Charley repressed a sarcastic rejoinder. "Certainly. I wouldn't want to intrude. I'll head for the camp."

"Don't get lost. Jaguars live out there."

Charley spared her a long look. "Don't be ridiculous. Jaguars don't attack humans."

"Some do." Exotic Ice Queen smirked. "*The New York Times* claimed there was a recent jaguar attack in this area."

Although Charley had read the same article, she shrugged off the cold shiver trickling down her spine and injected a note of moronic optimism into her voice. "I'm sure there's nothing to worry about."

"Don't say I didn't warn you."

Grunting, Charley wriggled into her backpack, looped the camera around her neck, and hoisted the duffel bag, then finally the laptop over her shoulder. Without a backwards glance, she staggered past Exotic Ice Queen and down the dock towards the palisade of trees festooned with hanging vines and mosses.

At the end of the dock, Charley obeyed the pilot's directions and turned left on the footpath that followed the shoreline. Tropical jungle immediately enclosed her in a cacophony of noise. Honking, chirping, clacking, screeching, rustling, and croaking filled the air. She inhaled a deep breath and grimaced. The fragrant scent of orchids did little to mask the jungle stench of moist earth overlaid by a darker odour of decaying vegetation and stagnant water. After ten paces, she faltered, lurched to a halt, and eyed the encroaching jungle with aversion. Sure, she had visited plenty of exotic locations for travel articles in the last few years, but this one was – *different.* An ominous undercurrent of pulsing energy prickled down her stiffened spine.

Unnerved by her illogical fear, she shuddered and picked up her pace again, picturing countless unseen furry and scaly creatures swarming, scurrying, and writhing through the underbrush only a few feet away from where she stood. She could almost feel a myriad of beady eyes boring into her back. With a small whimper, she straightened her shoulders and picked up her pace, keeping a wary eye peeled for hungry, hairy predators.

Charley consoled herself with the well-known theory that all natural noises ceased when big trouble crept up. Hopefully, the rumour was true.

The duffel bag gained weight with every step she took and the strap dug deeper into her throbbing shoulder. Halfway up a steep incline, she dropped her burden and plopped down beside it to wait until her breathing slowed to normal.

At first, the resonance was almost imperceptible. Heart pounding in her chest, she tilted her head to capture the sound and concentrated. Sure enough, the all-too-familiar buzz, reminiscent of a swarm of wasps filled the air. She clamped her teeth together to prevent them from chattering. The gesture of defiance did nothing to dispel the alarming sound that heralded another panic attack.

"Not again," she muttered in disbelief. "I'm supposed to be cured!"

The humming intensified and throbbed into her skull drowning out all other noises. Icy wind buffeted her body with powerful gales and sucked her breath away, stifling the howl lodged in her throat. This time, she felt she might not survive the attack. Helpless, she surrendered to a force she couldn't control.

Little by little, sensations receded, leaving Charley clammy and trembling. She opened her eyes to a foreboding and incomprehensible silence. Footpath, trees and rocky incline had disappeared, supplanted by graceful columns, which soared towards a carved wooden roof. Rocklike knobs jabbed her lower back, sending stabs of pain shooting up her spine. Her paralyzed body refused to obey her brain's command to shift to a more comfortable position.

In an attempt to conduct a self-survey, Charley rolled her eyes downward. A granite armrest supported an unfamiliar arm encased in jade-studded armbands from elbow to wrist.

The hand attached to the arm, bronzed and elegant, appeared smaller than her own, the fingers daintier and shorter. Artificial nails curved into elongated claws.

Fighting the panic bubbling in the back of her throat, she sucked in a shuddering breath. The other hand – she had difficulty viewing it as *her* hand – lay in her lap and cradled a human skull. Not just any skull, but a work of art made of volcanic glass overlaid with a mosaic of turquoise and coral. Inlaid mother-of-pearl eyes gazed back and what looked suspiciously like human teeth grinned in a permanent rictus of a smile.

The skull signifies the continuation of life after death.

Dammit. How did she know that? She took a long, deep breath and dredged up every ounce of mental strength she possessed to vanquish the horrifying hallucination.

And fell into a dark endless void.

The wavering call of a songbird penetrated the blackness that clouded Charley's brain. She stretched out one arm tentatively, then the other, rotating her wrists. Swallowing hard, she then twisted the turquoise ring on her middle finger, comforted by its familiar weight.

Oh, God! She must be losing her mind. Whatever she was experiencing, *this* wasn't her typical panic attack. This time, she could swear she'd been inside another woman's body – someone powerful, someone ruthless, someone, well … *evil*. Perhaps her true diagnosis should have been a multiple personality disorder.

Several inventive and unpleasant punishments for her shrink flashed through her mind. Three months ago, the therapist had nodded sagely and handed her some psychobabble about hallucinations, visual distortions, and panic attacks. The episodes, he informed her, would disappear, given enough Prozac, a change of scenery, and adequate rest. Bottom line – the quack didn't have a clue. Whatever their origin, the baffling attacks had ended her career.

Charley swiped the back of her arm over her face and straightened her spine. It would take more than a few lousy hallucinations to put this investigative journalist out of commission. All she needed was one kick-ass exposé to salvage her pride, her reputation, and her career. More to the point, a hefty cash advance would allow her to secure the essential treatment her mother needed. A few weeks in rehab and her mother would be as good as new.

She hoped.

When her heart rate descended out of the red-alert danger zone and her breathing returned to normal, she heaved herself upright and bounced on her feet in preparation for the final push to the summit. A snicker of semi-hysterical laughter bubbled from her lips. She was only climbing a puny incline, not scaling Mount Everest.

Grunting, she heaved the duffel bag to her shoulder once more, lowered her head, and ploughed up the steepest part. At the top, she sucked in a deep breath and scrutinized the criss-cross of roots and rocks studding the path ahead. Picking her way around the obstacles, she progressed slowly at first, then faster and faster, gaining momentum under the weight of her bag, until her feet moved in a frenetic step dance.

Chirping their alarm, a flock of tiny black and white birds burst from the jungle canopy ahead. The warning came too late. Still concentrating on her footing, Charley crashed into a warm, unyielding wall of muscle, and bounced backwards. A startled squeak popped out of her mouth.

"Oomph." The intruder gasped, clutching his stomach.

In slow motion, she teetered, lost her balance, and sprawled backward into a mossy depression beside the path, both hands clutching her camera out of harm's way. The backpack anchored her to the ground as effectively as a ball and chain.

A dark form blocked the sunlight.

She raised her head and squinted at the blue and maroon Argyle socks arising from scuffed hiking boots planted on either side of her knees.

Charley blinked. What kind of person wore Argyle socks in the jungle?

She allowed her gaze to travel up the endless pair of hairy legs straddling the path. Powerful thighs, bronzed and mouth-watering, ended at a pair of frayed khaki shorts encasing lean hips. A fuchsia aloha shirt, hideous in its fluorescence and patterned with palm trees and large-breasted hula dancers, completed the stylish ensemble.

She forced herself to look at his face while containing the insane urge to snicker at the incongruous socks. Tabloid photographs didn't come close to capturing the utterly masculine, almost elemental appearance of Dr. Alistair Kincaid.

She let out a tiny moan of mortification as the last faint hopes of making a professional first impression vaporized.

"Good God! Where did you come from? Are you hurt, lassie?" His deep voice rumbled over her, as smooth and rich as heavy cream. A dark, worried gaze swept over her sprawled frame. "You must be the geophysicist I'm expecting. But why a week early?"

A tidal wave of hormones coursed through Charley's veins leaving her limp and liquid with desire. The slight Scottish lilt completed her fast melt. Desperately aware that her curls had corkscrewed into a tangled mass of unruly frizz, likely resembling Medusa on a bad hair day, she struggled to come up with something clever to say. All that emerged was a hoarse croak. Quivering inside, she settled for a brief head nod. She could set him straight on the little issue of mistaken identity later. Much later.

He squatted beside her, chocolate velvet eyes positioned only inches from her own and brimming with concern.

"You could have killed yourself," he admonished. His musical accent made the words sound like a flowery compliment. "You should never run downhill unless you're sure of your footing."

Too true. This was hardly the sophisticated and businesslike image she'd hoped to project. She strained to rise and flopped back, humiliating herself further before finding her voice. "Ah, Dr. Kincaid, I presume?"

He swept aside her embarrassed attempt at levity. "Is anything broken? I hope you haven't sprained your ankle."

She moved her legs experimentally. "Everything's fine. And it wasn't your fault. I wasn't watching where I was going."

Before she realized his intentions, a large, warm hand grasped her right calf and capable fingers prodded her ankle, enticing a moan from her again, this time in ecstasy. He uttered a soft noise of satisfaction in the back of his throat and turned his attention to the other ankle.

Electric heat, unwelcome and bewildering, sizzled up her legs and nestled at the junction of her thighs. *Down, girl. Don't even consider going there again. Men, especially droolworthy hunks like this one, will only break your heart.*

"Nothing seems to be broken," he confirmed, kneading her flesh. "I hope you brought the new Geo-Survey magnetometer with you. I have something important I want you to scan as soon as possible."

"Um...." She gulped, feeling at a disadvantage as she struggled with the straps. How could she formulate a credible cover story, spread-eagled at his feet like a starfish?

A note of perplexity entered his voice. "What happened to the plane? I heard it leave. The pilot usually stays for a bite to eat and some gossip with our cook."

She bought herself some time before confessing her identity. "Uh ... do you think you could help me to stand? I can't seem to...."

A quick smile cut a brilliant slash through the two-day growth of heavy stubble. "You remind me of a turtle flipped on its back, legs kicking in the air."

She gazed in hypnotic fascination at the row of strong, even teeth. *All the better to eat you with*, she thought wildly, remembering his reputation with women. Apparently, jaguars weren't the only danger lurking in this jungle.

She gritted her teeth. "Do you think this is funny? Just help me up."

He let his hand linger a moment longer, then released her foot, leaving behind a warm tingle. No wonder women flung themselves blindly in his direction like lemmings scurrying towards a cliff.

"Always willing to oblige a beautiful woman who throws herself at me." He unhooked the straps that anchored her to the backpack and rose to his feet. "Here, give me your hand. We'll see to your equipment right away. I assume it's on the dock."

She could have sworn a glint of masculine approval lurked in his eyes.

Feeling positively petite for the first time in her life, she steeled herself against her visceral reaction and allowed him to hoist her upright. An unobtrusive knee flex confirmed everything was in working order. She turned away to hide the hot rush of blood to her face and brushed a dusting of twigs and mud from her butt. "Um ... thank you," she mumbled, hoping her conversational skills would improve over time.

For one heart-stopping moment, they locked gazes. He slid his arrogant inspection down to the camera she still clutched to her chest. Perhaps it was only her imagination, but she was certain his smile congealed.

Her heart twisted. She had a sneaking suspicion he had figured out her profession, but in case she was mistaken, she bent down with studied nonchalance and stuffed the camera into her pack, hoping he hadn't noticed the top-of-the-line brand name.

"You're not the geophysicist, are you?

Uh, oh. She shook her head.

"And that's not a portable magnetometer. It's a camera."

She nodded.

"Pretty fancy camera to be toting around the jungle." His glacial voice erased all trace of affability.

Her heart pumped a little harder. "Thanks. I like it."

"Aye. Professional quality." His eyes glinted with mistrust. A stray sunbeam teased out golden flecks dancing in their rich brown depths as his gaze probed her face, undoubtedly for traces of guilt. "We don't see too many cameras like that out here."

She fought the foolish alarm compressing her heart and practised looking innocent. "I like good equipment," she shot back. His dark brows drew together, and he mimicked a perplexed frown. "Now why would a beautiful stranger trespass on an archaeological dig while lugging around a big, expensive camera?" He looked as if he harboured several theories, none of them happy.

"I—"

He raised a hand to still her forthcoming explanation. "Wait. Don't tell me. Let me guess. You're not visiting anyone in camp because I authorize all our guests' visits." His frown deepened into a scowl. "I know. Might you be an innocent tourist who decided on a solitary exploration of this jungle paradise?"

Charley opened her mouth to interject.

He shook his head and spoke first. "Nope. You don't look that daft."

This wasn't going as well as she'd hoped. Too much was at stake to let the story slip through her fingers. "If you would let me explain—"

He cut her off again, his voice light and conversational. "Maybe you're an archaeologist trying to poach on my turf. I got rid of one of those last month. Sent him packing on the return flight."

Yeah, right. He was playing games, toying with her. A cleansing surge of irritation washed over Charley. "Now look here—"

He bared his teeth in a parody of a smile. "Or you could be a reporter searching for sensational gossip." His eyes narrowed. "My money's on the reporter," he said, his accent thickening.

The direction of this conversation was not in her best interest, and she'd been taught that the best defence was a good offence. She straightened her shoulders and looked him straight in the eye. "You haven't answered my question yet. You *are* Dr. Alistair Kincaid, aren't you? I've seen your face often enough in the gossip columns. I'm sure you dated some up-and-coming Hollywood star, Angelina-something-or-other, not to mention several dozen of San Francisco's most beautiful women. I hate to break it to you like this, but you're not living up to your reputation for manly charm."

His eyes flinty, Kincaid flicked off the predatory smile. "Aye, I'm Alistair Kincaid. Exactly who are you and why are you here?" In spite of his inhospitable words, he held out his hand.

This, at least, was progress. She forced herself to unclench her fist and clasped the outstretched hand. His firm grip engulfed her fingers sending a tingle up her arm. Her toes curled in an involuntary movement and she held on for dear life. "I'm Charley Underhill. Nice to meet you, Dr.

Kincaid."

His mouth tightened. "Call me Kincaid or Alistair." He extracted his hand from her clutching fingers. "We're not too much on formality around here."

"Right." She flicked a meaningful glance at his appalling socks. "I can see that."

"Charley," he repeated in an abstracted tone. "Unusual name for a woman."

"Charlotte Ophelia Underhill. Everyone calls me Charley. With an 'e-y'."

Recognition, followed by irritation, flickered across his face. "I only know of one other woman named 'Charley' with an 'e-y' – a San Francisco reporter noted for her exposés."

Charley stared at him, wordless.

"She blew the whistle on an illegal alien scandal. If I remember correctly, she screwed up during the assignment, nearly killed herself and her passenger in a car accident, and made the local headlines. I only paid attention because the driver was a reporter who had interviewed a couple of men who'd worked for me."

Right. The same two men who fled for their lives from your expedition and first raised my suspicions about your connection with the mysterious accidents plaguing the Olmec digs.

Charley's stomach knotted. Kincaid knew the grisly details of her disgrace.

He shrugged then shot her an intimidating stare. Mistrust saturated his voice. "Well, Charley with an 'e-y'. You shouldn't believe the gossip about my love life that you read in the tabloids. Reporters exaggerate and lie to manufacture a good story."

She felt an outraged flush start under the collar of her shirt and creep up her neck, knowing it had painted her face a fiery red. How could she have felt even the tiniest twinge of attraction for this churlish lout?

The liquid warble of a distant bird echoed in the ensuing silence. The searing heat stole every bit of moisture from her body.

His dark gaze drilled into her face – as if he were trying to plunder her thoughts. "Am I correct in assuming you're the reporter I described?" Kincaid stepped closer, invading her space, his body crowding her own.

Charley backed away and stumbled on an uneven patch of rock before she righted herself, her mouth full of cotton. A sudden awareness of her precarious situation washed over her. She had expected a challenge, but she hadn't expected to wander alone in the jungle, encountering intimidating and very large, albeit incredibly attractive, strangers. If he intended to browbeat her, he would be pleased to know he'd succeeded beyond his wildest dreams.

She sucked in a deep, fortifying breath, moistened her lips, and struck a defiant pose, thumbs stuck in her belt. He must never know how nervous she felt. "Okay, Kincaid. You've blown my cover. I confess. I'm the investigative journalist you described so tactfully, and I work for *The Golden Gate Times*." She swallowed. "At least I used to. I'm not so sure I still do."

"*Imigh sa diabhal*," Kincaid muttered.

That didn't sound like a compliment.

He let the silence stretch out until her nerves quivered.

Good interviewing technique. Her foot began tapping a nervous rhythm on the ground. *Forces the subject to spill her guts.* She had used it herself with great success.

He raked his fingers through dark wavy hair.

Good. He wasn't as calm as he appeared. She must demonstrate both confidence and firmness. She tightened her lips and resisted the urge to look away, determined to outwait her tormentor.

After thirty endless seconds, Kincaid sighed and caved first. "Okay. I'll bite. Why has *The Golden Gate Times* star reporter graced us with her presence?"

"Investigative journalist," she corrected, as if dealing with an obstinate child and stopped, listening. Was he grinding his teeth? Hastily, she arranged an earnest expression on her face and looked him straight in the eye, hoping she could convince him of her innocence. "It's rather a long story," she began.

He crossed his arms on his chest and leaned his lanky frame against a tree trunk. "I have all the time in the world."

She chewed on her lower lip and rocketed up a silent

prayer that he wouldn't detect the lie she would tell. Well, not so much an outright lie as a truth evasion. No way would she utter the dreaded words 'stress leave' or 'panic attack' – words that had all but terminated her career. She cleared her throat and began with: "I've been on an extended leave of absence, recovering from an illness."

He made a non-committal sound in the back of his throat that only Scots could make and quirked one dark eyebrow.

She took it as permission to continue. "Now it's time to get back in the saddle."

Kincaid pushed himself away from the tree and skewered her with a glare. "How did you hear about my dig?"

Charley shifted from one foot to another. She wanted to sit down on a log, but didn't intend to give him an additional height advantage. She paused, searching for the right words. "I was recuperating at a friend's villa in Puerto Escondido." *While tracking down the elusive Dr. Kincaid.*

"Go on."

Thus encouraged, she jabbered on. "I heard a rumor about your dig. A man claiming to have worked for you was shooting his mouth off in a local bar. You know, mysterious clues, lost city, hidden treasure, that kind of thing." Charley snapped her mouth shut to prevent more involuntary babble.

The crease between Kincaid's eyebrows deepened. "Aye. Daniel. I fired him a couple of months ago. So you heard about this place on the pub circuit and decided to drop in for a quick visit, did you?"

Charley cringed. Phrased that way, it sounded highly unlikely. "Not exactly. I conducted a thorough investigation first," she countered, wishing he'd drop the topic.

Kincaid shot her an exasperated look. "Get to the point."

Charley rattled on, avoiding his eyes. "A human interest article about your mysterious lost city and the ancient race inhabiting it, the Olmecs, would raise your prestige. Maybe help with your funding. I hope to sell it to *National Geographic*." That was much better. More businesslike. No need to mention the Curse of the Olmecs. Especially, if Kincaid was implicated in the series of tragedies that had afflicted the sites.

He rubbed the side of his nose thoughtfully while his

voice dropped to an ominous rumble. "How did you manage to find me?"

She forced her voice to exude bright perkiness. "I greased a few palms, and guess what? Your pilot volunteered to fly me in, for the appropriate remuneration, of course."

"I'll wring his scrawny little neck when I get my hands on him. See if he ever gets another free meal from me. He should know better than to bring a stranger to the site."

"Don't punish him." Charley cleared her throat, hoping to gain enough courage to confess the truth. "I told him you had invited me."

"You didn't consider phoning me first to get permission?"

Charley's mind screamed, *Keep your mouth shut, you idiot. Sarcasm will only make matters worse.* Ignoring her wise advice, she tossed the businesslike approach to the wind and ploughed ahead. "You're not exactly listed in the telephone book. Perhaps you could explain where I should have looked – under 'K' for 'Kincaid' or 'S' for 'Secret Archaeological Dig'?"

His lips twitched. "Why do I think there's more to your story than meets the eye?"

His searching gaze made her want to squirm. It galled her that he'd hit the nail on the head. The man's radar for truth evasion rivalled a polygraph test. The CIA should consider hiring him. "Dammit, Kincaid, I had hoped you'd appreciate a sympathetic article about your dig."

The scowl returned. "Wrong."

"Hey, I'm on your side. Word of your hidden city is bound to leak out."

"It already has."

"So far, nothing concrete, only rumours. I thought you'd want to give the story your own slant before someone else does. Sorry. My mistake." She stooped and picked up her backpack. "Let's go. We can't stand here all day."

He didn't raise his voice. He didn't need to. "Let me repeat – I don't want any stories or articles leaking out, sympathetic or otherwise."

His quiet vehemence was more disconcerting than outright ranting. Taken aback, she let her backpack fall to the ground and faced him. "It's inevitable. I'm only trying to help."

Kincaid combed his fingers through his hair again, then stopped. His head now looked like a poorly mowed lawn with unexpected tufts sticking out at random. When he spoke, bitterness laced his voice. "The day a member of the press helps me will be the day hell freezes."

Although several retorts, all of them rude, hovered on her lips, Charley struggled to remain calm. "No need to use that tone with me, Kincaid. I'm a journalist, not a tabloid reporter trying to dig up some smut."

"You're all cut from the same cloth."

She drew herself up to her full, impressive height of six feet, and still fell short of his eye level. "I'll have you know I'm a highly respected investigative journalist." Unthinking, she poked him in the chest to emphasize her point.

He restrained her from a second stab by grabbing her wrist, eyes narrowed into glacial slits. "Careful where you jab the finger, lady."

Her skin tingled under his grip. Appalled at her lack of professionalism, she jerked her arm away. "Sorry. Inappropriate behaviour," she muttered, then rallied. "But I thought you would appreciate a well-written article."

His voice roughened. "You're about to spread word of my dig far and wide and you think I should be grateful? Have you any idea how difficult it is to keep an archaeological discovery under wraps? How much damage you could do?"

Yeah, she had a pretty good idea. Shrugging, Charley ignored the twinge of conscience that threatened to undermine her resolve. She viewed any fallout from her article as collateral damage in the battle against her mother's alcoholism – accidental, regrettable, but justified.

"Damage?" she echoed, feigning innocence.

Kincaid rolled his eyes and threw up his hands to address an invisible audience in the canopy above. His brogue thickened with every mouthful of words, becoming virtually indecipherable. "Why don't we just install flashing neon signs in the jungle to invite thieves, bandits and envious archaeologists to swarm all over the site, shall we?"

Charley concentrated all her attention on his lips, trying to understand his accent.

"Signs saying 'Help yourself' or 'Dig Here for Priceless

Treasure'."

She perked up at the thought of a priceless treasure.

"Then I won't need to worry about unwanted visitors—" He broke off with a glare, then ended his tirade in a dramatic crescendo, "Because robbers will plunder the site and leave nothing of value for trespassers like you to gawk at."

Charley refused to give him the satisfaction of seeing her quake. Nothing and no one would stop her from writing an exposé to save her mother's life. "Sounds like you've made an important discovery." Her heart thundered at the possibility.

He drew his eyebrows together and rubbed his forehead, as if erasing lurking pain. "Look, Charley, There's more at stake here than you could ever guess. I can't afford any leaks until I'm certain I can protect.... " He broke off, probably aware he'd already said too much.

Protect what? Kincaid was onto something big and she'd stumbled into the middle of it. Suddenly, acquiring the fat fee for the Betty Ford Center didn't seem like such a remote possibility.

Kincaid eyed her warily, no doubt anticipating an inquisition.

She conjured up her best angelic smile. "Are we ready?"

He sighed. "I guess you'll have to sleep here, at least for tonight. The idiot pilot should have checked with me before taking off."

"You really know how to make a guest feel at home."

Kincaid cursed. "Bloody hell, woman. Are you always such a pain in the ass? I'd bundle you into the truck and drive you back myself, mournful eyes and all, if last night's downpour hadn't turned the goat path of a road into a quagmire." He eyed her balefully.

Charley's stomach flip-flopped. Naturally, there must be a road. She'd been a fool to overlook the small, crucial detail. She should have figured he'd own a truck. How else would he ferry in heavy supplies and equipment? Thank God for the rain.

"Too bad about the mud. So, where do I sleep?"

Her face must have mirrored her relief because Kincaid growled: "Don't start the celebration yet. I'll radio the pilot to haul his sorry ass back here tomorrow at first light. I can't have a nosy reporter—"

"Investigative journalist," Charley corrected.

He gave her a dark look. "As I was saying, I can't have a nosy reporter snooping around here, no matter how attractive she is. You'll be out of here before noon tomorrow. Count on it."

Charley suppressed a triumphant smirk. "Think again, Kincaid. The pilot has a six-day charter to Costa Rica, signed, sealed, and waiting. He won't return for another week." The Universe did, indeed, deliver.

The dismay on his face was almost comical. "No. Tell me it's not true."

"You won't find another pilot in the entire state of Oaxaca," she assured him. "I had to check the flights and nearly gave up before I found your pilot."

Kincaid's lips tightened into a compressed line of exasperation. "We'll see about that. In the meantime, don't leave camp."

"But—"

"And don't even *consider* sneaking off to the dig. As far as you're concerned, it's off limits."

He must be a mind reader. Charley looked away and studied the curtain of moss trailing from a branch behind his head, then straightened her shoulders and stiffened her spine. He'd soon learn he couldn't keep her a prisoner in camp.

Before she could open her mouth to utter a rejoinder, he stared grimly at a point behind her head and barked: "What the hell—" His inscrutable expression gave away nothing of his feelings, though a muscle in his cheek flickered.

"Dear God." He sucked in a shuddering breath and fixed Charley with an accusing glare. "Why the hell didn't you tell me *she* was here, too?"

Charley whirled around and stared. She masked her groan with a discrete cough and resisted the urge to smack herself on the forehead. How could she have forgotten Exotic Ice Queen?

The woman stood at the top of the incline, makeup flawless, a halo of sunlight glinting off the sweep of black hair and outlining graceful curves.

Charley loved riddles, and this one, she suspected, would soon be resolved.

Chapter 2

Charley couldn't tear her eyes away from Kincaid as he gaped at the woman posed at the top of the incline. He looked as if someone had sucker-punched him. A combination of fury, hurt and some other indecipherable emotion flickered across his face before a polite social mask descended.

Kincaid's intriguing reaction set all of Charley's journalistic instincts a-twitching. She edged away and brushed a spider off her arm before plunking herself down on a partially concealed log – an inconspicuous seat for the pending drama – wishing her tape recorder wasn't at the bottom of her backpack.

Kincaid sighed once, almost imperceptibly, squared his broad shoulders, and waited for the woman to tiptoe down the incline. His face revealed nothing except courtesy. "Leila. You are the last person on Earth I expected to see."

So Exotic Ice Queen had a name.

"Alistair! Darling! What a climb! How marvellous to see you again," she trilled, ignoring Charley's presence as if a journalist was beneath her notice.

Charley rolled her eyes. How phony could you get? Why do men allow themselves to be taken in by gorgeous women?

The husky voice carried on the still air as, arms outstretched, Leila approached Kincaid. "I can't believe it's been two whole years since we've seen one another. You look wonderful."

Kincaid sidestepped the intended hug, eyes frigid in his calm face. "So do you."

A tiny worry line appeared between Leila's eyes and faded so quickly, Charley wondered if the flicker had been real or merely a figment of her imagination. The smile had lost none of its brilliance although Kincaid's lukewarm greeting must have smarted.

"I tried to find you at the dig, but the *sweetest* security guard told me you'd stayed in camp after lunch, so I decided to track you down in camp."

He raised one eyebrow. "You've been up to the dig already? Fast work." His eyes narrowed. "This is the first time anyone ever referred to one of my guards as 'sweet'. I didn't hire them for their disposition. He probably booted your shapely ass off the dig."

Obviously undaunted, Leila reached for one of Kincaid's hands and held it captive in both of hers, effectively preventing his escape. "What a time I've had," she gushed, gazing up and giving him the full impact of her luminous eyes. "I missed you so much."

Charley allocated maximum points to Leila for using the ample ammunition Nature had bestowed.

"My life has been meaningless since I saw you last," Leila continued, seemingly undeterred by Kincaid's lack of response. "I need to tell you all about it. We have so much to catch up on."

His chest rose and fell in a gusty sigh. "So talk."

Leila shot a meaningful glance in Charley's direction. "Couldn't we go somewhere a little more private to chat?"

Charley pretended to be invisible.

Kincaid's mouth had tightened to the point where a white line rimmed his lips. He extricated himself by patting Leila's arm in a friendly gesture, then gently liberating his trapped hand. "I don't want to appear unfeeling, Leila, but you and I have nothing to discuss," he said lightly. "I said my piece to you two years ago."

Charley nearly fell off the log, straining to hear the low-pitched conversation. *What had happened two years ago?* She wished she could exert a fraction of the self-control Kincaid exhibited. His voice was calm and controlled, even friendly, although powerful emotions obviously seethed beneath the urbane surface. She'd love to scratch his veneer to find out what lay bubbling underneath.

"A lot has changed since then," Leila said softly.

"Aye, it has," he conceded, a glint of suspicion in his eye.

"What's wrong, Leila? Are you in trouble? Word is out, your project's been cancelled."

Her eyes flickered, then steadied again, as if determining the appropriate reaction to his simple statement. She settled on a wide-eyed, innocent gaze. "You didn't believe the silly old gossip, did you?"

"I heard you'd doctored your project results, just like you did on our last dig together when you seeded the site with artefacts. No wonder I couldn't raise enough funding this time. The archaeological community has a long memory for hoaxes."

Now Kincaid's lament about high stakes made more sense. Leila had destroyed his reputation along with her own. So how had he scraped up the money for his project?

Leila flushed and glossed over his jibe about her unethical conduct. "This time, my findings were perfectly sound. There was a stupid misunderstanding over a clerical error, and some spineless cretin claimed the results were suspect. The project is temporarily on hold. Management at the Institute is looking for ways to direct more funding to me. I'm sure it'll come through any day now and we can staff up again."

Yeah, right. Any century now.

Kincaid leaned against a tree and crossed one ankle over the other, his gaze speculative. "Who are you trying to kid, Leila? You thrive on politics and intrigue. You always did." He hooked a thumb in his pocket. "By the way, the academic grapevine is buzzing with the story of how your fancy Institute boyfriend – you know, the high-flyer you dumped me for – slithered away with his administrative assistant just before he recommended that your project be killed."

Leila's musical laughter rang out and she tossed her head in a way that caused the polished blue-black curtain of hair to swing over her shoulder. "Ridiculous stories are so easily spread, darling. Some people," she furrowed her brow, "I won't mention names, but suffice it to say, I have a few enemies who are jealous of my influence and success. They would love to see me fall flat on my face. You were right about one thing, though. Antonio was an idiot. I cut him loose over two months ago."

"Glad to hear it. I never saw him as your type of man. So now, I'm looking a little more interesting to you. Is that it?" Kincaid raised his eyebrows, his expression one of quizzical interest.

Leila's brittle smile faded, as if heavy clouds blanketed the sun – her plan, no doubt. Lustrous eyes brimmed with unshed tears and a lone droplet escaped to trickle down one flawless cheek.

Dammit, she was good. No streaming nose, no gulping sobs, no red-rimmed eyes or contorted mouth – just one single, pathetic tear, glistening on porcelain perfection. Too bad Kincaid had lost his hankie.

Leila's voice quavered. "I made a huge mistake when I left you, Alistair. I've missed you so much."

Kincaid pushed away from the tree and raked his fingers through his hair. "Come off it, Leila. You've never regretted a decision you've made for one nanosecond. Your unswerving conviction about virtue of your actions, regardless of truckloads of evidence to the contrary, always amazed me."

Leila flinched. "You always had a vicious streak, Alistair. I came all this way to help you." She laid a hand on Kincaid's forearm.

Charley had difficulty detecting the vicious streak Leila referred to. It sounded to Charley like Kincaid was the wronged party. She had dumped him for a newer model. If anything, he was displaying remarkable forbearance in a potentially combustible confrontation.

He shrugged Leila's hand away and gave her a look of sheer surprise, either at her audacity or at her unexpectedly kind offer. "Help me? With what? There's no place for you here. You should return to Mexico City and your own project." He stared longingly in the direction of the dock, as if conjuring up a floatplane bobbing merrily in the water.

Leila injected a note of sarcasm into her voice. "And how, pray tell, do you propose I leave this place, Alistair?" Catching herself, she lowered her voice to a sultry purr. "Besides, this project's far too big for you to handle alone, darling. I'm the only one who knows enough about the Olmecs to be of real assistance to you."

Kincaid shook his head. "Sorry. I've already filled my quota of archaeologists." His flat voice defied any argument.

Leila's veneer cracked for one split second, and Charley's bullshit detector immediately zoomed into overdrive. Grim determination blazed in the tear-studded, dark eyes, replacing pathetic dismay, before the shutters descended again. The flash of unswerving resolve disappeared as if it had never existed.

Leila's question about leaving the site must have reminded Kincaid that Charley sat behind him listening avidly to their exchange. His well-bred manners fell aside. He shot Charley an exasperated look over his shoulder then glared at Leila. "As I already explained to the meddlesome intruder here," he jabbed a thumb in Charley's direction, "who's been eavesdropping behind a shrub all this time, you're both history the minute I find a pilot."

Charley shot off her perch on the log and brushed off the decaying fragments of wood clinging to her jeans. "Hey, it's not my problem if you insist on airing your dirty laundry in public."

Leila ignored Charley and blinked away the unshed tears. "Finding a pilot might take you a long time, darling," she said with the merest hint of satisfaction in her voice.

Kincaid muttered an incoherent Scottish oath. "Don't think for one second you'll convince me to change my mind. Come with me, both of you." Bowing to the inevitable, Kincaid swung around and headed towards the camp without another word.

A small smile of triumph curved Leila's lips. "Where do you want me to sleep tonight?" she called, lengthening her stride to catch up with him.

Charley strained to hear Kincaid's reply as she fell into step behind the pair, jostling her duffel bag and backpack over her shoulders.

He turned his head and encompassed both women in his wicked grin. "I'm afraid we are not set up for guests." The unspoken rebuke hung in the air between them. His next words wiped the smile off Leila's face. "You'll have to share a tent. It's all we have."

He didn't need to sound as if he enjoyed the prospect so

much.

Leila turned her head and glared at Charley in icy silence.

Charley choked back her words of protest and struggled to hide her dismay as she strode along in the rear. "No problem," she responded nonchalantly. *Yeah, right. No choice.*

"What about my luggage?" Leila protested.

"A crew member will haul your suitcases to the tent."

Charley wrinkled her nose. *Only one crew member? Poor sucker. He'll be making at least five trips.*

Ahead of the women, Kincaid ran a hand through his hair, leaving more spiky tufts springing from the top of his head. Leila halted him by tugging on his shirt. He stopped and turned towards her, harsh lines bracketing his mouth. She reached up to smooth his hair, but he shot his hand out and grabbed her wrist. "Sorry, Leila. That won't work. Not today, not ever again."

Charley shivered. You could cut the undercurrents with a knife.

He released Leila's wrist and put distance between them by trudging away.

Leila caught up and kept pace with him and tilted her head. "Alistair. Give me a chance to change your mind. Talk to me. Hear what I have to say."

He veered away. "Not interested."

Undeterred, she moved her body closer to his, brushing against him. "I can help you. We've always worked so well together, right from the beginning."

Kincaid pressed ahead in a determined walk, again leaving Leila in his wake. "Not anymore," he said over his shoulder. "As you pointed out, things have changed over the last two years. We're divorced now."

Charley's jaw dropped. *Omigod!* She had read that Kincaid was divorced from a Dr. Romero. Leila was his ex-wife.

The week ahead promised to be fascinating.

She increased her pace, overtook Leila, and caught up with Kincaid just as he shook his head, unaware of her proximity, and muttered under his breath, "Jesus! This is the last thing I need. I've got to get rid of them both."

In the unguarded moment, he sounded so distraught, Charley could almost find it in her heart to feel a spark of remorse.

He flicked cold eyes towards Charley as she stole up beside him, then closed them for a moment, as if praying for strength. Or his visitors' magical disappearance.

She puffed along beside him in silence.

After a few paces, he relented and placed his hand on her arm, tugging her to a halt. "Hand over that duffel bag, Charley. It looks heavy."

She raised an eyebrow, but dropped the heavy bag with alacrity.

He slung it over his shoulder as if it was as light as a feather and tramped off without another word.

Kincaid tried to ignore the iron vice that compressed his forehead as he made a beeline for camp, leaving the two women to straggle along in his wake.

The promising afternoon had tumbled downhill with an astounding rapidity. In thirty short minutes, his worst nightmares had sprung to life. Kincaid massaged his right temple with the heel of his hand, as if rubbing would ease the discomfort, and considered his present dilemma. A meddlesome reporter on a crusade would have taxed his patience on a good day, even if serious financial problems weren't threatening his project, but a confrontation with his ex-wife and rival archaeologist, all in one shapely package, was too big a burden for any man to bear. A few rampaging bandits and a couple of jaguar attacks would round out his day nicely.

Lord, but what I wouldn't give for a glass of Lagavulin. He longingly pictured the unopened bottle of scotch in his cabin and could almost taste the dark, peaty taste in the back of his throat. He lengthened his pace and grinned when he heard Charley trip over a rock and curse under her breath. The reporter had plenty of spunk. Great legs, too.

The undergrowth thinned out and opened into an airy, tree-studded clearing the size of a football field. Kincaid paused, shifting Charley's heavy bag to the other shoulder, wondering if she had stuffed it with boulders. He waited for the women to catch up.

Charley stumbled into view and stood stock still, her chest heaving and tawny wisps of hair straggling damply around her face. She raised one hand to her brow, shading her eyes and panned the grove, scanning every inch of his camp. For some strange reason, it mattered to him that she approved. Not that he would let her stay.

Other than a faint wheezing, she remained silent.

Kincaid looked over the camp, this time through the eyes of a newcomer. Naturally, Charley's opinion of the place mattered to him for the simple fact that a description of it would probably appear in her article – an article she would write unless he kept her locked up in solitary confinement for the next week.

The camp looked well organized and comfortable for anyone who knew a thing or two about the nature of their work. A double row of tents and wooden cabins spread out along the waterfront, all linked by a raised wooden walkway and partially concealed within groves of trees and bushes.

Kincaid approached Charley, slightly ashamed of his inhospitable reception. Normally, he wouldn't dream of treating a guest that way, reporter or not, but it was her bad luck she'd caught him at a vulnerable moment.

Earlier today, one of his mule-headed financial backers had uttered threats about withholding money unless a spectacular discovery was forthcoming. Kincaid's line of credit was already stretched to the limit, with no other prospects on the horizon. Too much was at stake to allow an ill-timed article to jeopardize his future.

He pushed his financial woes aside and smiled his most hospitable, welcome-to-my-camp smile, hoping to make amends for his boorish behaviour. "We call this area 'the grove'. It's siesta time, so most of my team is hanging out, relaxing." He indicated four laughing students playing cards beside one of the cabins while an intertwined couple swung lazily in a hammock slung between two palm trees.

Charley waved away a cloud of mosquitoes and gave him a bemused stare, as if assessing his miraculous about-face from loutish brute to hospitable host. As if she took pity on his pathetic attempts at geniality, she waved at the entire compound and said: "Amazing. I had no idea what to expect. It's a complete community in the middle of the jungle, isn't it? Some of the cabins are huge."

"The larger ones sleep as many as six people, but most accommodate only two. A few of us have our own personal living quarters set apart from the others. Overall, they're very comfortable. Raised platforms keep the floor dry and rodent-free."

Her eyebrows rose cautiously. "Rodents? Tell me I heard you wrong."

She had an amazing voice, low and musical, even when she bitched. He could listen to her for hours. He smiled. "Ah, how do I break this to you gently? This is the jungle. Animals live in jungles."

She shuddered. "Tropical rodents probably grow to the size of Rottweilers."

His grin broadened. "Surely, a few harmless wee mice won't bother an intrepid reporter like you."

"Investigative journalist," she insisted.

Other than her automatic protest, she didn't dignify his teasing with a reaction. "What's that building?" She pointed to a taller building bearing a thatched roof on the opposite side of the grove.

"That's the heart of the community," said Kincaid with pride, dropping the topic of rodents. "The combined dining and recreation area. We serve all our meals there, and every evening, you'll find a card game."

They strolled across the grove. A distant radio blasted out steamy salsa music in the freshening breeze and a pair of students danced under an overhanging tree, grinding their hips together in time to the music.

Kincaid noticed that Charley averted her eyes and picked up her pace. "Makes me feel like a voyeur," she muttered in explanation.

"Aye. Young love abounds," he commented. "Not a lot of privacy here, mind you, but there's not much else to keep them occupied in the middle of the jungle. Cards, games, books, the occasional party night and sex – lots of sex. We've already had one marriage break-up and two young lassies have gone home pregnant."

Her eyes clouded. "How sad."

He shook his head. "There's no excuse for pregnancy here. We're very, how do they say? Proactive."

She screeched to a halt and looked at him as if he had lost his mind. "Glad to hear it," she said.

He felt compelled to explain. A warning of sorts so that there would be no misunderstanding. "Affairs and romances are so common around archaeological digs that condoms are considered a staple around here." *Bloody hell.* He was digging his grave deeper and wider with every word he uttered.

"Is that a fact?"

He took another stab at an explanation, shifting the duffel bag to his other shoulder. "Oh, aye. We hand them out to the students and archaeologists like Aspirin. You wouldn't believe the quantities we go through. There's a whole carton in the corner of the dining area beneath the radio, and more coming in with the next shipment."

Her face flamed an interesting shade of fiery pink. "Um, well." She scuffed her feet. "Very interesting. How considerate of you."

He groaned inwardly. Had he actually talked about condoms? He must be daft. She probably thought he was coming on to her. Not that the thought hadn't crossed his mind.

The faint sound of *Hot, Hot, Hot* by Los Rios filled the uncomfortable silence.

He decided a change of subject would be prudent. "You must be hungry and thirsty. Let's make sure someone takes care of you." He waved her on ahead.

Leila, who had lagged behind, no doubt trying to make him feel guilty, sauntered up in time to catch his last words. Kincaid noted her eyes had narrowed ever so faintly. He was positive she was biting her tongue to prevent a sarcastic rejoinder from jumping out and had trouble suppressing a smile when Charley whispered: "I'll just bet she'd like to see me taken care of – permanently."

Leila made a languid hand gesture. "Which tent do you

want us to take? I just want to settle in and—"

Charley chimed in simultaneously. "I'm starved. An in-flight lunch wasn't part of the package."

Kincaid grimaced at the contradictory requests. Bloody hell, he had a tiger by the tail. Make that two tigers, he amended.

He wouldn't have noticed the motionless figure standing under the huge banyan tree if he hadn't been scanning the camp for assistance. What the devil did his field director think he was doing, lurking under the twisted branches instead of stepping forward to greet them? Kincaid began to regret his hasty decision to hire the Mexican.

"Felipe," he called, dumping the heavy duffel bag on the ground. "I could use some help over here."

The dark figure took his time to emerge from the shadows.

Charley hadn't noticed him standing in the shade, partly because his dark jeans and shirt blended perfectly with the trunk, partly because overhanging branches had partially hidden him, but mainly because he'd remained immobile, as if hoping to avoid detection. She hated knowing she'd been under surveillance all this time.

The man sauntered towards the group, and Kincaid introduced Felipe Ortega, his field director and site supervisor.

Felipe scrutinized Charley, his smouldering gaze burning into her, as if he could read her every thought.

Charley blinked, faintly uneasy, and felt the telltale heat rise in her cheeks. His weathered face, all harsh angles and sharp planes, was compelling. Some might even call him attractive, if a tad austere. She cleared her throat and stretched out a hand. "Hi, Felipe, nice to meet you."

Felipe's broad smile did not reach the obsidian eyes that assessed her. "*Buenas tardes, señorita*. Welcome to our camp. If Dr. Kincaid permits, tomorrow you will visit our sacred city, *Ciudad de la Jaguar*."

Charley hid her faint trickle of unease and flashed him a beaming smile.

Before she could reply, Kincaid interjected: "Neither of

these women will be visiting the dig site."

Charley took one look at Kincaid's darkening expression and opted for discretion. "Thanks anyway, Felipe. Maybe another time."

Leila stepped forward, presenting Felipe with the luminous smile she apparently reserved exclusively for the male gender. "Pleased to meet you, Felipe."

He dropped Charley's hand and gazed at Leila. "I am most honoured, *señorita*."

Leila recoiled and opened her mouth as if to say something, but Felipe flicked his hand in a tiny, almost imperceptible gesture of denial. She settled back, a speculative look in her eyes.

Charley's radar clicked in. She'd wager a month's wages that Leila and Felipe recognized one another. She glanced at Kincaid for confirmation. The charged exchange of glances had escaped his notice, no doubt because the tantalizing freedom from his hostly duties was almost within his grasp.

"Felipe, please show Leila to the empty tent at the end of the waterfront row and find someone to haul her luggage from the dock. You can take Charley's duffel bag as well." He nudged the bag with the tip of his boot.

"*Si*, Dr. Kincaid. It is my great pleasure."

Charley shrugged a strap off her shoulder. "Thanks. I'll keep my backpack, but you can take my laptop."

Kincaid said: "Charley, you can either accompany them to your tent, or I'll take you to the kitchen. Your choice."

She shifted her backpack to a more comfortable position, then glanced at Kincaid. "Don't go to any trouble on my account. Just point me to the kitchen."

"We will find the tent," Leila said then whirled around to Kincaid. "And I will find you too, Alistair. That's a promise." She walked on, adding a toss of her hair.

It occurred to Charley that if Leila felt any resentment or disappointment at being dumped on a subordinate, she disguised it well.

Kincaid hissed out a ragged breath as he watched Felipe escort Leila across the grove towards her tent and out of earshot. "Bloody hell," he muttered under his breath, apparently forgetting about Charley. Catching himself, he returned her gaze, his expression grim. "Don't say another word."

He looked as if he'd explode if she uttered another smart-ass remark. The 'devil' made her say it anyway. "I can almost find it in my heart to feel sorry for you."

He rumbled another dark, Scottish-sounding oath. She stepped backwards. Perhaps she'd gone too far.

"I'd better feed you," he growled. "Then maybe I can have some peace and quiet for a few minutes."

Kincaid's words barely registered in Charley's startled brain. Frozen in place, she stared in horrified fascination at the fearsome apparition that emerged from a small out-building. The figure brandished a lethal-looking knife, while purposefully closing the gap between them. His gaze darted from one face to another, then focused like a laser beam on Charley.

Chapter 3

Kincaid followed Charley's gaze, wondering what had spooked her. She stared at the rapidly approaching figure swathed in a long white apron and brandishing a glittering butcher's knife. Her expression reflected the stunned fascination of a deer in the headlights combined with incipient amusement.

Kincaid had forgotten how strangers reacted to his friend's appearance. Wild, curly hair and a bushy black beard streaked with white gave Colin the appearance of a disreputable, middle-aged pirate. A hoop earring decorating his left ear combined with large square teeth that displayed a matching glint of gold when his grin broadened heightened the impression. The knife didn't help.

"Hey, Colin," Kincaid bellowed and waved his arm, thankful for the interruption. "Hurry up. I need to talk to you."

The older man bustled over. "Och, it's right here, I am, lad. No need to bellow like a rhinoceros in heat. I'm no' deaf." He checked out Kincaid's appalling socks. "Nice socks."

"Aye, thanks. My wee niece sent them last week for my birthday."

Charley uttered a soft sound. "Good grief. This camp is teeming with Scots. I'm surrounded."

"Kincaid, introduce me to this beautiful wee lassie."

Kincaid waited for Charley to bite off Colin's head with a few well-chosen words.

He watched in amazement as her lips twitched in mirth. "As you can easily see, I'm far from wee and no longer a lassie."

"Och, let me remove my foot from my oversized mouth. It was an innocent turn of phrase. No insult intended."

44

"None taken. It's a pleasant change to be referred to as wee." Charley clamped a hand to her hair as the freshening breeze tumbled honey-coloured curls into dancing eyes. "Do you always greet guests with a butcher's knife?"

"Someone has to keep Kincaid in line."

"I'm with you there."

Bloody hell, he's done it again. Another man, foolish enough to say the same thing, would be dead meat. Colin had the easy, natural way of a favourite uncle that allowed him to get away with outrageous banter, extravagant teasing, and joking insults that left women laughing helplessly at his absurdities. They trusted him instantly. Kincaid privately believed women instinctively sensed Colin's soft heart.

"Charley," said Kincaid, "This is Colin MacGreggor, chef extraordinaire. Don't be afraid. He doesn't bite, though he looks as if he might. Behind the hairy exterior, he's as gentle as a lamb, but a fiend in the kitchen. Watch out for the enchiladas if you value your taste buds. They'll take off the top of your head."

Charley threw back her head and her musical laugh rang out. It was the first time Kincaid had heard her laugh. She should do so more often. He continued with his introductions. "Colin, meet Charley, with an 'e-y', Underhill, our visiting ... er ... reporter."

"Investigative journalist," Charley corrected in her usual irritating manner. "Hi, Colin. Don't worry about toning down your enchiladas on my account. I eat anything, the hotter the better. I'm told I was born with a garburator instead of a stomach."

Colin roared with laughter and gave Kincaid a thumbs-up. "She'll do."

Kincaid rolled his eyes. "Would you mind preparing a snack for Charley?"

"Absolutely. I adore beautiful women." He addressed Charley: "Hold onto your hat, lass. I'm about to make you the happiest woman in the world. You'll be weeping with joy when I've had my way with you. They all do."

Kincaid studied the way her high cheekbones flushed an interesting shade of pink, the way her lush lips parted as she stared blankly at his friend. For one insane moment, he imagined how those lips would feel crushed against his own, then pushed the thought aside.

Eyes twinkling, Colin elaborated: "Treat you to a delectable snack, prepared as only a world-class chef knows how."

Charley grinned. "Uh-huh. I love modesty in a man. Watch out, though. If you're as good as you claim to be, I may just fall for you. The best way to my heart is through my stomach."

"Promises, promises."

Feeling the pressure building up inside his skull again, Kincaid interrupted the annoying banter. "You two seem to have hit it off. If you don't mind, I'm off to the dig to check my crew's progress."

Colin dropped his voice to an ostentatious stage whisper intended to carry to Charley's ears. "Kincaid, you've finally lost your marbles. What the hell's the matter with you? A gorgeous stranger lands on your doorstep and you leave her with me? Have you forgotten the affect I have on women? A half an hour with me and they're spoiled for other men."

Kincaid favoured Colin with a glare and dragged his friend aside, calling to Charley: "Please excuse us for a couple of minutes."

"Don't worry about me," Charley shouted after the two retreating backs. "I'll keep myself busy. You know, take photographs, snoop, pry and ask inappropriate questions." Her long, lithe legs carried her towards a spiny kapok tree covered in woolly white puffs.

When Kincaid figured Charley was out of earshot, he hissed to Colin: "I don't know what to do with her. She's a reporter. You know how I feel about reporters."

"That's the price you pay for being a celebrity." Colin sounded far from sympathetic. "In your heart, you know there was more than a wee bit of truth to the stories they printed."

"My private life is nobody's business but mine," Kincaid muttered, rubbing his tense neck muscles. "I don't need another one of your lectures right now."

Colin ignored the warning in Kincaid's voice and glanced at Charley, eyes warm with approval. "This one doesn't seem like all the rest."

"Oh, aye? What the hell does that mean?"

"It means Charley has some depth to her. She's bright and ambitious. Good sense of humour, too."

Kincaid made a derisive noise. "And you can tell all of that — how? Just because she laughed at your half-witted jokes – at my expense, I might add."

"At least give the lass a chance. That way, you'll have some control over the press release about your discovery."

"That lass, as you call her, spells nothing but trouble," Kincaid growled, wishing with all his heart he could put her on a plane and send her home.

"You're blithering. Look at that bonny face. The picture of innocence, it is."

Both men swivelled their heads and studied Charley while she snapped pictures of the kapok tree.

"Innocence, my ass," Kincaid growled. "I don't believe it's mere coincidence she landed on my doorstep just as I'm on the brink of one of the greatest discoveries of the last two centuries, sticking her long nose into places where it doesn't belong."

"Her distinctive nose gives her face character."

Although he secretly agreed, Kincaid ignored the interruption and continued: "I don't trust strangers, even sexy ones." He paused and eyed the way her skin-tight jeans encased a delectable ass. "Especially sexy ones."

Colin shook his shaggy head mournfully and patted his friend on the shoulder with mock sympathy. "Och, you're imagining things, Kincaid. Paranoia like yours requires intense therapy."

Kincaid swatted the large, hairy hand away, unable to suppress a laugh. "I can see whose side you're on."

"I can tell she's not like your string of bimbos back home," Colin persisted.

Kincaid ignored him. The man was more irritating than the cloud of tiny insects that swarmed around their heads, though honesty compelled Kincaid to admit there might be a speck of truth in his friend's assertion. "So, maybe I made a wee error or two in judgement. A man who's been dumped by his wife for another man is allowed a couple of mistakes."

"More like several dozen mistakes – all of them beautiful, all of them with boobs bigger than their brains, all of them shallower than a mud puddle. Not one of them with two intelligent words to rub together."

"I had a damned good reason for my dating frenzy," Kincaid muttered, remembering the searing pain of Leila's betrayal. The memory of his ex-wife's infidelity jolted Kincaid back to his waking nightmare. He raked his fingers through his hair, wondering how he could have forgotten his second visitor. "I must be cracking up. I have a worse catastrophe than a nosy reporter to deal with."

Colin made an inquiring noise.

"Someone else arrived on the same plane."

Colin's eyebrows drew together in a ferocious scowl. "Not—"

"Aye. Leila."

Words seldom escaped Colin, but this revelation rendered him speechless. At last, he spoke. "What's that witch doing here? I thought she was out of your life for good."

"I did, too."

"She must want something," said Colin.

"Oh, aye. I don't believe for one minute she'd be here if she weren't in big trouble. The question is: What does she want?"

"You."

The word hung in the air between the two men.

"Then she's out of luck," Kincaid said.

"I hope you mean that."

"Definitely." Kincaid hoped it was true. "But now I'm stuck with both of them for a week until the damned pilot returns. The road's impassable because of yesterday's rain." He rubbed his throbbing temples, wishing he could crawl into bed, pull the covers over his head, and sleep for a week until the plane arrived to end his torture.

With a speculative gleam in his eye, Colin craned his neck to shoot his friend a warning glare. "Don't you dare touch that bottle of Lagavulin you have hidden on the top shelf in your cabin."

Kincaid felt his mouth gape open and snapped it shut. "Damn, you must have eyes in the back of your head. How did you know it was there?"

"I've seen the way you look at that shelf, sometimes."

"I haven't touched a drop in years. You of all people should know that. I just need to know it's there."

"Aye. I get it. Kind of a security blanket."

"More than that. It proves I can resist the bottle." Truth be told, Kincaid didn't know why he kept the bottle in his cabin, but he wasn't quite ready to let it go. Not yet.

Colin eyed his friend. "Off you go for a good walk. I'll take care of the lass."

Torn, Kincaid hesitated. In the end, he couldn't resist the tempting opportunity to escape, if only for a couple of hours. "At least be careful about what you say. I know how much you like to gossip. Please don't blab about anything."

Indignation written on his face, Colin bristled. "I never blab. I'm the soul of discretion."

A feminine voice interrupted their discussion. "Are you two almost finished your squabbling? I'm famished."

Kincaid favoured Charley with a fulminating glare.

She stared back, as if issuing a silent challenge. Without breaking eye contact, she scraped her hair back with her fingers and fastened it with a blue clasp that matched her eyes. Her upraised arms caused her shirt to mould more closely to her torso.

Well, she definitely wasn't too skinny in all the places that mattered. As much as he hated the press and resented the notion of a reporter hanging around his camp, Kincaid had to admit that Charley presented quite an eyeful in her damp, body-hugging shirt.

Colin jabbed Kincaid in the ribs with his elbow and shouted: "Sorry about the wee delay, lass. We're finished. Don't mind Kincaid. He's just being himself."

Before Kincaid could open his mouth to utter a rude rejoinder, a huge black and tan, extremely scruffy apparition bolted out of the vegetation. It streaked straight towards its master like an arrow then twined around his legs, purring.

"Horrie." Kincaid scooped the cat into his arms. "Where the hell have you been hiding?" He stroked the silky fur between pointed ears. "He hates the plane's racket. Takes off every time he hears it."

"Horrie always hated Leila, too," muttered Colin under his breath. "An animal of discerning taste."

The cat closed his single yellow eye in apparent feline euphoria.

"Good Lord. I've never seen such a butt-ugly cat," Charley blurted.

It figured. Big city reporters probably preferred well-groomed, aristocratic cats. "Aye. He's no beauty," Kincaid admitted. He cooed nonsense into the cat's ear, then glanced at Charley. "Four years ago, I rescued poor Horrie from a gang of hooligans. He's been with me ever since."

"Horrie? What kind of name is that?" Charley asked, studying the animal with interest.

"He's named after Horatio Lord Nelson because he has only one eye. Horrie for short. But he's so mean-tempered most of the time, we usually call him Horrid."

Charley reached out to scratch his head.

"Don't touch him," warned Kincaid quickly, shifting the animal. "He'll take your hand off. Horrie tolerates no one but me and, occasionally, Colin, but only if tuna is involved." He eyed her. "On second thought, perhaps I should let him take a chunk out of your hide."

Ignoring Kincaid, Charley rubbed the fur under the cat's chin while crooning: "Aren't you the lovely boy?"

Horrid opened his eye, then closed it again. A wide yawn displayed a mouthful of extremely white, needle-sharp teeth and a dainty pink tongue. The throbbing purr grew louder.

"See?" Charley glanced at Kincaid, a smug look on her face. "He likes me. Cats always do for some strange reason."

Horrie reclined in Kincaid's arms, tail twitching blissfully, while Charley scratched him into a state of ecstasy with a rhythmic motion of her slender hand. She was close enough for Kincaid to smell the scent of coconut oil sunscreen combined with sun-warmed woman and the sharp tang of insect repellent.

As if sensing his friend's train of thought, Colin's voice sharpened and snapped Kincaid out of his trance. "Aye, weel, I thought you were off to poke around the dig, Kincaid. Don't let us stop you."

Reluctantly, Kincaid dragged his thoughts away from

long, slow caresses and leisurely stroking. "Right, then. See you at dinner." Out of the corner of his eye, he watched Colin proffer his arm to Charley with mock gallantry. The top of his shaggy head barely reached her nose. Her infectious grin flashed as she tucked her hand into the crook of his elbow.

Horrie leaped out of Kincaid's arms and followed the pair.

Kincaid almost changed his mind about leaving. Perhaps he had been a tad hasty in his unflattering assessment of Charley. If both Colin and Horrie liked her, she must have some redeeming features.

He shrugged and started towards the dig. He had an entire week to conduct a thorough investigation of those features.

Chapter 4

Leila followed Felipe towards the sleeping quarters. Although she intended to pry some answers out of the lying bastard, she hoped her neutral expression revealed nothing of her inner turmoil. She'd toyed with the idea of ratting him out to Alistair, but blurting the truth would have spoiled the sweet surge of power coursing through her veins at the thought of how Felipe's fate rested in her hands.

His quiet voice interrupted her reverie. "This is the tent. Your luggage will be here soon."

She turned on Felipe. "You son-of-a-bitch," she snapped. "I thought you were dead."

"You are angry with me. There is much we need to say to one another."

Damn right there was. "Not here. We need privacy for what I have to say to you."

"And I to you, so follow me." The note of quiet authority in his voice was unmistakable.

Leila stared at Felipe with growing interest. The transformation was remarkable. Gone was the quiet, obsequious man of her youth, and in his place stood a force to be reckoned with. "Your story had better be good."

Felipe led her along a narrow path that wound through lush, green vegetation until they emerged in a clearing beside the lagoon. Towering foliage and twisting vines dwarfed the tiny cabin that merged with the jungle, as if it was trying to return to its natural habitat.

"This is my cabin. Sit, please. We will talk." He indicated two wooden chairs bracketing a table, deep in the shadow cast by a wide porch.

Leila gnawed her bottom lip. Trees and exuberant underbrush enclosed the clearing on three sides and formed an impenetrable barrier. Perhaps she shouldn't have insisted on privacy. She doubted anyone would hear her if she screamed.

As if he could read her mind, Felipe said: "Sit. No harm will come. I will get drinks." He disappeared into the cabin and returned with two bottles of *Jarritos Tamarindos*. "This used to be your favourite soft drink." He drew up the second chair and sat motionless, eyes closed.

She sipped the drink. The sweet-tart flavour filled her mouth and lingered on her tongue, bringing back a jumble of memories. She allowed the brittle silence to lengthen until her nerves snapped. "So. We meet again, *Pedro*," she spat out, placing sarcastic emphasis on the name. Her voice hardened. "Pedro. Peter. Do you know the name Peter signifies 'the rock'? Strong, steadfast and reliable. All these years, I believed you couldn't possibly be alive. The Pedro I knew wouldn't have lied to me." She would never let Felipe know the devastating toll the loss of her friend had taken on her.

Felipe opened his hooded eyes and his unfathomable gaze collided with her own. The young man she'd met over thirteen years ago, uncertain of his fledgling powers, had disappeared forever. In his place was an enigmatic stranger.

"Please do not call me by the old name. The man called Pedro is long dead," he said in a voice that brooked no opposition.

Leila's fury intensified and her fingers itched to strangle the traitor. He offered no hint of apology for his abrupt disappearance. She toyed with the soft drink bottle and allowed a smile of sudden brightness to illuminate her face at the notion of smashing it over his head. With an impatient toss of her hair, Leila said: "No wonder Kincaid and Colin failed to recognize you, *Felipe*. You've aged beyond belief, and God knows, you even *sound* different. Less of an accent."

The dignified man facing her now bore no resemblance to the vital young worker who had befriended her on the first dig of her career. The Mexican must be thirty-eight now, she calculated, but he looked twenty years older. Life had taken its toll. A leather thong secured the longish hair, threaded now with more grey than black. Its severity accented his high cheekbones and broad, slightly flattened nose. Deep lines etched the bronze cheeks on either side of his mouth and furrowed the skin between his eyes.

"*Sí*. Life has presented many challenges. How did you know who I was when others did not recognize me?" he asked.

Leila considered the question thoughtfully. "Your eyes," she replied after a long pause. "I've never been able to forget your eyes. You've shaved your moustache and your hair is no longer black, but your eyes are still the same." She shivered. Was it her imagination, or did the unblinking, penetrating gaze hold a spark of fanaticism in its opaque depth?

"Deep anger blocks your energy field," said Felipe.

"You made me a promise, and you broke it. A promise you probably don't even remember."

Felipe raised his head. His stare pierced her soul in the old, familiar way. "I remember. You were my student, my acolyte. We shared a bond that extended far beyond the dig."

The deep, resonant '*jug-o-rum, jug-o-rum*' of a bullfrog boomed eerily from the opposite shore and heightened the silence.

So he did remember. During her first dig in Belize, she'd discovered an unexpected ally in Pedro – Leila still had difficulty thinking of him as Felipe – as an avid follower of the occult arts. Their mutual fascination with paranormal energies and mysticism had drawn the unlikely pair together.

An aromatic fragrance hung in the sultry air. Leila wandered over to a bush, snapped a branch, and sniffed. *Copal trees. How fitting*. The ancient Olmecs had used copal resin to produce incense. Felipe had always harbored a half-baked notion that he was a descendant of those same Olmecs. He'd once described how a spiritual guide from his village had taken him under his wing and trained him in the age-old shamanistic practices, beliefs and rituals.

Leila returned to the porch with the broken twig. "I wanted to learn it all. You told me I had a rare gift. You promised to teach me about shapeshifting."

"You demonstrated remarkable abilities." He smiled.

"I used to sneak away from Kincaid for the lessons. Even back then, he'd have found a way to get rid of you if he'd known what we were doing. My interest in that voodoo crap, as he always called it, horrified him."

Felipe twisted the copal twig from Leila's unresisting fingers, placed it in a three-legged brazier. He struck a match. A bright flame blazed as the twig ignited, flared briefly, then subsided to a smouldering ember. Fragrant smoke swirled towards them and caught in her throat.

Felipe laid a gentle finger on her arm as if testing her energy level then withdrew his hand. "The power still blossoms within you. You and I are not finished."

Leila pushed the soft drink aside. She wasn't letting him off the hook that easily. "You owe me an explanation. You promised to teach me. Why did you disappear without a word?" she asked without preamble to soften the question. The tightness of her voice betrayed her anger. The slight quiver had nothing to do with hurt.

"I was unable to stay," he said quietly. "The authorities would have blamed me for the explosion. With good cause."

The words, though hardly unexpected, caught Leila off guard. "You *were* involved." Her voice was flat, expressionless. "I wondered."

"It was an accident," Felipe said. "It happened while I still experienced the after-effects of an experiment with peyote."

Leila's breath caught in her throat. Peyote, cactus of the gods, source of visions. She hadn't thought about the plant since the long-ago summer when Felipe had introduced her to the substance that made mystic journeys possible.

She found her voice again and leaned forward. "I remember the day, I believed I jumped off the cliff and flew. Did our raven flight really happen, do you suppose, or was it just a peyote-induced hallucination?"

"You must decide for yourself."

"It seems unreal now – a fantasy I'd almost forgotten. The memory is like a dream – all swirly, in slow motion, as if the atmosphere had been thicker than normal."

Swooping over the camp that afternoon, clarity and certainty had overwhelmed her when she'd gazed down and understood how small, how insignificant, how ridiculous human beings were in the vast mystery of the cosmos. She was one of the elite with the audacity to overcome the laws of gravity and soar above it all, to throw off the shackles of petty human concerns and become one with the Universe. For the first time since she was a child, the gnawing emptiness inside her disappeared. A sense of God-like superiority crystallized in her heart. She made a solemn vow that she would never feel powerless again.

Leila strained to recall the sequence of events. Pieces of the puzzle started to click into place. She assessed his expression for traces of guilt. "The explosion occurred the same night, didn't it?"

"*Sí*. I was still hallucinating all evening. As you know, peyote's effects can last several days."

"Then what happened?"

He leaned forward and steepled his hands on the table. "Before going to bed, I went to the supply shed to get a new pick-axe – I'd broken mine that morning and needed another for the next day. The next thing I remember, I was in my own room with no memory of crawling into bed. Then, a terrible explosion shook the night and flames shot everywhere."

Leila schooled her face to show only surprise. "What caused the explosion?"

Felipe voice deepened, became more confidential. "As soon as the blast woke me, I knew what had happened. I must have left a kerosene lamp burning in the shed. Something, maybe a rat or a gust of wind must have tipped it over and set fire to the cartons. It was only a matter of time until the gasoline cans exploded." A small smile played around his mouth but didn't quite reach his eyes.

He was lying. Rats avoid open flames, and if the night had been windy, the fire would have consumed the entire camp. Thankfully, only a couple of sheds had burned down. Besides, his explanation was too glib, as if he'd rehearsed his speech.

Still, she decided to play along.

"If the explosion was accidental and nobody was hurt, why did you run?" Leila was curious to hear his excuses.

"I panicked. I was afraid someone had seen me leaving the shed."

"One of the workers *did* see someone, but the night was too dark to tell who it was."

"I had no way of knowing. If I had been recognized, they would have prosecuted me. My life, my mission, would have ended before it had begun. After all, I was a lowly, uneducated Mexican worker – the perfect scapegoat. I had no choice."

"You deceived me," Leila said slowly. "You could have told me the truth."

He shrugged his shoulders and wordlessly spread his hands. "I would have contacted you, but you married Kincaid. I could not be sure he would not tell the authorities if he discovered I was still alive. He never liked me."

Leila pointed out sweetly: "I could get you fired." She might as well keep him off-balance. At this moment, she had the upper hand.

Felipe's eyes narrowed at the implied threat. He started to pace the length of the porch. "You do not understand how much is at stake. No one else knows the Olmecs, or Xi, the way I do. They are in my blood. I cannot leave until my work is completed." He whirled towards her. "You must keep silent about my identity."

Felipe's enigmatic words left no doubt in Leila's mind that he was up to something. If she played along, perhaps he would let her in on the mystery. That way, if Kincaid wouldn't co-operate and share the glory, she would have a backup plan. For now, she would hold her tongue. There was no reason to divulge the truth to Alistair unless it suited her purposes. Besides, knowledge of Felipe's identity gave her an inside edge.

"Sit down, Felipe. You're making me dizzy. Perhaps we can find a way to make it worth my while to stay silent."

Felipe relaxed his posture. He drew up his chair again and composed his face into lines of calmness with a visible effort. "Have you ever been tempted to learn more?"

He understands what I want. "Yes." Leila allowed a tiny smile of triumph to curve her lips. "I have thought about it often."

"You have a rare mystical gift that must be cultivated or your talent will shrivel and die. All these years, I have searched for someone on whom the gods look with favour. The Master of Darkness, the revered Jaguar God, showed me your face in the flames, so I summoned you here."

"Nonsense. I came to visit Alistair," she retorted. But the truth of his words hit her like a hammer. An idle impulse to reconnect with her former husband had become an obsession.

"At a surface level, yes. But at the deepest level, you came here because I called to you and you heard my summons."

A wave of anger blazed through Leila at the thought of Felipe using his powers to manipulate her. "In that case, I trust you intend to make good on your promise to train me."

Felipe shrugged. "I wish to pass on the ancient secrets to an acolyte. You are the one person I have met who shows enough potential. Soon, I will join my ancestors. My knowledge cannot die with my body. The chain of power must continue, unbroken."

"You're about to die? Are you sick?" Now that he had reentered her life, she didn't want him to die until he had taught her all his secrets.

"No, not sick, not the way you mean. But I have seen my death. I don't know how or why, but I know death comes soon."

Her hands balled into fists under the table as she strove to present a calm façade. This was what she'd always dreamed of – to learn how to harness the occult energies of the Ancients. If he insisted on calling her his acolyte, so be it. Soon, the ultimate in power and dominance would belong to her. She managed a nod. "I learn quickly." That had damn well better be true if he was about to die soon.

"We will pick up where we left off."

She laughed with excitement. "How long will it take?"

"My remaining days are few. I will teach you for the length of time the gods grant me."

"When do we start?"

"Tonight. Meet me here at midnight. There is no time to waste. You will say nothing to Kincaid."

This was too good to be true. Her mind raced. Midnight would give her enough time to meet with Kincaid after dinner. If her reunion went the way she hoped, she might be late, but she'd invent an excuse to placate Felipe. "I have no reason to tell Alistair."

Felipe's gaze bored into her own. "That is not good enough. You will promise never to mention what I have revealed to you. If you betray me, you betray my cause, and I vow by the great Jaguar God of my ancestors, you will pay the price."

She stared. Felipe had drawn an invisible cloak of authority around himself. In spite of his rough, labourer's clothes, it occurred to her that he could no longer disguise his true identity – a high priest and an extremely dangerous man.

In spite of the heavy warmth of the afternoon, a cold chill skittered down her spine. She could still back out, but she loathed cowardice. For the rest of her life, she'd regret she lacked the wit and the will to grasp the opportunity. The promise of learning ancient secrets overshadowed his ominous threat. Ratting out Felipe was the last thing Leila intended to do. She might need this ace in the hole.

"I promise."

He lifted his bottle in a toast. "To the future."

Something in his voice stirred the hair on the back of her neck. When she gazed into his eyes, a feral glow of elation gleamed in their depths.

"To the future," she agreed. She clinked her bottle against Felipe's and drank deeply, wondering as she did so who had emerged the victor.

Chapter 5

The predator unsheathed lethal claws to slash into the unresisting body and rip out the still-beating heart. Blood geysered in a fountain that gleamed, black, in the firelight. A howl of agony, quickly silenced, tore the stillness.

The creature lowered her head and lapped with delicate precision.

The cry ripped through Charley's senses and dragged her back to semi-consciousness. A sharp, metallic taste lingered in her mouth and her pillow felt damp.

Disoriented, she stared around, then her memory returned. After lunch, she had headed to her tent for a nap. The distinctive scent of sun-warmed canvas filled her nostrils. Birds and insects continued their afternoon serenade outside the tent.

For less than a moment, fragments of the dream flickered through Charley's memory. Recognition hovered at the edge of consciousness before fading. Too exhausted to puzzle over a dream, she flopped back and curled into a tight, protective ball.

Sleep returned in an instant.

A half an hour later, an inhuman outcry tore apart the breathless afternoon stillness.

Charley bolted upright in her cot, trembling, heart thundering in her ears. She felt the blood leave her face and blurted: "Dear God."

Crouched under the thin sheet, she heard the whirring of wings as a flock of birds took to the air, screeching their alarm as they sped away. The brief flurry of activity culminated in an ominous silence. Another piercing yowl rang out, followed by a prolonged shriek that faded away in a series of agonized squeals, squeaks and bleats.

She sprang up and darted from her tent in time to see a pair of toucans burst from the jungle canopy and flap their way to safety. A passing student narrowly averted a head-on collision with her by grabbing her arm, preventing another ignominious sprawl in the dust.

Charley made an effort to get a grip on herself but couldn't prevent the slight quaver in her voice. "What is that God-awful racket?" Dumbfounded, she watched a broad grin split the student's bearded face. It occurred to her she could still be in the throes of a nightmare.

"Chill, babe," he reassured her. "This is my third year of suffering. You never really get used to Kincaid's bagpipes, but the shock fades."

Her brain whirled as she tried to make sense of the words. "Huh?"

"It's just the boss letting off some steam. He claims it helps him find clarity whenever he has a problem."

She felt her lips twitch into a reluctant smile. Ten to one, her presence in camp formed a huge portion of Kincaid's problem. "He's terrible. It sounds as if he's slaughtering a pig."

Louder and more discordant, mournful howls and shrill shrieks coalesced to form a continuous, wailing drone.

"Look over there." He pointed.

As she watched, a lone, colourful figure disappeared down the path surrounding the camp. The red and green tartan bag clutched under his arm warred with the fuchsia print of the aloha shirt that draped his lean torso.

The plaintive racket drilled into Charley's brain like a jackhammer. Slowly, her heart resumed a normal rhythm. "I've never heard anything quite like it," she whispered, scarcely believing her ears. "His playing is an insult to music lovers everywhere."

But somehow, the dreadful, off-key playing made Kincaid more human. Anyone who played that badly in public couldn't possibly take himself too seriously.

The young man grimaced. "This year, he graduated from the practice chanter to the full set of pipes. Much louder.

Much more difficult. Much worse for the listeners."

Kincaid should consider it a miracle someone hadn't destroyed the instrument of torture before now. Charley concentrated on finding the melody. Sure enough, a mournful bass-line moan underlined the distorted strains of *Amazing Grace*.

She turned her eyes heavenward and muttered a fervent prayer that Kincaid would find the clarity he sought in record time.

Kincaid arrived at the water's edge, whirled around after clicking his heels together, and marched in the opposite direction. He ignored the trickle of sweat dribbling down his forehead and focused his imagination on bleak, purple hills, blustering gales and chilling fog. He could almost smell the heather and feel the cool drizzle of a fine Scottish mist on his cheeks.

Drawing in a deep, shuddering breath through one side of his mouth, he forced the air into his bagpipes. His troubles disappeared like magic and he lost himself in his favourite fantasy – leading Bonnie Prince Charlie's highland charge, banners flying, to reunite the Scottish clans.

After half an hour of playing, Kincaid's cheeks were numb with the strain of maintaining constant air pressure in the bag. He made the wee mistake of loosening his facial muscles for a moment and the pipes let out the unearthly yowl his crew detested. Recovering, he exhaled mightily into the mouthpiece. A satisfying squawk and a renewed drone rewarded his efforts.

Colin exploded from the kitchen and barricaded the path, hands planted on his hips. "Enough, Kincaid. Truce. I can't take any more of this racket and neither can anyone else."

The bagpipes squealed their protest at the slackened air pressure. For some strange reason, his friends and crew never enjoyed his playing as much as he did. "Bloody hell," he growled.

Undeterred, Colin pressed on, as annoying as a gnat. "Only last night, your entire crew cleared out of the dining hall in under a minute when you brought out the pipes. Worked faster than a fire drill. If you keep this up, the staff will mutiny, and then you'll have some major unification to deal with in real life instead of in your imagination.

That was a low blow. "I never should have told you about my harmless wee fantasy. You're jealous of my talent. Always were."

"I might be if you had any. Do you want to talk about what's bothering you?"

Kincaid sighed and lowered the bagpipes. Colin was always there for him when he needed a friend. "Aye." He paused collecting his thoughts. "I suppose so. This problem's going to be worse than I thought. Let's keep walking – you need the exercise."

Colin threw Kincaid a dirty look, but fell into step while muttering dark insults under his breath about smart-assed, off-key, no-talent musicians. Amused, Kincaid ignored the grumbling and waited for his friend's curiosity to get the better of him.

Sure enough, after a couple of minutes, Colin broke off in mid-complaint and said: "Surely it can't be as bad as all that."

Kincaid rearranged the pipes under his arm. "It's a good job I visited the dig this afternoon. I helped the workers strip away the last of the creepers and vines from the cliff abutting the temple." He paused for effect.

"Spit it out, lad. Don't keep me in suspense."

Kincaid didn't try to hide his elation. "The cliff isn't a flat, unbroken wall," he announced. "There's an opening, just as I suspected. Tomorrow, Felipe and his crew can start removing the landslide that's blocking the tunnel."

Colin beamed from ear to ear. "Congratulations."

"Thanks. I have a feeling this is a major discovery."

"What do you expect to find in the tunnel?"

Kincaid raised his shoulders in an eloquent shrug. "I don't know. With luck, I might be the first archaeologist to find some preserved Olmec remains."

Colin glanced up with a quizzical expression. "Forgive me if I miss the point. Bones are bones."

Kincaid shook his head and explained: "Not in this case, they're not. No one has ever found more than a few useless scraps of disintegrating bone, probably due to soil acidity. This is different. If the stone floor protected any human remains, I could recoup my financial losses, clear my name and restore my reputation."

"And that would be bad – how?"

"Timing couldn't be worse. Word of the tunnel has probably spread through camp like wildfire. There's no way I can prevent our intrepid reporter from finding out about this breakthrough. Or my ex-wife, for that matter."

"Could you kindly walk a wee bit slower, Kincaid. I have to take four steps to your two," Colin protested. "I can't trot along and think at the same time." He remained stubbornly silent, panting, until his breathing evened out. "As I see it, you want to get Charley on your side."

Kincaid glowered at Colin. "Are you daft?"

Colin returned the glare. "You might try charm and civility instead of snapping and snarling at the poor, wee lass."

"Well, well," drawled Kincaid. "She certainly managed to wrap you around her little finger."

Colin shot Kincaid an assessing look that usually spelled meddling. "We had a nice cozy chat over lunch." He leaned closer and whispered: "She's not married, you know."

"Don't you go playing matchmaker with me, you old fraud. The woman's stubborn, ornery and an enormous pain in the ass."

Colin fingered his beard. "Stubborn, ornery, pain in the ass. Hmmm." He considered for a moment. "Reminds me of someone else. Can't think of who that would be, though. Never mind. It'll come to me."

Kincaid made a disgusted sound. "You can't be referring to me. I'm persistent, sensitive, and refreshingly outspoken."

"Och. You're a matched pair. Maybe that's why sparks fly when you're together."

"Give me one good reason why I should make an effort to be charming to a spying reporter."

"Because she's one of the best investigative journalists in San Francisco with a reputation for honesty and fairness. Her article might swing the extra funding you need."

As much as Kincaid hated to admit it, Colin had a point. "Maybe. But the last thing I want is for the story to hit the press right away. I don't have enough security guards. If bandits strip the place, I'll be the laughing stock of the profession. It'll be a miracle if I ever work in the field again ....." He broke off, thinking of his overdrawn line of credit.

"Aye, weel. I'm sure I remember warning you not to pump your entire life savings into the project."

Kincaid shot Colin a quelling glance. "I need more time. First, we'll remove the rocks. That could take anywhere from a few days to several weeks. Then, I'll hire more workers to remove any treasure we find. More security guards, too. We'll have to catalogue and crate the artefacts, and then—"

"I might have the answer." Colin paused, prolonging the moment of suspense. "Then again, you might think I was meddling, and I wouldn't want to overstep my bounds."

"Oh, aye?" asked Kincaid casually, feigning mild interest when what he really wanted to do was to shake the solution out of his friend. "What's your idea?" He knew it wouldn't take long to get the answer because Colin was quivering with excitement.

"Easy. Tell Charley you'll co-operate and provide all the information she needs for an exclusive, as long as she agrees to hold off submitting the article until you give her permission. Reporters have a fancy long term they like to use for it."

Kincaid looked at his friend in amazement. "You mean an embargo."

"Aye. That's the word."

"How do you know about embargos?"

Colin grinned. "Last year, I gave a fancy food critic one of my best recipes for haggis, but I made her promise not to print it in the paper until after the banquet for the Scots Heritage Society. I didn't want them chickening out when they read what they'd be eating for a midnight snack."

Kincaid stopped walking and stared at Colin in wonder. "Of course. You're a genius. You never cease to amaze me."

Colin nodded modestly.

Kincaid continued: "Every time I unload a problem, you manage to slice through all the bullshit and dive into the heart of the matter." He hooked his free arm through Colin's and swung his friend around in an impromptu highland reel.

"That's a disagreeable and nasty mixed metaphor, Kincaid," panted Colin. "Let go of me. I'm not finished."

Kincaid released his friend. "What else?"

"Put Leila to work. Don't piss her off. You can't get rid of her, either, so you might as well use her expertise." Colin shot Kincaid a scathing look. "Just make sure you keep your pants zipped up."

Kincaid glared and resumed walking. "I have no intention of being anything other than professional, but I'm guessing Leila may have a different agenda." Cold shivers ran down his spine as he contemplated the various forms her agenda could take. He hoped he had the strength to resist. After all, it had been months since he'd been with a woman, and he was only human.

Colin puffed along beside Kincaid. "Give her the most finicky set of tasks you can think of, something run-of-the-mill. As long as she's working here, she won't be spreading gossip."

Kincaid scratched his head thoughtfully. "I know just the thing. I'll turn over a few meters of the grid network in the merchants' quarters to her. It's painstaking work, and unlikely to yield anything significant."

Colin preened. "There you go. My job is done. I have dispensed wit and wisdom to those in need. All I want is your undying gratitude."

"Aye. It's yours. Back to your kitchen with you. Make sure it's an especially tasty dinner tonight. I have a couple of delicate situations to deal with and I'll need all the help I can get."

Colin sniffed and stalked away. "My dinners are always tasty."

"Colin," Kincaid called. "All your meals are delicious. And thanks for the advice."

His friend turned his head and grinned. "That's what friends are for."

Kincaid turned away and Colin's voice followed him. "Charley's special. Mind you're nice to her or I'll burn your porridge for a year."

Using her satellite telephone, Charley punched in her mother's number and waited for the connection, twiddling a pencil. She had just enough time for a brief chat before dinner.

A series of loud clicks ensued before the phone in San Francisco started ringing.

Charley's heart thudded and she gnawed her bottom lip. *Please God, let her be home.* After four rings, the answering machine clicked in and her mother's familiar voice rang in her ear: "You have reached the home of Audrey Huntington. I am unavailable to take your call, but please leave a message and have a great day."

"Hi, Mom. I'm calling from the dig I told you about. Are you home? Please pick up."

No response.

Now truly worried, Charley persisted: "Where are you? Are you still in bed at this time of the day? I hope you made it home safely last night. You really shouldn't drink and drive. I'm worried that you might have had another accident." She sighed, remembering the several narrow escapes and fender-benders over the last two years. It was a miracle her mother still had her driver's licence. "Call me as soon as you get this message. I'll keep my phone turned on." She sighed and broke the connection.

Her enforced stress leave had left her helpless, unable to act as her mother's watchdog, monitoring every step she took, every bottle she purchased, every drink she swallowed. Rehab would change everything.

A white-hot spear of pain lanced through both temples as she contemplated the monumental task of convincing her mother to sign herself into a renowned and extremely expensive rehabilitation centre. She shifted her shoulders uneasily and tapped the pencil against the arm of her chair. As soon as she cashed the fat bonus for her article, she could afford to hire an entire team of Sumo wrestlers, if necessary, to drag her unwilling parent, kicking and screaming, into the addiction treatment programme.

All she needed was a knock-'em-dead exposé – a goal Kincaid was determined to thwart.

Charley slumped, gnawing the end of her pencil, lost in

thought. She toyed with several ploys until a bold idea popped into her head. No longer plagued with indecision, she straightened her back.

It wouldn't be easy and it wouldn't be fun, but a girl had to do what a girl had to do.

Chapter 6

Tropical dusk fell with a swiftness that caught Charley by surprise. One minute the sun blazed on the horizon, flooding the air with a hazy, golden glow; seconds later, it disappeared, leaving only sweeping streaks of pink and orange fading into the deepening purple of the night sky. Electric bulbs strung between trees winked on and provided plenty of light for her to navigate the path as she joined up with the hungry horde hurrying to dinner.

The dining hall was filling fast. Charley climbed the steps to the veranda and scanned the room, searching for an empty seat. Preferably one as far from Kincaid as she could get. She adjusted the sleeves of the flower-studded jacket she wore over a black tank top and jeans. Her stomach clenched at the sound of a soft, unmistakable Scottish voice that stirred the wisp of hair beside her ear.

"I trust you'll sit at my table while you're here."

She whirled around. How did someone as large as Kincaid manage to get so close without betraying his presence? A tiny white adhesive strip graced the side of his chin. He'd taken the trouble to shave before dinner. And changed his shirt, she noted. This one boasted a tasteful pattern of yellow and green palm fronds scattered with red and blue parrots against a poisonous purple background. In spite of the awful shirt, an insistent fluttering stirred in the pit of her stomach.

It's only hunger, she reassured herself.

Charley took a cautious step backwards. "Why the change of heart? I thought I'd be the last person you'd want to talk to." Before she could stop them, the next words popped out of her mouth of their own volition. "I don't blame you for being angry with me. I owe you an apology."

"For your smart-ass comments and ornery disposition?" Kincaid said with a ridiculously hopeful look on his face.

They were blocking the entrance and causing a traffic jam. She drew him aside, away from the door. "Neither. They come with the territory, particularly the ornery disposition. I meant an apology for landing on you without any warning."

He quirked one dark eyebrow. "Are you admitting you made a mistake?"

Charley flushed. "I want to come clean. The pilot gave me your phone number, but I was afraid you'd refuse if I called and asked for an invitation. I preferred to meet you face-to-face. I had no idea I'd be stranded here. I was as surprised as you."

Charley's glib explanation met with ominous silence.

Her heart thudded. "You have every right to be angry. I hadn't considered the difficulties my article would cause. Tell you what. I'll make a deal."

He gave her an unreadable look. "You continue to intrigue me. I'm all ears."

"If you give me permission for an exclusive, I won't submit the article until you've reviewed it and approved its release. In the industry, it's called an embargo – a restriction on publication. The article won't go out until you're ready."

"Even if it takes another six months or a year?"

She heaved a gusty sigh. "Yeah. It breaks my heart, but I give you my word."

Charley hoped a bolt of lightning wouldn't strike her dead for the bold-faced lie. For the first time in her life, she intended to betray the journalistic code of professional ethics, and the knowledge corroded her gut like battery acid. The article would hit the press as soon as she returned home.

She had no other choice if she wanted to save her mother's life, even if it meant compromising Kincaid's career, his reputation and his bank account.

He rubbed his chin thoughtfully. "If I reject your offer, I could have my security guards bar you from the dig for the next six days. You'd never see the site."

"Don't count on it. I'd find a way." She collected her thoughts carefully. "Look, Kincaid. I can write an article that will knock their socks off. You, of all people should understand where I'm coming from."

"What are you talking about?"

She drew a deep breath and constructed what she hoped was a convincing argument. "As an archaeologist, you dig the truth from the ground. You piece together the history of an ancient race from relics, artefacts and analysis. Right?" She didn't wait for confirmation, but rushed ahead. "Well, believe it or not, I dig out the truth as well. Not from the ground, but from interviews, observation and research. I want the public to see the Olmecs as clearly as you do – what made them tick, how they lived, worked, died, their ceremonies and habits. I want the public to feel as if they know the Olmecs personally." The only fault with her argument was an error of omission. She would wait for concrete evidence until she mentioned the curse of the Olmecs.

A small smile quirked the corners of his mouth. "You make some excellent points."

Charley eyed Kincaid with growing frustration. What did it take to convince the man? Did he guess her true designs? She had the unsettled feeling that he enjoyed toying with her. "I'm grovelling here, Kincaid. I'm twisting on the hook. Enjoy the sight. I don't do this often."

A subtle spark danced in his eyes. "Okay. You have a deal. Now I have a confession to make, too. Honesty compels me to tell you that Colin had already convinced me to let you write the article, but I wanted to hear the reasons from your own lips."

Charley's mouth tightened. "You mean, you'd already made your decision, but you put me through the wringer just to see what arguments I would trot out? You miserable, unspeakable .... " It was easier to lose her temper than to let herself experience a twinge of remorse at what she planned to do.

He waved a finger under her nose. "Now, now. Don't say anything that might make me change my mind. Remember, that ornery disposition of yours needs some serious work."

She almost lost it before it dawned on her that he was trying his damnedest to throw her off-balance. With a superhuman effort, she swallowed the rejoinder that would prove his point and refrained from breaking the finger he waggled so temptingly in her face. She stretched her mouth into a phony smile, displaying a large quantity of teeth, and purred sweetly: "I warned you earlier. The ornery disposition comes with the territory."

"Could we call a short truce, at least through dinner?"

She glowered. "I don't believe you. Let me get this straight. First you make me beg for something you'd already decided to give me, then you insult me, and now you want a truce so you can enjoy your dinner in peace and quiet?"

"That about covers it. Please. I promise I'll try to mend my ways. According to Colin, I'm stubborn, ornery and downright nasty, and that's only the beginning."

"Did Colin also mention you were rude, irritating and obnoxious?" Charley snapped, then relented. "Okay. Truce. But only for dinner."

With any luck, Kincaid himself would give her permission to publish her article immediately, and she would have nothing to worry about.

Except collecting the money to save her mother's life. And living with her guilty conscience for the rest of her life.

Candles on every table added an unexpected touch of elegance to the dining hall. The flames flickered and danced in the light breeze from the open veranda. Charley sniffed the air appreciatively, her returning appetite heralded by a faint growl that she disguised with a spate of words. "Ahh. Something smells wonderful. I'm so hungry I could eat an iguana."

Kincaid seated himself beside her. "Apparently, you spend most of your life in that condition," he commented. "Didn't you finish lunch only minutes ago?"

A tinkling laugh interrupted the scathing retort that sprang to the tip of Charley's tongue. Leila swept towards them, accompanied by a cloud of the same noxious perfume she had worn earlier. "Here you are, darling, as unassuming as ever. I see you're still choosing the smallest table stuck away in the back corner. Do you mind if I sit down?" Without waiting for an answer, she pulled out a chair and sat down, leaning towards Kincaid like a flower towards the sun, and turning her shoulder on Charley.

The woman had balls. Even after his unenthusiastic reaction to their reunion, Leila had the temerity to sit with Kincaid as if there was no tension between them.

Oh, yes. This would be an interesting dinner.

Before Kincaid had a chance to respond, Felipe claimed the fourth chair at their table. "I hope you will not be offended if I join you, Dr. Kincaid," he said, smiling amiably.

Leila nodded warmly. "We would love it if you sat with us, wouldn't we, Alistair?"

Sounding resigned, Kincaid jutted his chin at the last unoccupied chair. "Felipe. Join the party"

Leila brushed Felipe's arm with the tip of her fingers, then turned away and leaned a little closer to Kincaid to whisper something in his ear. She studiously ignored Charley.

If she leaned over much further, Charley reasoned, her breasts would tumble right out of her blouse. Undoubtedly, that was exactly what she wanted. Charley shifted uneasily on her chair. She and Leila hadn't exchanged a word since the interlude on the dock. If they were going to share a tent for a week, some form of communication would be necessary. They couldn't both continue to pretend the other didn't exist. She decided to break the ice and ease the tension. "You must have settled in when I was asleep," she said lamely, searching for some common ground for conversation. "The cots are pretty comfortable."

Frost crackled in Leila's voice. "I could care less. I have no intention of spending much time in our tent." She slanted a sultry glance up at Kincaid.

Kincaid proved that a man could turn pale under a deep tan. Charley gave him full marks for ignoring Leila's innuendo. He then gestured to a long table that groaned under the weight of an astounding bounty of food. "Meals are served buffet style. Help yourselves to all you can eat. Watch out for the green salsa – it'll destroy your taste buds, your stomach lining and anything else it encounters."

Charley didn't need any more urging. Obviously, Kincaid believed in feeding the workers well. His sites were famous for their high quality food, and the spicy smells of Colin's cooking were making her mouth water.

After five minutes of careful deliberation, she carried the heavily laden plate back to the table in time to catch Kincaid's question to Felipe.

"Where were you this afternoon, Felipe?" Kincaid demanded. "We made an amazing breakthrough up at the temple."

This was news to Charley. She wished she could fish out her notepad and pencil, but they were in her tent.

Felipe's gaze slid away. "I had personal business to attend to. The workers told me about finding the tunnel behind the temple, but it has no significance. Besides, a rock fall blocks the entrance. You will never succeed in removing it."

Was it her imagination, or had Felipe's constant smile soured to a twisted grimace?

Kincaid scowled. "The tunnel could be the breakthrough I'm looking for – the reason the Olmecs chose this exact location."

"How is this possible?" Felipe asked, sounding baffled.

"I think the tunnel existed before the city. I believe the Olmecs deliberately chose the location of the pyramid and the placement of the temple against the cliff because of the crevice. The temple floor aligns with the entrance too perfectly to be accidental. Where else have you ever seen an Olmec pyramid built into the mountainside? To my knowledge, this is a first."

Charley replayed in her head everything she had learned about the Olmecs from her frantic weeks of research. She had never heard of them before she caught wind of the mysterious disasters plaguing recent archaeological digs – Olmec digs. She had read about Aztecs, Mayas and even Zapotecs, but never Olmecs. It turned out no one knew much about the ancient race, including the experts. According to her research, the Olmecs were the most sophisticated society in Mexico from about 1300 BC to 600 AD – long before any of the better-known races. Some archaeologists called Olmecs the mother culture of later Mexican civilizations.

Leila stopped eating, a forkful of salad poised halfway to her mouth. Her eyes gleamed. "What do you think you will find when the rocks are cleared away?" she asked, placing her cutlery on her plate.

Kincaid's eyebrows shot up, as if he'd forgotten her presence. "Oh, I don't know. Could be just about anything, maybe nothing at all," he said evasively.

Charley's heart galloped. She was certain Kincaid had deliberately downplayed his hunch about the tunnel.

"Dr. Kincaid, I beg your pardon," Felipe interjected. "I have no wish to see you endanger the men by trying to remove the rock pile. Let the crew excavate the area below the pyramid."

"They can do that later. Your main priority will be to make sure they open the tunnel."

"It could be dangerous. I've seen men crushed by falling rocks."

Charley continued to devour her dinner while following their exchange. Why was Felipe persisting in his quest to halt the rock removal when he was obviously displeasing his boss? Something strange was going on. She forked up a healthy bite of chicken dripping with dark, aromatic *mole* sauce.

Charley swore she heard Kincaid grit his teeth. His voice sharpened. "We'll take every precaution to prevent an accident. I won't permit anyone to take unreasonable risks, but mark my words – I intend to break through the barrier if I have to supervise the work myself."

The Mexican's voice was expressionless. "You will be removing rocks the Master of Darkness placed to guard and protect the gate to the underworld."

"You don't really swallow that old superstition, do you?" Kincaid leaned forward, frowning. "Not in this day and age?"

"What superstition is that," Charley interjected.

Kincaid replied: "Some experts think the Olmecs, like the Mayans, believed that any opening in the earth was an entry to the underworld."

"You place the men in great danger," Felipe persisted, although a sickly smile still hovered around his mouth.

Kincaid's jaw muscle twitched. "Enough. The work starts tomorrow, Felipe." His tone of voice brooked no more argument.

"*Sí*, Dr. Kincaid." Felipe subsided, but his gaze flicked away. Charley watched the smile, which had been a permanent resident on the Mexican's face, disappear. Although he maintained an outwardly calm expression, a dull film of anger clouded his eyes.

"Good. I'm glad that's settled."

Charley leaned forward and addressed Kincaid. "I find the whole idea of a link between the Olmecs and Mayans fascinating. Are there other similarities?"

Leila sighed, but held her tongue.

"There are many strong resemblances. The Mayans, like the Olmecs, worshipped the jaguar. They believed the jaguar was god of the underworld."

Charley's stomach jolted at yet another mention of jaguars.

"Is anything wrong?" Kincaid inquired, eying her sharply.

If jaguars were destined to be a recurring theme, she had better get used to it. "No, nothing. It's just that, well, are there really any jaguars around here?"

Felipe jumped in before Kincaid could answer. "There have been some signs in this vicinity. Today, one of the men found a fresh set of paw-prints down by the river – jaguars live in caves and canyons close to fresh water. Close to their prey, no?"

Kincaid shot him a quelling glance. "No need to frighten Charley needlessly." He turned towards her. "I don't think we have anything to worry about. Mexican jaguars are very shy and tend to avoid human habitation. They're close to extinction today. Mainly because of over-hunting and the encroachment of farms."

Leila addressed Charley for the first time, a malicious smile playing around her mouth. "Goodness. We've *never* found jaguars this close to camp before. Better not go anywhere alone."

Charley refused to react to Leila's spiteful taunt. She swallowed the tight knot of foreboding at the back of her throat and asked: "What did jaguars signify to the Olmecs?"

Kincaid's face lit up. "The jaguar was very important to the Olmecs," he began pompously.

Leila made a face. "Oh no. *Please* don't get him started."

Undeterred, Kincaid continued: "To the ancients, the jaguar was not simply an animal, but half of the most powerful supernatural force. It represented political or earthly power. The other half, the snake, represented celestial or cosmic power."

Oh, boy. Although Kincaid could be highly irritating, he was really cute when he went into lecture mode. All serious and knowledgeable and earnest. Charley had always found professors appealing. The gold flecks swimming in his deep brown irises mesmerized her.

Obviously, Kincaid was on a roll. "Olmecs recognized both the jaguar and the snake as *naguals*, animal-spirits so closely related to a particular person that if the animal died, the individual would surely die as well. Jaguars were considered the most powerful predators in the jungle and the alter egos of Olmec shamans. Ancient shamans performed dark and powerful ceremonies centered on the jaguar. They believed they could transform themselves into their jaguar *nagual* through a mystical power called shapeshifting."

Charley shuddered. Shapeshifting, jaguars, dark ceremonies. Terrifying pictures, almost memories, hovered on the periphery of her consciousness, tantalizing her with their elusiveness. Unexpectedly, she caught Felipe's eye. He was staring directly at her as if he could see into her soul. Now there's someone, she thought uneasily, who might actually understand. Somehow, the thought did not provide any comfort.

Kincaid launched into a lively sermon on the mysteries of 'were-jaguars', offspring of a feline father and human mother, a common theme in Olmec sculpture, when Colin strolled over to the table and caught the last words.

"Och, Kincaid, not those were-jaguars again. You don't want to put the wee lass to sleep at the dinner table on her first night in camp. You can continue the lecture some other time."

Charley hid a quick smile.

Colin addressed Charley: "You can thank me later for the timely rescue. Sometimes it's easier to stop a runaway train than to stop Kincaid once he's started discoursing on his favourite topics, particularly if he thinks he has an interested audience. The man can pontificate for hours without pausing for breath. Don't know how he does it. It's not uncommon for folks to nod off long before he runs out of steam."

Kincaid chuckled. "Colin always brings me down to Earth when I get carried away." He gestured towards an empty chair. "Join us."

"No thanks. I have to supervise my new assistant during kitchen clean-up." Colin grinned at the table's occupants, then stopped talking and mimed a dramatic double take. "Why, hullo, Leila. How delightful to see you again."

Had Charley detected the slightest wrinkling of Leila's finely chiselled nose, as if she'd noticed a faint, but unmistakable, bad odour?

Colin winked at Charley. "I came over to find out how you enjoyed dinner."

"He's fishing for compliments," said Kincaid. "Don't pander to his neediness. It'll swell his head bigger than it already is and then he'll have to sleep in the dining hall because he won't be able to squeeze through the door."

Charley ignored Kincaid. "Everything was delicious, Colin, especially the chicken. I've never tasted anything like it. The sauce was amazing – rich, spicy, complex. I'd love the recipe."

"It's yours for the asking. The secret ingredient is chocolate." Colin nodded his head in Kincaid's direction. "Has this one been behaving himself?"

"We got off to a slightly rocky start, but he has displayed exemplary behaviour since we sat down," Charley answered. "No sarcastic remarks and only one tiny snide comment all evening."

Kincaid leaned back in his chair. "Hey. Don't mind me, folks. Keep those compliments coming. Discuss me all night if you want. I can take it."

Colin leaned towards Charley and whispered confidentially: "He sucks the fun out of every conversation." He straightened up. "Now, I'd better get back to the kitchen before the new lad loses his battle with the Hobart machine – that's our temperamental dishwasher," he explained for Charley's benefit. "Good night."

A wave of exhaustion rolled over Charley, taking her by

surprise. She stifled a yawn and stood up. "'Night, Colin. It's been a long day, folks. If you'll excuse me, I think I'm headed for an early night."

Kincaid leaped to his feet. "Let me walk you to your tent."

Alone with a gorgeous man on a fragrant, star-studded night? She would have to be out of her mind to take the risk. "No thanks. I'm perfectly capable of finding my own way back in spite of lurking jaguars and other predators of the night." She hesitated. "But I would love a guided tour of the dig tomorrow, especially the temple."

Kincaid brightened. "Well, in the spirit of our agreement, I'll be glad to show you around – temple, pyramid, and all. We'll leave right after breakfast." He eyed Charley's strappy sandals doubtfully. "Better wear hiking boots tomorrow. Snakes love underbrush."

Charley suppressed a shudder. *So do jaguars.*

Leila, who had watched the exchange with narrowed eyes, said: "How touching – helping Charley to select her wardrobe." She turned her face towards Kincaid, like a flower following the sun. "If you don't mind, Alistair, I'll join the tour. Surely you can squeeze in one more guest."

Kincaid grunted and shot his ex-wife a piercing glance. "We need to talk. My cabin, half an hour."

Chapter 7

Two hours after dinner had ended, Kincaid struggled to the surface of sleep, unsure of what had woken him. A distressed yowl from Horrie provided the first clue. He was no longer alone in the cabin. Kincaid's eyes flew open. Disoriented, he still noted that the cat streaked away from his customary position, snuggled on the pillow beside his master, to slink under the mosquito netting and hide beneath a corner table. He then discerned a shadowy figure against the open window. A heavy, musky scent perfumed the air.

"Bloody hell, Leila. What are you doing in my cabin in the middle of the night?" he mumbled, sitting up and sweeping the mosquito netting aside.

"That's hardly the greeting I'd hoped for," Leila purred, moving closer to the bed. "Have you forgotten? You invited me here."

Kincaid focused his bleary eyes on the luminous face of his watch. "That was over two hours ago. At the very least, you could grant me the courtesy of knocking."

"I did – twice. But you were so sound asleep, I thought I'd wake you up another way."

Adrenaline pumped through Kincaid's veins, replacing all trace of drowsiness with a super-charged alertness. He leaped up and groped in the darkened room for the jeans he'd left lying on the floor, then pulled them up over his hips and fastened them with a snap. "Seems to me I recall mentioning half an hour," he grumbled and switched on the lamp.

"I don't take orders from anyone."

Kincaid squinted in the sudden brightness until his eyes adjusted. He heaved an uncomfortable sigh. Leila wore nothing but a flimsy robe that clung to her curves and revealed the outline of her shapely body – a calculated move on her part, he wagered. Dusky nipples and a darker shadow between her thighs contrasted with the pearly gold of her skin.

At the back of his mind, Kincaid had always wondered how he'd feel when he finally saw her again. Would he be strong enough to resist the pull? Now he knew the answer. As delectable as she looked, body gleaming like burnished ivory through the midnight blue of the sheer fabric, his gut no longer twisted with the familiar tug of lust and longing. Her sensual hold over him was broken.

He snagged a tee shirt from the chair and shrugged it on. That was better. Less exposed. A man should be fully dressed when confronting his ex-wife alone for the first time since she dumped him for another man.

He recalled with crystal clarity the fateful afternoon when she'd shattered his life into a million tiny pieces. Conflicting feelings of failure, futility and rage had torn him apart. Eleven years of his life disappeared down the toilet in the blink of an eye. Oblivion became his chief goal, and he'd succeeded beyond his wildest dreams. Throwing himself into work, he had pushed himself beyond human endurance trying to reestablish credibility within the archaeological community. He'd reserved evenings and weekends for the round of frenzied fun that had left him feeling empty and ashamed. Even though he no longer drank, he'd driven too fast, partied too much, and screwed far too many women. God help him, he couldn't even remember most of their names.

"A penny for your thoughts," Leila whispered, stepping towards him. "Aren't you at least a little happy to see me?" She traced one tapered, red-tipped finger down his cheek.

He grasped her hand and shoved it aside. "You don't want to know what I'm thinking," he muttered. After pacing the length of the cabin several times, he flung himself onto a chair.

Leila pouted prettily. "I've come down here to propose that we try to pick up where we left off." She glided over to where he sprawled, long legs extended. Slowly, she stooped, twined her arms around his neck and nipped his ear gently. Her robe fell open and her breasts spilled into view. "We

81

could make a good team again – just like old times."

He pushed her hands away and stood up. "Just like that?" He snapped his fingers together with a loud click to illustrate his point. "For God's sake, you talk as if you'd only taken a weekend break instead of compromising our project, then divorcing me for another man. Get it through your head, Leila. We're not a team anymore, personally or professionally. Do I make myself clear?"

Leila gripped his arm with both hands to prevent him from shrugging away, fingers pressing hard enough to bruise his flesh. She laughed softly. "Don't be such a grouch. I know you need to salvage some masculine pride, but I'm offering to come back and start again."

"Why?" The bluntness of his question reverberated in the air between them.

She turned her head away and stared blindly at the wall, but not before he'd caught a glimpse of the exasperation that darkened her face. "Because..., " she allowed her voice to falter, "because leaving you was the biggest mistake of my life."

Angry buzzing broke the charged silence. A hard-shelled insect battered its plump body against the screened window in a futile attempt to penetrate the invisible barrier.

Leila was up to something. She'd never once admitted a mistake in all the years he'd known her. Now that the scales had fallen away, he was able to regard her objectively. Why had he stubbornly refused to let go of his disastrous marriage? His self-assigned mission to rescue Leila from herself had been doomed from the start, but it had taken over two years after the divorce for him to admit he'd never had any control over the dark demons that drove her actions.

He tightened his jaw. "We can't go back, Leila. I'm not the same self-destructive fool I used to be."

She whirled around to confront him, face pale, eyes wide and glistening with unshed tears. "If only you'd been nicer to me, I wouldn't have turned to another man." A single tear rolled down her cheek.

A sick feeling bubbled in the pit of his stomach. How often had he fallen for those manipulative tears? "Oh, aye. Right you are. My fault, again. There I was, upset because you had perpetrated a hoax that nearly ended my career, so you traded me in for a more accommodating model. Well, I've reached my limit. I'll never play your game again."

She stepped closer and whispered: "We can start a new game, Alistair. I promise I'll never compromise our project again."

He glared at her incredulously. "A new game? You're dreaming in Technicolour."

"That's only your wounded pride speaking. Your feelings can't have changed so much in such a short time. We're too good together. You know you can't keep your hands off me. Admit it." Slowly, she opened her robe and placed his hand on a glorious breast.

He jerked away. "I'd sooner caress a rattlesnake."

Leila tossed her hair away from blazing eyes with a shake of her head. "Be careful what you wish for." With trembling fingers and jerky movements, she retied the sash of her robe. "You'll change your mind, but it may be too late."

Years of frustration and disappointment poured from his mouth in a bitter torrent of words, surprising the hell out of him. "For years, I loved you so much it hurt. I ignored your selfishness, your ruthlessness. I convinced myself that we didn't really need to have children to be a family, that what we had together was enough. I thought because I loved you, I could convince you to get the help you needed, but you were so hungry for power, you threw it all away."

Her mouth twisted. "You sanctimonious son-of-a-bitch. I don't need help. If anyone needs help, it's you."

"I made allowances for your tragic childhood and told myself your cold callousness was merely a protective shield to guard against more hurt and helplessness. But you'll never change, will you? I allowed you to control my life for over eleven years, but now I've regained my sanity. I owe you a debt of gratitude. Seeing you again makes it easy to put everything in perspective. It's over. We're over."

She threw her head back and laughed mirthlessly. "You need me, Alistair. Where do you think you'd be without me? Still sifting through the dirt looking for some lousy pottery shards."

"I've succeeded nicely without you for over two years. If I

hadn't, you wouldn't be here now, would you?"

Kincaid watched, curiously detached, as Leila struggled for an answer, her back rigid. She moved away and looked out of the window at the velvet darkness. A minute ticked by in silence, then another. When she finally turned and spoke, her brisk and businesslike tone belied the rage still smouldering behind her eyes. "Alistair, darling. I didn't come here to argue with you. It looks like we're stuck with one another for the next week, so you might as well make the most of another pair of hands. While I'm here, I want to help you with the dig."

"How altruistic of you." His suspicions grew stronger. What was she up to now? Everything Leila did served her purpose in some way.

"Not altruistic – practical. I'll go out of my mind with boredom if I don't have something to do to keep me busy."

True enough. Ever since he'd known her, she'd always manufactured a deliberate whirlwind of activity. She drove herself to distraction, tackling task upon task, generating artificial crises simply to hold her personal demons at bay. He couldn't see how allowing her to excavate a minor portion of the site could possibly pose a threat, and it might help keep her out of trouble.

He raked his fingers through his hair. "Okay. You might be able to help. Students need guidance and direction, and I don't have enough archaeologists to spread around. You could help them excavate the merchants' quarters we've uncovered in the Lower City."

"That's it?" she asked incredulously, her mouth twisted in a sneer. "All my years of Olmec expertise at your disposal, and you're giving me the *merchants' quarters*? Surely you can find something more challenging than baby-sitting a pack of neophyte students."

"Take it or leave it. It's the best offer you'll get."

Leila bit her lip. "Fine," she snapped. "I'll take it. You can show me the location of my exciting new job as part of the guided tour."

"Aye. I'll show you the entire site tomorrow, but after that, stay away from the pyramid and the temple. I don't want you nosing around up there or getting in my hair. I'll inform the security guards to let you onto the site but only in the Lower City. They'll make sure you don't go near the Ceremonial Centre, so don't bother trying."

Long lashes swept down to hide her eyes.

Kincaid stared at her suspiciously. He couldn't read her expression, but he knew her well enough to recognize that her meek capitulation over being rejected from his bed then banished from the most important archaeological discoveries had been too easy.

He hoped he wouldn't regret his decision to let her help.

Chapter 8

"Slow down, Felipe. Don't walk so damned fast," Leila panted.

The low midnight moon cast an eerie light, deepening the shadows and concealing pitfalls on the path ahead. She sensed, rather than saw, the faint animal trail they followed, more a thinning of vegetation than an actual path. The trail meandered up the darkened hillside behind Kincaid's dig, out of sight of the camp and, hopefully, the ever-vigilant security guards.

"How much further do you expect me to climb? What the hell's so special about the top of this hill?" Although the night air was crisp at an altitude of over one mile above sea level, perspiration streamed down her neck.

Felipe shrugged and kept walking. "All will become clear."

She hissed long and hard when a razor-sharp thorn grazed the back of her hand. When she sucked the wound, the coppery taste of blood filled her mouth. "You said the jungle would thin out as we climbed and you didn't mention anything about thorn bushes. Turn on the flashlight for a minute so I can see where I'm going."

"The moon provides enough light for our purposes. The guards must not see us."

Leila grunted, but plodded on upwards. Her mood, sour to begin with, was deteriorating by the minute. "This had better be good," she muttered. Anything would be an improvement on her evening thus far. Alistair's curt rebuff was an unexpected setback to her plans.

By the time she had stormed back to her tent from Alistair's cabin, it had been almost midnight. The romantic rendezvous had fallen far short of her expectations. Surprisingly, he had developed a backbone over the last two years. Well, let him cling to his petty grudge for the moment. She had one full week to convince him he couldn't live without her, and she could accomplish miracles in a week.

She'd discarded the filmy robe in disgust and hastily donned suitable attire for her rendezvous with Felipe – black jeans and turtleneck, heavy socks and supple hiking boots.

Leila's breath wheezed. The steep climb proved to be more difficult than she'd anticipated. Even regular workouts at the gym hadn't prepared her for scrambling up rocks like a mountain goat. The path flattened, and she walked more easily, lengthening her stride and letting her mind drift to what she considered her greatest asset – her body. She smoothed her hands over high, rounded breasts, tiny waist, and flat stomach, assessing herself critically. Although she was thirty-three, her figure was holding up pretty well, still firm and taut. Nature had been kind, but she didn't take her appearance for granted. Nobody, including Alistair, had any idea how fanatically she took care of herself – exercising like a fiend each day and depriving herself of all the foods she adored – all to retain the slim, curvy look men craved.

Beauty was power, as was sex, and she used both to her best advantage. Alistair wouldn't be able to hold out against her charms for more than a couple of days.

When they reached a large boulder, Felipe grunted: "We have arrived."

As far as she could tell, the desolate patch of rocky ground was devoid of ruins, buildings, vegetation, indeed, anything of interest. She flopped on the ground, hot, breathless and sullen. "We're not even at the summit. There's absolutely nothing to see here. I assume this is some weird test you dreamed up to torment me."

The screech of a night bird startled her. She raised her head. Felipe had disappeared. One minute he'd been standing beside her, and the next, he was simply gone without a sound. A superstitious shiver ran down her spine. Was this one of his tricks?

She hauled herself to her feet and squinted at the spot where he had vanished. A faint glow marked the concealed opening. An animal den? She peered into a crevice so well camouflaged with bushes and weeds and tucked away behind a rock that she would have walked past it without noticing, even at mid-day.

Her skin crawled. Did he really think she would join him in a dank, smelly hole in the ground? What if it was still inhabited and the occupant was anti-social? Worse, what if it contained bats? On the other hand, she had no wish to navigate the dangerous path back to camp, alone, in the darkness. She followed Felipe into the gloom, unable to see anything ahead except the dark outline of his figure against the dim gleam of the flashlight.

Felipe's voice reverberated off the rock walls. "Keep your head low and keep close."

Leila ducked her head. Her outstretched arms encountered smooth walls above her head and on either side of her. The tunnel was no more than three feet wide and five and a half feet high, smooth and dry underfoot, and sloping gently downward.

She started walking, placing one foot gingerly in front of the other, blood hammering in her ears. The oppressive weight of an entire mountain, tons of rock that could squash her like a bug if a tremor hit the area, hemmed her in. At one point, the ceiling lowered until she had to crouch in an uncomfortable duck walk.

More to take her mind off the claustrophobia clawing at her throat than out of genuine interest, Leila asked: "How did you find this tunnel?"

Felipe's distorted voice bounced off the walls. "I discovered it accidentally one day last month when I followed an animal trail. The path disappeared behind a rock and I grew curious. On closer examination, I found this tunnel descending into the ground."

"It looks like a volcanic tube."

"*Sí.* It is an underground lava tunnel. This entire area is volcanic. That is why the walls are glassy." He halted and touched her arm. "Watch out for the chasm. It has no bottom. I call it *el hoyo oscuro*, the dark pit."

Leila shuddered and edged around the gaping shaft. A faint rustle in the dark caused her to duck and cover her head with both hands. "Shit, Felipe. I just saw a bat," she whimpered, ashamed, but unable to suppress an involuntary shriek.

None too gently, he gripped her arm and dragged her away from the sinkhole. "Get back, you little fool. The bats will not harm you."

"I'm fine. You can let go now." When he dropped her arm and continued to walk ahead, she rubbed her throbbing elbow thoughtfully. *Damn, he might look old, but he is as wiry as tempered steel.*

After several endless minutes, the tunnel widened and she found she could stand upright. With a sigh of relief, she stretched, easing the kinks out of her back and neck. Felipe stepped aside, indicating that she should precede him. Wordlessly, he handed her the flashlight.

She stepped forward cautiously and played the narrow beam of light around the cave. Her discomfort fled as she gasped, lost for words at the sheer enormity of the rounded cavern. The roof soared into darkness above their heads. "I don't believe it," she said in a tight voice. "A lava bubble deep in the mountain. I've heard about how an air bubble sometimes gets trapped in molten lava, but I never expected to see one."

An intricate band of carvings encircled the walls and several dark openings promised more surprises. Inch by inch, she examined the carvings, spreading out her hand, touching the ancient symbols, sensing the shapes with her fingers.

She whispered in awe: "It's Olmec, isn't it?"

"*Sí.* Olmec."

Leila swung the flashlight around and illuminated a large, rectangular block of stone in the centre of the cave. Mindless of Felipe, she sprinted over and examined the carved surfaces, looking at them from all angles, then climbed up and lay down on the cold, hard slab. "I must be dreaming. This has to be an altar. There's even a depression for the head," she breathed then sat up. "But that's impossible. This entire cave is impossible. To my knowledge, this is the first record of a Meso-American religious centre buried in a mountain."

She hopped down and turned in a slow circle, trying to absorb the implications of the astounding sight. Her imagination conjured up visions of secret ceremonies and ancient sacrifices performed within soundproof confines. Tons of rock would have prevented any whisper of sound – screams, whimpers, pleadings – from reaching the curious ears of the masses.

At the far end of the cave, the light beam bounced off a huge pile of tumbled rocks. "A massive rockslide," she observed. "A tremor or earthquake must have brought it down."

Felipe's voice echoed in the cavern. "You are looking at the back of the rock pile Kincaid wants removed. The boulders block the entrance to this cave from the temple. If the gods are willing, Kincaid will never set foot in this sacred spot." He grasped her arm and lowered his voice, his breath hot and fetid on her cheek. "You will remember your promise to reveal nothing to Kincaid."

Leila's skin crawled. What was she getting herself into? She shrugged him off. "Don't worry. This is our secret." She did not intend to tell Alistair. For now. If necessary, she would use this secret as leverage to share in the rewards of the dig. She smiled grimly. At least her professional future was now assured, even if her romantic future was uncertain.

"What's in here?" she demanded, approaching the maw of one of the black openings.

Felipe blocked her way. "Do not stray from this main cavern. You could easily get lost. The entire mountain is honeycombed with tunnels."

What did he not want her to see? Reluctantly, she turned back, consoled by the thought that, for now, the discovery belonged to her, and her alone. There would be time enough to explore the subsidiary tunnels later. Right now, she wanted to examine every corner of the main cavern.

Half an hour later, Leila sank to the stone floor beside Felipe, overwhelmed by the magnitude of the discovery. Using a pile of sticks and twigs, Felipe had built a small fire in the shadows of the altar.

He sprinkled a handful of dry powder onto the blaze. Emerald green flames flared. A pungent, aromatic scent filled the cavern. The fire leaped higher into the blackness, highlighting his features, leaving his eyes deeply shadowed and sinister. Leila studied the enigmatic stranger sitting cross-legged on the opposite side of the fire. A cold shiver touched her spine. He could easily be one of the Olmecs' distant descendants, just as he claimed. It was no stretch to imagine him in ceremonial robes and the towering headdress of his people.

Her head began to spin pleasantly from the powder he sprinkled into the fire. As her uneasiness faded, she let her mind drift.

Felipe pulled a battered pouch from his pocket and untied the leather thong. His voice echoed from a distance, interrupting her reverie. "Tonight, you will use the sacred cactus to assist you on your journey. Soon your own powers will increase and you will not need help."

He shook out a few of the dry, brown objects into his palm.

Ahhh, peyote. The source of visions and power. Already, she could anticipate the dream-like trance.

Felipe handed half the buttons to her, one by one. Together they performed the ritual, chewing slowly and thoroughly, then swallowing the bitter pulp.

This time, she was prepared for her unpleasant reaction to the hallucinogenic plant. A touch of discomfort was a small enough price to pay. Again, she experienced the same mouth-parching thirst, nausea, heavy pounding in her ears, and the almost unbearable agony that had terrified her the first time. Then came the supreme moment she'd been anticipating – the transforming burst of insight and swirl of colour.

Her mind opened to the endless possibilities of the Universe. Elation bubbled at the back of her throat and she laughed aloud.

This was her destiny.

Felipe's deep voice, threaded with awe, broke the silence. "I am looking deep inside you and perceive an unusual duality."

Leila noted that his voice rose and fell like distant water tumbling over stones. How could he read the messages of her soul? "What duality?"

He stared deep into her eyes. "You are the only person I have ever seen who possesses two *naguals*. Great power will be yours if you learn to harness both."

Two powerful spirit-animals sounded good to Leila. "What are they?"

"One is the snake."

She curled her lip. "I hate snakes."

"To the Olmecs, the snake was half of the most potent god – a divine power representing the cosmos and transformation."

She forced her tongue to shape her next words. "What is my second *nagual*?"

"Your second *nagual* is the jaguar. The other half of the deity, signifying rain and prosperity."

"Both halves of the Olmec god," she mused. That should be power enough, even for her.

"Tonight, you will meet one of your *naguals*," Felipe explained.

She struggled to focus on his words. "Which one?"

"The Master of Darkness tells me you must start with the snake."

The cave swam with pulsing colours. Swirling blue, green and purple luminosity contracted and expanded rhythmically in tune with her heartbeat, so intense at times, the beauty hurt her eyes. She shrugged. Nothing could harm her. "What must I do?"

Felipe's voice was a distant echo in her head. "Tonight, you will find the spirit of the serpent. Make it your friend, get a psychic impression, and make its characteristics your own. This is the first level of shapeshifting."

She nodded, trying to concentrate.

"Tomorrow night, you will ascend to the second level. You will project your astral essence into its physical body while your human body remains here. Do you understand?"

Her numb lips slurred the words. "Are there other levels?"

"The Olmecs called the third and highest level *bè ta mè*. The name means 'unique state of comprehension'. Few people have ever ascended to this height, and I am one." His voice crackled with pride. "All who reach this level can manifest the creature that already dwells within themselves and change their physical form to become the animal."

"I will master all levels." She had never been so certain of anything in her life.

"If the Master of Darkness grants you the power. Now, lie down. You must call to the snake's spirit and ask it to recognize you. Take great care. If your *nagual* dies, so too, your human body must die. Do you see anything yet?"

She settled her back against the steps to the altar. Silently, in her mind, she called out to a presence so ephemeral, she sensed it only at the very fringe of her consciousness. Suddenly, she was aware of a connection with – *something* – a benign energy. Its essence surrounded and filled her, guiding her to an unknown destination.

Her spirit floated up, severing its ties to her body, leaving behind the shell of a woman sprawled like a rag doll against the stairs, one hand outstretched. She yielded to the insistent force sucking her into its energy field until she could no longer see the physical body below her. A cooling breeze lifted the hair from her forehead and a myriad of stars flew past her head in a blur of light. Guided by her *nagual,* Leila floated through space and time, anticipation fizzing in her veins.

Her journey ended in a dry sanctuary bounded by rocky walls.

She curled up on a low ledge, waiting, not sure what to expect, but knowing that this experience would change her life forever. A low hiss warned her of another presence hovering nearby. Her head felt like a pumpkin as she rotated it, trying to pierce the enveloping gloom. A sinuous movement in the darkness caught her eye and she threw aside the peyote-induced lassitude. Soon, she would savour the power she craved.

The snake undulated from the shadows, its long, thick body encircling Leila's, its rattle silent. Strangely enough, she felt no fear or revulsion, but remained motionless, welcoming the dry caress with a sensual shudder. The reptile opened its cavernous mouth, black tongue flickering, testing the air, and raised its head until their eyes were at the same level. Greenish eyes blazing with fierce intelligence stared into her own.

Unafraid, Leila caressed the reptile, feeling the sinuous strength of the creature. Rough scales rasped her fingertips. Meeting the snake was like meeting a long-hidden facet of her own personality, sensed but unacknowledged until this moment. They were two halves of the same whole.

Time belonged to another dimension. Without words, their two minds melded for what might have been hours, but could equally have been minutes, or seconds, or days, sharing the secrets of their souls.

Felipe's voice called out to her in the distance, signaling to Leila that her time with her *nagual* must end.

"Goodbye, my friend," she whispered. Tears of sadness trickled down her face as she tore herself away, feeling as if she was losing a part of herself. She touched the snake's cheek. "I will see you again tomorrow."

Going back was easy. She followed the sound of Felipe's voice and returned to the cavern where she had vacated her body. A loud *whoosh* followed by an electric hush signalled that her spirit had settled into its familiar trappings once more.

"Tell me everything," Felipe commanded.

Leila's memory of the adventure was already fading, as insubstantial as a dream. How could she forget the overwhelming emotions so quickly? She closed her eyes and tried to dredge up the memory. Focusing her attention inward, she described her experience of her *nagual*. When she finished talking, she opened her eyes and blinked. "That's all I can put my finger on. I wish I could tell you more."

Felipe nodded his approval, hooded eyes gleaming with satisfaction. "This is a strong omen. As I suspected, you are blessed with the natural abilities of a powerful shaman and sorcerer."

A surge of elation nearly unseated Leila. Soon, she would learn to command more power than she had ever dreamed of. The glorious daydream was so overwhelming, she nearly missed Felipe's next words.

He said: "You passed a crucial test tonight. Only true descendants of the Ancient Ones are granted the ability to shapeshift so effortlessly."

Leila shook her head in wonder as the meaning of his

words reverberated in her head. "*Me*? A descendant of the Olmecs?" she croaked, unwilling to believe.

"Think back to your birth."

She mulled it over, her brain churning with possibilities. Could the Olmecs be her distant ancestors? Her parents had both been born in a remote village in the region of Veracruz, ancestral home of the Olmecs. Perhaps an Olmec heritage explained why she had always been drawn to sorcery and the dark arts, not to mention her particular profession and area of speciality – archaeology, with a special focus on the Olmecs.

Perhaps she had inherited her ancestors' mystical gifts.

Leila wanted to whirl and spin in a dance of jubilation, but she schooled her face to remain impassive.

Envy roughened Felipe's voice. "The gods have bestowed on you the two most powerful spirit animals. Even I, a great shaman, possess only a single *nagual*."

Leila took a wild guess. "The jaguar."

"*Sí*. But you have both. The jaguar and the snake are the most sacred gods in the ancient Olmec religion – representing the cosmic and the earthly planes. Those who can shapeshift into one of those animals inherit its powers."

Cosmic powers. That suited Leila nicely.

Felipe continued: "You carry within you the combined forces of the Universe. For years, I have been searching for an acolyte to continue my work when I am no longer of this earthly plane. Until I found you, I believed I was the only person alive with a god-totem as a *nagual*. I thought everything I stood for would die along with me."

Leila couldn't believe her ears. The notion was insane, yet she couldn't deny that the power of the serpent still pulsed through her body. "You believe I am that acolyte?"

"There is no doubt in my mind. You answered my summons and you will help me with my mission here for as long as I am alive. The time to cultivate your gift has arrived."

Leila didn't answer. She doubted very much she would be following in his footsteps or helping him out with his mysterious mission, especially if her plans for reuniting with Alistair worked out the way she hoped. Soon, very soon, she would share in his triumph, and the scandal surrounding her last project would fade into obscurity. People had such short memories. She would, however, cultivate her gift, as Felipe so quaintly phrased it, for as long as possible.

"I have lost too much time already," he continued, taking her silence as assent. "We will continue our lessons each night when everyone else is asleep. Tomorrow, you will progress to the next level."

"But when do I get to sleep?"

Felipe frowned as if irritated at such a mundane question. "Sleep is irrelevant for the truly gifted."

Leila didn't much like the sound of that. When would she find time to help Alistair with the dig in order to win him back? But she'd give the experiment a whirl and do the best she could, at least for a couple of days. And if she missed a lesson because of romantic plans involving Alistair, so what? She would find a way to convince Felipe to continue her training.

"What about you? How are you able to work without sleep?" she asked.

He fed a twig into the fire and glanced up. "I take energy from the control I exercise over my mind."

She could do with a lesson or two in mind control as well, she thought, wryly. Then another niggling thought surfaced. "How do you expect me to help you continue your work here?"

"When you are able to command the power of both *naguals*, I will reveal more. Soon, you will develop a force so powerful, no challenger will defeat you. The ancient legacy must continue."

That sounded ominous, although the idea of the powerful force was interesting. Felipe was a fanatic. Unbalanced, verging on insane. She'd have to be careful while she picked his brains.

On the one hand, she craved the power and freedom of shapeshifting, and had no wish to jeopardize her training by turning against her teacher. At least, not yet. On the other hand, she wouldn't allow Felipe's fanaticism to hurt either Alistair or the dig. That would defeat her strategy. On the contrary, she hoped to share in the glory at Alistair's side. Best play along in order to receive her nightly lessons in shapeshifting.

"What do you have planned?" she asked with feigned nonchalance.

Felipe clambered to his feet and towered over her, an intimidating figure silhouetted against the flickering orange of the fire. "The desecration of this sacred cavern must be prevented. The path will be made clear to you when the time is right."

Leila flashed an uneasy smile and nodded her head, apprehension tightening her chest. Matching his action, she hauled herself to her feet and faced Felipe, her hands on her hips. "I can wait."

Leila wanted it all, and she vowed she'd find a way to do just that.

Chapter 9

In Charley's opinion, 6:15 am was an uncivilized time for a wake-up bell. She ignored it by pulling a pillow over her head. Half an hour later, the clamour of the ten-minute breakfast warning pierced the fog clouding her brain, and she jolted awake, disoriented and faintly apprehensive. A second later, her memory returned along with a jolt of foreboding. After last night's dinner, she'd flopped into bed, exhausted, and tumbled into an uneasy sleep punctuated by vivid nightmares. The dreams faded before she could capture them, but they had left a sense of impending doom in their wake.

She groaned and rolled over, eyes gritty from lack of sleep.

Shortly before midnight, a glaring light accompanied by a clatter of noise in the tent had torn her from a fitful sleep. Eyes squinting, she'd snapped: "Dammit, Leila. Do you mind? Some of us are trying to sleep."

Leila had snarled out a curse, tugged on a pair of heavy boots and disappeared into the night, leaving the table light on and an incensed investigative journalist, wide awake and seething with indignation, tinged with curiosity.

Unable to fall asleep again, Charley had resigned herself to an endless night of insomnia. Flipping open her paperback, she immersed herself in the heroine's trials and tribulations. Four hours later, she clicked off the lamp and curled up. Leila still hadn't returned.

As dawn bathed the interior of the tent in dim greyness, and a tiny portion of Charley's brain registered the fact that her roommate was sliding into the empty cot before deep slumber finally claimed her.

Now, as the last echoes of the warning bell faded in the still, hot air, Charley dragged her weary body upright. She probably looked as bad as she felt.

A quick glance at the other cot verified that Leila had, indeed, returned. She'd probably spent the night with Kincaid. Charley squelched the momentary pang and hopped out of bed.

For once, she was willing to skip breakfast. If all the meals were like last night's dinner, she'd be the size of a hippo after a week. Anyway, she needed time to prepare for the interview, arm herself against Kincaid's lethal charm.

Twenty minutes later, refreshed and energized from a lukewarm shower, Charley dashed back to the tent, clutching her robe closed and singing a vintage Eagles number under her breath. Still humming, she dressed in a snappy little sage green jumpsuit, chosen to emphasize her best asset – her legs. The perfect outfit for an archaeological tour. Casual chic. The tropical equivalent of a power suit.

Recalling Kincaid's warning about snakes, she dragged on her shiny new Sundowner hiking boots. Damned things had cost a small fortune. She tried to flex the sole and gave up. The boot boasted a full-length steel shank that made it as rigid as a drill bit. Charley laced them up and stomped her feet experimentally. The boots would be more than a match for any inhospitable snake bent on sinking venomous fangs into a visitor's unprotected feet.

She grabbed her travel bag and stowed the tools of her trade – tape recorder, notepad, pen and camera. As an afterthought, she tossed in a chocolate bar from the stash she took on every trip.

Birdsong mixed with beating wings greeted Charley's appearance. She shaded her eyes and blinked like an owl in the sudden glare. Steam clung to the ground and pearly ribbons of mist rose in ragged streamers from the calm waters of the lagoon. A great white heron spread its wings and flapped off carrying a flopping fish in its beak.

Charley sniffed the air. *Bacon and coffee.* Her appetite returned with a vengeance. Skipping breakfast was a lousy idea. Perhaps she'd cadge some leftovers from Colin before meeting with Kincaid.

Charley glanced at her watch for the fourth time and drummed her fingers on the table. She'd been cooling her heels in the kitchen for over an hour and Kincaid still hadn't showed up. Another five minutes, and then she'd head to the dig alone. Colin would point her in the right direction. She was getting used to the spooky atmosphere she had found so disturbing on the dock yesterday. Soon, it wouldn't faze her at all.

Four minutes and twenty-one seconds later, Colin waved to someone outside the window, then turned away and disappeared into the pantry. He might as well have hung an ostentatious 'Not Listening' sign on the door. A treacherous flutter curled in her stomach and she slanted a casual glance towards the veranda. Sure enough, Kincaid strode up the path towards her, smiling broadly, deep grooves creasing his cheeks and eyes crinkling at the corners. His momentum caused the rich, dark hair to whip around his face in casual disarray. A yellow and orange floral shirt hugged his body.

He looked even better than she remembered.

Kincaid leaped up the three steps in a single bound. "Good morning, beautiful."

A telltale burst of heat flooded her cheeks. She hoped he hadn't noticed. "Hi, yourself."

He straddled the chair across from her and leaned his elbows on the table. "I'm sorry I'm late, but Felipe didn't show up until fifteen minutes ago. I didn't want the men to waste time waiting for him, so I got them started on the rock removal myself." A perplexed expression crossed his face. "Strange. It's not like Felipe to be so unreliable."

Charley's mind whirled with possibilities. Her brain joined a few dots, and an interesting pattern started to emerge. Was it possible Felipe, not Kincaid, had spent the night with Leila? Perhaps her suspicions of Kincaid's participation in a sexual marathon with his ex had been a tad hasty. Not that it mattered in the slightest, Charley assured herself. Kincaid was off-limits.

"No problem. Colin fed me and entertained me." She eyed the riot of flowers that screamed across today's shirt. "That's quite a shirt you're wearing. Very ... er ... colourful. How many of those things do you own anyway?"

He brightened. "Dozens. Bought them last time I was in Hawaii. They have great taste on the islands. Fine colour sense. *Kanakas* know how to dress."

Charley made a non-committal noise. "So I see."

He leaned in closer. "I hope you were comfortable in your tent last night."

"Surprisingly comfortable, thank you," she said in a prim voice she hardly recognized as her own.

His mouth curved in a tiny smile. "Ah, good. I aim to please. We may be only a small establishment out here, and we may not have all the frills of a Hilton hotel, but there are a few advantages and amenities – *me* for example," he explained, modestly.

She nearly choked on a sip of coffee. "I'd rather have air conditioning."

Kincaid spread his arms wide in an expansive gesture. "Air conditioning? You can't mean that. Air conditioning is run-of-the-mill. Air conditioning is banal."

Charley retaliated: "Air conditioning is a necessity. How about an *ensuite* bathroom then?"

"Same thing. Boring, boring, boring. No sense of adventure with an *ensuite*. You'd never encounter the sights and sounds of the jungle at night. Never savour the freedom of the fresh air experience."

"Treats I could live without quite happily."

"Now I, on the contrary, am seldom boring, despite Colin's unkind claim to the contrary." He shot a baleful glance towards the open pantry door. "I'm one of the best tour guides in the world. I play the bagpipes so well the music will bring a tear to your eye, I clean up fairly nicely, and I seldom smell."

Charley found herself enjoying the verbal fencing. "The tear in the eye part is true enough. I heard your rendition of *Amazing Grace* yesterday."

"Then you know I'm telling the truth." He lowered his voice to a confidential whisper and leaned over to murmur in her ear. "You're by far the prettiest sight I've seen today."

Yeah, right. A typical Kincaid come-on line. A vivid recollection of some of the more suggestive tabloid articles involving Kincaid and buxom beauties sprang into her mind. She smiled sweetly and retorted: "You really know how to flatter a woman, you silver-tongued devil, you. But we both know the only people you've seen today are your crew of hairy workers."

"A compliment delivered from the heart, nevertheless." He looked around and raised his eyebrows. "It looks like it's just the two of us for the tour. Where's Leila?"

"Still in bed last I looked – snoring," she added maliciously.

His grin widened into a blinding smile. "No Leila, huh? You mean it's just the two of us? The day continues to improve."

"Don't get any ideas, Kincaid." She gazed right into his eyes. Big mistake. They were the kind of eyes she could get lost in. Deep brown with long lashes any woman would envy. A slow burst of heat curled through her belly. Mesmerized, her mind refused to focus on anything other than the fine specimen of captivating masculinity who drew her attention like a magnet.

Charley cleared her throat and found her voice again. "Stop leering at me like that. You look like a retriever on point, waiting to pounce on a fallen partridge." She shifted in her chair and focused on her fourth cup of coffee. "What's happening up at the rock slide? I assume Felipe arrived."

"Oh, aye. He showed up a full hour late, full of excuses and apologies. I could tell he was unhappy about supervising the job." Kincaid reached across the table and snagged a piece of Charley's half-eaten banana muffin, popped it in his mouth and chewed reflectively. "I don't know what's gotten into him. I've never seen him dig in his heels like this."

She pushed her plate towards him. "Help yourself. Felipe scares me. His eyes seemed to burn right into my head last night, as if he could read my mind."

"You have a vivid imagination," Kincaid mumbled around a mouthful of crumbs. "I've known him for nearly a year, and he's harmless. A bit whacked, but otherwise harmless."

"I'm not so sure. He looks dangerous. I wouldn't want to cross him."

"Enough pessimism." He pushed away from the table and walked around behind her. "It's a glorious morning and now that I've decided to forgive you for landing on me unannounced and burning with journalistic fervour, I intend to enjoy having you all to myself."

Charley bristled and craned her neck to glare at him. "How magnanimous of you. I trust I will live up to your expectations."

He grinned, taking in her boots. "I'm sure *you* will. Those boots are another matter. They look brand new. I can't see so much as a wee crease or scuff mark on the leather."

She stretched out one foot and displayed it. "Nothing wrong with looking smart. You might take a lesson or two from me," she countered, staring meaningfully at his scruffy footwear.

"My boots are well-loved and deeply treasured. They have that lived-in patina that takes years to achieve." He bent down to study Charley's boots and groaned: "Aye. As I suspected. These aren't even broken in. What are you thinking? I hope you can walk."

His unflattering doubts merely echoed her misgivings. She should have broken them in gradually before trying to wear them for an entire day. "The sales clerk assured me they're guaranteed to be comfortable and blister-proof or they'll give me my money back."

Kincaid scoffed: "And a fine lot of good a guarantee will do out here in the jungle." He narrowed his eyes. "Much as I'm looking forward to showing you the sights, I don't want to have to lug you around on my back. Maybe we should take the truck."

"Don't waste gas on my account, Kincaid. I'll be fine." She hoped it was true. To prove her point, she rose to her feet. "And I have no intention of letting you carry me."

An infuriating smirk spread across his face. "Okay, you're the boss. You can hobble back under your own steam. But don't worry. Colin has received the best first aid training San Francisco offers outside a medical school. Blisters are his speciality. Let's go. I've got water, sunscreen and insect repellent."

Charley favoured Kincaid with a dark scowl, then dumped the dishes in the sink. She raised her voice. "Bye, Colin. Thanks for breakfast. Have salve and bandages ready for my return."

Colin stuck his head out of the pantry, betraying his shameless eavesdropping. "Aye. They'll be waiting. Have fun and be good. Don't do anything I wouldn't do." He brayed with laughter.

Kincaid heaved a long-suffering sigh, and said: "Colin's scintillating wit never ceases to astound me." He hustled Charley towards the door. "I can't wait to see your reaction to our *Ciudad de la Jaguar.*"

Chapter 10

Charley discovered she was enjoying herself immensely in spite of her new boots, her reservations about Kincaid, and her qualms about the jungle.

It was a fine, bright day with just a whisper of a breeze to offset the heat. She and Kincaid walked companionably, shoulder to shoulder, along the rough trail that was barely wide enough to accommodate a vehicle. Branches interlaced overhead, forming a latticed tunnel of alternating shade and sun. Scarlet and blue flashes darting through the trees betrayed the position of a pair of painted buntings hunting for insects.

The boots refused to bend. They felt like cement blocks attached to her feet. Dammit. Kincaid was right. They should have driven to the dig. She glanced up and caught the wicked glint in his eye. "What the hell are you looking at, Kincaid?"

He slowed his pace to accommodate her shorter strides. "Is it my imagination, or are you limping already?"

"Of course not. The boots just take a little getting used to. They're heavy. Besides, that was definitely a gloat. Didn't your mother ever tell you it's not nice to gloat?"

"I wouldn't dream of gloating at your expense. It's only that we have quite a climb ahead of us. The city's built at the top of a hill."

"I'll be fine."

"I adore stoicism in a woman."

"Nothing to be stoic about. My new boots are as comfy as bedroom slippers."

"Ah-ha. You're talking about bedroom attire already and it's not even our first date. Is this a come-on?" he asked, leaning closer and sniffing the air near her ear. "Mmm-mmm, you smell delicious."

It was too easy to enjoy him. "Cut it out. No, it's not a come-on and leave my ear alone." Charley swatted at him, though her stomach turned, a slow, involuntary somersault. She dragged her mind back to the purpose of her visit. "Do you mind if I tape our interview for the record?" she asked in her most businesslike voice as she rummaged for her tape recorder.

He smiled as if he knew exactly how difficult it was to maintain her composure. "I don't mind at all. Where do you want to start?"

She clicked the on button and spoke distinctly. "Tell me how you discovered this place, what led you to it, how you excavated it."

For the next few minutes, the trail climbed steadily and Charley struggled to keep pace with Kincaid who happily expounded on his favourite topic – his dig. Although she'd read most of the story, it sprang to life in his lilting accent. Before long, she forgot the discomfort of her new boots.

Four years earlier, Kincaid had deciphered a legend carved on the wall panel of a newly excavated Zapotec temple close to Monte Alban. The myth described a major Olmec centre in the Oaxaca region of Mexico. He proceeded to explain how, in spite of the scandal Leila had caused on a previous dig, he'd raised limited funding for the expedition based on the strength of his translation. Determined to succeed and win back his colleagues' respect, he'd emptied his own bank accounts.

Charley averted her eyes and feigned interest in her camera. It would be her fault if he lost everything he had worked for. Publishing the article prematurely would serve as an open invitation to the *banditos* that plagued the area. To distract herself, she prodded: "Is it so important that your colleagues respect you?"

"Oh, aye. In this business, reputation is everything. This dig is my last chance. If I don't succeed this time, no one will touch me again, let alone fund another project. I might as well throw in the towel and open a trendy café." He threw up his hands. "Or worse, teach Archaeology 101 to a bunch of snivelling undergraduates."

"Would teaching be so bad?" Charley injected a note of

false optimism into her voice. "You love to deliver lectures."

He ignored her pretext of animation and scowled. "A wee part of my soul would die if I couldn't do what I was born to do. Uncovering the past is my purpose in life."

Charley cringed as the impact of his words sank in.

Unaware of her perfidy, he grinned. "Cheer up, lass. Everything is falling into place. My gut tells me the tunnel we found yesterday is the discovery of the century, but I digress. To finish my story; we spent many difficult weeks following the clues described in the legend, and eight months ago, we discovered the Olmec ruins I'm about to show you.

Charley tucked her guilt away in a dark place where she could pull it out for later examination. She had a job to do and she couldn't let misguided sentiment deter her. "You make it sound so simple. Find a lost sock, find a lost city. Do you mean to tell me you stumbled on an ancient city in the middle of nowhere, just like that?" She snapped her fingers together.

She watched with interest as his cheeks brightened under the tan and his ears glowed pink at the implied compliment.

"Well ... It was a wee bit more difficult than you make it sound. We made several trips into the hills and jungle between Oaxaca and the coast before we located the ruins. As you can see," he waved his arm at the surrounding jungle, "this area is virtually inaccessible. There are no real roads through the mountains, and only a few goat tracks to link the scattered villages."

"I would have thought the locals would have found the ruins long ago."

"Ah. That's the beauty of it. Locals avoid the area. They call it *El Sitio del Diablo*, or Devil's Place."

Charley raised her eyebrows. "Why?"

"Because of all the unexplained deaths over the years. Hey, watch out for that rock." He took her arm and steered her around a boulder. "The locals believe the area is haunted by ancient spirits and blame the curse of the Olmecs for the tragedies."

So others had heard of the curse, too. Lost in thought, Charley stumbled along beside him. She was on the right track, though she doubted that rumours of a curse would dissuade greedy thieves if the rewards were great enough. "Do you believe this curse exists?"

Kincaid hesitated. "I'm not sure. There's no denying that some strange things occurred during my search for the city, but I don't believe a curse caused them. For example, my second expedition ended in near-tragedy. A jaguar mauled one of my men. We had to carry him out, barely alive. The attack terrified my crew, and all of the men, except Felipe, skipped out on me during the night."

"You mean it's true? There really was a jaguar attack near here?" Charley squeaked and edged closer to the solid body beside her. "I thought jaguars didn't attack humans." She wasn't usually so skittish on an assignment, but prowling jaguars made her skin crawl.

"I didn't want to alarm you on your first night, but there's something you should understand. This isn't a sanitized Disneyland jungle, Charley. It's the real thing. You need to keep your wits about you at all times. Under normal circumstances, jaguars do avoid humans. My man must have stumbled onto its lair. Any animal, if cornered, will defend its young."

Somehow his explanation didn't make her feel any better, and she scanned the thick underbrush. "Do you think a jaguar will jump out at us?"

He shook his head. "No. If a cat hears us, it will get out of our way. Now snakes and scorpions are a different matter. Snakes are almost impossible to see among rocks, and scorpions will take refuge in your boots overnight. Make sure you shake out your boots before putting them on."

Charley thought of her new boots left overnight under the bed. "Great. I'm so glad we had this little discussion. Now that I know there's absolutely nothing to worry about, we can get back to your story. You continued to search in spite of the danger."

Kincaid lengthened his stride, apparently oblivious to her painful footwear dilemma. "It's not so dangerous if you know what to look for. I pulled together another crew for my third and final trip, but I had to recruit from a remote village where they hadn't heard of the curse. Only Felipe stayed with me."

Grateful for her long legs, Charley marched faster to

catch up, her mind whirling. Personally, she could sympathize with the defection. "Did anything else abnormal happen on your trips?" she panted, ignoring the pain in her left heel.

He studied her face and slackened his pace from a headlong gallop to an easy canter. "Well, some of our food mysteriously disappeared – an entire backpack containing rice, beans, pasta and some freeze-dried meals, but I didn't give it a lot of thought at the time. Oh, and two of the men deserted because they thought they'd heard something strange during the night. Luckily, we found ruins the next day, before any more of the crew decided to jump ship."

And she had targeted those same two deserters for her exposé on illegal aliens – her final assignment before her career had crashed down around her ears,

With much fanfare and enthusiastic hand-waving, Kincaid described how he'd found the city only because a worker had literally stumbled over a colossal stone head that was half-buried in the ground. Favouring her heel, Charley limped along and tried to forget that her blisters were probably gushing blood by now, when the path swerved around a hairpin turn, then ended in a sun-filled clearing.

She stopped dead in her tracks and drew in a breath. The vast open space of the main excavation area spread out in front of them, but that wasn't what captured her attention. Two disembodied stone heads stared at her with empty, slanted eyes. The monolithic sculptures were almost round and at least eight feet in diameter.

"What do you think?" he asked, his voice brimming with hopeful expectancy. "That's the original head over there." He pointed to the massive stone head directly in front of her. "We found its companion overgrown with creepers a few feet away. We excavated them and rolled them into what was probably their original position as guardians of the city."

"Guardians. I see what you mean," she said, taking in the statues' flattened noses, wide lips, tasselled headdresses and ferocious scowls. "Totally intimidating. Look at their size. Any self-respecting enemy would run for the hills."

She fumbled for her camera and snapped several shots from various angles. Satisfied, she tiptoed up to the closest head and ran her fingers tentatively over the massive mouth and nose. The warm stone pulsed and throbbed under her hand like a living being.

She gasped and jumped back as if stung. "Dammit." This couldn't be happening. Not here, not now.

Under Kincaid's amused contemplation, Charley forced her shaking fingers to touch the oversized features yet again. This time, she felt no more and no less than sun-warmed rock. She explained sheepishly: "For a second there, the stone almost seemed alive."

Kincaid's gaze caressed the stone. "Some say the colossal heads retain ancient memories."

Charley huffed out a silent sigh of relief. He hadn't detected her abnormal reaction to the heads. "I can see why. They make a powerful impact. What is their significance?"

"They're the Olmec equivalent of a celebrity portrait. Generally a ruler. Sometimes an ancestor. Occasionally, the subject lived to enjoy his likeness, but mostly, they were a post-mortem commemoration."

"Cheerful thought."

Kincaid directed her attention to the ancient city spread out in front of them. "Would you look at that view," he murmured. "I can never get enough of it. I feel as if the ruins are crying out to me to release their secrets."

Charley caught her breath at the sheer size and grandeur of the excavation. Directly in front of them, across a wide-open space the size of several football fields, a pyramid rose against the backdrop of dark cliffs, its polished marble, a dazzling white under the blazing sun. A double bank of stairs graced the front, and the sides dropped off in a series of steep terraces. Majestic ruins crowned the summit. Numerous mounds and crumbling walls in various stages of excavation dotted the perimeter.

A hawk soared overhead with a wild screech, and insects buzzed and whirred busily in the underbrush.

Lost in wonder, Charley snapped shot after shot of the view. Unaware of time's passage, she leaned against one of the colossal heads to steady herself.

An immediate wave of dizziness engulfed her again, only this time, she felt herself free-falling into inky darkness. From a distance, she heard the rumble of Kincaid's concerned voice, felt his arm around her shoulders just before her knees buckled. Unbidden and unwanted visions swept over her in waves. She knew this place. She had climbed those steep stairs to the temple on top. She knew exactly how many steps there were. Eighty-five. In her mind's eye, she walked the broad plaza teeming with people going about their daily business.

Her world tilted crazily and a cold void extended tentacles to engulf her senses. A banshee wind intermingled with loud humming, until her head threatened to explode. Oily coils of terror slithered down her spine and her breathing stalled as tremors wracked her body. She tried to call for help, but no sound emerged.

The child scuttled into the storage shed and hid behind a stack of woven baskets, her body shaking with fright. The day she had dreaded ever since she could remember had arrived.

"Zana." Her mother's voice was curt.

The child's body convulsed in fear.

Her mother called again, louder this time. "Come here immediately, Zanazca. Your new master awaits us. We must not delay. Where are you?" The voice grew louder still as her mother entered the shed. "There you are, you silly girl." She reached out a strong hand and dragged the girl from her hiding place.

"No, no! Please don't make me go! I don't want to leave you and live at the temple."

Zanazca's mother had the strength of two men. In vain, the child struggled to free herself from the powerful grip, tears of terror streaming down her cheeks.

The mother stroked her daughter's hair and held the small body close to her heart.

"Today marks five cycles since you came into this life. You must be brave. It is time for you to meet your destiny."

Zanazca knew the story all too well. Her father had died in battle before she was born and her mother waged a ceaseless war to put food in the mouths of her children. When Zanazca was an infant of twenty days, her mother had vowed her new daughter would have a better life than she herself could provide. She had swaddled Zanazca in a white, woven shawl and carried the baby up the endless steps to the temple. There, her mother had dedicated the child's life to serve as a priestess to the gods. She promised to deliver the girl to the temple and the High Priest, Kele-Pe, after five cycles had passed. A gift of incense established a pact that only death could dissolve.

"You will become a priestess, Zana. Kele-Pe will teach you writing, oratory and the art of prophecy. Great power will be yours. This is my last gift to you." Her voice broke as the tears began to flow. "I have ensured a life of wealth and wisdom for my child."

Zanazca flung her arms around her mother's legs and clung like a burr, but the woman pried the child's hands away, her face a twisted mask of pain. "It is for the best." She carried her daughter into the house to prepare for a new future.

The humming began again, faint at first, but increasing in volume until Charley thought she must surely cry out, although no sound escaped her constricted throat. Again, she spiraled crazily through endless darkness and shrieking wind with no sense of the passage of time.

The angry buzzing in her head receded and the nausea dissipated, leaving her body limp and shivering. And, by some miracle, alive. She sagged against the strong arm that supported her, grateful for the heavy warmth of the sun, hot and crimson against closed eyelids.

She opened her eyes. Kincaid's grave face, his eyes clouded with anxiety only inches from her own, betrayed his concern. His breath was warm on her icy cheek, and the steady thudding of his heart against her arm helped to steady her.

"Bloody hell. Thank God you're back." His accent was stronger than usual. "You scared the living daylights out of me. I've been shaking you for five minutes. Here, you'd better sit down." He relieved Charley of the tape recorder and bag, grasped her hand and led her to a large boulder.

Her legs buckled under her weight, and she slumped

onto the rock.

With both hands, he forced her head down until her nose almost touched his boots. "Put your head between your knees. You're greener than the fancy outfit you're wearing and shaking like a leaf."

She shook her head in bewilderment. That hadn't felt like any panic attack, but she couldn't very well confess she'd experienced a hallucination. Men in white coats would come and cart her away and there would be medical bills. But the child's emotion had seemed as real as Kincaid's dusty boots, now pressed against her nose. Could the vision have some deeper significance than merely an illusion conjured up by her feverish imagination?

She wriggled, trying to break away from the iron grip. "Let me up, Kincaid. This is uncomfortable," she protested in a muffled voice. Dammit, the man was strong. And persistent.

The grip tightened. "Not yet."

"I mean it. Let go before I throw up on your boots."

"Give it a minute more."

"Stop that, Kincaid."

The pressure relaxed. "Raise your head very slowly, but put it down right away if you feel dizzy again."

Charley didn't protest when he clasped her hand. His grip was warm, firm and comforting, and she hung on for dear life while she inched her head up. "I guess the sun was too strong," she muttered and waited for the trees to stop spinning.

He stroked her hair back from her face. "You should be wearing a hat. We'll sit here in the shade for a while. The excavation and the pyramid can wait until you're feeling better."

That was fine with her. Her legs still felt like limp strands of spaghetti. "I'll be up for it again in a few minutes." She'd make sure she was, even if she had to crawl through the dig on her hands and knees.

He thrust a water bottle into her hand. "Drink." His voice brooked no argument.

God, she hated taking orders, no matter how well intentioned. Muttering under her breath about bossy, arrogant Scots, she nevertheless raised the bottle to her lips and felt the cool, life-giving liquid slide across her parched tongue and down her tight throat. She lowered the bottle only to find it thrust towards her mouth again.

"More," he commanded.

She shot him a baleful scowl, but opened her mouth obediently, gulped and swallowed, then gulped again before pushing his hand away. "Enough. If you keep pouring water into me, I'll drown."

He let out an exasperated sigh. "Do you always argue like this?"

"Only when someone tries to boss me around. I've managed to stay alive all by myself for thirty-one years without someone forcing water down my throat."

"Water is the best antidote for heat stroke." He eyed her uneasily. "Are you sure you're okay? You're face isn't quite the sickly shade of greyish-green like before, but you still look shaky. Drink more water."

She brushed away his concern with an impatient shake of her head. "Later. If I promise to sit here quietly, will you tell me about the city?"

Distracted from the humiliating and unwelcome topic of her health, he launched into a lengthy dissertation, giving her a chance to collect herself. How feeble she must seem. She took great pride in her strength and self-reliance, and she'd practically fainted at his feet.

By the time she tuned in again, he was pointing out the shed where his team deposited artefacts for cataloguing and analysis. As he described the excavation process, his voice grew louder and his gestures more animated. He stood up to pace the path as if he strode a podium in a lecture hall, dark eyes flashing, arms gesturing broadly.

Too bad he didn't want to teach. He was a natural.

As Charley's eyes glazed over, Kincaid lectured on in his professorial fervour to impart knowledge to the student, blind to her information overload.

"To excavate is to destroy," expounded Kincaid earnestly, face pink with excitement. "Therefore, rigorous note-taking and recording is an essential part of the work."

Only an archaeologist, thought Charley, could get so worked up about squatting in the blazing sun, day after day, digging through acres of dirt with a dental pick, then, as if that wasn't enough, pressing the same mound through a sieve, then writing about it, to boot.

Deep trenches stretched away towards the pyramid. Students and specialists crouched in them, digging laboriously and placing the dirt in buckets. Others pressed the soil through large tripod-mounted screens or carried artefacts to the shed. The scene reminded Charley of a colony of ants.

In twenty minutes, she had learned more about archaeology than she'd ever dreamed possible. Recalling Colin's words of warning about Kincaid's long-windedness, she realized he would continue his lecture until someone stopped him. Out of a strong sense of self-preservation, she announced her full recovery.

As they strolled, she surveyed the proceedings around her with rapt fascination. "Unbelievable. What have you found so far?"

"The pyramid is the heart and ceremonial centre of the city. That huge rectangular open space in front of the pyramid is called the great plaza." He indicated crumbling stone walls, smaller mounds and heaps of rubble along two sides of the plaza. "Those are the remains of the buildings lining its perimeter."

Ignoring her aching feet, she climbed a small mound and snapped a dozen photographs. In her mind, she saw a row of white, stucco-covered buildings – shops and businesses. She edged her way down, feet skidding on loose shale and stared across the plaza, empty now of the laughing, jostling crowds she knew used to congregate for special ceremonies. "The pyramid's pretty impressive."

"Oh, aye. When we first arrived, we thought it was only a hillock of rubble piled against the cliff."

The dazzling display captivated her. "What made you take a closer look?"

He ducked his head. "The mound's overly regular shape made me believe it might be man-made. I pulled away some sod and creeping vines from one corner, and found carved marble underneath. We had to strip away centuries of underbrush to uncover the pyramid, but the result was worth the effort. Our stone masons have made some repairs."

Kincaid and Charley stopped at the foot of the pyramid. The cliff soared above the structure, solid and looming, dwarfing the insignificant efforts of ancient man to bring order into a chaotic existence. Charley peered up, squinting, her heart pounding in the stillness of the fine, golden morning. From the bottom, the stairs were too steep to catch a glimpse of the summit, but she knew that the temple crouched, sleeping, waiting expectantly for her arrival.

"You'll have to climb sideways," he warned, interrupting her trance. "They built the stairs steep and narrow on purpose to force people to zigzag up the face, similar to the movements of a snake. It must have made an impressive sight when dozens of people snaked in a single line to the top."

The spell holding Charley immobile dissolved. She gritted her teeth. "Let's do it."

"Are you sure about this? I don't want you tumbling down the stairs if you faint again. Blood stains the marble." He paused thoughtfully. "Though an artistic smear or two of blood might add a touch of realism, don't you think?"

She pinned him with a steely look. "Dammit, Kincaid. I told you, I'm fine. I didn't faint, and I didn't come all this way to sit like an invalid in the shade at the bottom simply because I felt dizzy for a couple of minutes."

Kincaid frowned, then relented. "Be careful then," he advised. "We'll take it in easy stages and I'll be right behind you in case you slip. Going up shouldn't be a problem, but coming down may be a different story, especially if you're prone to vertigo. Many people scrabble down backwards."

"Won't happen to me," she said confidently and started to climb.

Chapter 11

By the time Charley and Kincaid reached the pyramid's summit, her breath came in short puffs and her chest heaved like an old accordion. Beads of perspiration trickled into her eyes.

"Dammit, it's gotta be the altitude," she muttered under her breath, noting with resentment that her companion wasn't even breathing hard. Kincaid must be in great shape, but then, she remembered his finely muscled body only too well. Hadn't he cradled her against the hard planes of his chest after she had snapped out of her trance? With difficulty, she yanked her mind away from firm male flesh and massaged her burning thigh muscles.

"Give me a moment to catch my breath," she panted, wheezing like an eighty-year-old woman with emphysema. God, she wished she could kick off the boots that clamped her feet tighter than a bear trap.

As if reading her mind, Kincaid said: "The boots probably didn't help."

Charley flashed what she hoped was a carefree smile, but feared it bore more resemblance to a grimace of agony. "Thanks for your touching concern, but my boots are perfect. I think a good climb was just what I needed to break them in."

Kincaid looked unconvinced. "Right. Glad to hear it. Let me know when the pain transcends excruciating and becomes unbearable and I'll be happy to take you back to camp. In the meantime, there's something I want to show you." He pulled her to a spot with an unencumbered view. "Look. You can see the camp from here."

Across the emerald valley, overgrown with low, dense vegetation, a cluster of cabins and tents nestled beside the clear aquamarine waters of the sweetgum-lined lagoon.

Behind the camp, rank upon rank of purple mountains disappeared into the distance as far as the eye could see. Lost in a heat haze, the summits appeared remote and mysterious, full of empty vastness, hidden valleys and remote plateaus. A fragrant breeze infused with an elusive sweetness refreshed Charley's fiery cheeks.

She unclipped her hair and let the wind blow the tumbled mass of curls away from her face, savouring the sweet coolness against her scalp as the wind caught her hair. "That's quite a view," she said dreamily and wandered along the edge, putting a safe distance between herself and the man who threatened her peace of mind.

"Oh, aye. It certainly is."

The deep, quiet voice, unexpectedly close, made her jump. Dammit, how had he snuck up on her like that? Dark eyes danced a world of approval that had nothing to do with mountains and lagoons.

When would she learn? She would be wise to remember Kincaid spelled nothing but danger. Charley edged away and scraped the unruly mass of hair off her face with her fingers, intent on cramming it back into the clip.

"Leave it be." Kincaid leaned closer and twisted a curl around his finger, trailing his hand down the curve of her cheek in the process and leaving a burning trail in its wake. "I like to see your hair blowing free."

Charley backed away, her face warm and knees quivering. "Cut it out, Kincaid," she said, swatting his hand as if it were a gnat. "I'd look like Medusa if I let my hair fly loose in this wind."

Obediently he let go, but didn't move away. If anything, he moved an inch or two closer. Uncomfortably aware of his warm proximity, Charley felt the continued weight of his admiring gaze. For once, the rumours were on target, she concluded. The combined ammunition of lilting accent, killer smile and undeniable charm made her bones melt until she feared her legs would collapse.

"You look incredible," he rumbled. The look in his eyes caused her knees to quiver even harder.

Charley mustered every ounce of her wavering self-control and ignored the carnal messages her pounding heart and tingling nipples were hurling towards her brain. This time, she vowed, Kincaid had met his match. His smooth magnetism and compelling charisma might fool scores of unwitting females, but not this one. Instead of following her instincts and lunging towards him in a frenzy of lust, she waved an admonitory finger under his nose. "Kincaid. Let's get one thing straight between us right now. I'm here to write an article, not gratify your male ego by falling at your feet. I've read *all* about you."

He quirked an eyebrow. "Do tell."

She picked up a rock and fiddled with it, turning it around, hoping he wouldn't notice her unsteady fingers. "If you recall, the newspapers were full of articles about you and your countless romantic escapades." Charley didn't elaborate further, but the disdainful tone of her voice would leave no doubt in Kincaid's mind that she hadn't been impressed with what she'd read.

Amusement danced in his eyes. "Don't believe everything you read about a person, Charley. You're a reporter—"

"Investigative journalist." She dropped the rock and gave him a dark look.

"No matter. Either way, you should know better."

She flushed. He was right. She did know better, but damned if she would roll over and apologize – or anything else involving rolling over, for that matter. It was high time a woman demonstrated she could resist the famous Kincaid charm. "With dozens of women panting at your heels, I'm amazed you have any time left for finding lost cities," she said in a saccharine tone.

He took a step closer until his arm brushed hers. The heat electrified every cell in her body and made her libido stand at attention. She couldn't remember what they had been talking about.

"You've been reading too many society pages and tabloids," he said lightly.

She sidled away, breaking the charged contact that robbed her of all coherent thought. "Couldn't miss you. Every time I opened the paper, your face stared up at me."

"Those articles flatter me. I'd need the recuperative

119

powers of Superman to do all the things they claimed I'd done."

"You dated a different woman nearly every night," she reminded him.

Kincaid looked uncomfortable, as only a man being raked over the coals about the other women in his life could. "It's possible I may have gone a wee bit overboard for a year or two," he admitted. "The divorce shattered my life and sent me into a tailspin. I'm not proud of it, but I tried to kill the pain and anger with work and partying."

It was Charley's turn to squirm. "Um ... looks to me like you succeeded beyond your wildest dreams."

Kincaid relaxed and smiled. Before she could guess his intentions and move away, he placed his hand on the nape of her neck and rubbed softly. "My behaviour wasn't as bad as it looked."

Dammit, he could move fast for a man his size. Charley's brain issued an urgent flight command, but her body refused to move. She found herself wanting to whimper with pleasure and grant those warm, gentle fingers access to anything they cared to explore. Before she succumbed to those idiotic impulses, Charley peeled his hand away from its resting-place and turned her small sigh of regret into a question. "Then how do you explain the evidence against you unless the photographs were all digitally enhanced?" She looked away, appalled at her own rudeness. She wanted to die of embarrassment.

After a beat, he said: "Four of the photographs were publicity shots for the university, not real dates. And at least one was my friend's wee sister who did me a favour and accompanied me to the most boring party of the century."

"Well great," she mumbled, staring at the view but not really seeing it. With luck, her mouth would quit before it did any more damage. It didn't. "That sets my mind at ease. Five women explained, and dozens unaccounted for. Not that it's any of my business."

During the brief ensuing silence the clink of metal striking rock reminded Charley of the work party toiling within earshot. She considered bolting down the steps and hiding in her tent for the remainder of her visit. Only the steady throb of pain in her feet prevented the humiliating retreat. Instead, she shuffled to a nearby stone bench and sank down, wishing the rock would swallow her up. Was she out of her mind? She was blowing her golden opportunity – bickering with an interview subject who had a legendary reputation for avoiding journalists like the plague. The number of women Kincaid had dated was none of her business. Worse, he'd think she gave a damn.

When she raised her head, her discomfiture grew. Apparently, her rudeness had fallen on deaf ears. He had followed her to the bench. Now, his grin stretched from ear to ear.

"My, my. Do I detect a touch of wistfulness?" he inquired, settling himself beside her. "I'm a reformed man, Charley. I swear I've led a monastic existence for nearly a year. I never get involved with any of the women on my team." His voice deepened and so did his accent. "Fortunately, you're not a member of my team."

She stiffened and squirmed away. "In your dreams, Kincaid."

He heaved an exaggerated sigh. "Can't blame a man for trying."

"Then try with someone else."

"It's not often a beautiful woman drops in on my hidden jungle hideaway," he continued, heedless of her discomfort. Or deliberately ignoring it. "In fact, there's been a definite dearth of beautiful women around here until you arrived." He grinned.

An unwelcome pang of sizzling heat shot through her body and ripped the oxygen from her lungs. In spite of his reputation as a playboy, in spite of her most recent romantic fiasco and bruised ego, she couldn't deny that a tumble with Kincaid would be – mind-blowing.

When she refused to answer, he didn't give up as she'd hoped, but tried another approach. "I'm moving too fast, fool that I am. A woman as special as you obviously needs to be wooed."

"Wooed?" she echoed.

"Oh, aye. I can woo with the best of them. I'm a champion wooer. In fact, I can say with some assurance that

I'm probably the most accomplished wooer in the entire state of Oaxaca."

Charley's lips twitched, but she bit the inside of her mouth to prevent the bubble of laughter from escaping.

"I'll wine you and dine you and shower you with flowers. And if those all fail, I'll share my stash of chocolate with you as a last resort – I'm a closet chocoholic," he confided. "That would be a difficult sacrifice, but for such a worthy cause, the sky's the limit."

She closed her eyes for a moment, willing herself to resist the seductive offer and the equally beguiling notion that they shared a secret craving – sweet, dark, delicious chocolate. The temptation to lean into him was too strong and too dangerous. Instead, she pulled herself together and put up the invisible wall she fondly imagined would shield her from emotional damage. When she spoke at last, she was pleased her voice sounded cool and strong, betraying nothing of the inner agitation she felt. "Tempting and highly flattering, Kincaid – but no thanks. Let's keep our relationship strictly professional, shall we?"

Seemingly unaffected by her curt brush-off, Kincaid ratcheted up his smile from an eight to a perfect ten on the brilliance scale, but it seemed to Charley the teasing gleam drained from his eyes, leaving them sad and vulnerable.

Dammit, this was like walking a tightrope. She'd finally done irreparable damage to his fragile male ego. Relenting, she spoiled the businesslike effect she was striving for by adding: "Besides, I have my own emergency supply of chocolate in my bag if it hasn't already melted."

His quick laugh made her regret her stupid softening. She had only imagined she'd struck a nerve. This man was impervious to rejection.

He shifted his body, brushing his shoulder against hers and winked. "See? We have something in common already."

She inched closer to the end of the bench. "Are you going out of your way to be charming?"

"Aye. Is it working?"

"Definitely not."

"I tend to grow on people."

Charley snickered. "So does fungus." She turned away

and put some space between them. A safe distance made her feel better. *Yeah, right – less likely to jump him.* "Let's get back to work, shall we?" she said in a brisk, no-nonsense voice. "The workmanship of this temple is unbelievable. It must have taken years to carve it."

If she had offended him again, he didn't show it. "Okay. Have it your way for now. But I must warn you. Seven days is a long, long time and I'm a patient man."

"Six more days," she muttered through clenched teeth. *The six longest days of my life.*

"Six then," he said cheerfully. "To make amends for your brutal rejection, will you share some of your chocolate with me?" He waggled his eyebrows.

She sputtered out a reluctant laugh at the eagerness written on his face. "Sure. If you promise to behave yourself."

"I'll do almost anything for chocolate."

Charley noticed he'd avoided a direct response. Nevertheless, she rummaged in her bag and extracted the melting Snickers bar. Ripping off the wrapper, she studied the candy to avoid direct eye contact, and wondered if, at some level, she might be capitulating on more than mere chocolate.

Hiding a growing insecurity behind what he hoped was a slick and debonair grin, Kincaid slouched against the stone bench in a carefully crafted pose of careless negligence. He fought the urge to fidget, and concentrated his attention on Charley's slender hands as she divided the chocolate into two equal pieces. The prim precision of her movements captivated him. It had been a long time since any woman had reduced him to such a pathetic state of stomach-churning insecurity.

Most of the morning, he'd been almost certain he was making headway in his quest to seduce his quarry. After all, Charley had complimented him on his shirt, exchanged good-natured banter, and allowed him to comfort her after her bout of heat stroke, although her mulish disregard of his gentle suggestion to drink more water had caught him off guard. Hell, she'd even displayed a touch of jealousy about the women he'd dated after his marriage had fallen apart. Then, in the blink of an eye and for no apparent reason, she'd turned all chilly and businesslike. In total bewilderment, he wracked his brain to remember if he'd said anything a woman might interpret as offensive. All he could recall was the gargantuan effort he'd made to turn on the charm in order to impress her. What if he'd only been imagining the mutual attraction? Aye, well, what did it matter? He had bigger, more important concerns on his mind.

The hollow emptiness in his gut contradicted his nonchalance.

Damn, why were all females so complicated?

Kincaid's uneasiness grew by leaps and bounds. He couldn't help but notice Charley avoided looking at him as she fiddled with the chocolate. He had no idea what she was thinking. It was time to unleash his ultimate weapon – the world-famous Kincaid Touch Test – always an infallible indicator of a woman's true feelings. If Charley failed the test, he would throw in the towel and slink away without a whimper, tail tucked between his legs in shameful defeat. If, however, she passed the test, he vowed to re-double his efforts to coax her into his arms. And his bed.

A quick tumble in the sack, no strings attached, was all he needed.

Charley held out the sticky chunk of Snickers bar between thumb and forefinger, looking as if she thought it might bite. Or he would.

He tried to ignore his heart pounding against his ribs in a most unmanly fashion. Still grinning the most confident smile he could muster, he accepted the gooey mass of chocolate, trailing his fingers, as if by accident, over the back of her hand.

And watched.

And waited.

A gratifying glow rose from the prim neckline that begged his fingers to unfasten a couple more buttons. The blush crawled up her neck and painted her expressive features a bright peony. To Kincaid, mottled pink had never looked so good. Even better, she yanked her hand away so hard she nearly toppled off the end of the bench.

The extent of his relief caught him by surprise and he released a gush of breath he hadn't realized he'd been holding. Aye. No doubt about it. Her skittish reaction to his lightest touch indicated she'd passed the test with flying colours. She was definitely *not* indifferent to him, though, for a few minutes there, he'd started to question his instincts.

"Easy does it," he said, and reached out a hand to steady her.

She pushed his hand aside and snapped: "I'm fine."

This time, her rejection didn't sting at all. He smiled to himself and stuffed the chocolate in his mouth, chewing blissfully. "Ahhh. Chocolate. My favourite food group," he mumbled around a sticky mouthful that threatened to clamp his jaws shut. "Almost makes up for your crushing brush-off."

She polished off her half of her candy in silence. The sight of her pink tongue licking off the smears of chocolate from her fingers was the most erotic vision Kincaid could remember. *Soon*, he thought. *Soon, we'll be sharing more than a chocolate bar.* He had a few other moves in his arsenal, and he intended to show no mercy.

As if the unspoken contest had never transpired, Kincaid rose from the bench first, and said: "Now, we're ready for a guided tour of the temple – but only after you finish your water." He turned a deaf ear to her predictable protests and held out the water bottle.

Charley was a woman worth waiting for, and he was a very, very patient man. The cat-and-mouse game they played was just beginning to heat up.

Her mind in a turmoil, Charley limped after Kincaid, picking her way over patches of broken rock and loose shale. Dammit, the man was getting under her skin. Why had she mulishly refused his offer of water, especially when the chocolate had made her thirsty?

Perhaps because compliance is highly overrated. Gives men the wrong idea.

For the last couple of minutes, her companion had been uncharacteristically quiet. She glanced at the broad back draped in gaudy flowers. What was he thinking? *Probably devising a strategy for pumping six gallons of water down my gullet*, she decided, a secret smile curving her lips.

A loose rock nearly sent her flying, and she bit her lip to suppress a moan. If only she could rip off these boots from hell and go barefoot, she would be the happiest woman in the world. The unpleasant notion of snakes, scorpions and, okay, Kincaid's reaction, deterred her from following through on her impulse.

He stepped aside to let her pass. "Come this way, but watch your step. The roof is gone and some of the walls have collapsed, so there's plenty of rubble."

She tiptoed into the temple and stopped in the centre, overwhelmed with awe. Forgetting about Kincaid, forgetting about the pain, she circled the sacred space and allowed the enormity of his discovery to sink in. "Would you hand me my camera, please. I want to capture this on film," she said, a catch of emotion in her voice.

Kincaid handed her the camera and continued, every gesture betraying his pride. "This is one of the best-preserved Olmec temples ever discovered. The front face carries the carved image of the Jaguar God and many of the columns are still standing."

Charley forgot about the lethally attractive Scot by her side and her heart accelerated for a different reason. A flood of recognition washed over her at the sight of the altar – the carving around the sides, the towering jaguar rearing its snarling face over the head of the stone slab, even the deep groove encircling the top of the slab to catch the blood....

Charley shuddered. How could she know about the blood? None of the books she'd read while researching the dig had mentioned that little detail. Although over two millennia had passed since priests in ceremonial garb had chanted to the great Jaguar God while countless lines of Chosen Ones had walked those stones towards eternal life, she could visualize the shadowy figures from the past.

Charley licked her dry lips. "The Olmecs practised human sacrifice, didn't they?"

"Aye. They believed they were conferring a great honour on the poor devils they sacrificed to the gods. Except for slaves. Slaves were expendable and they killed them pretty much for the fun of it – that, and because they didn't want the cost of feeding and housing them. They staged special ball games to decide who would be killed."

"What?"

"Oh, aye. The contestants were slaves and the ball games were literally a matter of life and death. The winning team often won its freedom while the losers were sacrificed, but I've read accounts where they killed all the players, even the winners."

This chilling piece of trivia didn't surprise Charley. She must have read it in one of the research papers. "Pretty brutal," she commented, snapping several shots of the altar.

At that moment, six members of the work crew emerged from the shadows of the cliff face, the men chatting in Spanish, gesticulating and laughing. When they noticed Kincaid and Charley, one of them interrupted his conversation to wave and call out a greeting.

Kincaid swiveled his head and watched the men head for the steps of the pyramid. He frowned and looked at his watch. "Strange. I wonder where they're going. It's not even close to lunchtime. Will you be okay if I leave you alone for a few minutes?"

Charley's voice rose indignantly. "If you mean do I need a babysitter because I'm likely to have another dizzy spell, don't worry about me. Where are you going?"

"I need to check on Felipe and find out why the men are leaving. I'll be right back."

"Can I come? I want to see the tunnel, too."

"I'll show you later. Watch out for snakes, and for God's sake, stay right here. Don't wander down the pyramid by yourself."

"Are you always this bossy?"

"Are you always this stubborn?" He sucked in a deep breath. "Do you remember what I said about the dangers out here? You could get into trouble alone."

Charley sniffed at his dictatorial tone and opened her mouth to protest again, then snapped it shut. Solitude would give her a chance to explore the temple alone, to immerse herself in its atmosphere without unwanted distractions, and there was no doubt about it – Kincaid was a huge distraction. "Go ahead then. I'll look around the temple, take some pictures."

Kincaid tossed her a water bottle and looked at her sharply, almost as if he expected another argument. "Here, keep the water. You might get thirsty"

Charley smiled angelically. "Thanks. What are you waiting for?"

He nodded and turned towards the tunnel.

She watched until the last vestiges of the fluorescent yellow and orange aloha shirt had disappeared into the shadows of the overhanging cliff, swallowed up by the heavy gloom, before uncapping the bottle and taking a long, satisfying gulp.

Time passed in a blur for Charley. She loved this part of her job – immersing herself in the rhythm and heartbeat of a location, soaking up the atmosphere, becoming a fixture, as if she belonged there. She covered every square inch of the temple area, touching, marveling, taking pictures. And imagining.

Her nerves thrummed. Ancient and powerful energies still lingered, saturating the stones with pain and despair.

She glanced over one shoulder, then the other, the memory of her panic attack in the jungle flickering on the edge of her consciousness. White-hot sun baked the interior of the ruins. The temple was tranquil, walls crumbling and roofless, open to the elements after eons of erosion. Yet in her mind's eye, she could still see the place of worship as it had looked in its full glory, countless centuries ago.

She wandered over and touched a block of carved granite, then recoiled as if stung. Heart hammering in her chest, she examined the markings on the stone and sat down experimentally. This was the spot! Yesterday in the jungle, she had *seen* herself sitting in this very spot. The same lumps and knobs jabbed into the small of her back. Oh, sure, the roof had disappeared and the columns had crumbled, but the throne was identical to the one in her hallucination.

Charley straightened up and backed away slowly, staring at the chunk of stone in disbelief. She edged all the way to the tunnel entrance where Kincaid had disappeared.

If she stayed here alone for one more second of

peaceful solitude, she would explode clear out of her skin.

After Kincaid had reluctantly left Charley to her own devices, he'd stood inside the tunnel and waited until his eyes adjusted to the gloom. The heavy blackness wasn't absolute. Or completely silent. At the end of the passage, the faintest glow of a lantern reflected off minerals embedded in the rocky walls and revealed the rockslide's location, hidden from sight around a bend. A whisper of sound, little more than a vibration, disturbed the still air. As he padded towards the light, the alien sound coalesced into a low, guttural chant.

He held his breath and crept around the bend, keeping his back to the wall.

Encircled by light, a dark indistinct figure knelt, hands upraised, rocking rhythmically, in front of the jumble of stones and boulders. The eerie monotone swelled in volume, dropped, then rose again. Kincaid's skin prickled as the hairs rippled softly on the back of his arms.

"What the hell's going on here?" he demanded as he stepped out of the shadows and into the ring of light.

The chant choked off and the dark shape scrambled to its feet and faced Kincaid, chin raised, legs spread wide. Although the lantern hanging from the wall behind the man's head left his face in shadowy darkness, Kincaid recognized the figure without difficulty.

"Felipe? Answer me."

Felipe's disembodied voice replied: "I did not hear you approach."

It might have been the subtly defiant posture or it might have been the thinly veiled insolence in Felipe's voice, but Kincaid's gut warned him he couldn't trust the man facing him in the flickering light. An unfamiliar stranger had replaced the mild, obsequious field director he'd worked beside for the last year.

Kincaid fisted his hands on his hips. "You sent the men away. What's going on here?"

The insolent silence lasted so long, Kincaid doubted he'd get an answer to his question. When at last Felipe spoke, his voice resonated in the chamber. "I was begging the ancient gods for forgiveness."

Kincaid reached for the lantern, turned up the flame, and held it at shoulder height, illuminating Felipe's face. He wanted to read the man's expression. "Have you lost your mind? What are you talking about?"

Felipe turned his face away from the light, but not quickly enough. Kincaid caught the unmistakable gleam of fury in his eyes. "The Master of Darkness is angry. You make a dangerous mistake."

Kincaid gritted his teeth. Felipe's irrational and maddening refusal to remove the rocks grated on his nerves. "Exactly what is that supposed to mean?"

"You have woken the ancient spirits from their long sleep, and angered the gods of my forefathers. Great harm will befall you if you persist in this madness."

A chill slid down Kincaid's spine. Felipe had either lost touch with reality or he was dissembling in order to avoid hard and dangerous work. Damn. He hadn't pegged Felipe as lazy, cowardly or superstitious, and he considered himself an excellent judge of character. Clearing out the rockslide would be a backbreaking task, but that was why he'd hired a work crew.

"You're talking nonsense, Felipe. I want the men back at work."

Felipe's voice was implacable in spite of the thin smile distorting his face. "You must not remove the rocks that guard the underworld. I have protected you from your ignorance by telling the men to dig in the courtyard at the bottom of the pyramid."

"Bloody hell. Give that superstition bullshit a rest."

"If you anger the gods, great harm will befall you," Felipe persisted, his voice laced with venom.

Quivering with frustration at the man's insubordination, Kincaid raised his voice. "Enough." He caught himself and said in a quieter tone: "You've overstepped your bounds by a mile, Felipe. Make sure the men return to work this afternoon or I'll find someone else – someone I can rely on." He had every intention of following through on his threat.

Felipe's eyes blazed defiance before his face assumed its usual impassive expression.

Kincaid lowered his voice to a dangerous growl. "And never, *ever,* countermand my orders again. Do I make myself clear?"

Felipe's posture changed, his body seeming to shrink before Kincaid's astonished eyes. "*Si*, Dr. Kincaid," he said with a shrug and a conciliatory smile. "It will not happen again. It was only – well, I do not wish to trouble you with every tiny detail. You were busy with the reporter lady."

The harsh sound of a pebble grating underfoot caused both men to jump. Kincaid looked over his shoulder to find the reporter lady in question standing behind him, listening to every word. *Bloody hell.* "Charley. What are you doing back here? I thought we agreed you'd stay outside till I was finished."

"I agreed to nothing of the sort. You ordered me to stay put, then took off. I may have mentioned it already, but I react badly to commands."

Kincaid sighed. This woman brimmed with sheer orneriness, fighting him every inch of the way. Why couldn't she just do what she was told without an argument? He must be some kind of a masochist to enjoy fencing with such a royal pain in the ass. "I'll be with you in a minute. This is a private meeting," he said, more sharply than he intended.

Charley turned away, her reply muffled, and, to Kincaid's surprise, uncharacteristically subdued. "I ... well, I truly thought you'd be finished by now. I didn't want to stay alone in the temple any longer, and...." Her voice trailed off.

Kincaid caught the undercurrent of alarm that caused her voice to quiver and sensed controlled desperation in the stiffness of her posture. His eyebrows shot up. "It's okay. We're done here for now. Everything's fine." At least, he hoped it was.

Charley looked from one man to the other. "Are you sure?"

Felipe remained silent.

"Aye, I'm sure. Follow me." Kincaid led her towards the exit, feeling Felipe's hot gaze drilling a hole between his shoulder blades.

Kincaid and Charley stumbled out of the tunnel to find the sun had shifted until it was directly overhead. He took one alarmed look at her pallor, and changed his mind about climbing down the pyramid to redirect the men. That could wait. He gripped her arm and dragged her, compliant for once, towards a block of stone in the shade. "Sit here," he said. "You look awful."

"Thanks," she muttered, and sat.

No argument. How very uncharacteristic of Charley. She must be really upset.

He settled himself beside her and examined her face, taking in the way she gnawed the delectable lower lip with her teeth. "Now tell me what happened to upset you."

Charley turned her face to the sky and she sucked in a deep, shuddering breath of air. "Thank God I'm out of there. I always hated caves."

He would wager a month's salary there was more going on with Charley than a wee touch of claustrophobia. "Don't go trying to distract me with chatter about caves. That's not why you're upset."

She looked directly at him, blue eyes troubled. "I shouldn't have followed you in there. I knew you were talking to Felipe, but something about this temple.... " She shrugged wordlessly. "You were gone so long and I had to get out of the sun."

Kincaid wrestled with his guilt and wished he could erase the signs of strain from her expressive face. "I know. I'm sorry. I forgot about time." He peered at her, wondering what she was hiding. Although having several sisters had taught him a thing or two about women, he was smart enough to know he hadn't begun to plumb the depths of feminine complexities. "Did you faint again when I was gone?"

A healthy flush replaced the ashen pallor. "Absolutely not. What makes you say that?"

"I'm beginning to recognize that greenish tint to your complexion. I'd better get some water into you, and then we'll head back to camp." He uncapped the water bottle and handed it her.

To his relief, Charley drank deeply, then capped the bottle. "I guess I'm still experiencing the aftermath of the heat stroke I had earlier." She thrust the bottle towards him.

"I knew we should have gone back right away. I should have insisted." He handed the bottle back. "Drink some more."

For a second, Charley looked as if she wanted to argue, probably more as a matter of principle than actual disagreement, but she settled back and drained the bottle obediently. "Don't beat yourself up, Kincaid. You'd have had to lug me back to camp over your shoulder. I wasn't going anywhere until I'd seen the temple."

He found her determination both annoying and endearing at the same time. "We'll rest in the shade for a couple of minutes." He pulled out another water bottle. "Here. Take this."

She shot him a baleful glare. "Dammit, Kincaid. I'm not a camel."

He smiled to himself. "You take arguing to new heights. A rare talent. Just drink the water, for God's sake. It's the best antidote for heat stroke."

"Fine." Charley put the bottle to her lips once more and drank. "Are you satisfied?" She wiped her mouth with the back of her hand. "That was pretty weird back in the cave."

"How much did you overhear?"

"Not much. Something about countermanding your orders. I told you – Felipe scares me. He's always smiling. Never trust a man who smiles too much. It means he's hiding something."

"You may be right," Kincaid admitted. "I've never seen him act like this before. He's always been a devoted and tireless worker, almost too good to be true. I had no idea he'd get so riled up about ancient superstitions."

"What are you going to do?" She nodded towards the tunnel.

Good question. The very thought had never left his mind since he'd emerged from the tunnel. "If he persists in this attitude, I'll have to replace him in spite of his uncanny knowledge of the Olmecs."

"Do you know anything about his background?"

Kincaid squirmed. Her blunt question touched a nerve. "Not a lot," he admitted. "I may have been a wee bit hasty in hiring him, but he had perfect qualifications and his references all checked out – his previous boss raved about his hard work and honesty. Best of all, he agreed to trek into an area the locals all avoided."

In truth, Kincaid's intuition had been warning him for several months that something about Felipe didn't ring true. He suspected that today, he'd caught a glimpse of the authentic man behind the mask of subservient humility.

Charley frowned. "Where did he work before this?"

"On another Olmec dig north of here." Kincaid paused, considering. "Come to think of it, a fire destroyed the camp." And immediately, his suspicions about Felipe grew stronger.

She handed him the water bottle. "I'd keep my eye on him if I were you."

Feeling like a fool in front of Charley for not doing his homework better, Kincaid leaned towards her and nodded. "I'd better make a couple of phone calls when we get back, to find out more about the incident. No point in confronting him before I know all the facts. He'd only deny everything. But thank you for your kind words of concern. Does this mean you care about me more than you want me to believe?"

She flushed. "Relax, Kincaid. I just don't want him blowing you up before I write my article."

He loved the way she turned a remarkable shade of scarlet when she was flustered. "Your tender sympathy overwhelms me. I must be making progress in my attempts to woo you. In another couple of days, you'll be putty in my hands."

Charley bristled. "Give it a rest."

"Ah, good. Ornery again. You must be feeling better. Are you ready to hobble back to camp?"

Charley nodded and heaved herself to her feet, wincing. "You bet."

He stood up and watched her teeter towards the steps trying to disguise the fact that she could barely hobble. "Mmm-hmm," he said and steered her in the opposite direction. "We'll take the path down the cliff instead of tackling the front face of the pyramid. I think you'll find it easier in those damned boots."

She glanced up at him and gave him a brilliant smile. To

his surprise, he felt his heart pick up speed until it galloped in his chest. He would have to think about that later.

"Thanks, Kincaid. I think I may have a tiny blister," she said sheepishly. "Or maybe ten."

"Take my arm for support. I won't bite." Catching her glare, he amended: "Well, I might nibble a wee bit." He couldn't help imagining his teeth working their way down her neck to the tender hollow where he could see her pulse fluttering, then moving downward ....

Chapter 12

The return trip to camp was sheer torture for Charley in more ways than one.

The narrow trail bisected the cliff's face, skirted the pyramid, and snaked down the flank of the mountain. Leaning hard on Kincaid's arm, she tried not to think of the smooth muscles that bunched under her hand. In spite of the bright, shooting pain lancing her feet with every step, she felt his frequent glances searing her skin as they maneuvered down the path. She had a fair notion about the direction of his thoughts.

A shrill voice in her head nagged incessantly. *You're a coward. A lily-livered, scum-sucking coward. A gorgeous man pursues you, and you're too afraid to go for it. How stupid are you?*

No, not stupid, she protested. On the contrary, her reaction to Kincaid demonstrated a healthy prudence, foresight and discretion. Given his unparalleled track record with women and her own dismal failure with men, avoidance was the smart and sensible response – the only possible response if she wished to keep her sanity. She would never let a man get close enough to destroy her again. The memory of her fiancé's betrayal caused her to stumble.

"Watch your step," Kincaid said. "We don't want you harming yourself any more than the boots already have."

See? This one might be different. You're damaged goods, that's what you are.

Charley gave up arguing with herself. The tiny voice was probably right. She'd spend the rest of her empty life as a bitter, twisted old maid living with her alcoholic mother. And two cats. Old maids always had cats.

She must be seriously deranged. But at least she'd be

safe from more heartache.

When they arrived at the bottom, Charley's feet begged for mercy. She bit her lip to smother a whimper of pain and struggled along the path, clutching Kincaid's arm for dear life. He felt strong, solid. She damned her stupidity for wearing the cursed boots without breaking them in.

After fifteen agonizing minutes, she staggered to a halt, admitting defeat. She absolutely couldn't take one more step. Not if her life depended on it. "Enough. I hate to admit it, but my feet are killing me. I need to take my boots off." She suppressed a groan.

"You toughed it out longer than I thought you would. Hang in there. Only a little further to go." He drew her entire arm over his shoulder. Grasping her hand while placing his other arm around her waist, he half-carried, half-dragged her the rest of the way.

Very romantic.

"Here we are. Home at last," he grunted, releasing her beside the lagoon close to her tent. "You picked a hell of a way to get my attention, Charley, but it worked." The corners of his eyes crinkled although his face remained solemn. "You finally persuaded me to put my arms around you."

She snorted a reluctant half-laugh. "It was a tough job, but someone had to go out on a limb to help repair your poor, fragile ego."

"I think your cure might just be working. I'll probably need a second treatment soon, though, or I might suffer a relapse."

"Don't count on that happening any time soon."

"I can wait. I told you, I'm a patient man. Now, take off those boots and soak your feet."

Charley shot a dubious stare at the lagoon. "In there? You must be kidding."

"It's safe. Lovely and cool, very clean. We swim all the time."

"Are you sure? I'd hate to lose a toe or two to a hungry critter."

"Trust me. You'll never find alligators at this altitude, and there are no piranhas in Mexico."

Charley hobbled the last few steps and threw herself

onto a boulder at the water's edge. Moaning, she eased off the offending footwear and examined her burning, throbbing feet before immersing them into the cool water, half expecting steam to rise from the lagoon. She moaned again, this time with relief.

A frown of concern furrowed his brow. "I hope your feet heal quickly. You'll need boots if you plan to leave the tent."

"I guess I'll have to wear sneakers."

"Not good enough. A snake's fangs will penetrate rubber and canvas."

"Then I'll wear thicker socks with my boots."

He shook his head. "Sorry. You can't wear those things again until your feet are healed. Can't risk infection. I'll ask one of the students if she can lend you another pair."

A pang of conscience struck her. Kincaid was being so, well, *nice*. No recriminations, no sarcasm, only kindness and thoughtfulness. He deserved an apology. "Thanks, Kincaid. By the way, you were right about the boots. I was wrong. How's that for an admission? From now on, I'll never wear new boots without breaking them in. I've learned my lesson."

"Do my ears deceive me? Are you admitting you made a mistake?"

"Enjoy. It doesn't happen often."

He smiled. "The mistake or the apology? Never mind. I'm savouring the moment." He glanced at her feet. "Your poor feet look like raw hamburger, now, don't they? Don't go anywhere."

"As if I could."

"I have a first aid kit in my tent. I'll be right back. Drink more water while you wait."

Kincaid returned in less than five minutes and squatted beside her.

"Give me a foot," he ordered.

"More orders," she muttered. "I hope you don't have a foot fetish."

"You should be so lucky. Now, your right foot, please. Infection is always a danger here in the jungle. No one is allowed to ignore an open wound. Even you," he added sternly as she opened her mouth to protest.

Kincaid reached for one of her feet and cradled it in his

lap. Charley sucked in her breath at the warm, intimate contact. She sat perfectly still, incapable of movement or speech. Thank God she'd had the foresight to get a pedicure and leg waxing before her trip. Intent on his job, Kincaid blotted the water with a soft cloth, then feathered his thumb over the entire sole and heel, examining the throbbing extremity from all angles.

It would be easy to get used to this kind of treatment, Charley mused as he knelt in front of her. My, my, he was good with his hands.

Heat flooded Charley's body and pooled heavily between her legs. She could picture, no she could almost *feel*, those same long-fingered hands cupping other portions of her anatomy. She restrained herself from grabbing the shaggy, dark head bent over her feet by gripping the rock to give her hands something constructive to do – something that wouldn't land her in a huge pile of trouble.

For once, Kincaid appeared oblivious of erotic undertones. "Now, let's see what we have here," he muttered under his breath. "Look at this mess. I have to hand it to you – you have guts. I'm not sure I could have walked so far on feet this far gone. Poor wee lassie "

"Good God, Kincaid," she sputtered, grateful for something, anything, to distract her from the battle between her unruly libido and common sense. "First Colin, and now you too! Did women's liberation bypass all Scottish men to the point where they can refer to a woman my height and age as a 'wee lassie' and still keep a straight face?"

Kincaid grabbed a tube from the first-aid kit and spread a soothing antibiotic ointment on her blisters before raising his eyes. "Force of habit. Comes from having younger sisters." A wave of sadness washed over his features, but receded so quickly she might have imagined it.

Charley cringed. She'd gone too far this time. Not only was she lying to Kincaid about the embargo on publishing her article, but now she'd insulted him when his motives were nothing but kindness and compassion. "Sorry. Big over-reaction on my part. I shouldn't have snarled at you," she muttered. "I'm kind of sensitive about my height – five eleven is way too tall – and my mother considers me ancient enough to be an old maid."

"Too tall?" he mused in a thoughtful voice, all lingering trace of sadness gone. "I don't think so. I must confess I've begun to appreciate a woman whose chin reaches higher than my navel. You're exactly the right height. Makes dancing much easier and a lot less silly looking. Perhaps your mother – dare I say it – may be in need of glasses. You look more like a college freshman than a relic to me."

Charley groaned inwardly. The man even danced. Oh, yeah, he spelled trouble, with a capital 'T'. And she was an idiot with a capital 'I'.

Kincaid ignored Charley's fulminating silence and snapped a Band-Aid over each raw spot. "Give me your other foot."

The exquisite torment continued unabated. To take her mind off his clever fingers on her bare flesh, she prodded: "How many sisters do you have?"

He hesitated for a heartbeat. "Three. Only three. I had an older sister, but she died when I was fifteen and she was sixteen."

The underlying pain in his voice saddened her and could have kicked herself for stirring up painful memories. "I'm so sorry. How did it happen?"

"Suicide." His voice was bleak.

Charley wished she could pull back the thoughtless question. She hadn't expected anything like this. "What a horrible tragedy.

He smeared cream on her foot as if her life depended on it. "I always felt I should have been able to prevent her death. Done something, told someone. I knew there was a problem. She had changed, become moody and depressed. When I went into her room one night to tell her about making the rugby team, I found her crying, but she made me promise not to tell our mum and dad."

"It wasn't your fault. You were little more than a child."

"The rational part of my brain understands. But occasionally, a small part of me, deep down inside, still believes I could have prevented her death."

Charley placed her hand over his. "I didn't mean to pry."

He raised his head and stared at her, sudden pain flaring

in his gaze. "You didn't, Charley. You had no way of knowing, and it all happened a long time ago. You know, you're a lot like Mairie in many ways. She'd have liked you, I think."

Undone by his words, Charley's heart went out to the real person she'd glimpsed behind the charming façade. A man who still mourned his lost sister. Blatant flirting she could deal with, no problem. She wasn't so sure she could handle his vulnerability.

Kincaid continued his ministrations in silence. By the time he released Charley's foot, her blisters felt much better, but her stomach was doing those jittery somersaults again. She'd better get out of there fast, before she did something she would live to regret. Her orderly world was spinning out of control and she hated the feeling.

Tongue-tied and flustered, she struggled to her feet with a groan and a mumbled: "Thanks for the help. Gotta clean up, get ready for lunch." Avoiding eye contact, she flipped her hand in Kincaid's general direction, grabbed her boots and bag, and limped as regally as possible towards her tent.

"Ow," she squeaked when she stepped on a twig. The high-pitched yelp marred her stately exit.

Charley's undignified escape pulled Kincaid from his grief over his sister's death. The crushing pain should have subsided over twenty-one years ago, but some days, a mere word or a gesture triggered a flood of sad memories and a near-overwhelming desire to toss down a quick shot of whiskey – the same whiskey he'd turned to in those dark days when his teenaged guilt had become too painful to bear.

I might have dodged another bullet this time. But will my sobriety be strong enough to survive the next challenge life tosses at me? All he could do was live one day at a time.

Still hunkered down beside the lagoon, he followed Charley's unsteady progress with reluctant admiration. Those blisters must have hurt like hell, but she hadn't complained.

His elusive prize was definitely worth the effort.

A lazy smile spread across his face, and he hauled himself to his feet. Slowly but surely, his persistence was wearing her down, penetrating her carefully constructed defences. Her panicky flight only proved he was making significant inroads. He loved nothing better than a good challenge. Except, of course, winning the challenge.

Chuckling inside, he leaned against the rough bark of a towering palm tree, legs crossed at the ankle, and watched the ensuing performance a short distance away. She bent down and struggled unsuccessfully to unzip the tent flap with one hand while juggling her boots and bag in the other, her cheeks a brilliant beet-red. The green fabric of the jumpsuit encased her shapely butt like a tight-fitting glove, providing an interesting colour contrast against the crimson. A smear of mud emphasized the tempting roundness.

"You might have more luck if you used both hands," he shouted.

Charley stiffened, but she dropped her burden and tugged again, following his suggestion. Her awkward position presented a nice, long display of her delectable posterior. For once, he applauded her stubborn nature. Independence had side benefits for the spectator. When she finally coaxed the zipper loose after repeated tuggings accompanied by dire threats, she gathered her belongings with as much dignity as she could muster under the circumstances and disappeared inside without a backward glance.

"See you at lunch in a few minutes," Kincaid called to the closed tent flap. When she didn't reply, he sauntered away in the opposite direction, hoping she was peeking out.

Ever since his divorce, he'd preferred shallow, malleable women. Women who wouldn't complicate his life and jeopardize his hard-won peace of mind. Women who wouldn't penetrate his carefully constructed defences. *Women who wouldn't jeopardize his sobriety.* Charley didn't come close to filling the bill. Her feisty humour, quick wit and intelligence, coupled with unfortunate tendencies towards touchiness, obstinacy and general grouchiness added up to an irresistible package.

He hadn't been this intrigued with a woman since he'd first met Leila.

Fifteen minutes later, Kincaid ambled towards the dining hall, his organized brain already mapping out his next moves on Charley.

He planned to take advantage of the vast strides he'd made towards romantic conquest during the morning, striking while the iron was hot. A little more pressure, judiciously applied, and Charley would soon be warming his bed. He hoped. A speedy conquest was becoming increasingly important. The longer she held out, challenging him, intriguing him, the harder it was to dismiss her as another shallow adornment – a pretty bauble he could take or leave without any intellectual or emotional investment.

His heart tumbled around in his chest at the sight of Charley sitting quietly, legs crossed, at his personal table in the back corner.

She looked sensational. Sexy. In the short time since she'd bolted into her tent, she'd showered, changed her clothes and worked some mysterious feminine magic on everything else. The grubby, green jumpsuit had disappeared. In its place, a turquoise, silky blouse clung to her curves, revealing the tender hollow of her throat and emphasizing the fullness of her breasts. Tawny hair cascaded in a froth of curls around her shoulders, tempting him to bury his hands in the silken mass to find out if it felt as good as it looked.

Better still, she'd chosen to sit at his table voluntarily, without any arm-twisting, bribery or other coercive trickery on his part. His tactics must be working. He pulled out a chair and sat down. "Hi. How on Earth did you manage it?"

She looked at him blankly. "Manage what?"

"To look as if you've spent two hours in a beauty salon instead of twenty minutes in a tent?"

A mysterious smile flickered around her mouth. "Can't reveal all my little secrets, now can I? It would destroy the mystique."

"How are the feet?"

"Much better, thanks to your expert first aid. I'm afraid I ran off without thanking you properly. You must think I'm rude and ungrateful—"

A musical laugh interrupted Charley in the middle of her

apology. "If the shoe fits, honey. Sorry, just joking." Leila lowered her voice to a sultry drawl. "Mind if I sit down, Alistair?"

Charley shot Leila a look that would melt nails but kept her mouth closed.

Kincaid ground his teeth. So much for striking while the iron was hot. He'd have to wait till later to continue his conquest of Charley.

Without waiting for an answer, Leila slid into the seat beside Kincaid. "Darling," she purred and kissed his cheek, allowing her fingers to trail down his arm. "I am so terribly sorry I slept late this morning."

Amazing, thought Kincaid, staring at Leila dispassionately. She looked, smelled, and sounded wonderful. And he felt nothing at all. No tug of lust, no burst of excitement, not even a surge of anger. Only lingering sadness at wasted possibilities.

Leila placed her hand on his arm in a possessive gesture, and he couldn't shrug it off without seeming churlish. He felt stifled, uncomfortably aware of her cloying warmth.

Kincaid watched Charley bare her teeth, the sharp, white incisors gleaming in what he assumed was a parody of good fellowship. Her voice dripped with honeyed venom. "Why, Leila, honey. I'm sure you deserved a good, long sleep-in this morning. It must've been what, around dawn when you finally came to bed? No wonder you missed the tour."

"Yes," Leila agreed, shooting Charley a hostile glare. "You've blown my secret little vice. I'm afraid I got caught up in a poker game and forgot all about the time." She leaned closer to Kincaid. "You remember how much I love a good card game and how you used to beg me to come to bed."

Kincaid struggled to keep his voice even. Leila's gambling had been a major issue between them. "Aye. You could never resist an all-night poker game."

"I *do* hope the morning wasn't too tiresome for you, Alistair." Leila glanced meaningfully at Charley.

Charley's eyes narrowed and turned a cold, icy blue. He was beginning to read her moods like a book, and right now, she looked ready to go ballistic. He couldn't say he blamed her. The air around her head crackled with hostility as tangible as if she'd spoken aloud.

Kincaid prudently stepped in. "We had a great morning, thanks," he interjected, cutting off the caustic retort he was certain hovered on Charley's lips. "Charley was a great audience – asked all the right questions and kept me in line."

He ignored Leila's frown and winked at Charley, who subsided with a faint smile.

Leila's grip on his arm tightened like a vice. "I can hardly wait for the tour you promised me," she continued in an animated voice, which sounded artificial to Kincaid, given the death-grip on his arm. "I hope you don't mind taking me this afternoon. I want to see everything – including those silly merchants' quarters you want me to help excavate. When we're finished, we can discuss the important stuff – like the tunnel and what might lie behind the rock fall. It'll be just like old times."

Kincaid reached for the bread, effectively forcing Leila to remove her hand from his arm. "Too bad you slept in. Unfortunately, I can't get away again this afternoon."

For a single moment, Leila's mask cracked and he glimpsed her shock and disappointment before she regained her composure. "Why not, Alistair?" she pouted. "I didn't think it would matter if I wasn't there this morning. I thought you'd want to show me the site when we could be alone to analyze some of the findings."

Kincaid's voice hardened. "Sorry, Leila. You snooze, you lose. I'm needed at the rockslide this afternoon. I want to make sure the work is moving ahead."

Thankfully, she backed down. "Of course. I understand how much you care about your dig. Tomorrow then?" Leila's voice exuded a patience and tolerance that, in Kincaid's private opinion, was as phony as a Times Square Rolex. To his recollection, she'd never exhibited the slightest symptoms of either patience or tolerance during their marriage.

He sighed. She wasn't going down without a fight. He'd better put an end to the debate. "No, tomorrow won't work for me, either. But I'll find someone to show you around this afternoon."

He scanned the dining hall feverishly, feeling a quick pang of guilt for the task he was about to inflict on a hapless colleague. "I see the perfect person – there." He pointed out an animated redhead. "Karen's an archaeologist and can explain everything about the site as well as I can and maybe better. I'll tell her you'll be working on the merchants' quarters."

Although Leila's smile remained firmly glued in place, anger flickered in her eyes as though a switch had been flipped. "No problem, Alistair. We can catch up with one another later this evening. I'll look forward to talking to you about your findings."

Not if he could avoid it. He shuddered. That part of his life was over, but this was the wrong time to make the announcement. The inevitable showdown would come later.

The remainder of the meal passed in strained silence punctuated only by comments about the food. No one had much of an appetite. Even Charley, who usually tackled her meal with gusto, poked moodily at her salad, picking out the shrimp and chunks of avocado, leaving the rest.

When the meal had trailed to its uncomfortable conclusion, Charley pushed away from the table. "Gotta go. See you later." Before he could open his mouth to protest, her long legs had carried her out the door.

Kincaid caught up with her on the veranda. "Whoa, there. Don't run away so fast. What will you do with yourself this afternoon while I'm at the dig?"

"Rest. Relax. Give my feet a break. And I have the headache from hell. Probably the aftermath of my little heat stroke. I'll snooze while the coast is clear and Leila is otherwise occupied, then I'll type up my interview notes."

"Enjoy," he said. "But I should warn you – it's Saturday and the peace and quiet will end around 4:30. We hold happy hour before dinner and a campfire in the evening. Will you join me?"

Charley eyed him warily. "Are you inviting me on a date?"

She was really cute when alarmed. All fluttery and alert, eyes a deep ocean blue. "Aye. I suppose I am."

"I don't know. I don't think I'm ready for involvement. Besides, your ex-wife wouldn't appreciate it."

"It's only drinks and a wee campfire, not a lifetime

commitment. And Leila doesn't have any claim on me. She gave up all proprietary rights when she divorced me – and no, in case you were wondering, I'm not asking you on a date to spite Leila. I'm asking because I want to get to know you better."

Oh, bloody hell. Why did he go and say that? He must be a blithering idiot. What if he'd scared her off?

"Whew! That's a relief. I'll see you tonight at happy hour." Charley walked away.

"So we have a date?" he called.

She glanced at him over her shoulder and tossed her hair. "Not a date. Just a couple of drinks and a campfire."

Hot damn. That meant 'yes' in his book.

Chapter 13

Kincaid glanced at his watch, 4:45. Happy hour was well underway, and, based on the shrieks of laughter, a rousing success as usual. Alternating mariachi, salsa, and merengue blared from two loud speakers on the front veranda.

He paced up and down beneath a large jacaranda tree, scanning the faces. Ridiculous. He felt as if he'd been sucked into the gangling body of a fourteen-year-old again, cooling his heels in heart-pounding anticipation and horniness while waiting for his first date. Maybe he'd scared Charley off. He'd seen turkeys in November that were less skittish. Kincaid stole another glance at his watch. Five minutes past five.

"Don't worry. Charley will show up."

Kincaid jumped at the sound of Colin's voice. "You shouldn't sneak up on a person."

Colin handed him a Coke. "I thought you might be thirsty."

"Aye, thanks." Kincaid grasped the can, then scrutinized the glass of lethal-looking reddish liquid Colin balanced in his other hand. "Watch out for that swill you call rum punch. The last time you got into it, I had to listen to you complaining about a headache for a fortnight. Maybe you should stick to beer."

Colin sniffed, sounding aggrieved. "Moderation has always been my motto. You must be thinking of someone else." He changed the subject. "Why are you skulking behind a tree, anyway? You usually enjoy mingling with the team."

"I'm not skulking. I'm discretely avoiding a scene with the blonde over there." He nodded at a well-endowed young woman whose abundant assets spilled over the plunging neckline of her fluorescent yellow tank top. "She's got a crush on me and follows me around at every happy hour. You know my policy. I keep my hands to myself when it comes to my team members."

"Lucky for you, Charley's not part of your team."

Kincaid laughed, hearing the echo of the words he'd spoken to Charley. "Aye. Thank God for that. After way too many long and lonely months in the jungle, the prospect of a woman to warm my bed is a rare treat, and Charley is well worth the wait. I intend to pull out all the stops tonight. I'll give her my best moves – and some of them are superb if I do say so myself. Sooner or later, she'll stop fighting the inevitable."

Colin groaned and shook his shaggy head. "Kincaid, listen to yourself. You sound as cold-blooded as a shark. But I know better."

Kincaid relented, smiling sheepishly. "You know me too well. Just wishful thinking on my part. Actually, I'm scared shitless she'll blow me off."

"Oh, aye? I thought the three months of rehab and several years of therapy was supposed to help with all that insecurity."

"Most of the time, I'm fine." Kincaid recognized the defensiveness in his own voice. "Okay, *sometimes*, I'm fine."

"You must like Charley a lot."

"Hell, I'm more attracted to her than to any other woman I've dated since my divorce, and I think she feels the same way about me." Kincaid hoped his brave words were true. He feared he was becoming a little *too* interested in the fascinating reporter for his own good. He added, more for his own benefit than Colin's: "Nothing serious, mind you. We're two consenting adults thrown together in close quarters, no strings attached."

A brilliant flash of turquoise caught his eye. Kincaid promptly forgot about his misgivings. The tall, graceful figure approached the veranda, scanned the faces as if searching for someone, and plunged into the crowd clustered around the punch bucket.

"Excuse me. My date has arrived. I'd better go save her from the worst hangover of her life."

"You wouldn't be heartless enough to deprive her of the world's greatest beverage experience. I mix the king of rum punches."

Kincaid started to walk away, then stopped and grinned at Colin. "On second thought, a couple of glasses of your concoction might loosen her inhibitions."

"Kincaid," Colin called, a note of warning in his voice. "You mind your step and treat the wee lassie gently, or you'll have me to deal with, and I promise it won't be pleasant. She's just the woman you need."

"Don't worry," Kincaid tossed back. "I'll be gentle. I know what I'm doing."

You could learn a lot about a woman by catching her unaware. Kincaid smiled, following Charley's slow progress towards the bar. Whether she was selfish or thoughtful, shy or outgoing, happy or sad.

Charley hadn't noticed him yet. The porch was so crowded it would take a bulldozer to plough a path through the laughing, chatting mob. Kincaid gave up trying to reach her and stood motionless, sipping his Coke and watching her in action. Her glorious tawny mane flowed in loose curls around her shoulders and her eyes glowed a luminous turquoise, mirroring the tone of her silky blouse. She reminded him of a thoroughbred – all slim elegance with long legs, shapely hips and delicate feet and hands. And really terrific breasts. Not large, but perfectly formed, from what he could see, and ideally proportioned for her graceful body.

How could he ever have considered her too tall and skinny?

Charley handed a bearded student a glass of punch before filling her own. She threw back her head and laughed at whatever the young man had said and followed him through the crowd towards a group of young people who had thrown themselves into an uninhibited merengue.

The student stared at Charley, obviously mesmerized. Kincaid could practically read his love-struck mind. He was working up the courage to ask her to dance. *Bulldozer, be damned.* Kincaid discarded his empty can. He wanted to be her first dance partner. And only one. He elbowed and shoved his way through the milling bodies, working his way towards Charley. "Hullo, beautiful. Care to dance?"

She whipped her head around. "There you are. I wondered if you'd stood me up. Yes, I'd love to dance."

"Oh, hell." The student grimaced. "You stole my thunder, Kincaid. Any chance of the next dance?"

Kincaid gave the student his best shark-like smile. "Sorry, lad. You're not my type."

Kincaid led Charley into the sensual and elegant Latin dance.

She followed smoothly, without hesitation, her supple body swaying to the throbbing beat as if they had danced together a hundred times. Her smile flashed. "Nice rank pulling, Kincaid."

"What's the point of being the boss if there are no privileges? Besides, Latinos look on the merengue as a weapon of seduction used by a man courting a woman, and I'm damned if I'll stand there and allow one of my callow students to seduce you. It wouldn't be seemly."

"I'm overwhelmed by your concern about my reputation."

"Just doing my job as a dutiful host."

"Weapon of seduction, huh? Does this mean you're hoping I'll fling myself into your arms with abandon when the dance is over?"

"Aye. Is it working?" Women usually loved the frank approach.

"It'll take a lot more than one dance, Kincaid."

"Give me time." She felt so *good* under his hand – firm yet pliant, hips undulating. "Your feet must be feeling better."

"Much better, thank you. Pain killers and loose shoes work miracles."

Kincaid held Charley at arm's length as she executed a complicated series of small, hip swaying steps. Her gaze locked on his in an unspoken challenge, and he felt himself swell. If the dance didn't end soon, he would have to sit down or embarrass himself in front of his team.

Fortunately for both his image and his peace of mind, the music ended with a blare of prolonged trumpet notes. Kincaid swept Charley into a dramatic finale and reluctantly released his grip on the armful of hot, flushed female to a spatter of applause and catcalls.

"Not bad for an old man," shouted the bearded student.

"Pretty hot," commented another.

Kincaid bowed. "Take a lesson from the master, lads. I'm not ready for the rocking chair yet."

The music started up again and he swung Charley into another dance, then another.

When the fifth dance finished, she collapsed against him, breathless. "Enough, Kincaid. Have pity," she wheezed.

He wrapped his arm around her shoulder, enjoying the way her body moulded to his. "Let's get some drinks and go somewhere quieter. I want to show you something," he said, wanting to herd her away from the crowd.

She dug in her heels, eyes wary, cheeks rosy from exertion. "I'm enjoying myself. I like dancing and I'm not so sure I want to let you drag me away from the party."

He hoped she wouldn't pick tonight to exhibit more of the mule-headed stubbornness she'd displayed earlier. "You're arguing already and the evening hasn't begun."

"I'm stating my preference, not arguing. I hate arguing and I usually make it a point to avoid domineering men."

"You love to argue. In fact, you live to argue. And I'm not domineering, merely dynamic and resolute."

She heaved an exasperated sigh. "Why are we sparring like this?"

"It's fun, that's why. We both enjoy a good verbal challenge," he answered, thinking how adorable she looked when she was flustered. The way her eyes lit up turned his insides to butter.

"I give up. What do you want to show me?"

Ah. Persistence paid. For a moment, he'd been afraid she would refuse if he pushed any harder. "It's a surprise. No, don't look at me as if I'm about to drag you off by the hair into my cave. I show all the visitors to camp this surprise. Get your drink and bring it with you."

She grabbed her glass from the table and examined it suspiciously. "Do you have any idea what's in this thing? It looks dangerous." She sipped the concoction and her face lit up. "Hey, it's really good. Hardly tastes as if there's any alcohol in it, though." She took a larger gulp.

Kincaid's conscience got the better of him. He wouldn't wish the rum-punch hangover on his worst enemy. "Slow down there. It contains three kinds of rum and God-knows what else. Colin won't disclose the exact recipe, but everyone tells me his concoction tastes like heaven and packs the kick of a mule. Look at the rowdy crowd if you don't believe me. That student over there drank it only once and spent most of the next day wishing he was dead. I was afraid we'd have to fly him out for treatment."

"Thanks for the warning." Charley returned her glass to the table. "Beer it is. Besides, Leila would gloat if I made a fool of myself." Charley scanned the faces in the crowd. "Speaking of Leila, she's not here. Does she know about the happy hour?"

"I forgot to mention it. Did you tell her?"

She shook her head. "Do I look like a masochist to you? The further away she is, the happier I am. She's probably asleep since she was out all night. Just as well, because I might have throttled her by now." Charley flushed a bright scarlet. "Oh, my God. You must think I'm a spiteful bitch, insulting your ex-wife. We just don't seem to hit it off. I doubt we'll ever be buddies."

"It's okay, I understand. Leila tends to have an adverse effect on people." He remembered only too clearly how Leila's cruelty wounded those on the receiving end. "She's another reason to get out of here. I'll grab some drinks, we can get a couple of things from my cabin, and then I want to show you the roosting tree before dinner."

"Is that some new form of jungle seduction I've never heard of – like showing me your etchings?"

With a wee bit of luck, it might be. "Patience. All will become clear."

Kincaid and Charley strolled side-by-side along the shadowy path leading from the grove to his cabin. At one point, the trail narrowed, forcing them to walk single file. Kincaid ushered Charley ahead. He couldn't help noticing the enticing movement of her nicely rounded ass inside the tight jeans she wore. He enjoyed the view for a brief moment, then took a couple of rapid strides to catch up.

He had high hopes that cold beer, good food, laughter

and a few songs around the campfire would lure her into his arms at the end of the evening. "We'll need a blanket for later," he said, following his train of thought to its logical conclusion.

Charley stared at him blankly.

Had he really blurted out his innermost thoughts? Thinking fast, he explained: "It gets cold when the sun goes down. These mountains are higher than they look. You'll thank me for a warm blanket."

They stopped when they reached a cabin set apart from the others. "Home sweet home. Come in while I find the blanket, some insect repellent, and a flashlight." Juggling the beer and Coke in one hand, he opened the door and ushered Charley inside.

She gazed around. "Very impressive. A queen-sized bed, table, chairs, even a chest of drawers."

Her subtle fragrance of lavender and soap was driving him mad. "The bed's very comfy. Best in camp. Want to try it out?" he inquired hopefully.

"In your dreams, Kincaid. Don't get any ideas because I accompanied you to your cabin."

"Wouldn't think of it. I'm a proper gentleman," Kincaid asserted, making a joke of her rebuff. "As a matter of fact, I carry gentlemanliness to new heights. I wouldn't even consider thinking an improper thought."

So, why did he find himself uncomfortably aroused at the notion of Charley, sprawled out on his spacious queen-sized bed, wearing nothing but her ring and a brilliant smile? Ever since she'd collided with him on the path yesterday afternoon, his fingers had itched to bury themselves in the glorious mass of honey-coloured hair that curled around her face. Damn, but the woman was jumpy. During their first dance, he could have sworn she was attracted to him; by the time they'd finished their fourth, he'd optimistically envisaged a blissful week of carnal pleasure. Now it looked as if he'd better tread gently or he'd scare her off.

To his surprise, Charley emitted a loud squeak. A furry shape whizzed through the open door, brushed against her leg, and flew onto the bed where it collapsed on the pillow and licked its paw with great concentration.

"Horrie." Charley gave an audible gasp then laughed. "You nearly gave me heart failure."

The cat stopped licking his paw and stared at her with his one yellow, unblinking eye.

As Kincaid watched in amazement, Charley perched on the edge of the bed and scratched between the cat's ears. Horrie's one good eye immediately closed in contentment and loud purring filled the cabin.

"You chose an excellent time to become my babe magnet, Horrie," said Kincaid. "Good work, lad. You've enticed her onto my bed. I'll make sure you get an extra can of tuna for your supper tonight."

Charley laughed. "Enjoy the sight while you can." She tickled Horrie's chin, and the cat obediently collapsed onto his back, presenting a round, white tummy for her ministrations.

The purring increased two decibels.

"You like that, baby, don't you," cooed Charley.

"Who wouldn't?" mumbled Kincaid.

Charley paused and looked up from under her lashes, smiling. "I thought you were going to show me the roosting tree. Just the two of us."

He stared at her in mock amazement. "Are you flirting with me?"

Her face pinkened. "Maybe a little. By accident."

His pulse quickened at her admission. So what was holding him back?

Kincaid's noble effort to push all erotic thoughts aside came as something of a shock to him. This was a new and perplexing development. He wasn't sure he liked it. But one thing he was sure of – if he moved too quickly, he would scare Charley off.

To his unending surprise, he didn't want to lose her.

He gathered up everything, including the drinks, flashlight, insect repellent and blanket and stuffed them into a gym bag. "Right you are. Let's go, before I forget my good intentions about being a gentleman."

Chapter 14

A discordant squawking, chattering and chirping filled the air.

Kincaid enjoyed watching visitors' incredulous reaction to their first sight of the ancient fig tree overhanging the lagoon. Charley's thunder-struck expression exceeded his expectations. She gazed up at the network of branches silhouetted against the sunset, disbelief etched on her expressive features.

She shouted to be heard above the din. "It's amazing. Miraculous. I didn't know anything like this existed."

He positioned his mouth close to her ear. "Every evening at dusk, the green parakeets return to this tree."

The branches contained so many birds, all jostling for position, the entire tree seemed to be in constant, fluttering movement. More birds hovered and swooped, searching for a place to land.

"There must be thousands of birds. I love it."

"I come here most evenings before dinner to watch the show. As soon as the sun sets, they'll all shut up and fall asleep. Let's sit down over there, away from the racket. There are some chairs beside the lagoon and we can watch the sun disappear behind the mountains."

Two minutes later, Charley settled in a chair while Kincaid deposited the gym bag on the ground and extracted the contents. He placed the drinks in the water to keep them cool, keeping one beer and a Coke aside, then passed the insect repellent to Charley.

"You'd better use this or you'll be eaten alive. The mosquitoes are enormous out here." He watched as Charley sprayed those portions of her body that she could reach.

A light, citrus scent mixed with eucalyptus filled the air.

He took the can and applied the spray liberally to his free

hand. Before she had time to realize what he intended to do and bolt for freedom, he swept her hair away from her face. Its springy softness startled him.

She fixed her startled gaze on his eyes. He took her silence as permission to smooth the oily concoction on the back of her neck, ears and face.

As he drew his hand over the curve of her cheek, the light contact turned into a silky caress. "Mosquitoes love unprotected, tender areas like this," he whispered and drew his finger down the front of her neck.

Eyes wide with alarm, she jerked back. "Just worry about your own skin, Kincaid, not mine."

Give her time, you daft fool. You're moving too fast.

Kincaid sprayed himself and sat down. "Now enjoy the evening and stop fretting."

The clamorous chirping of a tree frog emphasized the surrounding hush. He could hear the distant music and laughter of the happy hour.

Suddenly tongue-tied, he busied himself, prying off the beer cap to buy himself some time. This was unthinkable. He'd skilfully manoeuvred her away from the crowd, and now that they were alone, words escaped him. He wracked his brain to find something meaningful or at least witty to say, but failed miserably.

Kincaid handed Charley the beer and opened a Coke for himself.

"Thanks." She looked at him curiously. "Wouldn't you rather have a beer?"

Her innocent question caught him off-balance and he answered without thinking, his voice harsh and grating in his ears, "I don't drink."

"Oh," she said, sounding surprised and a little hurt. "I'm sorry I pried."

"No harm done," he muttered, feeling like a fool. "I just never learned to like beer. Or, maybe I should say, booze doesn't like me."

An uncomfortable silence thrummed between them. She deserved an explanation, but spilling his shameful story would kill any chances he had of ever winning her over. He simply couldn't bring himself to describe his battle with the bottle.

Finally, he cleared his throat. "What led you into journalism?" he asked, knowing his Scottish burr was thicker than normal. That only happened when he was angry, nervous or in the throes of passion. Since he was neither angry, nor regrettably, in the throes of passion, that left only nervous.

He'd asked an inane question. Charley must think he was a blithering idiot or a tongue-tied fool. Or both.

Kincaid prided himself on his smooth-tongued glibness around women. His uncanny knack of saying exactly the right thing at the right time had led to most of his highly pleasurable successes in the bedroom arena. Tonight, when he actually gave a damn, his easy gift of the gab deserted him with a careless disregard for his ego.

As if unaware of the triteness of the conversational gambit, she replied: "I've always wanted to write, ever since I first learned the joys of reading. Stories, articles. That sort of thing. I loved English in high school, won a couple of essay-writing prizes, and it seemed only natural to study journalism. One day, I intend to write a novel."

Thank God. She'd taken pity on him and was striving to engage in a halfway normal conversation.

In the fading light, Charley's extraordinary dark-lashed eyes turned his insides to butter. Her shoulder brushed Kincaid's arm and he immediately lost his train of thought. Amazing. This couldn't be happening to him. He hated feeling out of control and vulnerable. All he wanted was a quick fling with no complications, no strings.

"Wonderful," he said feebly. "I can't imagine how you authors do it."

"It remains to be seen whether or not I can pull it off. Writing a book takes an enormous amount of discipline, and I'm not sure I have the patience and stamina."

"If you want something badly enough, you'll find a way."

He was almost certain he caught a glimpse of pain in her eyes before she turned to study the glory of the sunset as if it contained the secrets of life. He must have said something to make her uncomfortable, but damned if he knew what it was.

Her voice betrayed a tell-tale tightness. "This place is

mind-blowing. Not at all what I expected. Your camp even has running water, showers and electricity."

Now this was a topic near and dear to his heart. "Oh, aye. We installed as many amenities as possible out here in the jungle. The team will be here for a long time and I want them to feel at home."

"Did you build it yourself?"

He laughed and relaxed, all trace of discomfort vanished. "No. I'm a man of many and varied talents, but mechanical aptitude isn't one of them. You'd be amazed at the damage I can do with a screwdriver and a wrench. Let's just say there was an unfortunate incident involving a toilet and an uncontrollable geyser just before I left San Francisco. I don't like to talk about it," he said, straight faced.

"Very traumatic, I'm sure. I'll respect your privacy." Although her face was shadowed against the darkening sky, he could swear her eyes glinted with suppressed laughter in spite of her solemn tone.

Fighting every urge to move too quickly, he shifted closer. "You're a very thoughtful woman."

This time, she didn't shift away.

Yes, he definitely wanted to get to know her better, preferably, in his bed. Tonight. Not that he wanted a serious relationship. His experience with Leila had proven how uncomfortable emotional entanglement could be. But a wee dalliance with a beautiful and intelligent woman for the next week or so – that was a different story.

The musical tones of *The Star Spangled Banner* rang out, causing them both to jump.

"Dammit. That's my satellite phone. Oh, my God, I forgot to call my mother this afternoon," Charley explained. "Excuse me." She fumbled in her pocket, extracted the phone and punched the connect button. "Hi, Mom."

He stared as she bolted out of the chair and stalked away, clutching her beer, following the path along the lagoon until thick underbrush concealed her. Her agitated voice disturbed the roosting birds, and a few disgruntled squawks and sleepy chirps drowned out her words.

As hard as he strained, Kincaid couldn't make out what she was saying, but one thing was certain – Charley had severe mother issues.

After six infuriating minutes on the phone with her mother, Charley broke the connection and glanced over her shoulder towards the chairs where Kincaid waited. She hoped he hadn't heard her end of the conversation. That would be too embarrassing. Surprised to discover the sun had almost disappeared, she hurried back. Soon, it would be too dark to see anything.

Kincaid studied her face with worried eyes as she approached. "Is everything okay?"

He was too damned perceptive for her comfort. She sat down, mouth dry, palms slick with sweat. "Yes. No. Dammit. My mother makes me stark raving mad. Sometimes I think tormenting me is her primary purpose in life."

Kincaid removed the empty beer bottle from Charley's unresisting hand. She hadn't realized she had drained it.

"Looks like you could use another." He retrieved another Corona from the water and opened it without waiting for her answer. "Amazing creatures, mothers. Where would we be without them?"

Charley raised the bottle absently, took a long swig, and brooded. Ice-cold beer trickled down her throat, easing the parched dryness, loosening the tight knot inside. She put the bottle down and glared at it balefully. Drinking definitely wasn't the answer. As the pressure built inside her chest, she drummed her fingers on the arms of her chair.

They both sipped their drinks during the strained silence until Charley thought her nerves would snap.

Finally, Kincaid's voice, deep with sympathy, rumbled in her ear. "Want to talk about whatever's bothering you?"

Every cell of her body snapped to attention, acutely aware of the large, warm body beside her, his arm brushing hers. Near darkness lent a false sense of intimacy, and she had protected her mother for too many years. If she didn't talk to someone, she would explode, and Kincaid was offering a friendly ear. She clenched her hands into tight fists until fingernails dug into flesh and plunged ahead: "I really dread her phone calls. D'you think it's possible to love someone so much you'd die for them, yet want to strangle them at the same time?"

"I think so, aye."

Charley cleared her throat and prayed her voice wouldn't waver. "My mother likes to, ah, mould her environment, especially after she's had a couple of glasses of wine. And she's had more than a couple by this time of the day."

"You mean the wine controls her and she tries to control everyone and everything around her. Take no prisoners, no holds barred?"

Kincaid's acute perception astonished Charley. She wasn't sure what reaction she'd expected from him. Disapproval maybe, disgust, even dismissal, but not sympathetic understanding. She nodded. "Exactly. Ever since I can remember, Mom has always loved her wine. Too much for her own good, or mine. I grew up thinking we were normal. Only recently, I finally admitted the truth to myself – my mother's a drunk." She picked up the beer bottle and poured out the contents to form a frothy puddle at her feet.

He shifted his body and stretched out his long legs. "It's hard to stand back and watch someone we love poisoning themselves."

Charley stared at him in shock, straining to read his expression but unable to decipher it. "I can't just stand back and watch. Someone has to step in, or she'll harm herself. I have to take care of her, you know, check up every day, drop in unexpectedly, phone her, make sure she doesn't get into too much trouble." Her voice dropped. "If I don't, God only knows what will happen."

"Trying to rescue someone when they don't want to be helped is a huge burden," he said.

Charley fiddled with the label on the bottle, shredding it into little pieces. "You've got that right."

Kincaid's large hand covered hers, stilling the jittery action. "As strange as it may seem, the best way to help your mother might be to let her make her own mistakes until she's willing to seek help."

She yanked her hand away. A sane person wouldn't propose such an idiotic idea. "I don't believe it. You're telling me to sit back and let her drink herself to death. Not bloody likely."

His voice was compassionate. "Are you able to curb her drinking? Slow her down?"

"Apparently not," Charley admitted. "She just sneaks behind my back."

"Then trust what I'm telling you. Let her go."

Charley's stomach twisted. "I can't abandon my mother."

"That's not what I meant. Naturally, you don't want to abandon her. But if you try to control her life, you'll destroy your own."

"What would you know about it?" Even to her own ears, she sounded surly.

His voice deepened. "More than you might think. The bottle took over my own mum's life after my sister died. One day, after an afternoon of drinking, she picked up my sisters at school, drove through a red light, and broadsided a Fiat. Luckily, no one was badly hurt. Booze damned near killed her."

Kincaid sounded so sad, Charley wanted to smooth away the lines she knew furrowed his forehead. Instead, she reached across and linked her fingers with his. "Did your mother ever stop drinking?"

His grip tightened and he moved closer. "Aye. When she decided she wanted to live more than she wanted to die. But by then, I ...." He broke off and gazed at the darkening horizon in thoughtful silence.

She twisted to look at him. "What?"

"Oh, nothing. Just another memory. The important thing is that she quit."

"Then there may be hope for my mom." *There'd better be hope.* A wave of bitterness nearly suffocated her. She was sacrificing a lot to save her mother – her values, her reputation if word of her unethical conduct leaked out, her budding friendship with Kincaid.

"There's always hope, Charley. Your mother is probably stronger than you think. What did she say to upset you?"

"She thinks my love life is a mess and has made it her mission to rectify the situation."

He transferred the Coke to his other hand, making it easier to drape his arm over her shoulders, his fingers brushing against her bare flesh in scorching contact.

"*Is* your love life a mess?"

Charley smiled to herself at his hopeful tone and fought the urge to lean into his solid body. "Forget it, Kincaid." She shrugged his arm away. "Anyway, Mom insists on introducing me to as many eligible bachelors as she can find."

He removed his arm without protest and made a non-committal sound of sympathy. In Charley's opinion, he could at least have put up a token fight.

"Her latest brainwave is to host a trendy little dinner party starring yours truly and yet another likely candidate. She phoned to find out when I was coming home so she could make the arrangements. I told her to forget it. No more blind dates."

"Let me guess. She didn't jump up and down with joy at your ungrateful and unfilial reaction."

"Totally pissed off."

"Don't worry. It'll pass. Besides, you're down here, she's up there."

"Never stopped her before. You might remember my mother. When I mentioned your name, she told me she had met you at a charity event. She goes by her maiden name, Audrey Huntington."

Kincaid peered at Charley, Coke can frozen halfway to his lips. "*You're* the daughter?"

Charley put down her bottle with deliberate calmness and stared at him. Horrible certainty blossomed. Her mother had succeeded again – found another way to humiliate her. "She tried to set us up, didn't she?"

"Damn. I shouldn't have opened my big mouth. Last year, Audrey invited me over to the house for dinner before I left San Francisco."

Charley's face burned with mortification. Thank God for the darkness. "Obviously, you declined," she said stiffly.

His voice softened. "I would have accepted if I'd known it was you."

Charley wished the ground would swallow her up. "I'm so embarrassed. I don't know what to say. How awful of her to humiliate me like that. She never mentioned anything to me."

He swept her embarrassment aside. "Don't let her get to you. She recognized me as a bachelor of the highest calibre and couldn't help herself. After all, look at me." He pointed dramatically to his chest. "I just can't turn it off," he joked.

"Mmm-hmm." He was doing a good job of smoothing over an awkward moment.

"Not that I wouldn't be interested in getting better acquainted with you now that we've finally met," he hinted broadly. "Your mother would be pleased. After all, I meet a few of her eligibility criteria. I'm definitely single, don't drink, have a wee bit of my own money and occasionally, but only under duress, move in rarified social circles."

Charley stifled the giggle that threatened to bubble from her lips.

Undeterred, he continued: "I still have all of my own hair and most of my teeth − I had a couple of wisdom teeth yanked when I was sixteen − and, last but far from least, I'm a very snappy dresser. A woman would be proud to be seen with me." He gestured modestly at the aloha shirt, mercifully toned down by the darkness, then pulled back his lips in a huge, exaggerated grin. His teeth gleamed a dazzling white in the glow of the rising moon.

"My, what a lot of teeth you have," Charley said, her mouth twitching with suppressed laughter. "You're absolutely correct. No man could possibly score higher in the eligibility ranking than you. What was I thinking? I'd be out of my mind not to swoon at your feet. Except for one teeny, tiny fly in the ointment."

"Oh, aye?"

"I have no need for a man in my life. Especially one my mother endorsed. In my humble opinion, all men are rats."

He bristled. "We're not all bad. Why are you so bitter about men?"

Should she tell him? Why not? After all, she would never see him again after she stabbed him in the back. She reached for his Coke and took a large swallow, then threw caution to the wind. When she spoke, she tried to keep her voice light, dismissive. "I was engaged to be married last year."

"What happened?" Clearly, Kincaid had a clue for his

voice was kind.

"A week before our wedding, I found my fiancé in our bed with our maid of honour, my former best friend. Bye, bye wedded bliss."

His voice rose in utter surprise. "He must have been an idiot."

She shrugged.

He gave a brief grunt. "The two-timing, double-dealing, slimy bastard should have been suspended by his thumbs. Or other vital appendages."

She gurgled out a surprised laugh. "I agree. Do you want to know the clincher?"

"Aye."

"My maid of honour had a tattoo of Bugs Bunny on her butt. And it was huge. Absolutely enormous. The tattoo, I mean," she snickered. "She always refused to undress in front of me. Now I know why."

Kincaid released a deep guffaw. "You paint quite a picture." When his laughter subsided, he shifted his chair closer and engulfed her hand in his warm, comforting grip again. "I can imagine how much it must have hurt."

She fought the urge to lean into his comforting warmth. "Yeah, right. This wasn't the first time a man betrayed me. I'm now the proud possessor of an unbroken chain of trashed relationships spread out like road kill across ten of the fifty states and north into Canada. Hell will freeze over before I'll trust another man."

"You deserve better, Charley. Much better." His breath stirred her hair.

Charley knew she should drop Kincaid's hand. It was the only sensible thing to do. Instead, she ignored her sage advice. Deliberately, she turned her hand so that their fingers intertwined. Big mistake. Kincaid feathered his thumb across her palm. The gentle caress caused her lower body to throb with a dull ache. Flustered, she snatched her hand away. She didn't understand why her revelations hadn't succeeded in driving him away. On the contrary, he had moved a little closer, his warm body almost touching her own.

A shiver tingled down her spine and she replied quickly, "Think again, Kincaid. I'm not remotely interested in dating anyone right now. Men are trouble. At least the ones I pick certainly are."

"Hah. That sounds like a challenge. I love a good challenge."

She'd already figured that out. He'd been playing a subtle mating game with her for the last hour. "I'd be out of my mind to get involved with you."

"And I'd be out of my mind to let you go without a struggle."

Kincaid played with Charley's fingers. The flutter of breath on her cheek warned her of his proximity. A slow heat circled her belly, filling her with longing. All she needed to do was turn her head and—

Fear boiled in Charley's belly. She yanked her hand away in an act of panicky self-preservation. There was no point starting something he wouldn't want to continue. To put an end to the turmoil of feelings awakened by his slow seduction, she jerked to her feet, her abrupt motion toppling the chair. *Nice move. Smooth and sophisticated.* To cover her acute discomfort, she sniffed the air, and chirped: "I swear I can smell charred meat, Kincaid. Isn't it time to eat?"

Charley felt rather than saw Kincaid's assessing look before he bowed to the inevitable and pushed himself upright with remarkably good grace under the circumstances. He straightened the chair and shook his head. "Okay, Charley. You win for now." His voice reflected resigned amusement. "I'm beginning to believe the best approach to use with you is through your stomach. Let's grab a burger before the campfire starts."

Chapter 15

After the sleepy glow of the campfire, the path seemed a lot steeper and darker than it had at the beginning of the evening. "I can't see where I'm going," Charley said, trying to discern the outline of the path, and immediately tripped over a protruding root. Pain pierced the ball of her foot. "Ouch. Dammit."

Kincaid moved closer. "I'll get you another pair of boots for the morning. Take my arm. It'll be easier."

Seeing no other alternative, she gripped his arm to steady herself as they clambered up the steep slope.

"We're nearly there," he said. "It's only midnight, so you should be able to get a decent night's sleep."

"Great," she mumbled. Sleep would probably elude her for hours while she relived the campfire.

The unexpected richness of Kincaid's singing voice had washed over Charley and brought a lump to her throat. Why, oh why, did he have to possess a glorious voice that made her toes curl? Surely, she wasn't a pathetic groupie to be swayed by a silken voice and easy magnetism wrapped up in a too-attractive package. She mistrusted his charm and pledged a silent vow to resist. She was willing to forgo the temptations of a handsome face and lithe body. But the voice! That velvet voice had touched her soul and come close to battering down her carefully constructed defences.

She was wide-awake now. Painfully so. Every fibre of her being vibrated at a high frequency, acutely aware of the shadowy figure beside her.

His deep voice rumbled in her ear. "I have to do something before I take you back to your tent."

"You do?" Charley halted in surprise. "Right now?"

"Yes. I've been thinking about it all night, wondering

what it would taste like. Very distracting. I have to do it right away before you panic and run."

Her heart hammered against his chest. She knew what he planned to do, but her leaden arms refused to push him away.

Kincaid stepped closer and pulled out the clip holding her hair in place. "You should always wear it like this," he whispered and cupped her cheek in his palm. "You are so beautiful, I feel humbled." His warm mouth slanted over her unresisting lips, gently at first, then more insistently.

Her heart melted and she closed her eyes, surrendering to the hot, erotic sensations flooding her body.

He deepened the kiss as if he had all the time in the world, one hand buried in the mass of loosened hair, the other pressed into the small of her back.

She inhaled his masculine scent – an intoxicating combination of healthy male overlaid with a subtle aftershave, reminiscent of ocean mists mixed with Scottish moors. The tang of wood smoke clung to his clothes.

Part of Charley's brain retained a shred of sanity and knew she should be pushing him away. Her disloyal arms slid up and locked around his neck, drawing his head down as she surrendered to the sizzling heat. Her body melted against his.

So much for her head ruling her actions.

"Oh, sweet Mother of Jesus," he muttered huskily as his body hardened unmistakably against her own. "You're driving me insane." He ran his hands down her back.

The electric jolt coursing through her body shocked her. White heat flashed through every cell, leaving in its wake a deep, pulsing ache and feminine moistness. She quivered slightly and buried one hand in his thick, dark hair to keep him close. "Your mouth should be registered as a lethal weapon, Kincaid," she muttered.

His lips slanted over hers again with exquisite slowness. His tongue teased her mouth open and demanded more. She met his questing tongue with thrusts of her own. One hand moved over her throat, paused then inched down to cup a breast through the light material of her blouse.

Charley lost herself in the sensation. Her mouth fused

with his as she responded with all the passion of her soul. It would have been easy to push his hand away as it had wandered down her body to her breast. She understood that its slow progress was Kincaid's unspoken invitation to stop, if that was what she wanted.

She didn't.

Surely, she hadn't made that primitive moaning sound.

Unconsciously, her hips began to undulate against the hard fullness pressing urgently against her belly.

A tug of desire made her legs tremble, forcing her to face the cold, hard facts. She wanted this man. All of her protests had been meaningless denial. God, how she wanted him. Too much for her own good. How could something so wrong feel so right? She had hoped she would never again feel this terrifying sense of *neediness*, this loss of self in another human being, this feeling of being out of control.

Drawing on a hard core of inner strength, Charley slammed on the brakes and drew away, pushing hard on his chest. "I can't do this. Sorry, Kincaid. I promised myself never to go there again."

A soft groan escaped his lips. His breath hitched in his chest and his stomach muscles quivered under her hand. "You can't mean that. Goes against nature," he said through clenched teeth.

Charley shook her head, mute. He was right, but she did not intend to debate the issue.

He permitted her to put an inch of space between their bodies. "Look at you. You're trembling. I know you feel the heat as much as I do."

"Just chemistry, Kincaid. Nature at work. Hormones and pheromones and endorphins and whatever else gets all stirred up under these circumstances."

"I can't get enough of you, Charley," he whispered hoarsely. "You're addictive."

"I'm sure there must be a twelve-step programme somewhere for that sort of thing," Charley said, her voice husky. "They have one for almost everything these days."

His body tensed, then relaxed. "Just a few more minutes," he wheedled, running his finger over her lower lip.

She sighed and leaned back in his arms, striving to even

out her breathing. "Did anyone ever tell you that you're a very persuasive man, not to mention persistent?"

"Aye. My mother might have mentioned something of the sort when I pestered her night and day for five months straight to buy me the red bicycle in McTavish's window."

"Did she ever give in?"

"Eventually. I can outlast anyone when I've a mind to. And I'm definitely of a mind to make you see the error of your ways." Kincaid cupped Charley's face in both hands and moved his lips over hers, tasting, then nipping gently. "Mmmm. You taste of toasted marshmallows. One of my favourite things in the whole world."

"I think I'd better find my tent," Charley said, relieved to find her breathing and her voice under control once more. She'd better make her getaway while she could still say 'no'.

The darkness couldn't hide the sudden white flash of his smile. "Sweet dreams, lovely Charley. Think about me. This isn't finished."

Kincaid flung himself on his bed and pounded the pillow. He ached in places that hadn't ached since he was eighteen and he'd spent a frenzied hour necking with Martha McLeod in the steamy back seat of his dad's old Vauxhall. The abrupt appearance of Mr. McLeod's face in the car window had put an untimely end to what had promised to be an auspicious interlude.

It had felt every bit as unpleasant now as it did then.

He suppressed a groan *I should head to the showers. Cold water will cool off the lads down there.*

From the second he'd laid eyes on Charley, he'd sensed she was unattainable. Far from being a deterrent, he'd found her aloofness irresistible.

Kincaid could never resist a worthy challenge. Was he totally nuts?

He cast a longing glance at the bottle of Lagavulin he kept on the top shelf, then decided against it.

Unable to lie still and relax, he heaved himself out of bed and flopped onto a chair. Charley had spent the entire evening firing a barrage of mixed messages at him until his head spun. At every opportunity, she'd made it crystal clear she had no intention of getting involved with another man. Ever again. At the same time, Kincaid's finely tuned radar had picked up the unmistakable, high frequency, you-turn-me-on signals she emitted.

The lass wanted him. He felt it in his bones.

Unfortunately for his serenity, he reciprocated the feeling. He found Charley's combination of sassy independence coupled with fragile vulnerability irresistible. Never mind that she possessed a killer body, an abundance of brains and a face that would haunt his dreams tonight, assuming he slept. His imagination painted a delectable picture of her slim, naked body writhing in uncontrolled passion beneath him.

He had pulled out all the stops, ignoring the flashing warning signs that spelled danger to his hard-won peace of mind. He'd listened to her personal problems with genuine understanding and sympathy. He'd tried his best to be funny, witty and attentive. Hell, he'd even sung a few songs in the hopes of impressing her. Many women found a man who could sing a turn-on.

His reaction to the kiss had astonished him. The punch of pure lust tinged with tender protectiveness had stolen his breath. Then, when things had started heating up, he'd allowed her to shove him away.

What a gentleman. He thumped a fist on the table, feeling a sharp pain shoot up his arm. What a virtuous fool. He must be losing his mind. When Leila had walked out, he'd promised himself he would avoid all serious relationships in the future. Now, with little more than two years passed, he was mooning over a flighty female who toyed with him mercilessly.

Charley reminded him of Horrie – the way the cat tormented a frantic mouse before executing the killing blow, letting the poor wee creature limp away intact, always pulling it back kicking and struggling when it ventured too far, before ending its futile struggles with one quick swipe of his paw.

Life after Leila, he thought ruefully. 'Love 'em and leave 'em' was his new motto. He had no desire to become entangled in the sticky snare of another long-term relationship. Or any relationship, for that matter. The 'R' word spelled disaster. Women liked safe words like 'commitment' and 'forever'. He didn't know those words anymore, and when he saw a white picket fence, he wanted to take a chainsaw to it. If he ever fell in love again, it would be for all the right reasons, based on trust and friendship and loyalty – not because a woman represented a compelling challenge to be rescued or a tasty temptation he couldn't resist.

But that didn't mean they couldn't enjoy one another. A week was a long time. Undoubtedly, she'd want to visit the site again tomorrow. His mind raced as he contemplated the numerous opportunities to get her alone.

A slow smile crossed his face and he climbed back into bed. He drifted off to sleep, still thinking about how soft, warm and utterly *right* Charley had felt in his arms.

Charley's head pounded and her mouth tasted as if Genghis Khan had ridden his entire army through it. She checked the glowing face of her watch, 3:30.

Water. She needed water. And Aspirin.

She groped for the bottled water on the table beside her bed and took a long, grateful swig. Where were those painkillers? She scrambled to the foot of her cot and rummaged in the backpack. She pried loose a couple of loose tablets stuck in the side pocket. Never mind that they'd been there since the beginning of time and were covered in a disgusting layer of hairy fuzz from God knows what. This was no time for fastidiousness. She washed them down with another gulp of water.

No more beer, ever again, she vowed, tugging down the oversized purple tee shirt she wore as a nightie. Was this how her mother felt most nights?

As her head slowly cleared, the events of the evening returned with appalling clarity. Happy hour with Kincaid, serious conversation with Kincaid, dinner with Kincaid, the campfire with Kincaid, laughter and singing with Kincaid, and then – recollection smacked her squarely in the face.

She moaned softly. Oh God. What had possessed her?

She'd practically thrown herself at him. Another couple

of minutes, and she'd have torn his clothes off along with her own. Never in her life had she craved a man so strongly. Never in her life had a kiss felt so right.

Her body tingled as she recalled how she'd melted in his arms. She'd nearly let him take her right then and there on the path outside her tent. Alistair Kincaid was downright dangerous. No wonder he had such a way with the women.

No way, girl. Don't even think about it. He's nothing but trouble. You won't become the newest member of Kincaid's harem, even if he's incredibly, impossibly sweet. He'll only break your heart.

Aspirin and water finally worked their magic. Her headache receded to a dull throb, fading by the minute, and her eyelids drooped. She didn't want to think about what had nearly happened with Kincaid. *In the morning, I'll make a plan and get my life under control again.* Comforted by the thought, she rolled over, closed her eyes and willed herself into a deep slumber.

The respite didn't last long. In less than an hour, Charley stirred uneasily, tossing and turning on the narrow cot. She whimpered softly in her half-sleep as bright, spearing coldness knifed straight through her heart and a loud humming filled her ears. She tumbled helplessly into the chaos, all the while thinking that this was not a mere dream.

Zanazca followed her master, Kele-Pe, to the altar and adjusted her feathered robe, savouring the way it whispered around her ankles. The towering gold headdress she wore for the first time strained her neck and made her head ache with a dull throb, but she was willing to pay the price to enter adulthood.

Kele-Pe ignored the excited crowd gathered in the Great Plaza below and grasped both her hands. "Ten cycles have passed since your mother delivered you to the temple, daughter of my heart. Today, you are an adult. Today, you will prove you are worthy to become a handmaiden of the all-powerful Jaguar God, Master of Darkness. My beloved son, Nama, joins with me to celebrate this auspicious occasion."

Zanazca's heart thundered in her ears until she thought

it would leap out of her body. She glanced under her lashes at her friend, Nama. He nodded encouragement and smiled. She took a slow, deep breath. "I am ready, Master. Long have I waited for this moment."

Many times, she had watched the Chosen Ones mount the marble steps of the grand pyramid. Some climbed stoically, unassisted, while others begged for deliverance from their fate. Some of them were so overcome by terror, several priests had to carry them to the top.

Many times, envious, she had watched Kele-Pe guide Nama's hand when he delivered the gift of death.

Kele-Pe led Zanazca to the altar. "Come," he said. "You have seen the cutting ritual many times, and I am here to help you if you falter."

She smiled sweetly. "I need no help. You have taught me well."

The Chosen One lay on the altar, arms and legs bound by leather thongs, chest arched upwards. Liquid, dark eyes brimmed with terrible comprehension.

Zanazca clutched the broad-bladed, obsidian knife and gazed in horrified fascination at the man spread-eagled across the altar. His beseeching gaze sought hers. "Who is this young man, Kele-Pe?" she asked, looking away, unable to tolerate the naked pleading.

"A prisoner and trouble-maker. The Master of Darkness is hungry, Zana. You must not delay."

The young man stuttered a few words in a guttural tongue she didn't understand.

"What does he say?" she whispered.

"He absolves you of all blame and asks you to release him quickly from the burdens of this life."

Zanazca gazed into the young man's eyes, so clear, so full of life and despair. She shook her head. "He is too young to die. I am not sure I can do this. Surely he would make a useful slave."

Kele-Pe's deep voice rumbled. "He must die. Do not look into his face. Concentrate on the gift you are giving the gods and hold the knife in both hands. Like this." Kele-Pe positioned both her hands on the knife. "Now raise it."

The razor-sharp blade glinted in the rising sun.

Kele-Pe barked an order. "Now."

Unthinking, Zanazca took a deep breath and obeyed her master. With strength she did not know she possessed, she plunged the knife deep into the young man's chest, rotating it to separate the ribs, as she had been taught. When the gaping hole was wide enough, she reached into the yawning, red cavity with her left hand, grasped the healthy heart, severed the major links to the body, and wrenched it, still beating, from his chest.

The youth's high, thin scream shattered the stillness and hot blood spurted in a crimson geyser.

She stepped back and held the dripping heart high above her head.

The crowd roared its approval.

Zanazca stared into the young man's eyes at the exact moment his soul took flight from his inert body. In that moment of absolute power, she absorbed his life force into her own. A triumphant smile curved her lips. Her laughter was lost in the crowd's outcry.

The fading clamour ripped through Charley's senses and dragged her back to consciousness, her heart racing. Whether the episode had been a dream or a panic attack, Charley didn't know or particularly care. All she wanted was for the episodes to stop.

Another cry, fainter this time, ripped the stillness of the night. She flinched. Just a nocturnal predator on a hunting expedition. The law of the jungle reigned supreme.

Heavy silence blanketed the camp once more.

The potent spell relinquished its hold on her, and she willed herself back to sleep, grateful that Leila hadn't returned yet. This time, no disturbance marred her slumber.

The cavern walls pulsed with unearthly colours.

Leila crammed another peyote button into her mouth and chewed. Immediately, her mouth puckered with the bitter taste and nausea gripped her gut like a vice. She ignored the unpleasant sensations and reached for another button.

Tonight, she would become one with her *nagual.*

When Felipe pried her fingers open and removed the peyote from her grasp, she heard herself moan with a combination of frustration and pain.

His voice, urgent with worry, reached her from a distance. "Slow down. Do not eat them so fast."

Suddenly, she could hardly talk through the parched dryness of her mouth. "Water," she choked. "I can't stand the thirst. I need water."

She felt Felipe hold the water bottle to her lips, his hand supporting her head. Cool, life-giving liquid flooded her mouth and dribbled down her chin. She swallowed and whispered: "More."

"No more. You will be ill."

Her body convulsed in agony. Someone screamed. From a distance, she recognized her voice.

Felipe grasped her hand, giving her his strength. "Ride the wave. The worst of the pain will soon end."

Darkness threatened to drown her.

"Listen only to my voice."

Leila gagged and as an unbearable thirst clawed at her throat, but in the midst of the chaos, she hung onto both the hand that supported her and the voice that guided her.

"You must find your *nagual.* Concentrate."

All sensations except the hypnotic cadence of Felipe's voice vanished, and Leila realized the pain and thirst had faded. Everything was all swirly, as if the atmosphere was thicker than normal. Her entire body started to tingle, not unpleasantly, but as if a mild electrical charge surged and crackled over her skin.

"Send your spirit soaring to find the snake. Only after you master this lesson, will you find your true strength. We have no time to lose."

A lust for power, hot and urgent, blossomed inside Leila. She emptied her mind of everything except the snake. In her mind's eye, she recreated her friend, picturing the sinewy body and broad reptilian head, the flat, greenish eyes that stared into her soul, beckoning, until she knew what she must do.

The smoky darkness of the cave receded and Felipe's

voice grew fainter until only her heartbeat and the ragged sound of her hoarse breathing echoed in her ears. Heat sizzled along her nerves as she spiralled fearlessly through the darkness. The journey ended with an audible *whoosh* that sucked her into the body of the snake, as if filling a vacuum.

One minute she was Leila, a human being, the next minute she was – a serpent. Snake memories mingled and fused with human intellect in a bizarre union that defied description.

Evening air bathed her body in delicious coolness. Sharp, insistent hunger pangs stirred in her belly. Experimentally, she uncoiled her powerful body, throwing off the lethargy that had gripped her during the heat of the day, and raised her head, sensing the air. She allowed her tongue to flicker out of her mouth and taste the breeze. A juicy agouti had wandered within striking distance. Swivelling her head in all directions, she could feel the animal's body heat radiating in the darkness.

A low vibration alerted her to the animal's panicky attempt at escape. The snake lifted the tip of her tail and sensed, rather than heard, the loud buzzing that knifed the air. She reared her head towards the heat source and struck. Hollow fangs connected with the warm, furry body and injected powerful venom into the unresisting prey.

The brief flurry of movement ended quickly.

The snake glided to the fallen animal, her body carving graceful, sinuous curves over the rock surface. Hinged jaws gaped wide as she encircled the motionless agouti with her mouth. Slowly, deliberately, she strained to force the meal down her gullet, expanding her throat and engulfing the animal with her body until only the tip of its tail emerged from her mouth. With a huge final effort, she gulped again, and the tail disappeared.

Satisfied, the snake curled up under the ledge and slept.

Chapter 16

Operation Avoidance kicked in bright and early the next morning and had entered full deployment by the time the breakfast bell rang.

Charley figured her short-term plan should be easy enough to implement – evade Kincaid until she had wrestled her libido under some semblance of control. It was simply a matter of choice and strength of character. With enough effort, she could put the previous evening behind her and pretend the steamy kiss had never happened.

Her long-term plan was still dismayingly hazy.

She eluded Kincaid over breakfast easily enough by arriving late, knowing he would have left for the temple.

To Charley's satisfaction, the plan worked perfectly. The next hour and forty-five minutes flew by in a flurry of breakfast, chatting, photography and note taking, interspersed with intermittent pacing.

Ignoring the lure of the temple by working, she returned to the tent to compile notes and strategize. Suffocating heat buffeted her face when she opened the tent flap. Leila stirred in protest, then grunted and rolled over, tugging the thin sheet over her bare shoulder.

Charley aimed a vicious kick at the filmy navy blue nightie that had snaked its way to her side of the tent. She picked up the wisp of fabric. Pure silk and delicate Belgian lace dripped from her fingers – an expensive confection. Her roomie had come prepared for a different kind of heat. Charley flung the garment on the foot of Leila's bed. Perhaps this scrap of cloth was a clue to her mysterious nightly absences. Leila might have been lying about the poker game and been hanging out with Felipe both nights. Neither had turned up at last night's campfire.

For the second night in a row, Leila had returned to the tent at dawn. She'd flicked on the lamp, oblivious to the fact that Charley might not appreciate being rudely awoken, then puttered around for ten minutes, undressing and clattering objects before rolling into bed.

Charley eyed the sleeping figure in the other cot with distaste, then shrugged and pulled out her laptop. Quiet clacking filled the tent for the next half-hour as she immersed herself in the task of typing up her notes. A sense of peace settled into the marrow of her bones. She'd never understood why other people detested this task. Assembling coherent notes from scraps and snippets of information gave her a huge sense of accomplishment. Typing crystallized her thoughts, lined them up, rearranged them like a fluid jigsaw puzzle. Patterns emerged from the chaos of what initially seemed like a jumble of unrelated facts. It never failed. As her fingers flew over the keyboard, a story, still nebulous, still embryonic, but a story nevertheless, started to take shape on the tiny blue-green screen. Her brain was definitely connected to her fingertips.

Finished at last, she stopped and reread what she'd written. Yes, the answers to some of her questions might lead to a blockbuster story. What mysterious treasures hid behind the rockslide? Why did Felipe insist on leaving the rocks untouched?

Or they might just be dead ends.

The breathless heat finally defeated even Charley. She stood and, pushing the chair aside, stretched to release the tightness between her shoulder blades. One of her feet accidentally jostled Leila's cot.

Leila yawned and sat up, clutching the sheet to her chin. She glared at Charley through slitted eyes. "Do you mind? I'm trying to sleep," she snarled and flopped back onto the pillow.

Charley swivelled around and shot a fulminating scowl at the back of her inconsiderate roommate's head. Perhaps it was the heat, or perhaps it was because Leila had awoken her before dawn, but Charley's simmering resentment exploded. She bit out the words: "Let me try to understand, Leila. It's okay for you to wake me up in the middle of the night, but I'm not to move around in my own tent?" Her voice rose, along with her temper. "Everyone else in camp has been up for hours. If you went to bed at a normal time, this wouldn't be a problem."

Leila glared. "Shut up if you know what's good for you."

Charley counted to ten. It didn't work. She took a deep breath and allowed full vent to her anger. "D'you think you're the only one living in this tent? Where do you get off banging around in the middle of the night, waking me up two nights in a row?"

Leila's dark eyes glittered in a furious white mask and her lips drew back from perfect teeth in an ugly snarl. "I'm too tired to argue, so why don't you get the hell out?"

She's not beautiful right now. Charley wanted to tear off the covers and throw the other woman in the lagoon, but sanity prevailed. "Sure. No problem. Boy, it's hot in here, don't you think? I think I'll change clothes first. Now, where did I put my new blouse?" Charley rooted through her clothes, moving them from one shelf to another and back again. She knew that baiting Leila wasn't the smartest move of her life, but couldn't resist giving the woman a taste of her own medicine. "Dammit, I know it's here somewhere."

Leila scowled and flopped back on her pillow. "What the hell's wrong with you? Just find the damned thing and move your ass out of here."

Triumphantly, Charley yanked out the blue and white striped blouse and waved it over her head. "Ah. Here it is. Under my jeans. Why on Earth would I put it there when my blouses are supposed to be on the bottom shelf? I won't be long now." She changed out of her long sleeved shirt while walking around the tent, making mindless conversation calculated to annoy Leila. "I have no idea what made me dress in long sleeves in the first place this morning. I guess because it gets cold at night. Have you noticed? I think—"

Rage clouded Leila's eyes and thickened her voice. "Is this your idea of a joke or are you getting up my nose on purpose?"

Hiding a grin, Charley stacked her papers neatly, replaced the laptop, and zipped up the case, taking care to lock it. The heat in the tent had soared beyond suffocating, and now hovered around the intensity of a blast furnace.

"Don't you wish we had a fan in here?" she chirped. "You should mention it to Kincaid if you insist on sleeping this late every day. I'm going outside where the air is fresh and cool. Nice breeze from the water today." She unzipped the door. "Enjoy your beauty rest."

"If you've finished, get the hell out."

Charley fired off a final volley for the sheer pleasure of messing with Leila's head. "I'm heading on up to the temple and see how Kincaid is faring with the rock removal."

Leila jerked upright. She tugged the sheet higher and dropped her voice to an ominous snarl. "You're going to the dig? I'm warning you. You don't know what's waiting for you out there."

Charley disguised a violent shiver as an indifferent shrug. "Your concern for my welfare is touching and unexpected. If I didn't know better, I'd think you were jealous."

Leila spat out a curse. "You've been drooling over Alistair ever since you met him. I'm not blind and I'm far from stupid. If you know what's good for you, keep your hands off him or you'll regret it."

In spite of the threat, Charley stubbornly refused to back down though her heart hammered in her chest. She felt like a dog with its hackles up. "He's a very attractive man, isn't he? I can't imagine why you left him. I'll coax him to take a quick break or grab some lunch and we'll take it from there." She stuffed the laptop under her bed and padlocked it in place to make sure nobody, especially Leila, tampered with it. Snagging the backpack containing camera, notepad and tape recorder, she ducked out of the tent.

As an afterthought, she stuck her head back inside and smiled sweetly. "I can't vouch for Kincaid's intentions towards me, though."

Palpable hatred twisted Leila's mouth and vibrated in the air between them.

Perhaps she had pushed the wrong button with her empty threat, Charley thought, belatedly nervous. She had no intention of visiting Kincaid at the temple. He was the last man on Earth she wanted to see.

She zipped the door shut before Leila could act on the transparently murderous thoughts written on her face.

Still questioning the advisability of goading Leila, Charley tied the door flap snugly to prevent any whisper of air from entering the tent to cool off its fuming occupant. She turned to stomp away and stubbed her toe on the pair of heavy, lace-up boots blocking her path. She looked in all directions, but saw no one.

Her heart leaped when she realized Kincaid had remembered his promise. Trust him to display thoughtfulness when she was doing her best to forget him. That wasn't playing fair.

The boots bore signs of hard use – scuffs and scratches marred the leather surface – but they looked sturdy and a lot more comfortable than her painful hiking boots.

She shook out her new footwear, ensuring they were empty of unwanted scorpions and other vermin. Satisfied, she slipped off her sneakers and replaced them with the new boots, stuffing her jeans into the tops before lacing them up. She flexed her toes and stomped her feet experimentally. They fit perfectly.

She ought to thank Kincaid for his kindness. Surely, he deserved an expression of her appreciation. Only a man with several sisters would know a woman's shoe size. He must have gone out of his way to find size nine boots, extra narrow.

A quick visit to the site, she rationalized, would be therapeutic – similar to treating a phobia by saturating the patient with the stimulus in order to reduce the fear. Only by confronting Kincaid could she prove to herself she was in control of her emotions. Operation Avoidance was the coward's way out.

She needed a different plan.

Her decision made, Charley's heart felt lighter. She swung by the kitchen to grab a water bottle and a couple of cookies. Suitably provisioned, she positioned her sunglasses on her nose and closed the kitchen door carefully.

Charley strode boldly down the path leading to the dig, feeling rather like an explorer headed up the Amazon. Humming *Peaceful Easy Feeling*, she hoped that tranquility would magically manifest itself in her heart through the power of suggestion. "Fake it till you make it," she muttered under her breath between songs, and switched to *Take it Easy*.

After five minutes, she stopped singing and walked faster. Her heavy boots beat a rapid rhythm on the path. She wanted nothing more than to reach the dig where the work party and – honesty kicked in – Kincaid would alleviate her sense of isolation. Yesterday, when they had hiked the path together, she hadn't given a second thought to the solitude or the dangers the jungle might pose for a woman stupid enough to walk alone. Today, mysterious rustlings and furtive movements in the underbrush seemed magnified and ominous.

The pathway meandered between thick walls of impenetrable thorn bushes, tall, yellowing grasses and patches of emerald ferns. Occasional massive trees propped up by buttress roots towered above the low-lying jungle. Unseen, a troop of monkeys crashed through the canopy, screeching and chattering as they played and fought, and small, hidden creatures scurried through the grass foraging for food. Warm odours of decaying wood mingled with the light scent of orchids, reminding Charley that life and death co-existed in close proximity.

She thought of turning back to camp, but the dig was closer. Scanning the underbrush for signs of stealthy movement, she picked up the pace.

The hairs on the back of her arms prickled. She could almost swear a creature moved through the underbrush beside the path, matching her step, never moving far away. She could *feel* its gaze on her. She stopped and listened. The monkeys had disappeared. Only bird calls broke the solitude. When she started walking again, the stealthy rustling accompanied her.

She removed her sunglasses and fought down the bubble of panic. This was no time to lose her head. Striving for calmness, she skimmed her gaze over the ground, searching for a stick or rock – anything she could use as a weapon against the stalking predator. If she panicked, she was finished.

She froze to the spot as a snake slithered from the concealing underbrush and coiled itself in a patch of sunlight at the side of the path. The reptile must have been six, maybe seven, feet long, its greyish body as thick as her thigh, and marked with bold, black chevrons. If she had taken another step, she'd have tripped over it.

The creature raised its broad, triangular head. A black forked tongue flickered towards her. The air filled with a loud, whirring buzz that started slowly, like the sound of dry bones clacking together, and grew in intensity until individual clicks blended into a strident blur.

Charley leaped backwards without conscious input from her brain. Slowly, as if it had all the time in the world, the snake moved towards her, its sinuous body carving a graceful pattern in the dirt.

A wave of fear slammed through her body. Feeding her terror, a vision of Kincaid finding her body, bloated with poison and lying beside the path, flashed into her mind.

Her brain barked out a message: *Do something! Fast!*

Panting convulsively, she forced her feet to move, heedless of direction.

The rattlesnake followed, hissing.

A tree blocked her retreat, and she cursed. She had blundered off the path.

The creature reared its head back and weaved hypnotically. It fastened greenish, reptilian eyes on her face and she swore it could read her mind.

The snake feinted a strike and drew back, tongue flickering. A dark intelligence lurked behind the cold flatness of its hooded gaze. It darted its wicked head again.

There was no doubt in her mind the snake enjoyed toying with her, terrifying her before executing the killing strike.

She whirled, intending to run as far into the jungle as she could, and found herself sprawled on the ground, face-first and helpless. Twisting, she cursed the fallen branch entangling her feet, and glanced over her shoulder, panic building in her chest.

The rattle buzzed a warning, and Charley rolled away,

drawing up her knees with instinctive speed.

The triangular head flashed in a blur of speed. Lethal fangs embedded themselves in the thick leather of her boot. The rattlesnake's body whipped viciously as it struggled to withdraw.

She cursed and kicked desperately, bracing herself against the rough tree trunk.

The snake sprang loose, a clear, yellow liquid dripping from its fangs.

Charley lashed out again. One steel-reinforced toe connected with the wicked-looking head. The force of the blow flung the snake backward into the underbrush, out of sight but not out of earshot.

Her blood froze as the furious rattle gathered in volume.

She scrabbled her hands in the dirt and her fingers connected with the forked branch she had tripped over. Fear gave her arms strength. Gripping the heavy piece of wood, she vaulted to her feet and swung the weapon above her head like a battle-axe. "Come here, you bastard," she screeched. "I know you're in there somewhere."

After an eternity, the snake appeared again. Its thick upper body towered from the grass in a high, sinuous coil. A malevolent gaze locked with Charley's in an outlandish contest of wills.

The attacker darted its head forward in a lightning-fast move, but Charley had foreseen its intentions and leaped away. The strike fell short and the snake dropped to the ground.

Adrenaline combined with her attacker's sudden movement turned fear into rage. "I'm not as helpless as you thought," she shouted and swung the branch, trying to pin the creature to the ground.

The snake hissed in fury, writhing to escape. It eluded the forked stick and raised its head to stare at her before it slithered away towards the jungle.

Swaying ferns on the far side of the path marked its progress.

"Coward," Charley shrieked. "Come back here. I'm not finished with you."

Bushes swam in front of her eyes and her legs wanted to

collapse. Nevertheless, she tucked the stick under her arm and forced her feet into a quick jog. If the snake returned to finish her off, it wouldn't find a helpless victim awaiting her fate.

After five endless minutes, during which Charley thought her heart would burst, the path widened. Two colossal heads gazed impassively at the jungle and the ancient city spread out in front of her. She sank to the ground, cradled her face in her hands, and allowed the shuddering sobs to burst loose. After several minutes, she blinked back the tears and groped in her backpack for a tissue to wipe her running nose. Then, she stood up and walked deliberately to the edge of the path.

And threw up.

Chapter 17

Thankful to be alive, Charley sprinted towards the pyramid and safety, praying she'd kicked the rattlesnake hard enough to discourage it from following. Without stopping, she bolted across the open expanse of the Great Plaza, then bounded up the endless steps of the pyramid. The gym teacher who had proclaimed that running wasn't one of Charley's strengths was dead wrong.

She flew up the shallow stairs as if her feet had sprouted wings.

Only when she reached the top did she feel safe enough to flop on a block of stone, her chest heaving and lungs straining. She figured she was safe at last. Snakes could climb, but surely, there was no way the rattler could hoist its super-sized bulk up eighty-five steep steps.

A shudder wracked her body as she allowed herself to think about her narrow escape. What if she'd been bitten? Worse, what if she'd been killed? What would her mother have done without her? On the other hand, what did it matter? We all must die some day. She put her head between her knees, trying to catch her breath and regain her equilibrium.

Straightening, she ordered herself to stop shaking. She had always prided herself on being able to cope with any danger life threw at her, and a snake attack was no exception. After all, the creature hadn't done any real damage. She looked down at her boot. Small punctures perforated the leather and a yellowish smear of venom gleamed in the sunlight like bright death. Another tremor caught her by surprise.

Still crackling with nervous energy, she jumped to her feet and paced the temple. She craved movement, to touch and be touched, to reaffirm that she was still alive, safe and unhurt. To prove that life was worth living.

She needed Kincaid.

"I see you found the boots."

Charley whipped her head around at the deep, familiar voice, and blinked once. Kincaid looked different today, but she couldn't put a finger on the disparity. Then she got it. He was wearing black jeans and a black work shirt instead of his customary aloha shirt. He looked harder, more dangerous and wickedly sexy.

Her heart jackhammered in her chest as she took a step towards him. "Kincaid. Come with me." She grabbed a fistful of shirt and led him to the side of the temple where a pile of rubble performed the task of hiding them from prying eyes.

"What's this all about?" he asked, his eyes widening in surprised disbelief.

Instead of answering, she stepped forward until her body brushed against his, then threaded her fingers through his hair in unspoken invitation. He was warm and solid – a perfect antidote to the feeling of flat futility that had enveloped her since her near brush with death. A shudder of sexual delight coursed through her veins. "Kiss me, Kincaid. Hold me." Hungrily, she raised her lips, allowing a primitive mating urge sweep her rational qualms away.

He made an inarticulate groan before drawing a finger down her neck, sending licks of flame flickering along her quivering nerves. Catching her chin in his fingers, he slanted a hot, hungry kiss on her lips. His tongue entered her mouth – firm and velvety and demanding. He was fully aroused already, taut and hard.

The cold, twisted knot deep inside her started to thaw. Ragged breathing caught in her throat. Flinging common sense to the wind, she ground her hips against his with a desperation she hadn't known she possessed and reached down to rub his erection through the fabric. Liquid fire smouldered and coiled inside her belly. If she didn't find her release soon, she'd go out of her mind.

"I need you." She gasped between ragged breaths.

"Oh, sweet Jesus. Slow down, Charley. If you do that, there'll be no turning back."

In reply, she captured his lips with her own in a frenzy of need and desire, and gave herself up to the raging inferno that consumed her. Wordlessly, she unbuttoned her blouse and brought his hand to her breast.

He kissed her neck and delved lower. She could swear he muttered: "*Mhuirnin.*"

"More," she panted and arched her back, allowing her head to fall backwards and exposing her throat and breasts to his questing lips. A wave of primal heat tightened her body. Through filmy lace, he captured her nipple between his teeth and tugged. Dimly, she heard her soft, throaty whimpers turn into urgent entreaties. An unbearable pressure built between her thighs and she tugged his shirt loose then raked her fingers down his back, aching to feel the touch of flesh against flesh.

Dazed and throbbing, lost in the searing blaze of sensation, she tugged his shirt out of his jeans. Why did they make the damned fasteners so difficult to undo?

An iron hand grasped her wrist and yanked her hand away. "Stop. Have you lost your mind? What the hell are we doing? We're in a public place, acting like a pair of animals."

She opened her eyes, shocked out of her sensual reverie by the note of warning in his voice. "I need to *feel.*" She gasped in shock as he pulled away. "Why are you stopping? I thought this was what you wanted."

He tucked in his shirt before refastening his jeans with shaking fingers. "I do, lass," he panted, "but not here, not like this. I don't understand what's going on. Last night, you couldn't get rid of me fast enough, and today, you're ready to tear my clothes off without a thought of the men in the tunnel only a few yards away."

Shocked into silent humiliation, Charley cast a horrified glance at her own clothing. Face burning, she re-buttoned her blouse and smoothed her hands over her hips.

"I have no idea what got into me," she muttered, unable to meet his eyes. "Sorry about that." Sorrier than he'd ever know. *God, please make me vanish*, she pleaded silently.

Kincaid hissed an inarticulate sound between his teeth.

"I guess I should thank you for exhibiting unusual restraint," Charley continued briskly, wrestling her emotions under control. She slanted a sheepish glance at him. "I, ummm, hope you're not too uncomfortable."

He glared at her and found his voice again. "I'll survive," he bit out, still breathing heavily. "But why? Why here? Why now?"

She studied the ground. "I don't know. I guess I did it because I needed to reassure myself I was still alive."

"What the hell are you talking about?" Kincaid gripped Charley's chin, tilted her head back, and gazed at her face, his forehead wrinkling with concern. "*Mo Dhia,* lass! What happened to you? You look like you've been in a battle. Is your cheek bruised?"

"It's probably just dirt. Y-you should see the other guy."

His eyes darkened and a dangerous flash glinted in their depths. "Did someone attack you? I'll kill him. Hanging will be too good for the bastard that hurt you. Let me look." He traced the line of her jaw, his fingers feather-light on her over-heated skin.

Charley shuddered. "Not someone – *something.* I made a three-point landing trying to get away from a snake. Look what it did to my boot." Charley pointed at the two puncture marks and smear of toxin on the leather.

Kincaid frowned, his voice adamant. "Sit here." He pointed to the rock. "You look awful."

A sense of déjà vu washed over Charley. He'd said exactly the same words to her in this exact same spot yesterday. Meekly, she collapsed on the stone, the strength leaving her legs. "This is becoming a habit."

Kincaid lifted her leg with both hands and examined her boot. Anxiety etched his voice, sharpening it. "Do you have any idea what kind of snake it was?"

"Rattlesnake," she whispered.

Waves of shock and horror washed across Kincaid's face. His voice cracked. "Did it break the skin? We need to get you back to camp right away. We have antivenin serum in camp and it only works within the first four hours. Do you feel any nausea or pain? Numbness?" He raked shaking hands through his hair, his eyes wild. "That was a daft question. If the fangs had broken the skin, you wouldn't be sitting here discussing it."

Her voice shook. "I'm not hurt. Just shaken. The boots saved my life. Tucking my jeans inside probably helped, too."

Kincaid touched the puncture marks. "This must be your lucky day. From the looks of it, the snake was a monster. I've spotted only one rattlesnake the entire time I've worked here. The snake was more afraid of me than I was of it – and I was scared shitless."

"This snake wasn't afraid of me. Far from it. You may think I've gone over the edge, but I don't think this was a normal snake."

"What do you mean?"

She thought about the attack. "There was something, I don't know, vindictive, even calculated, about the way it stalked me. It moved when I moved, stopped when I stopped. Then, when I tripped and the snake cornered me, it didn't strike right away. It taunted me and enjoyed my fear. When I looked into its eyes, I could swear I saw intelligence and malice."

"Impossible. Reptiles have no cognitive reasoning capabilities."

Charley bristled. "I wasn't imagining things. The snake was trying to scare me. And it damn-well succeeded."

"Aye. Fear can play strange tricks on our imagination. I'll order the men to carry machetes or shotguns and keep an eye open for a large rattler. We'll kill it if we find it."

"Yeah, right. I'm not sure I believe it myself." She examined the toes of her boots.

He tilted her chin upward with gentle fingers. "Look at me, Charley. I believe you are an incredibly brave and resourceful woman. Most people would have panicked, but you kept your head, stood up to the snake, and came out of it alive."

A distant rumble shook the temple. Hoarse shouting followed the tremor.

She stared at Kincaid in alarm. "Did I imagine it, or did the ground just shake?"

"Aye. It sounded like it came from the tunnel."

A choking cloud of dust belched from the tunnel's mouth.

Chapter 18

Before the rumbling echo of falling rocks faded, an agitated shout broke the spell of disbelief that held Kincaid immobile.

"Are you still out there, Kincaid? Where are you?" Seconds later, a young man exploded from the darkness at the rear of the temple and skidded to an abrupt halt. "Oops – didn't realize you had company. Hey, Charley."

Charley recovered first and wiggled her fingers at the student.

A wave of guilt washed over Kincaid. While he'd been oblivious of everything except the sexy siren bent on tearing off his clothes, something had gone terribly wrong in the tunnel. "What's going on?" he called, thankful the interruption hadn't occurred five minutes earlier.

"There's been an accident at the rock face. The shoring collapsed and a worker is hurt."

Bile rose in Kincaid's throat. He swallowed hard. "How bad is it?"

"Can't tell. He's alive, though."

Kincaid closed his eyes in silent thanks. He was responsible for the safety and wellbeing of his men. He should never have left them alone in the tunnel. If he hadn't gone outside hoping he might find Charley picking her way up the pyramid, he might have prevented the accident.

"Show me." He waved the student ahead with an abrupt gesture.

Charley grabbed his arm. "I'm coming, too."

He shook his head. Damn, she was stubborn. "It could be dangerous in there. You'd better stay here until I find out what happened."

"Still trying to give me orders, Kincaid? You'd better hurry."

The student turned and disappeared into the yawning tunnel. Kincaid followed hard on his heels, aware of her footsteps behind him.

"I told you to stay outside," he growled over his shoulder, not slowing his step. "I don't know what we'll find in here."

"I'll take my chances. Can't be worse than the snake."

The tunnel was clear for thirty feet. At the end, a lantern illuminated the rockslide that blocked the passage. Piles of lumber rested against the wall. In front of the tumble of rocks, a group of four men clustered around a fifth who lay slumped on the ground.

Kincaid crouched down beside the injured worker, ignoring Felipe who edged away into the shadows. "Tell me where it hurts."

The worker rubbed his head and started to sit up. "*No es nada, señor*. Only a scratch on my forehead."

Kincaid gently but firmly pushed him down. "Lie still and don't move until I figure out how badly hurt you are. Did you pass out or throw up?"

"Neither. Do not worry about me, *por favor*. It is only, how do you say? *Un pequeño dolor de la cabeza*, a small headache."

Kincaid planted his hand firmly on the man's chest, pinning him to the ground to subdue his struggles to rise. "Someone please pass me a flashlight."

The student thrust a small pocket light into the outstretched hand. Kincaid trained the thin beam of light on the injured worker's face and winced at the gory sight. Blood streamed over his forehead and cheek, dampening the ground. He parted the matted hair with gentle fingers. Thankfully, the hairline cut appeared shallow. Some bruising and lots of blood, but he gauged that stitches were unnecessary.

"Now I'll check for a concussion." He shone the light into the wounded man's eyes and heaved a sigh of relief when the pupils contracted normally.

"You're extremely lucky. It must have been a glancing blow. There doesn't seem to be any concussion, but it could have been bad. Let's put a bandage on the cut and get you to camp." He slid an arm under the worker's shoulders and helped him rise to a sitting position.

The man groaned and closed his eyes for a second.

"I want you to stay quiet for the rest of the day."

"Thank you, but that is not necessary," protested the worker. "The dizziness passes. I can continue working."

Kincaid hauled himself to his feet. "I don't want you taking any chances with a head wound." His tone brooked no argument and he passed the flashlight to the student.

At Kincaid's signal, the two other workers hoisted the injured man upright. With friends flanking him and the student trailing behind, the small group headed towards sunlight.

Out of the corner of his eye, Kincaid saw Charley move closer to the rock pile and extend one hand to touch it. He moved swiftly, yanking her away. "Move back," he said curtly. "Those rocks are dangerous."

Thank God she didn't protest. He was in no mood to argue.

He scanned the looming shadows for Felipe. His field director stood motionless and silent ten feet away. "Felipe. Why the hell are you standing over there in the dark? Kindly come closer and explain to me how this accident happened."

Felipe stepped into the circle of flickering light, his expression solemn. "It is all my fault, Dr. Kincaid. The support we installed to shore up the roof gave way and some rocks tumbled down. One of them struck that man." He wrung his hands together in a dramatic gesture. "I should have checked the wood more thoroughly before we started. It must have been rotten."

Kincaid ran his hands over a portion of the shattered beam that projected from the rubble. If the lumber was rotten, he'd eat it for dinner. Every splinter. He had hand picked the best wood himself and supervised the stacking of it inside a dry shed. The mishap was no accident. Felipe's humble demeanour didn't deflect Kincaid's suspicions, but he couldn't prove his field director had caused the accident.

Kincaid held his temper and said evenly: "I want work on the rock pile to continue this afternoon, Felipe, so please make sure everyone except the injured worker returns after lunch. Since you'll need another pair of hands, I'll join the work party."

"You cannot be serious, Dr. Kincaid." Felipe gestured at the unstable rock pile. "The lumber is rotten. The rocks are unstable. Someone could get badly hurt."

"I'm very serious, and I have every intention of continuing. I've had experience in shoring up tunnels, so I'll lend a hand – double check the wood, make sure there are no more accidents. If we're not careful, the National Institute of Culture will be breathing down my neck wanting to shut us down. I'll never hear the end of it if the NIC gets wind of this."

Then again, he thought, perhaps that's exactly what Felipe was hoping for.

"*Sí,* Dr. Kincaid." Felipe's voice was flat. "Now, I must see to my man if you have no objections." Without waiting for a reply, he extinguished the light and strode away in the direction his men had taken, leaving Kincaid and Charley alone in the darkness.

She inched closer to him until her shirt brushed his arm. "Let's get out of here."

"Aye," he said, reaching out in the dark to take her hand. "You and I have some unfinished business to take care of."

When Kincaid and Charley stepped out of the tunnel and into the courtyard, the late morning sun almost blinded him. He slipped on his sunglasses, partly to protect his eyes and partly to conceal his thoughts. As they picked their way towards the pyramid steps, he promptly put the thorny issue of Felipe out of his mind. Instead, he concentrated all his attention on the woman walking silently beside him A cool and distant stranger had replaced the woman who had writhed in his arms in an uncontrolled burst of passion.

Charley posed an enigma he resolved to figure out.

A kaleidoscope of sensual memories circled in his head – her head thrown back in mindless ecstasy, the petal softness of her skin, the way her breast had filled his palm and thrust against his fingers. He cursed silently as a torrent of blood drained from his head and pooled in another part of his body. He tucked her arm into his and cleared his throat. "About that unfinished business ...."

She wrenched her arm away and shot him a look that

195

would freeze a volcano in mid-eruption. Only her flaming face betrayed the turmoil behind the icy façade she had erected. "I would prefer to forget that the unfortunate incident ever happened."

He straightened his back, too proud to show how much her words had hurt. "Oh, aye? The 'unfortunate incident', as you term it, happened all right. As I recall, you had me halfway out of my clothes." He removed his sunglasses and fixed her with a stare.

Charley's eyes looked away to focus on a point behind his left shoulder. "Don't remind me. That was a temporary aberration caused by a close brush with death," she stated crisply, as if reading from a textbook. "The need to reaffirm life is quite common for survivors of traumatic events. Something about a primitive desire to procreate."

He placed a finger under her chin and tipped her head back, forcing her to meet his gaze. Frustration crackled under his calm words. "Fair enough. But you picked *me*. Are you trying to tell me you'd have used any man who was handy to scratch your itch?"

Charley's jaw muscles quivered. He sensed the iron control she clamped on her emotions, and her mask remained in place. "Nice choice of words, Kincaid, but since you insist on tormenting yourself – yes. After the snake attack, I needed to prove to myself I was still capable of feeling, and then you appeared on the scene. Impeccable timing. The rest is history."

He raked his fingers through his hair. "*Mo Dhia.* Then prove there's nothing between us, Charley. Kiss me. I dare you."

She backed away, eyes wary. "I don't think kissing you would be a good idea."

He followed, crowding her against a half-crumbled wall. "You're afraid to kiss me in case you lose your head again."

She placed both hands against his chest and shoved. "In your dreams, Kincaid. Not even if the snake attacks me again." She softened her voice, no doubt taking pity on his ego. "Look, I'm not ready to get tangled up with anyone right now, and certainly not with a womanizer who's only interested in a one-night stand."

His eyebrows shot up, but he backed away, noticing her body relax. "Who said anything about a one-night stand?"

"It's your pattern. Don't bother trying to deny it."

Kincaid gritted his teeth. He had only himself to blame for his reputation. "Okay, okay. I'm not proud of it, but I admit you might have a point. After Leila dumped me, I used anything and anyone I could find to deaden the pain – work and women. But all that's behind me now. A man can change when he meets the right woman."

He opened and closed his mouth, speechless at what he'd said. When had Charley suddenly become the right woman? *Since you learned you had almost lost her, you fool*, came the prompt reply.

"Yeah, right. I'm not falling for that old line."

Thank God, she hadn't taken his assertion seriously. He ran his thumb down her cheek. "You can't be indifferent to me. No one who responds the way you do can possibly be indifferent."

Charley shrugged away, her eyes betraying inner agitation. "All the more reason not to get involved."

Kincaid took care to hide his elation. She'd practically admitted she had feelings for him and she would be as furious as a gorilla with its balls caught in a vice if she realized what she'd said.

He lowered his voice. "We just need more time to get to know one another better. We can take it slowly, one day at a time."

"That won't make any difference, Kincaid."

He sighed. This wasn't going the way he'd planned, but it was too late to back off now. "I know you don't trust men. With good reason. But I want you to believe me when I tell you one thing – I will never lie to you."

Her voice quivered. "I'm not ready for this." She turned her back on him. "Everything's moving too fast."

"I'll make you a deal." He swung her around to face him and clasped her hand in both of his. "I've never forced myself on a woman, and I don't intend to start now. I promise I'll try to keep my hands to myself. It won't be easy, but the next move will be up to you. I won't touch you – well, unless I forget – until you tell me you're ready – and, preferably, willing and eager as well."

Her eyes flickered, then widened in surprise. "Hmmm. Clever. You're putting me in the driver's seat."

He didn't feel so clever right now. "Aye. Another of my many virtues," he said, wishing he could retract his promise.

"Don't hold your breath waiting for me to change my mind," she warned with a steely smile.

He hid the queasy feeling with a forced grin. What, in God's name had he been thinking? He should have moved in when he'd sensed that, with just a wee bit more convincing on his part, she would have conceded defeat. "This doesn't mean I'm giving you up without a fight." He furrowed his brow to emphasize his next words. "I intend to use my killer wit and fatal charm in every devious manner dreamed of by man and beast to convince you to change your mind."

"Suit yourself." Charley clamped her mouth shut in a stubborn line and set off down the steps.

Chapter 19

The second Charley set foot in camp, she redeployed Operation Avoidance. What a fool she'd been, to abandon her well-laid plan.

Her afternoon dragged by in a combination of recurring waves of humiliation coupled with mind-numbing boredom. By dinnertime, she had rethought her position. Escape and evade was the wrong approach. If she continued to act like a timid schoolgirl, she could never hope to regain a normal footing with her host and main source of information. Her situation called for immediate action. It wouldn't hurt to swallow her pride and invite Kincaid to join her for dinner. They could still be friends, couldn't they?

She stalked towards the dining area, mentally rehearsing an offhand approach. It was foolish to be nervous. Unfortunately, the message hadn't reached her agitated stomach.

Overhead lights clicked on in the darkening grove and shed a golden glow over the path. The night was alive with noise. Cicadas, frogs and crickets filled the air with an incessant, high-pitched drone punctuated with rapid chirps. Ignoring the fairytale appearance of the camp, she scowled and kicked a small twig off the path.

Her carefully conceived plan never got off the ground. When she entered the dining room, Kincaid was nowhere in sight. Perhaps he was avoiding her, too. *Just as well.* She squelched the pang of dismay. She should be stretched out on a therapist's couch for even contemplating fraternizing with the enemy.

"Hey, Charley. Over here." An archaeologist she had met during lunch waved her over to his table. "Tell us about the snake attack." His eyes glowed with admiration.

She laughed and drew up the empty chair. "My, my. The jungle drums have been thumping."

"Kincaid spread the warning," said another. "We've never seen a snake that size."

With a little more urging, she launched into a vivid description of the harrowing attack and narrow escape. While she talked, she wondered where Kincaid was hiding himself.

Ten minutes later, she got her answer. The entire work crew entered the dining hall in a flurry of excited chatter and gesticulations. They squeezed together at Kincaid's table. Charley noticed Felipe sat as far away from Kincaid as possible. If Felipe's scowl and Kincaid's grin were any indication, work on the rock removal was progressing satisfactorily.

Next, Leila made a late and dramatic entry, breezing in from God-knows-where, accompanied by a sinus-clogging cloud of perfume. She eyed Kincaid's table.

Luckily for him, it was too crowded to squeeze in another person.

Charley's eyes widened as Leila came nearer. Only a sharp eye would discern the faint discoloration marring the flawless complexion. The left side of her face was swollen and she had attempted to disguise a large, purple bruise with skillfully applied makeup.

Charley shook her head, dismissing the ludicrous suspicion that drifted into her mind. There was no logical connection between Leila and the snake. As her roommate breezed by, Charley snagged her arm. "Nice shiner there, Leila," she said. "Another fight? Looks like you lost."

Leila glared at Charley, a murderous spark in her eyes, before she collected herself and smiled sweetly. "Just a tiny accident on the job. I started excavating the merchants' quarters and tripped over a shovel some idiot left lying on the ground."

Charley forked up a huge bite of enchilada dripping with cheese. "Looks painful."

Leila's light laugh set Charley on edge. "I assure you, it's not, but thanks for your concern. I hear you tangled with a snake."

Charley chewed and swallowed. "It was nothing. The

snake got the worst of it."

Leila's eyes were frigid behind her smile. "You'd better watch your step. Snakes can be dangerous." She turned and swept away towards another table.

Charley stared after the woman then shook her head, cursing her overactive imagination. Leila hadn't issued a veiled threat, only a warning.

The evening meal ground to its conclusion. Apparently, it would be a quiet evening in camp. Quiet suited Charley just fine. She had other, more important, things to do than moon over Kincaid. Her article still needed lots of work.

When she looked up, Kincaid was picking his way across the still-crowded dining area, balancing his coffee cup and heading in her direction with the economical movements of an athlete. A whisper of awareness stirred her senses and drove away all thoughts of writing.

He looked down at her with a crooked half smile, his eyes crinkling in the way she loved. "If I didn't know better, I'd think you were avoiding me."

Under the mocking humour, a touch of uncertainty lurked at the back of his eyes. The acerbic remark Charley was about to make died, unspoken. She smiled a welcome. "I'm glad you came over."

He set his cup on the table and straddled a chair, pulling it so close she could feel his body heat. An undercurrent of sexual awareness ripped through her, but she refused to give in to the urge to bolt from the room. Her face felt warm. She hoped she wasn't blushing.

Kincaid leaned closer. "You're looking much better than the last time I saw you. How are you feeling now?" He ran a roughened finger down her bare arm, blazing a trail of heat.

Her foolish heart did a quick flip. Obviously, Kincaid had forgotten his promise to keep his hands to himself, but somehow, she didn't want to remind him. "Much better, thanks." She moistened her lower lip and mentally cursed her awkwardness. "How was the afternoon? Any luck at the rock pile?"

He moved his hand to the nape of her neck where his thumb painted small swirls. "Aye. We cleared out several feet of tunnel and shored up the ceiling so it won't collapse again.

I told Felipe we'd be there again tomorrow morning, bright and early."

She shivered with sensual pleasure and tried to concentrate on his words, figuring that a world-class massage in no way qualified as making a move. "So that's why he looked so angry at dinner."

"Let's just say he wasn't happy." His fingers dug into her mass of hair and massaged the back of her scalp, sending delicious shivers down her spine. "I wouldn't be surprised if we broke through tomorrow or the next day."

"I think you're right," she said dreamily, lost in the exquisite sensation of his touch. "You're very close, you know."

He stilled his hand and quirked one eyebrow. "How on Earth would you know that?"

Charley blinked and crashed back to reality. All afternoon, she had found herself fighting an inexplicable and compelling urge to return to the rock fall. Inside the tunnel, a powerful sense of vast, sacred recesses behind the rocks had overwhelmed her. Without understanding how, she *knew* the men were close to a breakthrough. She also sensed that whatever had lain concealed behind the rocks for millennia was now drawing her closer, pulling her in against her will.

She stretched the truth. "Oh, all the archaeologists think so." No need to mention her premonitions. At best, he'd think she was a flake, and, at worst, a lunatic. She shifted her shoulders and changed the subject in a businesslike voice. "I intend to flesh out my article this evening. What about you?"

He took the hint and withdrew his hand, leaving a cold emptiness behind. "Working, damn it. I wish I could entertain you. Organize a party. Play the bagpipes."

Charley bit the inside of her cheek to suppress a laugh at the thought of Kincaid playing the bagpipes as a form of entertainment. "Another time," she assured him, keeping a straight face.

"Aye. People tell me I play well. Unfortunately, I'll be in the administration shed all evening. My paperwork is piling up."

"No problem. I can keep myself occupied. And I have to call my mother to let her know I'm still alive and kicking."

"You mean, you want to make sure she's still alive and kicking."

She avoided his eyes. Man, he was too observant. "Maybe."

"After you recover from the phone call, why don't you drop by the admin shed and drag me away for a nightcap with Colin?"

"Er...."

He must have sensed the evasion hovering on the tip of her tongue because he added hastily: "I'll behave myself, and Colin makes a vigilant chaperone. Just give me a couple of hours."

"I might need a drink at that," she conceded. "To settle my nerves. Nothing else." A small smile tugged at the corners of her mouth.

He drained his coffee and stood up. "Deal. Nothing else – unless you change your mind."

Thoughtfully, Charley watched Kincaid stride towards the door with a fluid grace that was as innate to him as his Scottish accent. She feared it might be too late to pull back into her hard, protective shell. She had inadvertently released a monster and it was resisting all efforts to cram it back.

No matter how hard she tried, she might never be able to stuff her loosened emotions back inside, where they were safe.

Chapter 20

The system froze defiantly for the third time and the dreaded 'Exception' message, otherwise known as the Blue Screen of Death, flashed on Kincaid's monitor. "You will lose any unsaved information in all applications," the message warned.

"Oh, no. Please. Not again," Kincaid groaned and pounded the desk with his fist. He unleashed a fluent stream of curses in English and Gaelic for three minutes straight, without repeating himself once.

"What the hell's wrong with you this time?" he muttered, rubbing bruised knuckles. "What have I ever done to you to make you hate me?"

The administration shed was Kincaid's least favourite place in camp. The small, prefabricated building housed several computers, a printer, a photocopier, several ancient filing cabinets and boxes of office supplies. The only thing it had going for it was an air conditioning unit, an unnecessary luxury in the coolness of the night. A breeze from the open window stirred his hair.

He sighed and rebooted again. On previous digs, everything had run like clockwork. Leila had always taken care of the accounting. Left to his own devices on this project, he had forgotten to hire someone for the hated chore, and now he was stuck with the job.

His evening had passed in a hectic flurry of activity, leaving no room to dwell on Charley. He'd ironed out two thorny accommodation problems, visited the injured worker, placed e-shopping orders for everything from hardware supplies to toilet paper via a satellite uplink, written twenty-two cheques to go out on the next plane and was now immersed in his final task – posting several dozen financial transactions that had accumulated in his 'In' basket.

He glared at the screen and called up the accounting software package.

"I should take a sledgehammer to you," he threatened.

"Treat it gently and it will co-operate," purred a throaty, feminine voice.

Kincaid shot out of his chair, then sank back. "Leila. Don't sneak up like that. You could cause permanent damage."

Damn. He didn't trust her motives, and he had no desire to be alone with her, especially dressed for success the way she was. He cast an uneasy eye at the filmy blouse, carefully calculated to reveal more than it concealed. Obviously, she wore nothing under it but silky skin.

She dangled a thermos and two mugs in front of his eyes. "Please don't be cross. I come in peace. I thought I'd drop by and offer you some hot chocolate."

He glanced at his watch. If Charley was coming, she'd be here soon, and he didn't think she'd be too happy if she found him sharing a cozy mug of cocoa with his semi-naked ex-wife.

"I don't dare stop now. There'll be hell to pay if the suppliers cut us off and Colin doesn't get his next shipment," he said evading her invitation, wishing she'd just go away and leave him in peace.

Leila glided closer until she stood behind his chair. "Serves you right for procrastinating. From what I heard while I was standing here waiting for you to notice me, it's time you quit. If you're nice to me tonight, I'll take a look at it for you tomorrow."

Kincaid craned his neck to look up at her. Her dark eyes glistened with sincerity. For less than a heartbeat, he was almost tempted. On the one hand, it was difficult to refuse an offer like that – Leila had a way with computers and a head for numbers. On the other hand, he had a fair idea of what she had in mind when she asked him to be 'nice' to her tonight, and it involved a lot more than sharing a thermos of cocoa.

Easy decision, difficult execution.

Since he had no wish to hurt her feelings or antagonize her any more than he had to, he tried to duck the proposition as diplomatically as possible. Turning his attention to the screen in front of him, he closed the accounting application. "Thanks for the offer, but I think I'll just turn in for the night. My head's pounding. You know how I feel about numbers and computers."

He really did have a throbbing headache, but he wasn't sure whether it was caused by his futile battle with the computer or Leila's sudden appearance.

Her warm breath stirred his hair. "Lean back, darling. This will help."

Before he realized her intentions, he felt cool hands expertly massaging his temples and scalp. God, she still had magic hands. In spite of his qualms, he leaned back and let the tension seep out of his body as delicious shivers ran down his spine.

She moved her hands lower.

Kincaid tensed. His eyes popped open as her fingers slid under his open collar to caress his chest. If he didn't move quickly, it'd be too late. He'd been alone in the jungle without a woman for many long months, and she knew exactly how to turn him on. Cursing himself for being ten kinds of an idiot, he peeled her hands away and stood up to face her. "Enough," he said, more irritated by his own involuntary reaction to her clever fingers than by her seduction attempt. "I'm not interested in what you're offering."

She injected a note of hurt into her voice. "You never used to object, Alistair. I thought you'd be pleased to see me."

He twiddled a pencil as he contemplated his options. Her blatant strategy filled him with an anger he hadn't realized he possessed. Unfortunately, bodily eviction wasn't his style. "You lost the right to touch me when you dumped me."

"You always wanted me. I don't believe that has changed."

Kincaid ground his teeth together and snapped the pencil in half. Had she always been this manipulative? Too often in the past, the sight and touch of her flawless body had succeeded in taking his mind off his grievances.

He tossed the broken pencil into the trash and growled: "I thought I'd made it clear you're wasting your time."

Leila flushed. "It's the insipid, blond reporter bitch, isn't it?" Her lip curled with distaste. "You're hot for her – oh, don't bother trying to deny it. It's written all over your face. What's she got that I don't have?"

He was so angry by this time he almost tripped over his words. "Don't bring Charley into this. It's none of your damned business. You and I have been finished for over two years. Your choice. Your betrayal damn near killed me."

He watched as her huge, dark eyes shimmered with tears. *Damn*. She knew how much he hated to see a woman cry. This time, however, the heavy artillery only succeeded in making him angrier. Manipulation wouldn't work. Not this time.

"That was the biggest mistake of my life," she whispered. "Not a day has gone by that I haven't regretted my actions. If I could do anything to change the past, I would."

Remembering the anguish of her final betrayal, her words only served to fuel his rage. "And then there's the wee matter of your suicide threats," he bit out, his words dripping with irony. "I didn't take them lightly. They stopped me from walking out long ago and saving my sanity."

Leila widened her eyes. "I—"

He cut off her protests. "You knew suicide was a hot button because of my sister's death, didn't you? I'll never forgive you for that."

"I'm truly sorry, Alistair. You have to believe me."

He felt his face stiffen into lines of disbelief. Superb acting like Leila's was a trademark of pathological liars.

Face contorted, she clutched his sleeve. "I know I was wrong, but I couldn't think of any other way to make you stay. I want to make it up to you."

Her touch, once so coveted, now repelled him. He shook off her hand and moved out of reach in case he yielded to the overpowering urge to throttle her. Even when she had walked out on him, he'd kept a tight rein on his temper, suppressing the churning combination of hurt and rage. He'd then compounded the problem by ignoring his fury for over two years, dealing with it in his own unique way – a poisonous combination of manly denial combined with work obsession and a joyless immersion in the frenetic San Francisco party circuit.

No wonder his pent-up rage threatened to explode, like a toxic geyser.

Kincaid drew in a deep breath, feeling only glacial distaste for the beautiful woman in front of him. "I never saw the remotest sign of a conscience in you for the eleven years we were together, Leila, and I don't believe you've magically acquired one now. Genuine remorse is a foreign concept to you."

"But—"

His voice hardened. "Let's just try to stay out of each other's hair until the plane arrives, shall we?"

Her tears dried up in an instant. A narrow, malevolent glare replaced the sad, dewy-eyed demeanour. The change was so sudden, so complete, it seemed as if another person inhabited her body.

Kincaid took an involuntary step backwards.

"You bastard. I'll never forgive you for this," she hissed. "Never."

He exhaled slowly. "It doesn't have to end like this. We can still be civil to one another."

"Civil?" Her sardonic laugh was tinged with hysteria. "You want to be civil? Do you hear yourself, you pathetic, patronizing worm? You and that pitiful excuse for a woman deserve one another."

For one brief instant, she looked scarcely human. Before his disbelieving eyes, her outline seemed to blur and shimmer. A murderous glint lurked in the narrowed eyes, more green than brown in the reflected light. Her once-lovely mouth stretched and tightened into a thin, narrow slit. A strange combination of light and shadow tricked him into believing her pupils had mysteriously elongated into the elliptical shape he'd seen only once before – in a poisonous snake.

The hair on the back of his neck prickled.

In the sudden, electrically charged silence, a wave of energy pulsed towards him, as powerful as a blow from an unseen fist. He staggered once and grabbed the back of his chair to steady himself. When he looked again, her face had resumed its natural appearance as though nothing abnormal had happened.

He shook his head and rubbed his eyes.

A sinister glow animated the dead flatness of Leila's eyes and her voice dropped to a whisper. "You can't hope to understand the powerful and ancient forces at work here."

"Bloody hell. Not that occult crap again."

Her face tightened. "You'll be sorry you rejected me, Alistair. I would have protected you, but now you've sealed your fate."

He grabbed her wrist. "Don't threaten me. I don't scare so easily."

She wrenched her arm away, her mouth twisted in fury, "You'll beg for death before I'm finished with you." She slipped out into the night and slammed the door behind her.

Chapter 21

Eavesdropping was wrong. Unscrupulous. Dishonest. Sneaky. Charley had done it anyway.

As soon as she'd realized Kincaid wasn't alone in the administration shed, she had drawn back, intending to take the high road and walk away. But when Leila started talking about the insipid blonde reporter bitch, all bets were off. The temptation to find out what they were saying about her far outweighed any scruples.

Charley spent the next twenty excruciating minutes of her life crouched beneath the open window listening with spellbound attention, twisted like a pretzel to avoid the prickly thorn bush.

When the door burst open, she shrank back into the concealing bushes, heedless of the twigs clawing at her neck and face. For a split second, enough illumination streamed out to spotlight a face so contorted in rage, she barely recognized it as Leila's before the door slammed shut with a savage force that shook the shed. Charley figured she'd better hold her breath lest the slightest movement betray her presence.

The other woman swept past only inches away. Charley squeezed her eyes shut and shivered, overcome by a sudden chill. A tangible wave of hatred and rage buffeted her body and sucked the air out of her lungs. A trickle of dread crawled down her spine and burrowed into the marrow of her bones.

It's not real. None of this is real. Quelling the urge to burst from the bushes and run for safety, Charley concentrated on a searing pain, which shot down her arm, compliments of a thorn that skewered her shoulder, but she refused to twitch. Perhaps, if she didn't blink, didn't move a muscle, she might be lucky enough to escape detection.

Over the steady pounding of blood in her ears, Charley heard Leila's footsteps thunder by and fade away in the opposite direction, away from the administration shed, away from their tent, and, strangest of all, away from the camp.

Only half-aware of the scalding tears that flooded her cheeks, she filled her lungs with a shuddering breath of clean, sweet air. The overwhelming sense of doom receded, leaving only glacial tendrils that slowly dissipated. Even after Leila's footsteps faded, Charley remained motionless, dubious of her ability to walk. After an endless five minutes, she rose on wobbly legs and, half crouched, risked a peek in the window.

Kincaid slumped on a swivel chair, very still. He rested his elbows on the desk, his hands supporting his drooping head.

Charley's elbow connected with a two-inch thorn. She let out a squeak of pain, too agitated to remember she was in deep trouble if Kincaid caught her with her nose pressed against the window.

She found herself peering through the window into shocked, peat-brown eyes.

Kincaid rose slowly to his feet, never losing eye contact with Charley, whose expression reflected the stunned horror of someone witnessing a train wreck.

He found his voice first. "Why in God's name are you crouched under the window?" he asked, almost afraid to hear the answer.

Charley's mouth opened and closed several times, but no sound emerged.

"Stay right where you are. I'll be right out." Several long, determined steps carried him out the door and around to the side of the cabin where Charley huddled, looking as guilty as sin.

"You were eavesdropping!"

Charley straightened up slowly, avoiding eye contact. She moistened her lips and whipped up her most ingratiating smile. "Eavesdropping is such an ugly word. I prefer to think of it as inadvertently overhearing a private conversation."

Kincaid felt his neck stiffen into an iron bar. Frowning, he took a step closer to Charley. "You were very quiet. How long have you been listening outside my window?"

"Long enough."

"Why didn't you just knock and come in?"

She collected herself enough to give him a look of undisguised forbearance. "And interrupt Leila's attempted seduction? I don't think so."

Bloody hell. He rubbed the nape of his neck where the muscles had kinked. "You've missed your calling as a spy."

A wave of misery clouded her face. "It wasn't what you're thinking. Let me explain...."

He watched with interest as a shamefaced blush spread over her face and down her neck.

"Yes? Go on."

"Well ... I spent all evening in my tent working on my article." She looked at him imploringly.

He gave her his most encouraging nod.

Her eyes pleaded for understanding. "This isn't easy ... um ... by the time I looked at my watch, it was 11:15. When I arrived at the shed, I discovered Leila had beaten me to the punch. I was going to turn around and leave, truly I was, when she mentioned an insipid, blonde reporter bitch. How could I not listen?"

Something deep inside of him loosened and his neck pain disappeared as if by magic. He breathed deeply, noticing the heavy perfume of night-blooming flowers. "I don't blame you. I'd probably have done the same thing."

"I haven't felt this guilty since my grade nine homeroom teacher ferreted out my corrupt but brilliant, not to mention lucrative, parental note forgery business."

Kincaid smiled, then laughed aloud. Charley had mastered the knack of entertaining him with her wry sense of humour. "Sounds to me like creative writing has always been your gift."

Hope blossomed in her eyes. "Then you're not angry?"

"Well ...." He pretended to consider. "You could find a way to make me forget this unfortunate incident ever happened."

At first, her face expressed incomprehension, but he could tell the exact moment his words registered. Her voice sharpened with suspicion. "I'm almost afraid to ask."

He could see her face clearly in the dim light filtering from the window. She looked delicious, her full lips slightly parted, comprehension dawning in those huge, luminous eyes. He wrapped one arm around her waist and drew her towards him. "One kiss. That's all I ask." He touched a finger to her lips, savouring their softness.

He felt a light shudder ripple through her body.

"What about our deal?" A faint tremor shook her voice.

He let his hand roam through her hair, feeling the silky weight slide through his fingers. "That was before I caught you eavesdropping. You owe me a forfeit."

"I thought we agreed you would have done the same thing."

"Doesn't make it right."

"You're not playing fair." She sounded defeated.

"Neither is eavesdropping."

Kincaid watched as Charley gnawed on her lower lip. He figured she was debating her options and his mind screamed, *Idiot, idiot, idiot. Your stupid trick backfired.* An owl hooted somewhere nearby. Its mournful call underlined his sudden fear that he had just lost the best thing that had happened to him in years.

After what seemed like a year, she whispered: "Well ... maybe one, and then we're even."

He let out his breath. "Deal!"

With unsteady hands, he tipped Charley's head back. He felt as if he had been waiting for this moment forever. She surged towards him in a fluid motion, her laugh of triumph turning to a low moan when her lips found his.

He ran his hands over her back and down her flanks. In response, her hips ground against his lower body and he could feel the steady pounding of her heart through thin layers of cloth. His knees threatened to buckle as a combination of lust and tenderness overwhelmed him.

Charley strained against him and he deepened the kiss. Her eager mouth, hot, spicy, impossibly sweet, responded with an intensity that promised more than he had ever dreamed of, and left him gasping for breath. The erotic innocence of her familiar lavender and soap nearly undid him.

Shattered by the kiss he had initiated as a harmless joke, Kincaid dragged his mouth away. If he let the kiss draw them to the logical conclusion, she would never forgive him. "Not now, Charley. Not as a forfeit," he groaned.

Her lashes fluttered. He found himself staring into smoky blue eyes, the passion in them rapidly dulling into flustered comprehension. She placed her hands against his chest, pushing. "Maybe this wasn't such a good idea."

He gave her a quick peck on the tip of her nose and forced himself to take a step backwards. "The kiss was a great idea, Charley. But next time, you will initiate it."

"There won't be a next time."

He smiled, trying to mask his uneasiness at her threat. "Let's join Colin before he packs it in for the night," he said and reached for her hand.

She dug in her heels and refused to budge, a mutinous glint in her eye. "Only as long as you don't mention my eavesdropping."

"I'll be the soul of discretion. We won't mention that you inadvertently overheard a private conversation."

Charley allowed Kincaid to tow her towards the back door of the dining hall on legs that threatened to buckle. She figured she was experiencing a delayed reaction to the stress generated by Leila's threat, compounded by her ignominious exposure as an eavesdropper.

It certainly wasn't the unexpected heat of the kiss, though she couldn't deny she had enjoyed it. Far too much for her peace of mind. She slanted a glance at Kincaid's face. He didn't need to look so damned smug.

At their entry, Colin glanced up and grinned. "Aha, at last. I thought you'd changed your minds. Help yourselves to a drink. I'm making bread and my hands are covered in flour."

Kincaid pried the lid off a metal cookie tin sitting on the counter, placed a stack of crisp-edged cookies on a plate, and offered them to Charley. She shook her head. Her stomach still churned with tension. The mere thought of food made her queasy.

Kincaid glanced at Charley in obvious concern. "It's not

like you to refuse a cookie."

"Observant, aren't you," muttered Charley. "I think I need a drink."

Kincaid poured himself a coffee while Charley took her time debating over a beer or Coke. In the end, she pulled a beer from the refrigerator and opened it, willing her hands to be steady, then wandered back to the wooden counter. Kincaid was perched on a stool, munching a huge oatmeal cookie, and laughing over Colin's nonsense. Everything looked safe and normal.

Colin gathered up a large lump of dough and plopped it in the middle of a mound of flour. It landed with a soft *thud* and a puffy cloud of white powder coated his beard. "Something happened, didn't it? You both looked a wee bit fashed when you arrived."

Charley jumped in. "Kincaid just had a huge fight with Leila."

Colin stopped kneading and raised his eyebrows expectantly. "Spill it."

Charley pointed to the mountain of dough. "Let me help you out. They say kneading dough is therapeutic."

Colin glanced expectantly from one face to the other. "This story must be good if you're in need of therapy. Go wash up while I prepare you a spot."

When Charley returned, Colin draped an apron over her head and she rolled up the sleeves of her denim shirt. Plunging in with both hands, she pressed the dough against the marble slab, enjoying the feel of the soft mass squelching through her fingers. While she worked the elastic lump, she listened to Kincaid describing his version of the acrimonious words in the administration shed, glossing over the massage part and the tiny fact that Leila had practically stripped naked and jumped him on his desk. Charley wasn't sure if the tactful omissions were for Colin's benefit or her own.

When Kincaid finished his recital, a wrinkle creased Colin's brow. "Where were you when all this happened, lass?"

She felt embarrassment paint her face bright scarlet and concentrated on her hands. "Uh...."

She could have hugged Kincaid when he jumped in, preventing her from confessing her crime. "Charley

215

inadvertently overheard part of the conversation."

Colin's eyes crinkled. "Eavesdropping, huh? That's my girl."

She looked up, startled. Was she so transparent?

Colin winked at Charley and turned back to Kincaid without losing a beat. "So Leila uttered a death threat, did she? I'd watch my back if I were you. I always said she was trouble. I never understood what you saw in her."

"Aye, well. For once, it turns out you were right. I tried to make allowances for her tragic childhood, but I'm beginning to believe she's damaged beyond repair." He selected another cookie and sank his teeth into it. "Mmmm. Good."

Charley thumped the dough viciously, not wanting to hear about Leila's vulnerable side. Then she sighed and succumbed to the curiosity that consumed her. "I'll bite. What happened?"

Colin answered for Kincaid whose mouth was full. "Och, when Leila was only a wee lass of two, she was involved in a horrible car accident. Her car seat in the back protected her from serious injury, but the front of the car was squashed like an accordion. She had to listen to her parents die, screaming, before help arrived."

Kincaid finished the story with his mouth full. "After the accident, I gather she was unmanageable. The system bounced her around from one foster home to another." He swallowed. "She told me once she would never allow herself to feel powerless again."

To her great surprise, Charley felt a reluctant stab of pity for Leila. "How horrible. But a childhood trauma doesn't excuse her actions now, as an adult. Anyway, there's more you should know about her – something I haven't told you."

Kincaid selected another cookie, took a bite and made an inquiring noise.

Charley concentrated on the dough she was kneading, unable to look him straight in the eye while she ratted out his ex-wife. "When Leila left the administration shed, she didn't head back to our tent. She took the path leading to the dig." She risked a glance at Kincaid.

Kincaid's eyebrows shot into his hairline, his cookie forgotten. "No one in their right mind would take a midnight stroll through the jungle alone."

Colin tugged his beard and shrugged. "If she's headed for the dig, we can find out tomorrow from the security guard."

Charley squeezed the dough, avoiding both pairs of eyes. "I think the situation might be even worse. It was too dark to see much, but I felt...." She chose her next words carefully. "Oh, hell. You'll think I'm paranoid or crazy, but when Leila left the shed, she radiated ... I don't know how to describe it ... some sort of weird force-field or dark energy that wanted to destroy everything in the vicinity. If she had caught me hiding in the bushes, I hate to think what she'd have done."

"You have a smudge of flour right here." Kincaid rubbed the tip of her nose with his finger and grinned. "Then I guess you're lucky that I blew your cover instead of Leila."

Charley caught her breath in disbelief. He wasn't taking her seriously. She had to find a way to make him understand. "It's no laughing matter. I think she would have killed me without a qualm."

The crease in his cheeks deepened as a smile spread from ear to ear. "Are you sure you're not over-reacting a wee bit? Kill you? I know the pair of you aren't best buddies, but I doubt she'd murder you in cold blood – even over a mouth-watering prize like me."

Charley drove her fist into the dough in frustration, pretending it was Kincaid's fat head. The stubborn idiot refused to listen. "Not everything boils down to a petty female cat-fight," she muttered in sheer frustration.

Colin gently removed the mass of dough from Charley's clenched fists before she could destroy it and placed it carefully in a greased pan. "I think you might be right about Leila, lass." He turned to Kincaid. "This is the wrong time for jokes. There's a dark side to Leila that always scared the shit out of me."

Charley turned to Colin in relief. "Thank God, *someone* around here believes me. What do you think Leila meant when she warned Kincaid about 'powerful and ancient forces'?"

Kincaid summoned up an annoyingly superior smile. "Leila was just upset. You can't seriously believe she can

217

summon up ghosties and evil spirits."

Colin covered the pan with a clean tea towel and spoke over his shoulder. "Leila always displayed an interest in the occult, and you know it."

Charley ignored Kincaid. "The occult, huh? Sounds intriguing."

Colin leaned his hands on the counter, his eyes gleaming, his voice confidential. "Och, aye. Thirteen years ago, when I first met Kincaid and Leila – she was his girlfriend at the time – she and a young Mexican lad, Pedro, I think his name was, would disappear into the hills to chew peyote and mess around with supernatural experiments. She thought Kincaid didn't know about her wee research projects, but eventually, he found out. Nearly drove him crazy, though he kept his mouth shut, hoping she'd stop of her own accord. If you ask me, the peyote fried her brain. She's never been the same since that summer."

Charley processed this information. A picture was beginning to emerge. "What if Leila is up to something? She's been out of the tent all night, every night, since we arrived. I know because she always wakes me up coming in at dawn."

Kincaid leaned forward, his disbelief forgotten. "You're kidding. Where does she go?"

Charley shrugged. "Who knows? Sometimes, I think she meets Felipe. Doesn't he believe he has a spiritual connection with his ancient Olmec ancestors?"

"How did you leap to that conclusion?"

Charley had the grace to look sheepish. "I overheard your argument with Felipe when I followed you into the tunnel, and...."

Kincaid interjected: "The first time I caught you eavesdropping."

Charley's face grew warm, but she continued as if he hadn't interrupted. "Felipe was babbling on about how you had angered the gods of his forefathers." She smiled sweetly. "I assumed you understood the implications."

"Kincaid always was a wee bit thick, lass."

Kincaid ignored Colin and fixed her with a stare. "That's a wee bit farfetched, don't you think?" But he didn't sound convinced.

Charley shrugged. "Oh, I don't know. Felipe has had a few unexplained absences himself this week. He's an attractive man in a forbidding sort of way and besides, he looks as if he believes in the supernatural."

Kincaid growled: "You find him attractive?"

She wiped her hands on a cloth and worked at ignoring Kincaid's scowl. "Some women like that kind of man." She smiled sweetly. "Okay, Colin, how else can I help?"

Colin plopped the slab of dough he'd been kneading in front of Charley. "You can roll this into a rectangle for cinnamon rolls."

She grabbed the rolling pin and plied it vigorously, glad to have something to do with her hands. "About those ancient and powerful forces Leila mentioned—"

Kincaid uttered the curious glottal sound in the back of his throat. Charley thought the sound probably indicated exasperation. Maybe disgust. A cookie crumb caught in his throat.

She turned the dough and floured it, then slanted a glance at him. "I take it, Kincaid, you don't believe in the existence of anything you can't see, hear, touch, smell or taste."

He set his mug down before answering. "Of course not. Nobody in his right mind would believe Leila's occult crap. She was just trying to scare me."

Hoping for support, Charley turned to Colin. "What about you, Colin? Do you believe in supernatural forces?"

Colin scratched his beard absently, a sign of deep contemplation. "Och, aye. I suppose I do. And now that you mention it, this place possesses an energy unlike anything I've ever experienced." He looked at her shrewdly. "Why do you ask?"

She avoided Kincaid's eyes and addressed Colin. "Sometimes, I imagine I can feel the spirits of the dead."

Kincaid seemed to be at a momentary loss for words. As the import of her words sank in, his eyes widened in disbelief. "Surely, you can't be talking about *ghosts?*" He sounded as though he thought she might be losing her mind.

Colin overrode Kincaid's scathing comment. "Sometimes I feel the spirits too, particularly when I'm near a burial site or sacred place of worship. Ancient energies seem very close at those times."

"*Imigh sa diabhal*," said Kincaid, shaking his head.

Charley figured perhaps tonight wasn't the right time to spring her strange hallucinations on him. She chewed her lip, selecting her next words with care, testing, probing. "Do you think the dead can return? Do you believe ancient energies can exert power over us?"

Kincaid merely shook his head in disbelief.

Colin eyed her quizzically. "That's a very deep and metaphysical question for this time of night." He paused then added: "Are you asking these questions for any particular reason?"

Charley took a deep breath and ploughed ahead, feeling Kincaid's gaze boring into her. "I'm beginning to believe this dig may have stirred up something strange – I don't know, memories and feelings, past energies, for lack of better words and—"

Kincaid cut her off. "No offence, but surely an intelligent woman like you doesn't believe in mystical bullshit."

He didn't know the half of it. What would he say if she told him that Zanazca's extraordinary life had been unfolding in her imagination ever since she arrived? Charley pushed aside the sinking feeling in the pit of her stomach and ignored the interruption. "Do either of you believe deeds committed in a previous lifetime can affect our lives in the present?"

Kincaid let out a sceptical snort. "You're kidding, right? You sound as if you're talking about karma and reincarnation."

Before Charley could get the words out, Colin interjected: "I'm surprised a scientist like you even knows the words, Kincaid."

"What if I *am* talking about karma and reincarnation?" countered Charley.

Kincaid's twisted smile looked more like a grimace than a grin. "Only the naive and the gullible believe in reincarnation. There's absolutely no scientific proof."

Colin patted his friend's hand. "Why don't you take a stab at broadening your narrow, wee outlook, Kincaid?" Pity dripped from his voice. "Science doesn't resolve everything.

I'll have you know that reincarnation is a fundamental tenet of some of the world's greatest religions."

Kincaid looked at both of them in turn, shaking his head slowly. "And I suppose you both believe in that nonsense?"

Charley swallowed her retort.

Colin flicked Kincaid a scathing look. "Aye, lad. Furthermore, I happen to know for a fact that this is my twenty-fifth lifetime," he announced in a tone that brooked no opposition.

Charley knew her jaw had dropped open so she snapped her mouth shut. An inquiring and open mind was one of the qualities that had made her a star journalist. Maybe she wasn't as crazy as she thought. While she turned the idea over in her mind, trying to process the implications, Colin calmly prepared a sugar and cinnamon mixture to sprinkle on the dough.

Kincaid appeared to be at a momentary loss for words. He raked his fingers through his hair then asked faintly: "How did I end up discussing reincarnation with a pair of lunatics like you?"

Charley found her voice at last. "Just lucky, I guess. We'll make a convert out of you yet and you can apologize. Flowers are good, chocolate even better. I believe I'll take you up on the cookie now."

As pieces of the puzzle clicked into place, a bubble of excitement expanded in Charley's chest. If Colin could have past lives, so could she. What if her hallucinations were really flashbacks of a previous lifetime? That would explain everything.

Chapter 22

Much later, Charley's restless brain denied her the sleep she craved.

After a couple of hours of tossing and turning, she berated herself for not filching a couple of her mother's kick-ass sleeping pills – just in case of emergency insomnia. Her mind churned and whirled, reminding her of a hamster she'd once owned as a child. All night long, Frisky had scampered on his squeaky wheel, running desperately, going nowhere, and accomplishing nothing.

Squeak-squeak. Squeak-squeak. Round and round.

Reincarnation. Karma. Round and round.

After another hour, Charley finally felt herself drift off when the familiar chill engulfed her body and humming filled her ears. This time, she embraced the sensations. If these strange attacks were flashbacks to a past lifetime, she wanted to experience the next one fully.

There was barely enough time to open her mind to the possibilities when the howling darkness swept her away.

A burst of power, more intoxicating than the goblet of fermented pulque she'd drained at the banquet, fizzed through Zanazca's veins. Today, she had crossed the invisible line separating woman from child. She had held a hot, still-beating heart in her hands and absorbed the man's life force into her own.

Her body throbbed with an urgent energy, and she intended to find the release she craved. "Nama," she whispered. "Come with me."

Nama smiled, his expressive face creased with pleasure. "You did well today, Zana. You were very brave – for a girl."

Zanazca laughed at the private joke they shared. Two years younger, she had always been the adventurous one, the rebel. Nama, a born peacemaker and student, was always anxious to placate Kele-Pe, their demanding master. Many times, Nama had taken the blame for her heedless pranks.

She took his hand and pulled him towards the cave entrance. "There is more I must learn today."

A startled expression crossed his face. "Kele-Pe forbids us to enter the sacred cave without permission."

"Risk it one time. For me."

Torches flickered in wall sconces, lighting their way as she coaxed him through the sacred cave and into a short, dark tunnel that led to a smaller cavern. Only a faint reflection of light penetrated the heavy darkness of the inner cave.

"No one will think to look for us here," she whispered.

Zanazca turned towards Nama and feathered her hands over his bare chest until they rested on his shoulders. "Today, I am no longer a girl. I want you to teach me the pleasures of being a woman. We have loved one another for many cycles."

He tensed under her touch. "Our master will kill us both."

"Kele-Pe will never find out. You want me, Nama. I have seen you watching me when you thought I was not looking. Touch me. Show me. I want you to be the first." She opened her robe and guided his hand to her breast. At first, she thought he would pull away, but his rigid fingers softened, then cupped and stroked, kneading the sensitive nipple. She moaned softly in the back of her throat as heat built in her lower body. His drugging kiss stole her breath away and she met his tongue with her own.

After a minute, he dragged his mouth away and sucked in his breath. "Zana," he groaned, pulling away. "This is wrong. You are my sister." The thickening length of his stirring erection nudged her belly and belied his words.

"I am no more your blood sister than Kele-Pe is our blood father." She reached down and unfastened his tunic. It slid to the ground with a whisper and he stood proudly naked in front of her. She grasped him with her hand and closed her fist around the hot, smooth flesh.

His hands slid under her robe and grasped her buttocks. She felt his mouth on her breasts. He lowered himself until he was kneeling at her feet. His mouth slid lower, over her belly, tongue investigating her belly button and leaving a scalding path as it travelled lower. Gently, he parted the dark curls between her legs.

Obediently, she spread her legs, allowing him free access. She clutched his head in both hands and gasped as his hot tongue glided over the sensitive bud.

The long, clear tones of the conch trumpet reverberated through the cave. Nama and Zanazca sprang apart as the sound tore through the darkness.

"Kele-Pe summons us to the temple," Nama said, fumbling for his tunic and tying it around his hips. "He told me there will be an important ceremony when the sun sinks below the horizon. We must return before he comes in search of us. Late tonight, I will come to you."

When Charley opened her eyes, she grew aware of a heavy ache and embarrassing dampness between her legs. One thing was certain. If she was experiencing flashbacks, her past life certainly hadn't been boring.

Fully aroused, she shifted uncomfortably on her cot. Too bad an affair with Kincaid was out of the question. Mentally, she reviewed all of the iron-clad reasons she shouldn't indulge in a romantic interlude – she had too much pride to join his harem, he would only dump her and break her heart, her mother would approve, he was a man and, by definition, men couldn't be trusted.... Given enough time, she was certain she could think of dozens more equally good reasons.

She glanced at the luminous face of her watch and pounded her pillow.

The epiphany arrived at 4:56 am in a burst of clarity that washed away her lingering fears and changed her attitude about relationships. With men. Specifically, with Alistair Kincaid.

It was so simple, so obvious. Why hadn't the insight occurred to her sooner? Wide-awake now, she sat up in bed.

A brief fling might be just what the doctor ordered to get

Kincaid out of her system. They were both adults, footloose and fancy-free, and she would be going home in a few days, leaving him behind. She'd be long gone before he could hurt her.

This time, she would do the leaving.

She laughed softly to herself. For the first time in her life, at least in this lifetime, she planned to seduce a man. She wasn't sure how and she wasn't sure when, but one thing was certain – Kincaid didn't stand a chance.

Chapter 23

Rage lent wings to Leila's feet. The trip from the administration shed to the hidden tunnel had never seemed so short. She couldn't afford to let herself acknowledge the pain that fuelled her anger. Lingering regrets would get in the way of what she had to do. Alistair would pay a heavy price for rejecting her.

When her booted feet thudded into the cave, she stopped and took a couple of seconds to calm down and erase all traces of anger from her face. No need for Felipe to know that a burning thirst for revenge rather than concern over the violation of sacred relics was her only reason for joining him tonight.

Felipe's voice rang out. "You are late."

Hiding the quick spurt of anger by injecting a conciliatory note into her voice, she turned in his direction. "I'm so sorry, Felipe. When I saw the time, I ran most of the way."

He had already ignited the wall torches. They produced a dim glow that cast flickering shadows and left much of the cave in darkness. A fire crackled in the centre of the cave. As she approached, he jumped to his feet and lit the incense in the three-legged stone burners, one at each corner of the altar and another in the mouth of the stone jaguar that loomed over it. Aromatic smoke drifted through the cave and billowed in clouds to the ceiling where it dissipated through hidden cracks.

She settled herself on the cold cave floor, struggling to control her agitated breathing. The finality of Alistair's rejection had begun to sink in. Only vengeance would extinguish the raging fury that had coalesced into a white-hot core. She brushed a pebble aside and shifted her body, trying to arrange her legs in a more comfortable position beneath her. Her sheer blouse, perfect for seduction, gave little protection against the chill of the night air. She'd planned to stand Felipe up tonight in favour of seducing Alistair, but his brutal rejection had forced her hand. Soon, he would pay the price.

Nobody rejected Leila Romero.

The sound of Felipe's chanting jolted her back to reality. She hid her impatience. The endless preparation would soon be over and they could get down to serious business.

Finally, he seated himself, cross-legged, on the opposite side of the fire. Flickering flames highlighted his aquiline features, leaving the hooded eyes in dark shadow.

"We will start," he intoned.

"Alistair continues his work on the rockslide," she said in an off-handed voice. "He must be nearly through the barrier."

Felipe's large hands resting on his knees clenched into fists. "*Sí.* One, maybe two days at most. I have tried everything in my power to make him change his mind, but the man is blind to reason. The time to act approaches."

Leila leaned forward to convey sincerity. "I want to help stop the sacrilege. I am ready to learn more."

Felipe grunted. "Your natural ability to shapeshift is more powerful than my own. It took me many years and much effort to transform myself into my *nagual.* You, on the other hand, succeeded on your second attempt."

Her heart pounded. Unlimited power was within her reach, if only she could compel Felipe to cram the remainder of her lessons into a single night. "Tonight is the night I want to transform into my second *nagual,* my real *nagual,* the jaguar."

"It is too soon."

"I must learn tonight. As you said, time grows short." She closed her eyes, held her breath and waited for his answer.

After an eternity, he handed her a leather flask. "Drink this."

Felipe sat in the flickering darkness studying the flames. A tiny worm of panic slithered through his gut. Leila's life force had been gone too long for her first transformation into a

227

jaguar. The woman's empty body sprawled on the floor like a waxen statue, arms limp at her sides. He willed her to move. Only the shallow rise and fall of her chest bore testament to the spark of life still stirring within her body.

His brow furrowed. He had heard of instances when a person's spirit remained trapped in the *nagual* for several years, leaving the human body in a state of suspended animation. Unless the spirit returned to its physical incarnation, the animal's eventual death spelled the person's demise as well.

In the recesses of his mind, he sensed that the challenger to Leila's supremacy was within striking distance. What if the powerful threat had already struck?

A slight movement drew his eyes to Leila's face. Was it his imagination, or had her lips fluttered? He held his breath.

She lay motionless on the ground for another minute, then stirred. As the vital spark returned to her body and reanimated it, she opened her eyes and blinked.

Felipe licked his dry lips and heaved a mighty sigh of relief. "You succeeded."

A satisfied smile spread over her face. She pushed herself upright into a sitting position and stretched luxuriantly, cat-like. "Shifting to a jaguar was the most awesome experience of my life. I've never felt such power, such speed, such incredible strength. I did not want to return, but I had no choice." She shivered and drew closer to the fire.

He shrugged out of his rough woollen jacket and draped it around her shoulders. "Be patient. Soon, you will have complete control over the power. Already you have accomplished more than most do in a lifetime. Tell me what you experienced."

He listened in silence as Leila described her first killing experience as a jaguar – how she had stalked the tapir and pounced on it, how her jaws had clamped around its skull, crushing it as the victim uttered its final squeak of terror. "And then, I feasted," she concluded, flicking a pink tongue around her mouth, as if she could still taste the hot, salty blood. "I won't want to eat for days."

Felipe chuckled. The half-eaten carcass close to camp coupled with jaguar prints might make Kincaid think twice about risking his men's lives. Unless he could prevent the discovery of the cavern and its priceless contents – the remains of his ancestors, the graves that only he was aware of – he must make his final move. He needed Leila's help.

"You did well. But the hour grows late."

She did not leap to her feet as he expected. Instead, she fixed him with an intense gaze. "What shall we do about Alistair? He inches closer to the cavern every day."

His heart leaped. Hard work and training had paid off. Leila, like himself, believed she had an obligation to protect the secrets of their ancestors. He intended to take full advantage of her change of heart.

He lowered his voice to a confidential whisper. "I have devised a strategy to prevent Kincaid from despoiling our forefathers' secrets. The priceless artefacts must never suffer the indignity of being placed on display for the entertainment of the vulgar masses." He still did not trust her enough to mention the bones of their ancestors, hidden in the inner cave.

She leaned forward, her hair hiding her eyes. "Tell me your mysterious strategy."

Felipe considered Leila's request in silence, wishing he could see her expression. The edge roughening her voice caused his back to stiffen. There was time enough to explain about the dynamite if such drastic measures were required. "When the time is right," he hedged. "Kincaid may fail in his attempt to reach the cavern."

Her voice failed to hide her derision. "Not unless you do something to make him stop."

He knew she was right, and he almost hated her for it. He shrugged and spread out his hands. "I have tried many things. Nothing worked. Not the accident, not the theft, not the sabotage."

Leila curled her lip. "You have not tried hard enough. You need to do something drastic."

He concealed his quick flare of anger at her arrogance and asked quietly: "What do you suggest?"

She sat in contemplative silence, staring into the fire. Finally, she raised her head, eyes gleaming. "You must kidnap the reporter bitch and bring her to the cave. I promise you, Alistair will have everybody in camp scouring the area for her. Removing the rockslide will be the least of his worries."

Felipe considered Leila's suggestion in silence. He could see no flaw in the idea.

"Your idea is sound. The reporter woman will disappear and you will deliver a ransom note stating she will be released only when Kincaid dynamites the tunnel. That way, no one will ever violate the cave. When that is done, my work here will be finished."

"Then what?"

"I will disappear."

Chapter 24

Kincaid's restless night had taken its toll. Four cups of Colin's train-oil coffee and the fresh, flower-scented morning air had done nothing to rouse him from his somnolent state or lighten his mood. Yawning and preoccupied, he stumbled towards the dig, trailing behind the rest of the work party.

Yesterday, when the afternoon's breathless heat had penetrated even the depths of the tunnel, his decision to start work on the rock pile at dawn the next day had seemed like a stroke of genius. That way, he'd reasoned, they could quit before the temperature soared into the stratosphere.

He hadn't counted on losing a night of precious sleep.

The disturbing scene with Leila in the administration shed had left him shaken and upset, more with his reaction than with hers. He'd always prided himself on being easy-going and laid back, never losing his temper, and never, ever indulging in shouting matches, no matter how great the provocation.

Until last night.

Chagrined, he admitted to himself he had indulged in a spectacular outburst of temper, scorning Leila's proclamation of love, calling her a liar, and pushing her away. Naturally, he had discounted her dramatic warning – something about powerful and ancient forces – as her usual occult nonsense, but her parting threat about how he would beg for death had echoed in his head most of the night.

To compound matters, Colin had taken him aside and demanded to know whether or not he had told Charley yet that he was a recovering alcoholic. Kincaid had snapped back that it was none of Colin's business and pointed out that, somehow, he didn't think dropping that little bombshell on her would earn him a free passage into her bed. Nevertheless, his idiotic knee-jerk response to his best friend's question, not to mention his shameful little secret, had prodded his conscience.

As if those worries weren't enough to keep him awake, Felipe's strange behaviour had continued to gnaw at the back of Kincaid's mind like a turbo-charged rodent attacking a sack of grain. Instinct warned him Felipe knew more about yesterday's accident in the tunnel than he was letting on, but he could hardly confront his field director without concrete proof.

Even that wasn't the worst of it. Every time his exhausted body had begun to relax in preparation for sleep, a tantalizing picture of Charley, head thrown back in passion, had popped into his mind. She was driving him crazy. He wanted the reporter desperately, both in his bed and, to his dismayed surprise, out of it. Oh, bloody hell, he actually *liked* her – a lot – and he couldn't remember when he had last felt this way about a woman.

He wasn't enjoying the sensation.

He eyed the gleaming pyramid balefully. Under normal circumstances, he would think nothing of racing to the summit without stopping to catch his breath. Today, the eighty-five crumbling steps represented a painful and humbling challenge. He shook his head to clear it and pulled himself together, focusing all his energy on achieving his distant goal.

"Mind over matter," he muttered and plodded upwards.

The sooner they started, the sooner they would finish.

Five hours later, exhausted and drenched with sweat, Kincaid rested his pickaxe against the wall and swiped his arm over his dripping forehead. "Good work, men. We've been at it for nearly five hours. That's enough for today. Let's have some lunch and enjoy the afternoon."

The men groaned with relief and tossed their tools into a corner.

They hadn't made as much progress as he'd hoped. At this rate, it would take several days to break through the barrier of rocks.

If they ever did, he thought dismally.

The men straggled back towards camp in single file, their usual banter dampened by fatigue. The prospect of a cool shower before lunch lent Kincaid renewed energy, and he picked up the pace. The camp was almost in sight when Felipe halted and called out: "Dr. Kincaid. Look." He pointed to the soft earth beside the path.

Kincaid's blood turned to ice. "A paw print," he said, kneeling and placing his outstretched hand over the deep impression. The imprint was bigger than his hand, claw marks clearly outlined. "Something large. A jaguar, from the looks of it."

Felipe, crouched beside Kincaid, crumbled a handful of earth in his hand and let the reddish soil slide through his fingers. "The ground is still damp underneath. These prints are only a few hours old," he announced in an ominous voice, standing up and brushing off his hands on his work pants. "The animal is close."

The men burst into a torrent of agitated Spanish, gesturing and peering into the jungle.

Kincaid sprang to his feet, silently cursing Felipe's big mouth. If he had intended to incite panic, it had worked. He held up a hand to quell the developing hysteria. "Don't panic. If it's a jaguar, it's probably long gone by now. They feed at dawn and dusk. Besides, they prefer to avoid humans."

Felipe closed his eyes and making, a dramatic sign of the cross, uttered: "*Dios!* This animal does not avoid humans. It comes close to camp."

Kincaid ignored Felipe. "Stay here, men, and don't move. I'll check it out." He was uncomfortably aware that he sounded like the great white hunter uttering soothing platitudes to his loyal followers.

Sweat trickled down his forehead and over the bridge of his nose as he contemplated the potential dangers he faced. Heart hammering, he grabbed one of the shovels as a makeshift weapon and followed the prints leading into the deep emerald shadows of the jungle.

As he pushed his way through the network of branches festooned with clutching vines, mosses and creepers, shovel raised in front of him, he scanned the encroaching bushes for any sign of movement. Although he didn't really expect an indignant jaguar to spring out at him, it paid to be cautious.

The jungle thinned out and opened into a sun-dappled clearing. Flattened grass and a pool of drying blood surrounded by clouds of bloated flies indicated that a life-and-death struggle had taken place here. Kincaid became aware of the high-pitched buzzing – the unmistakable sound of millions of tiny insect wings. Simultaneously, he collided with the sweetish odour of putrefaction.

He gagged reflexively and clapped his hand over his nose and mouth.

The mangled body of a young tapir, killed by something big, powerful and very hungry, lay sprawled on the far side of the clearing.

Three black vultures surrounded the carcass, their beaks stained with blood. By nightfall, nothing except bones and a few patches of hair would be left of the carcass.

He returned to his men.

"It was a jaguar, no doubt about it," he announced. "I found the remains of its last meal in a clearing, so at least it isn't hungry."

Felipe addressed Kincaid, a glint of defiance flickering in his eyes: "You do not know that. It might come back." Kincaid's hand itched to throttle him."

The morning flew by for Charley in a cheerful flurry of activity. Strange how her decision to seduce Kincaid had changed her outlook on life. A different perspective lent a spring to her step and a lilt to her voice as she hummed the morning away. The sun shone brighter, the flowers smelled sweeter, the birds were more musical, too.

A half an hour later than usual, the work crew clattered into the dining hall in a flurry of excited gestures and chatter. Kincaid locked gazes with Charley, grinned and waved.

She felt her insides tighten while her bones did a long, slow dissolve. Yes, she'd made the right decision. His hair, still damp from a hasty shower, had started to curl. In spite of the garish aloha shirt sporting giant hibiscus blossoms against a scarlet and gold sunset, he looked good, really good.

A hand gesture signalled he'd be over directly. He turned off the radio and strode to the centre of the room where he stood on a chair and motioned for silence. Over the roar of laughter and clatter of cutlery, he shouted: "Listen up, people."

All heads swivelled in Kincaid's direction. Gradually, the room stilled.

"I have an important announcement to make." He raised his voice so that it would carry to the kitchen. "Colin, you and your kitchen staff had better come out here. You'll want to hear this as well." Kincaid waited.

The kitchen door flew open. Colin and his two assistants trooped out. "Better make it quick, Kincaid," Colin growled. "You don't want me to burn your lunch."

"Burn my food, and you'll know the real meaning of trouble."

Laughter greeted the joking insults.

Kincaid's face sobered. "I'll get right to the point. On our way back to camp this morning, we saw signs of a large jaguar not five minutes away from here. I followed its tracks and found the remains of a young tapir it had killed. The blood wasn't quite dry."

The announcement raised goose bumps on Charley's bare arms.

An excited buzz broke out as everyone talked at once. Tapirs, it appeared, were large animals, not so easy to take down unless the predator was very powerful. She'd seen a picture of a tapir once in a magazine. The animal looked like the result of a mad geneticist gone amok while crossing a pig, a horse and an anteater.

When the room quieted, Kincaid continued: "Until further notice, I don't want any of you to leave camp alone. Always travel in groups, the larger the better. I don't need to remind you that under normal circumstances, jaguars avoid humans, but we don't want to take any chances. Make lots of noise so that you don't surprise the animal, and carry a knife or machete with you at all times. Keep your eyes open, and please report any jaguar signs to me. I don't anticipate trouble, but we may have to take more drastic steps if the animal doesn't leave the area."

An excited outburst filled the room. Charley marvelled at how easily Kincaid restored order. He took questions one by one, answering calmly and concisely. In ten minutes, he had defused a potentially explosive situation. When the hubbub had subsided to the normal lunchtime babble, he squeezed his way between the tables and made his way towards her.

She had already cleared some space. "Hey, Kincaid. What were you thinking of, chasing after a jaguar? You might have been killed."

Kincaid sat down, his face wreathed in a smile. He reached for a roll. "Does that mean you're a wee bit concerned about my tender hide?"

Her heart thudded. "Of course I am. It also means I need someone to take me swimming this afternoon."

His eyebrows drew together. "*Swimming*? This is hardly the ideal time to go swimming."

She shrugged. "I could use the exercise and you need a break. Besides, the jaguar will be sleeping off its meal."

Exasperation tinged his voice. "Didn't you hear a single word I said?"

"Of course I heard. You said it was okay to leave camp with a companion and I can't think of anyone I'd be safer with than you."

"I'm flattered, I think."

She looked at him from under her lashes and smiled. "Come on, Kincaid. Please come with me. It'll be fun."

"All right, all right. You win. How can I resist when you put it that way? What time shall I meet you?"

She favoured him with a brilliant smile. "I'll come by your cabin in two hours."

She would give him the aquatic adventure of his life.

Chapter 25

Two hours on the dot after Charley had issued her invitation, Kincaid found himself pacing the front porch of his cabin. He forced himself to sit down, legs crossed, feigning nonchalance. It wasn't a good idea to look too eager.

Horrie meowed and twined around his legs. Kincaid leaned down to scratch between the cat's ears. He'd heard that stroking an animal helped release tension. If that was true, he was about to make Horrie a very happy cat.

"What do you think, lad?" he asked Horrie. "Charley asked me to go swimming."

Horrie's ears twitched.

He stroked the cat's silky head. "Aye. Swimming! A blatant euphemism, if ever I heard one. She's definitely making the next move."

In response, Horrie sprang into Kincaid's lap, circled twice and curled into a tight ball, his tail wrapped around his body.

"Make yourself at home, why don't you?" Kincaid stroked the cat's back. The rhythmic purring escalated and Kincaid took it as a sign of encouragement. "I'll bet she's a knock-out in a bathing suit. And looks even better out of it."

Horrie yawned.

"I can tell you don't give a damn."

The very thought of Charley's golden body clad in nothing but a skimpy bathing suit, possibly a bikini, no, a red thong bikini, made Kincaid's mouth water. He leaned back in his chair, taking care not to disturb Horrie.

He looked at his watch for the fifth time in as many minutes. What mysterious spell had she used to reduce him to a quivering mass of jelly? Hell, he was a grown man who had dated dozens of sophisticated and beautiful women. He shook his head, irritated by his own eagerness.

Mo Dhia. Charley could spell trouble for a carefree bachelor. His hand rested, motionless, on Horrie's back.

Horrie flexed his claws and fixed Kincaid with one unblinking, yellow eye.

"Ow. Okay, okay. I'll pay more attention to what I'm doing." Kincaid resumed stroking his cat, concentrating on – and almost achieving – the therapeutic effects of heightened tranquility and reduced pulse rate.

Kincaid's relaxation was short-lived. His breath caught in his chest at the vision striding towards him, carrying a small gym bag, her hair piled in a burnished mass on top of her head. Denim cut-offs displayed miles of shapely leg and a crimson tube top moulded her breasts like a second skin and bared her taut belly. Sturdy boots completed the outfit.

Charley was breathtaking.

Kincaid waved and scooped up an indignant Horrie in order to stand and greet his date. He let out a long, low wolf whistle. "Hullo, lass. You look amazing."

She smiled and kissed his cheek, a slight flush betraying a trace of nervousness. "Hello, yourself." She scratched Horrie under his furry chin. "Is he coming, too?"

"No idea. He does pretty much what he pleases." He released the cat and studied her face. The kiss was a very good sign. So was the nervousness. With difficulty, he restrained himself from grabbing her and raining kisses over every square inch of the gorgeous body – and a few more places her skimpy outfit attempted to conceal.

She must have read something of his thoughts because the rosy blush spread to her neck and chest.

Taking pity on her confusion, Kincaid dragged his gaze away and slung the bag over his shoulder. "I've packed some cool drinks, snacks, towels, sunscreen and my bathing suit."

"Snacks. Good thinking. Swimming always makes me hungry. Never fails. Do we need those?" She pointed to the weapons leaning against a palm tree.

"I don't imagine we'll use them, but I'm not taking any chances." He picked up the machete and shotgun. "All set. Let's go swimming."

Horrie stalked in the opposite direction, tail held high.

The water felt like cool silk on Charley's skin as she kicked upwards towards the dappled sunlight. Seconds later, her head broke the surface several yards from the flat rock that had served as her impromptu diving platform.

She smiled to herself, recalling the expression on Kincaid's face when she'd let her towel drift to the ground, revealing her naked body. Enjoying his bemused expression, she had raised her arms with calculated deliberation and unpinned her hair, letting it flow over her shoulders. Turning her back on him, she had poised on her toes for two seconds and executed the cleanest dive of her life.

Treading water, she looked towards the shore. He was still frozen on the exact same spot, a mixture of disbelief, excitement and hope flickering across his features.

Good. That had shaken him out of his masculine complacency. He was beginning to clue into the fact that she'd turned the tables on him.

The sight of Kincaid in a bathing suit robbed her of breath. Smooth, deeply tanned skin covered the lithe, well-muscled frame of an athlete. She contemplated his chest, feathered with dark hair that tapered to a 'V' and disappeared beneath his trunks. Her insides turned to jelly at the thought of what lay beneath the thin covering of cloth. His torso narrowed to a flat stomach. Slim hips supported long, muscular legs, furred with the same fine, dark hair as his chest.

She threw back her head and gurgled a low, wicked laugh, causing a flock of birds to burst from the trees on the opposite shore and flap away, squawking their protest. "I forgot to pack a bathing suit. Why are you standing like a rock, Kincaid? Are you chicken? I dare you to take it all off and join me."

The result was a foregone conclusion. A white smile slashed across Kincaid's tanned face as he captured her gaze with his own.

She remained motionless and silent, afraid to breathe, afraid to break the spell.

A gleam of anticipation shone in his eyes as he hooked

his fingers in the waistband of his trunks and worked them down his legs. He stepped out of the garment, kicking it aside with a casual nudge of his foot. He made no attempt to hide his body, but straightened up and stood proudly, legs apart, gentle breeze ruffling his hair.

He was magnificent, she thought, staring greedily, her heart dancing a wild conga in her chest. An imposing erection jutted from the thicket of dark hair at the junction of his thighs.

With a swift motion, he bunched up his muscles and launched himself into the water. Moments later, his dark head, sleek as an otter, surfaced beside her.

She splashed a fistful of water in his face. "You'll have to catch me first." Evading his reach, she flipped away with a strong stroke.

He laughed. "You'll not get away so easily." Powerful strokes propelled him through the water in hot pursuit, but she succeeded in staying a hair's breadth ahead of his grasp. Just as she thought she'd make good her escape, he caught up with her, grabbed her flailing ankle and hauled her back, giggling, into the now waist-deep water and his waiting arms.

"*Mo Dhia*, you're fast," he panted.

She was as breathless as he was. It's the exertion, she told herself. This was what she had wanted. She'd chosen the time and the place, and now she intended to choose the means of his seduction. She had never been the seducer before. But she was a quick study. She'd get the hang of it before long.

"You didn't tell me you could swim like a fish. Another few yards, and you'd have had a drowned man on your conscience." His laughing words belied the intensity of his expression.

Slowly, sensually, she trailed a finger down his chest while holding his gaze with her own. His eyes were amazing – an exotic, gold-flecked chocolate brown with a slightly lighter rim around the irises, surrounded by lashes that seemed impossibly long when spiky with dampness.

"I didn't want to scare you off, Kincaid. Lots of men are intimidated by athletic women."

He cupped her face in both hands. "Not a problem. I've always loved athletes. You're beautiful, *Mhuirnín*, You leave me breathless."

Her heart melted. He was making the seduction easy. She raised her mouth to his and nipped his lower lip, and, sucking gently, drew it into her mouth with exquisite care before releasing it. She heard his quick intake of breath. He smelled of sunshine and fresh water.

"What does '*Mhuirnín*' mean?"

"It means 'sweetheart' or 'dearest one' in Gaelic," he answered as his hand captured one of her breasts and his thumb circled the nipple, teasing the bud until she wanted to scream.

Her heart thundered in her ears. "How lovely it sounds." Her voice trailed off as his questing fingers found her other breast. She twined her arms around his neck, melting inside, arching her body backwards to give his questing mouth easier access to what it craved.

"You are exquisite. Exactly the right size," he muttered before his mouth found an eager rose-coloured nipple. He sucked gently at first, then harder, flicking the nipple with his hot tongue until she cried out softly. His strong hand clasped her hips and pressed her body against his, and she could feel the evidence of his arousal hard against her naked belly. A surge of lust coursed through her veins, as powerful as a shot of straight whiskey.

As she twined her legs around his waist, the tiny rational portion of her brain that still functioned started chattering in her head. She tried to ignore the voice, but it was too loud. Whatever was she thinking? She pushed his chest. It was like pushing a rock, she thought, panicking slightly. She pushed harder.

"Wait. Stop, Kincaid. Not in the water. Let's go back to shore," she panted.

Her worried tone of voice must have pierced the haze of sensuality clouding his mind and he loosened his grip. "What? Why? Have you changed your mind?" he asked tightly.

"No, no. Nothing like that. But we can't do it here. We need protection."

His eyes widened as the realization of what she'd said registered. "Don't know what's wrong with me. I didn't bring anything," he muttered, his face a mask of dismay. "Must be lack of blood to the brain."

"I brought them," she announced smugly. "I was a Girl Scout when I was growing up. Their motto is: 'Be prepared'."

Kincaid spread out the towels in the shade.

He devoured Charley with his eyes. She strode unselfconsciously over to the pile of clothes she had dumped beside the rock, knelt down and foraged in the pockets.

Her body was, in Kincaid's opinion, perfectly proportioned, like pure poetry – all dips and hills that glistened with water droplets and mysterious valleys that invited closer investigation. High, firm breasts, palm-sized and perfect, thrust impudent nipples towards the sky, as if inviting his touch. Her slender body sloped in gentle curves into a tiny waist, then flared out again into shapely hips that drove him into a frenzy of desire again. A fluff of golden curls concealed the shadowed cleft between her legs.

Desire dried his mouth, and a wave of searing heat engulfed him.

"Got them." She pulled them out the roll of condoms with a triumphant gesture and waved them in the air.

The roll unfurled in the breeze.

"Good God, woman. What kind of a sex machine do you think I am? I may have great stamina, not to mention superlative recovery power, but I doubt I can do justice to all of those." He nodded in the direction of the condoms. "Not all in one day at any rate."

"Promises, promises." She laughed. Deliberately, she walked over to the towels where Kincaid reclined and knelt beside him. "Now, where were we?" she asked, and bent her head to capture his lips with her own. Her tongue slipped between his unresisting lips. Gripped with dazzling heat, she tasted, tested the slickness of his mouth and the firmness of his teeth.

His head spun. Her mouth tasted spicy, exotic, fresh. He wasn't sure if he moaned or if she did. He didn't care. He only knew he wanted her to go on and on.

"I've been thinking about this since we met," she

whispered in his ear, nibbling the lobe.

"*Mo Dhia*—" he managed as her warm, wet mouth left his ear and wandered down to his neck, where a frantic pulse hammered. Her lips lingered on the indentation above his collarbone before descending to lick a tight, masculine nipple.

He groaned. She filled his senses. He felt her lips trail a blazing path down, down, to his waiting shaft. Slowly, she grasped it in her hand, stroking, caressing until he groaned aloud. His world had narrowed to the exquisite sensations. Unbelievably, she took the entire length of him in her gorgeous mouth and worshipped him with her tongue, tousled hair tumbling over his lap, until he thought he'd explode.

His heart turned over in his chest. Never had a woman been so generous in her loving. The openhearted gift of her entire being moved him in a way he had never anticipated. He had to end this exquisite agony or it would be over for him long before her release had begun.

"*Mhuirnín*," he whispered hoarsely, his entire frame rigid with the iron restraint he imposed in order to retain control and prevent the explosive climax his body craved. "If you don't stop for a couple of minutes, there'll be no need for a condom."

She raised her head, eyes dark with passion. Her lips parted in a provocative smile. He shuddered at the loss of her warm, clever mouth, but he rolled over and gently pressed her body down before she could protest, reversing their positions so that she reclined on the towel. Her skin was golden velvet, lush, satiny, irresistible.

She laughed in triumph when he pinned her hands above her head and nudged her legs apart. He gloried in the sight of her body arching towards his with desire, her core open to his greedy gaze.

He leaned down and suckled one upthrust breast. Her skin was flushed and hot, and she made small, animal noises in the back of her throat. She tugged her hands loose and he felt her nails on his back, urging him on as he turned his attention to her other pouting nipple.

He feathered kisses over her stomach, his tongue investigating her belly button as he pressed his hand over the soft curls covering her sex. She moaned and placed her hand over his. Spinning on the verge of control, he slipped his fingers into the hot moistness of her feminine recess, toying, playing, rubbing until she shuddered in a paroxysm of sexual delight.

Already moist and swollen, ready for him, she bent her knees and opened her legs wider, arching her hips in wordless invitation. "I want you inside me," she whispered. "Now."

He grabbed one of the condoms with shaking hands, ripped off the wrapper and unrolled it to sheath himself. Kneeling between her legs, he lowered himself and probed gently, and eased into the dark, feminine mystery of her body with slow insistence.

Charley forgot about the hardness of the ground. Oblivious of everything except the pulsing ache building in her lower body, she clutched his hips with both hands, wrapped her legs around his waist, and wordlessly urged him deeper.

He ground his mouth onto hers, muscles quivering, desperate for his release, but delaying the final thrust until he knew she was ready.

She savoured the power. She, and she alone, had brought him to this brink. He whispered something in Gaelic into her ear, and the tenderness in his voice undid her, sending her over the edge.

"Ahhh, Kincaid," she whispered, helpless, as her world exploded into a million brilliant sparks around her in a shuddering climax that left her breathless.

Kincaid groaned and thrust himself deeper into her willing and pliant body, quicker and quicker, until he stiffened and called her name.

She stared into his face, glorying in her power, as he exploded.

For several minutes, before her brain started functioning normally again, Charley gloried in the warm weight pressing her to the ground and smiled dreamily. Never in her life had she been so consumed by passion. Kincaid's lovemaking had affected her in a way she had never experienced before. She could easily fall in love.

An alarm clanged a warning in her head as reality

returned with a thud. How could she have been so stupid? Why hadn't she seen it coming? Making love with Kincaid wasn't supposed to feel this good. This right.

Fall in love? That's only the afterglow talking, she reassured herself. The feeling would soon pass. She wasn't foolish enough to lose her heart to a man ever again, especially to a rogue like Kincaid. This was merely an entertaining way to while away a bright afternoon with an attractive man in a romantic setting.

Who the hell are you trying to kid? The voice in her head persisted. *You know you're a goner.*

Charley gritted her teeth. She may have lost her heart, but she still owned her pride. She'd never give Kincaid the satisfaction of knowing she'd just made the biggest mistake of her life.

She tried to wiggle away, shoving with all her might. "Kincaid, I think a sharp rock is going to cause permanent damage to an important part of my anatomy if you don't roll over and let me up," she said, a note of alarm in her voice.

He groaned and heaved himself up, taking the brunt of his weight on his elbows. He studied her for a moment, then feathered soft kisses on her mouth, eyelids and the tip of her nose, before rolling off to sit on the towel.

Her heart melted at his gentleness. She might as well take what he offered while it was available. She'd have plenty of time to nurse her shattered heart when she returned to San Francisco.

He looked down at her recumbent body. "You're very quiet all of a sudden."

"I didn't expect to enjoy myself so much," she said truthfully. "Makes me nervous."

"I've never been seduced before," he said, running his hand possessively down the curves and slopes of her body. "It could become addictive."

She couldn't help smiling. "First time I've tried the seduction route. I'm either a fast learner or a natural. Maybe with a little more practice when I return home—"

She got no further. He silenced her mouth with a leisurely kiss that left her nerve ends tingling and came close to destroying her composure. She pulled him on top of her again.

Later, when she found her voice again, she whispered: "I don't want this afternoon to end."

"We have hours ahead of us before it starts getting dark."

Two hours later, the sun made its slow descent towards the purple-hazed mountains.

The jaguar crouched in the bamboo thicket, yellow eyes gleaming with rage and frustration. The animal eyed the shotgun and machete lying within arm's reach of the laughing couple intertwined on the towel while part of her feline brain debated the advisability of attacking them immediately.

The jaguar bared her teeth in a soundless snarl, then turned and padded away on silent paws. A low growl rumbled in the back of her throat.

The perfect opportunity would present itself before long.

Chapter 26

Charley fluffed up her pillow and studied the two sleeping forms in bed beside her. Kincaid slept on his side facing her, one hand under his head and the other resting on her thigh. Horrie, cuddled up in the crook of Kincaid's legs, had rolled onto his back, legs splayed in an undignified position. Both jaws hung open, both chests rose and fell peacefully.

A smile touched her lips as she remembered how she had floated through the rest of the day and evening in a sensual haze. She still didn't trust Kincaid as far as she could throw him, but she was willing to toss her bleak mood aside and make the most of her one-night stand. Or, to be more precise, her *four*-night stand. Regrets and recriminations could come later.

When Kincaid had invited her to move into his cabin, she'd accepted eagerly. At least she wouldn't need to worry about Leila's disturbing proximity – only his.

She sighed, rolled over, and snuggled her butt against Kincaid's warmth. He mumbled something in Gaelic and flung his arm around her waist, drawing her closer to his bare chest. Her last thought before dropping off to sleep was that she couldn't remember feeling this happy and secure in her entire life.

The vivid nightmare shattered Charley's slumber. She stirred in her sleep, kicking off the thin blanket.

In her dream, she looked down at her body and wasn't surprised to see a thick pelt of mahogany fur patterned with underlying blotches of ebony rosettes covering powerful legs and paws.

Her entire body jerked from the effort of slicing through tissue and bone.

The dream became fragmented and blurred, sliding

away in a confusion of more blood, butchery and betrayal until she knew she must run to save her own life. Her legs refused to move and her feet felt as if they were stuck in quicksand. Danger crept closer on stealthy feet.

She jerked awake to find herself crouched, shivering and naked, on a hard wooden floor, her heart pounding like a jackhammer. She cast frantic eyes around the unfamiliar room and scrabbled backwards until her back touched the wall. A shadowy form materialized above her and she felt a pair of firm hands grasping her bare shoulders. A jolt of sheer terror sizzled along overstretched nerves.

Kincaid's low, familiar voice broke the spell that immobilized her. "Wake up, lass. Hush. It's only a bad dream."

She gasped, then relaxed. "Kincaid. Thank God it's you."

"Take it easy. You're trembling."

The tension in her chest started to ease. She tried to haul herself to her feet and flopped back onto the floor. Tears of terror dampened her cheeks. "W-what happened?"

"That must have been some nightmare." He shook his head in disbelief. "You woke me up."

She clung to the strong arms that grasped her shoulders. "It was horrible. There was blood, so much blood, so much…." Her voice trailed away uncertainly.

"I'll get the light."

The golden glow dispelled the last remnants of her dream. Kincaid returned with a box of tissues and crouched beside her again. He pulled out a fistful and handed the wad to Charley. "Blow."

Mortified, she turned her head away and blew her nose before making a stab at the mop-up job. She wished he'd turn off the light. She never looked her best with a streaming nose.

"Come away to bed. You can tell me about it in the morning." Meekly, she allowed him to pull her to her feet and didn't complain when he put his arm around her as she stumbled back to bed.

Too drained to protest, she huddled close to the warm form beside her and closed her eyes. The faint memory lingering on the edge of her consciousness slipped away, along with her knowledge of the truth.

Some time later, she awoke with a start, her head filled with loud buzzing, a sure precursor to one of her flashbacks. This was no dream. Kincaid slept, oblivious of the humming and eerie coldness seeping into the cabin, but Horrie leaped off the bed and disappeared into a corner. Unable to utter a sound, Charley surrendered to the pull and allowed the swirling darkness and noise to draw her into her past life.

The last echoes of the conch trumpet faded.

Zanazca noted with envy that Kele-Pe, seated in regal splendour on the massive granite throne, drew the gaze of every person in the vast crowd. She and Nama, his acolytes and surrogate children, flanked the throne. All three were clad in ceremonial garments and headdresses, as befitted the auspicious occasion.

Zanazca stared in wonder at the throng. Nobility from Kele-Pe's Xi territory and high-ranking dignitaries from the northern and eastern lands clustered in the courtyard. More spilled over the edge of the platform and down the steps of the pyramid. Merchants, farmers and commoners filled the Grand Plaza. The moving, heaving mass chanted its approval.

She lowered her eyes and smiled to herself. This could mean only one thing. Her mentor would announce his successor today. The beloved land of her forefathers stretched from the great-water-that-had-no-end, to the neighbouring allied lands on the east and north, and the hostile, primitive races of the south.

Zanazca had long believed she was the logical choice to be Kele-Pe's successor as High Priestess and ruler of the vast western Xi territory. Countless times, her master had confided his wish that Nama possessed her agile mind, her courage, her leadership.

Kele-Pe's benign smile creased his face. He raised his hands.

A hush fell over the crowd. The wild cry of a circling eagle was audible in the sudden stillness. Zanazca raised her eyes to the sky and gave thanks. The eagle, a symbol of power and transformation, represented an auspicious omen to mark her official presentation as Kele-Pe's acolyte and successor.

Kele-Pe's voice rang out, its rich tones filling the temple and carrying far. "People of the Xi, I wish to thank you for your presence. Today, I wish to make two announcements."

Zanazca turned her head to gaze at Nama, and smiled. He would be happy for her, and delighted to pursue his own passions of anatomy and surgery.

"First, I wish to announce my successor."

Zanazca held her breath.

"I name Nama, son of my heart, as the next High Priest and ruler of the Xi."

The crowd buzzed with excitement.

Zanazca shook her head. There must be some mistake. Kele-Pe would not betray her in this way. She opened her mouth to protest, but no sound emerged.

"I have a second proclamation to make. I wish also to announce the betrothal of my beloved Zanazca, daughter of my heart and handmaiden of the great Jaguar God, to U-Kix-Chan, ruler of the greatest city to the east. She will remain here for thirteen more moons to learn the mystic arts before she travels east to meet her betrothed."

Kele-Pe lifted his voice. "Thus, my succession is ensured and my daughter's marriage will bind our territories in the strongest alliance the world has known."

The crowd's murmur swelled into a full-throated roar of approval.

Zanazca's heart fell to the pit of her stomach. Unaware of her movements, she darted to stand in front of Kele-Pe, her hands clutching his in supplication.

"Disappointment fills your heart, little one," he whispered. "We will talk later." He arose and stepped between Nama and Zanazca, raising his hands. When the crowd stilled, his voice rang out. "My announcement today marks a new era of peace and prosperity that no man or woman dare contravene.

250

Chapter 27

The first thing Kincaid saw when he opened his eyes in the predawn greyness was a tumble of tawny curls on the pillow beside him. The owner of the curls slept on her side with her luscious butt nestled against his growing erection.

Life didn't get any better than this.

Charley rolled over onto her back and muttered a string of unintelligible words. When her elbow connected with Kincaid's arm, her eyes flew open, blinked twice and focused on his face. A lazy smile curved her lips. In her half-sleep, she'd thrown one arm over her head, like a defenceless child.

Kincaid knew that her fragile appearance was deceptive. Under the vulnerability ran a gutsy streak of independence coupled with a will of iron that rivalled his own. Admittedly, she'd taken too long for his comfort to make the first move, but when she finally made up her mind, she went after what she wanted with a vengeance. Happily, she wanted him – at least in the short term.

A pang of uneasiness gripped Kincaid's belly at the thought of how large and empty his bed would feel without Charley in it after she returned home.

Get a grip, lad. A quick fling was what she wanted, and a quick fling was what she'd get. No strings attached.

A brief affair was all he wanted, too.

He leaned over to press a light kiss on her forehead. "Good morning, *Mhuirnín*," he whispered, winding a curl around his fingers. Her eyes darkened and her rosy lips parted. He pulled her head towards him for a long, drugging kiss.

When he released her, she stretched and smiled like a contented cat. "For a split second, I didn't remember where I was. Then I saw you, and it all came rushing back. You *did*

251

tell me to make the first move, didn't you?" She reached up and stroked his cheek.

Kincaid turned his head to dig his teeth gently into the fleshy part of her palm. "Aye. And a fine, thorough job you made of your first move, not to mention your second and third."

She lowered her eyes modestly. "My mother always told me, 'If a job's worth doing, it's worth doing well.'"

He swept his hand down the silky length of the lithe body stretched out beside him. "Remind me to thank your mother. By the way, what took you so long to make up your mind?"

She grinned and shrugged. "Cold feet, nerves, pride, all of the above. I'm still in a state of shock that I scraped up the courage to seduce you."

He traced a slow, sensual pattern down her body with his finger and heard her soft sigh as she snuggled closer. A dark, hot hunger rose within him. "I'm very happy you did," he whispered against her lips, "but this time, it's my turn to make the first move."

He drew her closer and buried his face in the softness of her neck, inhaling the light fragrance of her skin. He intended to make the most of the precious remaining time.

He would make Charley care about him so much that when he dredged up the courage to confess his youthful substance abuse, she would be able to overlook his dependency and see the real person behind the disease.

A long time later, Charley lay curled on her side, her head nestled on Kincaid's shoulder, intensely aware of the warm, muscled arm pinning her to the bed. One by one, he was slowly toppling her carefully constructed barriers against men. Despite the afterglow of a woman who's been well and truly loved, dispirited thoughts crept into her head. She tried to block out the memory of the desperate, shattering passion of her response to his lovemaking.

She had lived without him once, and she'd learn to live without him again. Now was not a good time to deal with the conflicting emotions churning in her chest.

Kincaid's breathing was deep and even in her ear, but

she knew he was awake. Disentangling herself, she swung her feet over the side of the bed and grabbed her robe. Injecting a note of levity into her voice, she said: "We can't lie in bed all day, Kincaid. Don't you have men to manage and rocks to move?"

She watched his jaw tighten as he raised himself on one elbow. "Are you going to tell me what's wrong?" he said in a neutral voice. "Did I hurt you? I got pretty carried away."

She widened her eyes in genuine surprise, taken aback by the question. "Absolutely not." Her voice softened. "I loved every minute of our lovemaking. I'm just afraid I'm distracting you from your work."

He raised one eyebrow. "Are you sure there's nothing else bothering you?"

He was too damned perceptive. "No nothing. Really." She stretched her mouth in a bright smile. "I'm a little tired."

His body relaxed slightly. "Can't say as I'm surprised. You had a rough night."

Worse than he would ever know. "I did?" she said lightly, feigning a memory lapse.

"Do you want to tell me about it?"

Dammit, Kincaid's uncanny ability to read her mind was unsettling. The truth would only raise dark suspicions about her sanity. Evasion was the answer. Although he didn't realize it, he'd already witnessed a couple of her attacks, thinking they were heat stroke. If she admitted to dreaming she was a jaguar or experiencing flashbacks about being an Olmec priestess, he'd dump her in the blink of an eye. She wouldn't blame him.

Charley forced another brilliant smile and perched on the edge of the bed. "I guess I had a nightmare. I don't remember much of it. Funny how even the scariest dreams fade away."

"You were talking about blood," he prompted.

Dammit. She hadn't realized she'd spoken aloud in her dream. "That's a scary thought. The truth is, this place gets to me. Too much imagination, too many ghosts."

He kissed her on the nose and said lightly: "I'm glad to hear it has nothing to do with the ridiculous notion of reincarnation this time. Now, much as I wish I could stay and make love with you for the rest of the day, you were right. I need some breakfast and then I'll head up to the tunnel."

She controlled the urge to shake some sense into his thick, cynical skull and jumped to her feet again. "Great. I'll come, too. I want to interview some of your archaeologists, and I don't want to walk to the dig alone. I might run into another snake, or worse, the jaguar."

He threw back the sheet, revealing the entire bronzed length of his body to her avid gaze. "You'll be on your own when we reach the dig site," he warned. "I want to keep an eye on the crew, particularly Felipe, so I'll be working all morning in the tunnel."

He wrapped a striped towel low around his hips in preparation for a shower. The man looked good – mouth-watering good. Charley dragged her mind away from the sensual thoughts swirling through her head. "Okay. When I'm finished my interviews, I'll wait for you in the courtyard."

"Aye, then. Don't be going off anywhere alone."

Her interviews completed, Charley climbed the pyramid slowly, taking in the view. She gloried in the sweep of dappled, mountain-borne clouds against the deepening blue of the sky.

The archaeologists had answered her questions graciously, she thought with a touch of satisfaction. She'd compiled an entire volume of notes about the Olmecs – everything from preferred cooking methods, to ritual weapons used during human sacrifices, to surgical procedures, at which, her informant asserted, the ancient race was skilled.

None of the information had come as a surprise to Charley.

The interviews had eaten up the entire morning, and she was eager to tell Kincaid she'd finished her work for the day. She smiled to herself. Perhaps she could convince him to spend another lazy afternoon at the swimming hole. A man needed some fun after hauling rocks all morning.

She eyed the tunnel with distaste and felt a pang of sympathy for the men working in the breathless heat of the claustrophobic space. If she let Kincaid know she would wait for him outside, she could enjoy the serenity of the courtyard in peaceful solitude.

Mission accomplished, she exited the tunnel and sucked a cleansing breath into her lungs, grateful for the fresh air. Then she sank onto a boulder and let the breeze ruffle her hair. A bee buzzed around her head. What was a bee doing at this altitude? The sound increased in volume until it sounded like an entire swarm. *It can't be happening again. Not so soon*, were her last thoughts before the spinning darkness sucked her up.

Zanazca fluttered her eyelashes. "Meet me at midnight inside the sacred cave," she told Nama in her sultriest voice.

His eyes kindled with joy. "I thought you hated me. You have refused to talk to me or even to look into my eyes for two moons."

"I feel no anger in my heart," she lied. "Only sadness over my departure."

"Grief fills my heart also, but we must obey Kele-Pe. Our master does what he thinks is best, Zana," he said earnestly.

Nama must not suspect the rage smouldering in her heart. She smiled sweetly and widened her eyes to disguise her bitterness. "I know he feels boundless love for us. I will bow to the destiny he has chosen for me." She stepped into Nama's arms and submitted to his kiss, letting her mind wander.

For two moons she had held her peace and plotted careful revenge against the two men who had betrayed her. She cast her mind back to the fateful afternoon that had changed her life and the existence of those around her, in ways they did not yet comprehend.

The look of stunned joy on Nama's face at Kele-Pe's announcement would remain imprinted in her mind forever. The young man who had professed to love her, who had always bowed to her superiority, had preened with satisfaction at his unexpected rise to favour. Nama's reaction to Kele-Pe's fateful proclamation had sealed his fate.

Tonight, she would exact her revenge.

Some day soon, Zanazca thought, she would take care of her master as well. First, he must proclaim her as his successor. If he was willing to sacrifice her happiness in favour of appointing a weakling as his acolyte and heir, then she was willing to make him pay the ultimate price for his betrayal.

She thrust Nama away. "We must make the most of our remaining time together," she whispered. "Now I will go. People must not see us talking or their lips will flap."

She felt Nama's heated gaze following her departure.

At midnight, Zanazca entered the cavern, confident that Nama would be waiting.

He opened his arms and she flew to him, allowing her lips to feather his cheek. She placed his hand on her breast, smiling at the expression of avid lust on his face. "See how my heart beats for you, Nama," she whispered, feeling the unmistakable evidence of his arousal against her belly. That was a good sign. He'd follow her anywhere. After a lingering kiss, calculated to leave him breathless, she grasped his hand and tugged. "Not here. I will take you into the tunnels where no one will spy on us."

He pulled a torch from the wall and followed like an obedient puppy.

Deeper, deeper into the labyrinth, she pulled her willing captive.

"Isn't this far enough?" he asked plaintively.

Zanazca stopped. "We are in the right spot. Let me take the torch and free up your hands." She tucked the burning torch into a crevice where it continued to burn.

She stroked his face once. "Now, I am ready. I have long waited for this moment." Both palms against his chest, she put all her weight behind the sharp shove.

Nama's eyes registered surprise, then bewildered horror as he teetered for an endless moment on the edge of the yawning abyss before he cartwheeled out of sight.

His drawn-out shriek lasted longer than she thought possible before it ceased abruptly.

The sinkhole had served its purpose. Before the mourning period passed, Kele-Pe would name his rightful successor – Zanazca.

An anxious voice penetrated Charley's fog-filled brain. "Wake up. What's wrong with you? Should I, like, get you some help?"

Charley opened her eyes and squinted at a blur of vibrant pink floating in front of her face. The numbing chill faded as the sun warmed her skin. At first, her eyes refused to focus. She rubbed them and blinked. After a few seconds, the hazy face of the buxom student who had been hanging around Kincaid like an annoying shadow swam into view. The hot pink tank top finished off the job of clearing her vision. Charley opened and closed her mouth then found her voice. "I'm fine. I must have dozed off."

The student looked at her sceptically. "It must have been some dream you were having. You were shaking so hard I thought you'd fall off the boulder. I've been, like, trying to wake you for the last five minutes."

Charley pulled herself together, blood pounding in her ears. The flashbacks, increasingly disturbing, were coming closer together. She couldn't face making inane conversation with this young woman right now. She forced a smile. "Thank you for wanting to help, I'm fine. I'd like to be left alone here for a few minutes to clear my head."

The student frowned, then shrugged. "Knock yourself out," and walked away. When she was almost out of sight behind a pile of rubble, Charley heard a muttered: "Bitch."

Charley's peace was short-lived. Thirty seconds later, the crunch of approaching footsteps alerted her to a nearby presence.

Chapter 28

Kincaid cast his gaze around the empty temple area and courtyard and frowned, glancing at his watch. He was fifteen minutes later than he'd anticipated, but he wasn't worried. Charley had said she would wait outside in the courtyard and her backpack was slung on the bench. He didn't believe she would leave without an explanation.

Impatience changed to gnawing anxiety.

The entire area was devoid of life. His crew had set off down the pyramid steps towards camp and their lunch.

A movement behind the altar caught his eye and he heaved a sigh of relief. "Charley. Are you there?" he called, heading towards the flash of fluorescent pink.

The blonde, well-endowed student straightened up and stepped away from the stone carving she'd been tracing. Her eyes glinted with a flirtatious light. "Will I do?"

Kincaid recognized her immediately and hoped his disappointment didn't show on his face. He'd been avoiding this young woman ever since the last happy hour. "Maybe you can help," he replied, ignoring her blatant innuendo. "Have you seen Charley?"

Her face fell. "Oh, sure. She was here."

Kincaid's impatience mounted. He raked his fingers through his hair. "Did you see where she went?"

"Um, yeah. She was acting all weird. Claimed she had fallen asleep, but I could tell she was more, like, unconscious."

"I seriously doubt that."

She shrugged. "Whatever. After I shake her for five minutes, she wakes up and blows me off, all embarrassed. Then Felipe comes out of the tunnel and cozies up to her. She doesn't seem to mind chatting with *him* for a couple of minutes. Next thing I know, they're heading down the path together." She indicated the narrow trail carved into the steep hillside and smiled spitefully. "Better watch out, lover-boy. I think your field director may be giving you some tough competition."

Something inside Kincaid went very still. Felipe had left the tunnel in a tearing hurry, leaving Kincaid and the men to finish up and stack the tools – almost as if he was following Charley. He couldn't imagine her leaving with Felipe voluntarily.

Kincaid peered down the path. "I don't see them."

"They, like, took a cutoff halfway down and disappeared over the top of the next rise."

"Thanks," Kincaid muttered and took off down the path at a gallop.

Overcome by a sense of wrongness, Charley dug in her heels and halted.

Felipe grunted in surprise as he skidded to a stop to avoid crashing into her back.

She must be out of her mind, traipsing off with Felipe because he claimed he knew a secret that would guarantee her a journalistic prize.

"What is wrong?" he asked.

She turned and eyed him warily. She didn't like the wild look in his eyes. "We've walked far enough, Felipe. I can't see the temple anymore and I left my backpack behind. I'm not taking another step until you tell me what's so confidential you don't want Kincaid to know."

Felipe blocked her retreat, his lips compressed in a white line. "I am taking you to a secret place to show you proof of Kincaid's guilt."

"Guilt?"

"*Sí*. He is the cause of all the accidents on the dig."

She placed her hands on her hips. "You're out of your mind."

Felipe drew his lip back from his teeth in a lop-sided snarl. "Any normal man would have given up. If Kincaid was not so persistent, I would not need to go to these lengths to preserve my ancestors' privacy."

Charley stared, a trickle of fear shimmering in her heart. "What the hell are you talking about?"

"He intrudes on the sanctity of my ancestors. I must stop him."

Charley placed one foot behind the other, edging backwards. This man was seriously deranged. Did he really believe he was a descendant of the Olmecs? More pieces of the puzzle clicked into place. "You mean, *you* caused the accident in the tunnel?" she asked, trying to keep her voice steady.

"My duty is clear."

Her blood ran cold. The man was clearly unbalanced. She cursed herself for not slipping her Swiss army knife into her pocket before leaving Kincaid's cabin. It might not have been much of a match for the machete swinging from Felipe's belt, but it would have been something.

Charley found her voice. "Kincaid respects the mysteries of the past. He would never do anything to disrespect your ancestors."

He lowered his voice to a confidential whisper. "Some mysteries must remain so. If I do not stop Kincaid, he will destroy everything."

She tightened her jaw, pulse racing. "I'm heading back to the temple. I was crazy to come with you in the first place."

"No. You will come with me."

The note of determination made her skin crawl. Frantic thoughts skittered around in her mind like frenzied mice. Felipe had obviously crossed the line between sanity and madness. She couldn't allow him to abduct her without a fight. She had to say something to distract him.

"Your ancestors would not want you to do this."

Felipe's eyes were feral. "The desecration must be halted."

He was too far-gone to listen to reason. She took a deep breath and summoned up enough bravado to answer. "You'll never get away with abducting me."

A combination of rage and frustration darkened Felipe's face. "You take his side," he snarled. "The gods demand retribution." He snaked out his hand and grasped Charley's arm before she could run, and started speaking in a guttural language – one that was neither English, nor Spanish.

She listened in disbelief, her mind whirling. The sense of the words penetrated her brain even as she tried to squirm away. He spoke an ancient tongue, but she understood every word of the blood-chilling threat he uttered.

His hand felt like a hot, leathery vice clamped around her wrist. She tugged, terror fuelling her resistance. "Let go."

He merely tightened his grip and pulled her along the path, his face contorted with rage.

Using her free hand, she raked her nails across the hand gripping her wrist. Caught unaware, he cursed and staggered backwards, releasing her arm. Seizing the opportunity, she darted to grab a rock and flung it with desperate strength. It flew towards his head and sailed harmlessly past, missing its mark by less than an inch.

"You will pay for that," he barked, and lunged at her. His hand whipped out and nearly dragged her arm from its socket as he hauled her towards him and slapped her across the face twice, openhanded. Her knees buckled but he yanked her around with a brutal jerk, forcing her back against his chest and holding her immobile by hooking one arm around her neck.

Charley's ears rang with the force of the blows. She nearly fainted from the pain that mushroomed in her head. He tightened the pressure on her neck, squeezing her windpipe.

A snarl twisted Felipe's face into a mask of hatred. "I always knew you spelled trouble. Tonight, your blood will feed the Jaguar God."

Charley gasped for air and her blood ran cold. How could she have been so stupid as to follow Felipe meekly into the hills? Determined to buy some time until Kincaid found her, she fired up a frantic prayer for inspiration.

The answer exploded into her head.

Out of the corner of her eye, Charley could see Felipe's feet, clad only in leather *huaraches*. He'd claimed he had no need of boots – snakes did not attack him. She raised one knee as high as possible and smashed the reinforced heel of her borrowed boot down on his unprotected foot with all her weight. It landed with a satisfying crunch.

Felipe screeched with pain, but refused to release his prey, his breath hissing in her ear.

Charley was sure she'd broken some of the small bones in his instep. She'd heard something snap like a dry twig.

He shifted his grip, hands scrabbling to clutch her neck.

Big mistake. He'd find out she wasn't a mere helpless female. She lashed backwards again, this time at his shins.

With uncanny accuracy, he seemed to sense her intentions and tried to dance away, hampered by his broken foot.

Charley felt a rush of satisfaction when her foot connected solidly with bone.

The Mexican howled again.

Felipe tightened his crushing grip on her throat, breathing heavily on the back of her neck and spraying her with saliva. His iron fingers tightened.

Charley panicked, clawing at his arms in a futile attempt to drag his crushing hands away. Using her nails, she raked his skin, slashing until blood gushed.

He cursed at the unexpected onslaught and slackened his grip.

The momentary loosening was enough for Charley to drag in one tortured breath before her throat closed up again. The pain was unbearable. Her vision darkened and she slipped to the ground. Her entire world had narrowed to the stench of his breath on her face.

An appalling high-pitched bellow ripped the stillness.

The dreadful roar pierced the black mist that threatened to obliterate her senses. Small hairs on her arms stood on end. Felipe turned to meet this new and fearsome threat and the pressure on her neck ceased abruptly.

She slumped to the ground and wheezed in deep, life-giving breaths of air. When her brain started to function normally again, it dawned on her that the terrifying sound was the savage battle cry only an irate Highlander could utter.

Recognition and relief overwhelmed her.

Felipe whirled and pulled the machete from his belt. Sunlight glinted off the wicked-looking blade.

Transfixed with horror, Charley watched, helpless.

A deadly fighting machine, Felipe swung his lethal

weapon at Kincaid's head.

Quick reflexes saved Kincaid's life as he ducked away.

Felipe advanced slowly, blood streaming down his outstretched arm to the hand that gripped the broad, heavy knife.

Kincaid maintained eye contact while he backed away. "You'll never get away with this, Felipe."

Felipe's face contorted with rage, his eyes wild. He brandished the machete, bellowing: "Willingly, I sacrifice myself for my cause. I will see you in hell before I let you desecrate the dead." Spittle flew from his mouth in a foul froth.

Kincaid backed up until his retreat was blocked by a tumble of large boulders.

Felipe held the weapon in a practised hand, swaying hypnotically, brandishing it at shoulder height, ready to slash.

Kincaid followed the horizontal arc with his gaze and tensed his legs, crouching slightly, balanced on the balls of his feet.

Felipe raised the machete to deliver a killing blow and lunged.

As soon as the weapon started its downward path towards his unprotected head, Kincaid danced away.

Charley gasped in horror as the razor-sharp blade grazed a path of red, slicing Kincaid's shoulder. A blossom of blood unfurled on the front of his shirt.

He regained his balance, ramming his fist into Felipe's belly.

The Mexican grunted with pain and doubled over, straining to remain on his feet, still clutching the machete. He spat, then straightened up, and advanced slowly, favouring his injured foot.

Crouched on the ground, Charley could smell the rich, ripe sweat drenching Felipe's body. The potent force of Kincaid's blow had slowed him down for only a moment. The madman advanced, robot-like, balancing the machete in front of him.

"You have nowhere to run, Kincaid. You are a dead man." Again, Felipe threw all his weight behind the swinging blow.

Kincaid leaped backwards.

Heart in her mouth, Charley watched the lethal dance. It almost looked choreographed, the movements surreal against the hot, glaring backdrop of rocks and scrubby yucca and prickly pear baking in the white-hot sun.

Kincaid weaved in front of Felipe trying to stay alive, barely an inch from the flying knife-blade.

Felipe charged blindly towards the taller man, sweat streaming down his face. He bellowed with rage and frustration as his flailing blade met with empty air again. He continued the deadly pursuit, hampered by his disabled foot.

Kincaid's unwavering gaze never left the machete. When the weapon reached the furthest arc of its outward sweep, he planted his feet firmly in a forward stance, then whirled around and launched himself in the air. His foot connected with the Mexican's chin in a perfectly executed snap kick.

After a sickening crack, they both went down in a tangle of arms and legs.

Kincaid raised himself painfully to his elbows, pushing Felipe's dead weight aside. He felt for a pulse and heaved a sigh of relief. The bastard was still alive. He dropped the wrist he was holding and staggered towards Charley.

Unmoving, she stared at him, then launched herself into his arms. So great was Kincaid's relief, the pain of his wound barely registered.

"Thank you," she croaked. "You saved my life."

Kincaid folded his arms around Charley, feeling the steady thump of her heart beating against his chest. After a moment, he ran his hands over her back, her neck, her face, reassuring himself she was unhurt. "I knew something was wrong when you weren't waiting in the courtyard." He heaved a deep breath. "You wouldn't go far without telling me."

"I thought he would kill you," she said and burst into tears.

It's only the aftermath of an adrenaline rush, Kincaid told himself, but the unexpected depth of her emotions caught him unprepared. He wrapped his arms around her again and simply rocked her against his chest. When the storm subsided, he drew back and cradled her face, using his thumbs to wipe away her scalding tears. "When I saw Felipe choking you, I thought I'd lost you. I was ready to tear the bastard apart, limb by limb, with my bare hands." He trailed his fingers down to skim her bruised throat. "I should have killed him for hurting you."

She winced. "I'll live. I'm only bruised." She drew back, her eyes filled with concern. "You're the one who's badly hurt."

Kincaid pulled the torn fabric aside to examine his shoulder and poked gingerly at the wound. "It's not too deep. I don't think I'll even need stitches."

Charley closed her eyes for a second. When she opened them, he was surprised to see tears swimming in their depths. "I've never been so afraid in my entire life." Her voice wavered. "I thought I'd lost you forever."

The desolation in her voice led Kincaid to believe that perhaps Charley's feelings ran deeper than she'd admit. He allowed the faint burst of hope to expand and growled: "The bastard was hurting you. Do you seriously believe a madman wielding a wee machete could stop me?"

She looked away. "I'm so sorry. It was all my fault. I tried to get away from him, but—"

"Shhhh, lass."

"What do you plan to do with him?" She jerked her chin at the spot where Felipe had fallen. Her mouth opened and closed, but no words emerged.

He turned and followed the direction of her shocked gaze. Sun-baked rock in a landscape devoid of life spread out before him, barren and empty. The machete, harmless now, lay half-buried in the dirt.

"The bastard's disappeared!" Kincaid grated out: "He's probably hightailing it to the nearest village."

Charley shuddered. "I'm afraid we haven't seen the last of him."

Kincaid's eyes hardened as he thought of how close Felipe had come to killing Charley. "If he returns, he'll regret the day he was born."

Chapter 29

Charley watched Kincaid's chest rise and fall while the antibiotic Colin had administered coursed its way through his bloodstream. Tears filled her eyes at the pain he had endured on her behalf. She stroked his forehead and brushed the damp hair off his face before she tiptoed out the door of his cabin into the afternoon brightness.

Thoughts and impressions she'd suppressed rushed back. The events of the day swept over her in a confused jumble of danger, pain and violence that set her nerves jumping. She moistened dry lips with the tip of her tongue. Felipe had nearly killed her. Worse, her unthinking stupidity had almost caused Kincaid's death as well.

She plopped down in the wooden chair and sighed. Kincaid had leaped to her rescue, confronting Felipe with no thought for his own safety. And soon, very soon, she was going to show her gratitude by betraying him to save her mother.

What kind of monster was she?

Her brain skittered away from the unthinkable deed she was determined to commit. Unable to contemplate a future of certain loneliness and self-loathing, she forced herself to focus on Felipe's attack. Her skin crawled as she recalled the threat he had thrown in her face. He had intended to sacrifice her on the altar. Her flashbacks must have opened a channel of communication she'd never known existed, because she had understood every word of the Olmec language he'd used.

Her stomach lurched. She sensed the flashbacks were inexorably drawing her closer to uncovering the truth — revelations she wasn't a hundred percent certain she was ready to face. In some mysterious way, the past had started to intertwine with the present and was trying to send her a message.

Until now, every flashback had occurred involuntarily. She had no idea how to invoke one but intended to find out. Unsure how to proceed, she called to mind meditation techniques. *Relax. Empty your mind. Focus on your breathing. Concentrate on the in-breath ... now, the out-breath.* Her brain settled into stillness. A bee buzzed somewhere nearby, drawing her deeper. Relaxing, she drew inward, back in time, until the humming carried her away to a distant past.

Would the old man never die? Zanazca sighed. Kele-Pe had already ingested enough poison to kill three men, but his stubborn heart refused to stop beating.

"Can I get you anything, my father?" she asked, wiping his forehead with a cool cloth.

He reached out a dry, papery hand and grasped her wrist. "Zana, my little one. You have brought me much joy."

Suppressing the shudder of distaste, she extricated her hand and held the goblet of poison-laced kakawa to his lips. "This drink will make you strong again. You must drink it all."

Obediently, he sipped the bittersweet concoction of liquid chocolate. The grimace of agony twisting his face indicated that the poison flowed through his veins. He closed his eyes and turned his head towards the wall, his breathing harsh.

Zanazca sat beside him, watching the rise and fall of his chest, willing the movement to cease. She itched to press her fingers into his windpipe and crush the life out of his frail body, but she dared not take the risk. The poison would claim his life soon enough. Only then could she begin her reign as High Priestess and ruler of the land of her people.

An hour later, Kele-Pe opened his eyes and spoke in a thready voice. "The underworld beckons. Hold my hand."

Reluctantly, she gripped his hand, feeling the frail bones shift beneath his skin.

He whispered: "My eyes grow dark, and I have much to tell you."

"What, my father?"

"Zana, you are strong and courageous, but I have long sensed a ruthlessness and streak of cunning in you. That is why I named Nama as my successor instead of you." He closed his eyes.

Her nails bit into the palm of her unencumbered hand, but she kept her voice calm and soothing, as if talking to a child. "Yes, my father. Nama showed his cowardice at your great gift and disappeared without a word of farewell."

A tear escaped from his closed eyelids and trickled down his leathery cheeks. "I never believed he would betray me."

"Now I am your successor," she prompted.

He struggled to suck in a breath of air and opened his eyes to stare at her. She shifted her weight uncomfortably and lowered her lashes. Ever since she could remember, he had always seen too much.

"My child, I had hoped I would have more time to teach you compassion before my days were ended. You must learn to temper your harshness with mercy and gentleness."

No longer trying to hide her bitterness, Zanazca raised her eyes and let Kele-Pe see what was in her heart. "You take your last breath of life, old man. There is nothing more you can do to prevent me from achieving my destiny."

A terrible realization filled his eyes before they clouded and dimmed. His last words escaped in a tortured whisper, "You will pay a terrible price," before his body went limp.

Zanazca waited for a minute then leaned over the still form and checked for a pulse. She smiled, then raised her head and called: "Uxatle. Come here."

A young girl glided into the room, eyes lowered beneath a fringe of lustrous black hair. "Yes, Mistress."

The girl raised long lashes and stared at the body on the bed. Dark eyes glowed, hot with ambition, in her impassive face.

"Kele-Pe is dead. Tomorrow, I will sit on the throne as High Priestess and you will stand by my side."

Chapter 30

Leila choked on the acrid scent of wood smoke that overpowered the cloying sweetness of incense. Eyes stinging, she peered through the murky haze swirling in the cavern, certain she would find Felipe cowering in a corner. Where else would he go? She should never have entrusted the fool with Charley's abduction. The only way to get the job done properly was to do it herself.

A voice grated from the shadows beside the altar. "What delayed you? For many hours, I have awaited your arrival."

She squinted and made out a crumpled figure sprawled on the altar steps. How dare he imply she was at fault for not dashing to his rescue? She bristled and swung her hair. "We agreed to meet at midnight, not earlier. I brought you some food, water and a blanket." She tossed a bulging canvas bag at his feet and sauntered closer, studying him.

Felipe looked like hell, and he'd look worse tomorrow. Blood caked his arm and a large bruise purpled the left side of his face. Strips of torn fabric encased his foot and ankle.

"What happened with the abduction?" She already knew the answer, but wanted to hear his version of the disaster.

Felipe dug into the bag and took several huge gulps of water. After he wiped his chin on his sleeve, he bit out: "Kincaid and the reporter overpowered me, but I escaped. There will be no ransom for the woman."

She flung herself onto the second step of the altar, taking care to leave plenty of space between herself and Felipe. "In other words, you messed up."

Felipe appeared oblivious to the accusation. "I deliberated for many hours and have reached a decision. Kincaid and the woman who calls herself Charley are dangerous. They must die. My ancestors demand the

269

sacrifice." His eyes burned with a fanatical fire and his gestures took on a fevered animation. "The jaguar will strike when the time is right."

Shocked into an uneasy silence, Leila stared at Felipe in a combination of disbelief and excited horror. She tried, but failed, to read his face. If he succeeded in carrying out his threat to kill Alistair and Charley, her hands would be clean and all her problems solved. Both her archrival and the man who had rejected her would die, leaving her path free and clear to take ownership of the dig.

Felipe's harsh bark of laughter chilled her blood.

"*Sí*. As the *gringos* say, I will kill two birds with one stone and rid myself of my greatest enemies while I pacify the gods of my forefathers. Then, you and I will commit our final undertaking together. Come. There is much to do."

She dug in her heels. She was not going to soil her hands doing Felipe's dirty work. "What final undertaking are you talking about?"

"You will help me move my revered ancestors' bones to a safe place deep in the caves."

Her eyes widened. "Bones? What bones? Are you telling me there are sarcophagi in here, and you haven't seen fit to mention them?" she hissed in disbelief.

"There was no reason to tell you."

Glad that the darkness hid her expression, she forced a note of patience into her voice. "Why should we move the bones?"

Using a stick as a crutch to assist his painful ascent, Felipe dragged himself upright, favouring the injured foot. His voice was ice-cold and resolute. "When I blast the cave tonight, the ceiling will collapse. We must move my ancestors' remains to a safe place inside the tunnels where they will rest, undisturbed, forever. I brought blankets to wrap around the bodies."

"No," she blurted, unable to prevent a dismayed gasp from escaping her lips. Her mind whirled. The fool was on the brink of a severe psychosis. He wanted to demolish the cave, destroying one of the most significant discoveries of the century – and her dreams. As long as she still had breath left in her body, she wouldn't let it happen.

"I have already placed explosives inside the cavern and at the back entrance to the caves. The devices are well-hidden and wired to satellite phones, which will act as triggers. All we need to do is move the bodies to safety before I detonate the blasts with this." He held up a satellite phone and waved it at her. "I programmed the numbers on speed-dial."

She leaped up and moved away, placing the altar between them. "No."

"Do not worry." His condescending tone angered her further; he'd spoken as if dealing with a slightly stupid pupil. "We will be perfectly safe and miles away before I press the button. I learned about remote detonation in a course I attended two years ago in Paraguay."

"You must be mad." She edged away.

He seemed surprised. "Not mad. Brilliant. No trespasser will ever enter the tunnels again."

Not if I can stop you first. She quivered at the thought of the wanton destruction he planned. The Olmec remains were her ticket to success, and she had no intention of allowing Felipe to pulverize the cave. In spite of her efforts at nonchalance, her voice quivered. "Surely, there must be a better solution."

Bleak eyes hardened as understanding dawned. "All this time, you have been lying to me. All you wanted was the power."

"No, really. I am on your side, but you must not destroy the cave."

His eyes glittered as he limped towards her, brandishing the phone. "Traitor. I thought we held the same beliefs, the same values. I have taught you everything and now you betray me."

There must be a way she could reach the man behind the madness. She waved her hand around the cave and dropped her voice to a placating whisper. "Destroying priceless artefacts is not the answer, Felipe. You cannot reduce this record of your ancestors' lives to a worthless pile of rubble. There must be another way."

A combination of rage and frustration darkened Felipe's face. "It is too late for you to change your mind now, *puta*.

You betray me." His voice shook with hurt and anger.

Leila's head whirled at the speed with which she had lost control of the discussion. Uneasiness gripped her as she began to realize she, too, might be in real danger. She edged away, but his fist shot out and grabbed a handful of her blouse, dragging her towards him.

"What are you planning to do?" Her voice cracked.

Eyes burning, he placed the phone in his back pocket still grasping her blouse with his other hand. She stared blankly at the evil-looking ceremonial knife that materialized in his hand. Flames glinted off the obsidian blade. He threw his head back and giggled wildly, his laughter filling the cavern with incongruous mirth. "You will die tonight. The gods demand retribution."

Felipe's laughter terrified Leila more than any of his threats. He was on a rollercoaster careening downhill, and she did not intend to let him drag her down along with him. Her sudden sideways jerk caused the delicate fabric of her blouse to rip.

Free of his grasping hands, she darted towards the altar and grabbed one leg of a stone incense burner, startled by its weight. The missile missed its target, but it had the desired effect. Burning embers scattered in Felipe's face like angry bees.

His roar echoed in the cavern and bounced back, magnified. He shook his head to dislodge the particles that burned into his skin. Flailing his arms, he dropped the knife. "You will pay, you traitorous bitch," he bellowed.

She didn't stay to find out what happened, but whirled and ran. Her feet tangled over Felipe's makeshift crutch. She righted herself, but not in time. He lunged before she could leap aside. Iron talons dug painfully into both her shoulders and his foul breath scalded her face. As he drew back one fist to deliver the killing blow, Leila remembered a fragment of the self-defense class for women she had taken as an undergraduate. She drew up her right knee and drove it as hard as she could into the junction between his legs.

Felipe gasped for air and doubled over in agony, clutching himself.

She staggered backwards towards the spot where he'd

dropped the knife. Silently, she sank to her knees. "Please, let me find it, please let me find it." Her hands scrabbled over the cold stone.

She should have known his fanaticism coupled with his special powers would permit him to overcome even the debilitating agony she'd inflicted. A quick glance confirmed her fears. He loomed above her, his mouth twisted in a snarl. Before she could back away, he reached out, as fast as a viper, and grabbed a handful of the long hair she was so proud of. Yanking hard, he jerked her to her feet.

An involuntary whimper escaped her throat and her eyes watered with the scalding pain.

He lowered his face until it was inches from her own. "*Puta.* You must die. I will make sure your suffering is great."

She saw the blow coming, but, immobilized as she was, she couldn't duck. His fist descended with the force of a sledgehammer.

The blow silenced her cry and flung her backward against the wall where she slumped to the ground, struggling to hold onto a thread of consciousness.

The pain was incandescent. Her head clattered with a thousand brilliant lights, as if a pinball ricocheted around in her skull. She clamped her mouth shut to prevent the moan from escaping, certain the throbbing, pulsing agony indicated that he'd shattered her cheekbone. She had to convince him she was unconscious.

Only cold determination prevented her from blacking out. Either she must kill Felipe or die trying. Consciously, she relaxed all her muscles and lay perfectly still, blocking out the pain that thundered through every cell of her body.

Several minutes passed in absolute silence. It seemed like hours. Her heart pounded in her head until she thought he must surely hear it.

Motionless, she risked a glance under veiled eyelids and controlled the telltale jolt of horror. Felipe had shed his clothes and now wore only a ceremonial cloak and a loincloth. He had found the knife, and now loomed over her body, his eyes dark, empty caverns in his impassive face.

There was only one solution.

Leila closed her eyes and cleared her mind of all

thoughts. Her spirit left her body and soared beyond the confines of the cave and into the whirling, sparkling darkness of the cosmos, seeking her *nagual*.

Where are you, my friend? She called in her mind. *Show me your resting-place. I need to occupy your body.*

Vibration and heat hummed throughout every cell. Never had her powers been so concentrated or the transformation so effortless. She felt her essence pulled into the jaguar's body by the irrevocable forces she had set in motion.

A hoarse, coughing growl lodged in her throat as she savoured the power surging through her sinewy body. The night wind ruffled her fur and she sniffed the air before gathering her legs beneath her haunches and bounding up the hill towards the tunnel and her enemy.

Felipe flung Leila's inert body onto the altar, grunting with the effort. The bitch would die, but not until she was fully conscious, aware of her fate.

"Oh, Master of Darkness," he intoned," I, your humble servant await a sign."

Several minutes passed in silence.

A furtive movement caught his eye. A sinuous shape that hadn't been there a second ago materialized from the mouth of the cave. He blinked and strained his eyes, staring in disbelief as the head and neck of the jaguar emerged from the gloom. The animal crept stealthily, padding closer on velvet paws, its belly almost touching the ground as it stalked its prey – him. Step by stealthy step, the jaguar glided closer to the altar.

The terrible truth, as impossible as it was, registered. Comprehension flooded him with terror. Leila should have been incapacitated for hours by the blow he had administered.

A series of hoarse grunts from the animal turned Felipe's insides to liquid.

How had she succeeded in shapeshifting under these circumstances? Even using peyote, he had never been able to execute the transformation so quickly or effortlessly.

The predator crouched as low to the ground as possible

without making actual contact, every muscle of her lithe body as still as a rock. Yellow eyes glowed, hot with hatred, reflecting the torchlight. The twitching tail tip flagged a wordless message of vengeance.

In a single, effortless bound, the jaguar leaped to the top of the altar, side-stepping the woman's motionless body, and poised, muscles coiled, ready to spring, Felipe backed slowly away, then turned and bolted in a futile attempt to escape the lethal claws. The searing pain in his foot and groin were irrelevant nuisances.

Felipe recognized the death shown to him not so long ago by the Master of Darkness. "No, please, not yet. I'm not ready to go into the darkness," he pleaded as he tried to out-run Death.

The last thing he felt was a crushing blow on his back and shoulders before he dropped to the ground like a stone. A feeling of lassitude crept over his body and numbing cold crept into his belly. Then ... nothingness.

The faint crackle of burning twigs marred the heavy silence of the cavern. Leila opened her eyes and blinked. Memory returned in a flash of horror. The insane bastard had intended to sacrifice her on the altar.

Thank you, my friend, she whispered into the darkness. *Thank you for saving my life.*

Numb and shaking, she pushed herself into a sitting position and tested her jaw. Perhaps it wasn't broken after all, but it ached like hell. Seconds ticked by as the magnitude of what she had done sank in.

She had killed another human being.

Hysterical laughter bubbled from her lips, surprising the hell out of her. Shouldn't she feel contrition or at least a twinge of remorse?

Whatever other emotions she had anticipated, it certainly wasn't elated disbelief. With Felipe dead, she was the sole possessor of mystical powers far exceeding those of her mentor – she'd shapeshifted effortlessly without using a chemical crutch. Even better, at the moment of Felipe's death, the moment when his life force fled his body, she had leaned over and absorbed his essence. Now, she owned his power.

She threw back her head and convulsed with laughter until tears rolled down her cheeks at the irony of the situation. The chain of power continued, unbroken, exactly as Felipe had dreamed.

Well, maybe not *exactly*. He probably hadn't factored his own murder into the plan.

Leila's throbbing cheek drew her back to reality. If she didn't put ice on her face soon, she'd look like a punching bag by the morning. Speculation about her nocturnal activities was the last thing she needed. The sooner she disposed of Felipe, the sooner she could take care of her swollen face.

She stared down in frustration and nudged the broken corpse with her toe. With Kincaid on the verge of a breakthrough at the rock pile, she couldn't simply leave it here. Felipe's remains would raise too many questions.

She knew the exact spot to conceal the body.

She gathered up Felipe's discarded clothing and dumped it on top of his corpse, then remembered the detonator. With shaking fingers, she extracted the satellite phone and stuffed it in her pocket.

Who knew when a little added insurance might come in handy?

Straining and heaving, Leila dragged her blanket-wrapped burden along the tunnel. Damn, Felipe was heavier in death than he'd ever looked in life.

When she reached the spot where the floor of the tunnel veered towards the drop-off, she stopped and wiped her forehead, chest heaving. "Good-bye, you bastard," she grunted before pushing the body into the dark void. "Now you can rest forever, along with your sacred ancestors."

She stepped back and listened, counting. When she reached six, she heard a faint thud and a rattle of stones at the bottom of the pit. *El hoyo oscuro* wasn't bottomless after all, but by the time anyone found the body, it would be a pile of scattered bones.

Soon, very soon, Alistair and his whore would join Felipe

for all eternity. The Master of Darkness had so ordained, and Leila would obey.

A faint rustle alerted her to the presence of bats before she saw them. She let out a whimper and flicked the light around her head, flailing her arm to ward off an attack. The faint beam illuminated the pair of sinister shadows darting up from the sinkhole, disturbed by the commotion. Emitting high pitched squeaks, they flapped towards the exit, leaving her feeling shaken and more than a little foolish.

Chapter 32

In spite of Felipe's disappearance, work on the rock pile entered another grueling day. Two hours of backbreaking labour had taken its toll on the men. The pungent odor of sweat from six straining bodies permeated the narrow space and Kincaid admitted to himself he was almost ready to quit if they didn't break through soon.

Although he tried to favour his shoulder as much as possible, his wound throbbed mercilessly. Sweat trickled down his neck and over his naked shoulders, leaving a clean trail through the rock dust clinging to him like a grey body stocking. He cursed as he strained to wedge in an unwieldy piece of wooden shoring more securely, then grunted with satisfaction as it eased into place.

Chest heaving with exertion, he stepped back from the rock face and examined his handiwork with satisfaction. Using his forearm, he mopped his streaming forehead, but feared he'd only succeeded in transforming the dirt into mud.

"Well done, men. Time for a short break." He nodded to the men. "Have something to drink."

He felt rather than heard the collective sigh of relief. One of the men reached into his pocket for a crumpled pack of cigarettes and tried to light a match. The flame died.

The worker grumbled loudly.

Kincaid's head whipped around. "Try again," he said, his voice taut.

The same thing happened.

His heart beating faster, Kincaid forgot about the heat, forgot about his shoulder, and stepped closer to the rock pile. A faint whisper of air fanned his face.

Blood rushed to his head and thundered in his ears. "There's a breeze coming from behind the rocks. That's why

278

you can't light a match. We're nearly through."

Countless days and nights of dedicated studying, compounded by years of back-breaking labour, not to mention the political tightropes he'd walked in order to get funding for his dreams had finally culminated in this lightless tunnel deep inside a mountain. In less than an hour, he would know whether his hypothesis was correct – that the tunnel led to a tomb containing the first intact Olmec remains to see the light of day.

Perversely, Kincaid found himself wishing he could postpone the moment they removed the last rock. What if he was wrong? Sometimes a cave was only a cave. He shook away the pessimistic thoughts. No, he was on the right track. His tenacity had paid off. This could be one of the most significant archaeological finds of the century.

He wanted to bellow out his triumph and jubilation to the world but feared the vibrations would bring down another several tons of rocks. Instead, he raced outside, followed by the nonplussed workers.

Safely out of the tunnel, he clenched both fists in the air, threw back his head, and released a war cry. The howl bounced off the surrounding mountains until the Mexican jungle sounded as if it had been invaded by a pack of wild Scottish highlanders. A flock of blue-winged parrots burst out of the jungle canopy and screeched their terror as they fled from the unearthly sound. Two of the men grabbed one another's arms and executed an impromptu dance, while the rest slapped one another on the backs, grinning from ear to ear.

They had succeeded in accomplishing the impossible.

As the excitement subsided, Kincaid regrouped the men and directed the last stages of the work, watching every move like a hawk and guarding against the slightest shift of the rocks. It would be too easy to lose focus and make a careless error this close to the finish line.

The workers spent the next hour shoring up the last couple of feet of the tunnel, removing the remaining rocks and stacking them outside the entrance. Finally, they created an opening large enough for a man to squeeze through if he turned his body slightly.

Everybody stepped back and looked at Kincaid with expectant eyes.

He sucked in a deep breath and grabbed a flashlight with trembling hands. "Let's do it," he said and stepped into the unknown.

The passageway continued on a downhill slant deep into the mountain where it angled to the left for several yards in a sharp dog-leg, then opened up into a cavern. The cave was as large as a cathedral. He switched the light off for a few seconds, and total darkness enveloped them – the kind of unrelieved darkness that pressed on the eyeballs. The oppressive silence felt almost alive, malevolent, with a breathless texture and weight.

He switched on the light again and shone it around the walls, inch by inch, illuminating carvings of figures and glyphs encircling the cavern. The flashlight's beam wasn't strong enough to illuminate the ceiling. As Kincaid tried to absorb the amazing scene in front of him, the thought occurred to him that they were probably the first people to set foot in this cavern for countless centuries.

"Oh, aye." His voice hitched with emotion. "There's no doubt about it. This was a place of worship. Probably more sacrosanct than the temple outside. I would guess the cave was reserved for special ceremonies and sacrifices the priests wanted to hide from public view."

The men were silent, gaping at the vastness of the sacred space. Kincaid's breath sounded loud in his ears. "*Mo Dhia*. Look at the workmanship on the altar." He pointed to the stone altar on top of three wide steps set in the middle of the cave. An enormous head and gaping maw of a jaguar, similar to the one in the temple outside, reared above one end. Scarcely believing his eyes, he bounded up the steps and reverently ran his hand over stone, marvelling at the smooth, unweathered surface. "It looks as if it was carved only yesterday. I've never seen an altar in such excellent condition."

Kincaid knew he was talking too much, but couldn't prevent his jubilant babble. "Look at the detail of those features. Every hair is perfectly carved. Amazing workmanship. I've never seen anything quite like it. The beast looks as if he's about to growl—"

"Do you think there are any human remains in here?" The student's hollow voice echoed in the cavern, interrupting what had promised to be an enjoyable half-hour dissertation.

The sound jolted Kincaid back to the present, reminding him of his number one priority. He shone his light around the cave, seeking the sarcophagi he was certain the darkness concealed.

Only a vast, echoing emptiness met his disappointed eyes.

He raked a hand through his hair. With jerky movements, he moved to the perimeter of the cave and examined the walls, foot by foot. How could he have been so wrong?

At the farthest end of the cavern, two breaks marred the solid rock.

He released a gusty breath. "Ah. There must be other passages and caves. Locals say the mountains in this region are honeycombed with them."

He directed the light into one of the openings, trying to pierce the darkness. Another narrow, dark tunnel disappeared into the bowels of the mountain. Reluctant to explore the labyrinth of caves without the correct equipment, he turned his attention to the other break in the wall. The short tunnel appeared to end in another cave.

"We'll try this one." He entered the smaller cave, followed by his crew.

He skidded to a halt and whispered in awe: "The burial chamber."

The flashlight beam bounced off glinting surfaces. Intricate carving and writing surrounded this cave, too. Moving in for a closer look, Kincaid gaped at the rich mosaic of what looked like turquoise, jade, pearls and other semi-precious and precious stones set into the wall. But the jewels that decorated the walls were not what captured his attention.

Goosebumps stippled his arms.

In the centre of the cave stood two stone sarcophagi standing side by side. It appeared that the rock fall had deterred the bands of roving marauders because massive stone slabs still provided a tight seal on each.

Heart hammering in his chest, Kincaid took several long steps towards the sarcophagi, then stopped. All his life, he had waited for this moment. He could wait another half-hour.

"Someone go get Charley," he said.

Chapter 32

The breathless worker arrived at the cabin to summon Charley, informing her in broken English of the breakthrough. Kincaid wanted her in the cave to witness the opening of the sarcophagi.

Tears stung Charley's eyes and tenderness welled up out of nowhere. Even in Kincaid's moment of greatest triumph, he hadn't forgotten her.

Twenty minutes later, she entered the cavern, lagging behind the group of archaeologists crowding in front of her, chattering like magpies. She wanted, no, *needed,* to immerse herself with reverence and respect in the sanctity of the once-familiar space. The cave contained the key she needed to make sense of her life, to answer the unspoken questions that eluded description. All she had to do was listen.

She closed her eyes and opened them again to the silence of absolute stillness. Memories hovered at the fringes of her consciousness, tantalizing her with their whisper. In vain, she waited for the blinding flash of insight. Very quickly, she realized the answers she sought still eluded her.

As her eyes grew accustomed to the darkness, she realized the blackness wasn't absolute. A faint pinpoint of light pierced the shadows at the far end of the cavern.

Charley groped her way towards the light.

The unaccustomed brightness in the smaller cave made her blink. She tiptoed in and joined the party, craning her neck to see the attraction.

A floodlight illuminated the furthest recesses of the chamber and threw two massive stone sarcophagi into harsh relief. She rubbed her arms, feeling goose bumps spring up. Chilling apprehension skittered down her spine at the sense of familiarity that swamped her senses. Long ago, the exact meaning and significance of every nook, rock, and cranny had imprinted itself in her memory. Unable to restrain herself, she pointed to one section of the wall and spoke. "This mosaic represents an unbroken chain of power and knowledge," she said, a note of certainty in her voice. "Look at how intricately woven the pattern is...." Her voice trailed off in confusion.

As one, all of the heads turned towards Charley, varying levels of surprise evident in their stunned expressions. Leila, who wormed her way into Kincaid's limelight, voiced the question everybody else was probably thinking. "How did you know the meaning of the mosaic?"

Dammit, she'd revealed too much. Charley jolted out of her near trance-like state. "I'm either a fountain of knowledge or an exceptionally good guesser," she muttered, embarrassed.

How, indeed, could she possibly have known that tidbit of information – unless she had been here in a previous lifetime?

Luckily, Leila held her tongue.

What would Kincaid say if he knew the truth? Charley held her breath and watched as he ran his long, sensitive fingers over the intricate carving and writing on the sides of the sarcophagi.

Although he spoke quietly, the walls of the cave magnified every word. "Look at the detail in the carving. The people buried in these sarcophagi must have been very important. I'd guess either priests or rulers."

Charley's heart pumped a little harder. "Is this significant?"

Kincaid turned his head towards her, dark eyes glowing with smouldering excitement. "This is a huge discovery, the discovery of a lifetime. To this very day, archaeologists have found only poorly preserved traces of Olmec remains, and scholars dispute even these remnants," he explained. "No skeletons have ever survived through the centuries because the soil is too acidic. If these sarcophagi are air-tight, they will have kept the bodies dry, so there is a remote possibility some human remains may have survived – bones, an entire skeleton, even desiccated skin and flesh."

Charley shifted uneasily, her stomach queasy.

Oblivious to her discomfort, he continued: "This writing was carved over two thousand years ago. I can't translate all of it right now." He traced one of the passages. "But I'm pretty sure the person buried here was called 'Kele-Pe'."

Charley tried hard to listen, but suddenly her head throbbed and buzzed, making it almost impossible to concentrate. She clenched her teeth and willed the swirling darkness away, determined to avoid another flashback in front of an interested crowd of spectators.

Kincaid moved to the second sarcophagus. "This sarcophagus is slightly larger and more ornate, possibly more important. Look at the full-sized jaguar carved into the surface." He squinted, then looked closer. "*Mo Dhia*, unless I'm mistaken, the person buried here was a woman. Her name was 'Zanazca'."

Charley swallowed the bile rising, hot and bitter, in her throat. Her head throbbed and her stomach churned with sudden nausea as the dizziness struck. Uncaring if anyone noticed, she staggered out of the cave and returned to the sunlight where she plunked herself down on a rock, head between her knees, and surrendered to the past.

To Zanazca's muddleheaded surprise, her rubbery legs buckled. Confused, she slumped heavily to the ground beside one of the pillars. Was she ill?

A low, soothing voice murmured in her ear, "I will help you, Mistress. Lean on me."

Her head spun. "I am tired, so tired. I must rest."

A familiar laugh tinkled in her ear. "Soon, you will sleep. Trust me."

Zanazca strained to focus her blurred gaze on the shadowy figure crouched beside her. When she recognized Uxatle, the woman she trusted and loved as if she were her own daughter, she drew in a sigh of relief. All would be well.

Unquestioning, the priestess allowed her acolyte to pull her to her feet and welcomed the supportive arm around her waist. Leaning heavily, she savoured the warmth of the lithe body gliding beside her, and allowed Uxatle to lead her deep into the darkness of the sacred place within the mountain. The home of the Master of Darkness.

After that, Zanazca knew nothing for many long minutes.

When she regained consciousness, acute awareness of the cold, unyielding stone pressing into her back jolted her fully awake only to discover she was lying, spread-eagled, across the altar, unable to move her arms or legs.

Her mouth was dry and she had trouble speaking. "Why have you done this, my daughter?"

But deep down, she already understood.

A guttural, coughing growl drew her attention.

She recognized the jaguar and the betrayal cut deeply. The person dearest to her in this lifetime crouched above the altar in the form of her nagual.

Zanazca had trained her acolyte well. Her successor's affinity for evil was unsurpassed.

The jaguar's eyes caught the light of the fire and gleamed with a fierce, yellow glow. The cat bared sharp, white teeth in a soundless snarl. Or was it a smile?

One last time, Zanazca wanted to embrace Uxatle, but could not. How often had she, herself, watched her victims stretched out on the altar from her vantage point as High Priestess? Now she was one of The Chosen. The power to escape lay within her grasp if she allowed her nagual to emerge, but acquiescence offered delivery from a life grown intolerable.

To her humiliation, hot tears filled her eyes, more from a sense of loss and betrayal than from terror. A momentary rush of panic seized her and she steadied herself with an effort. She would die a courageous death, a death worthy of Zanazca, the jaguar she knew herself to be.

Her life flashed before her eyes. The evil deeds she had done. The pain she had caused. The power she had enjoyed. Oh, yes! The power, the god-like supremacy of life and death. How could her life, so full of promise as a child, have turned out so wrong?

Evil was like an undertow. It sucked you under.

Zanazca delivered her last words with a sinking heart. "You will regret this, my child. I have seen the future. I will permit you to kill my body, but you will never kill my spirit.

Your soul, like mine, will be damned for all eternity – unless one of us finds redemption."

A series of coughing grunts filled the air with anger and hatred.

Through blurred vision, Zanazca saw the quick flash of claws, then felt a powerful blow on her chest.

Her last surprised thought was that she felt no pain. A cold darkness engulfed her, then … peace.

Charley raised her head, heedless of the tears streaming down her cheeks. Now that she remembered everything, she wondered how she could ever have forgotten. She scrubbed her eyes. No wonder this place had looked familiar. No wonder a sense of recognition had struck her at the sight of the sarcophagi. After all, one of them belonged to a man she had loved and betrayed so long ago.

The second was her own grave.

Charley slipped back into the small chamber, unnoticed. Every gaze was riveted on the drama in front of their eyes as Kincaid and the workers strained to remove the stone slab sealing the larger sarcophagus.

Zanazca's sarcophagus.

The stone moved with a loud, grinding noise.

"Aye. That's it. Just a few more inches," grunted Kincaid. "I don't want to remove it completely. Only swivel it enough to see if the remains are intact. We'll bring in the proper equipment to move them to the university laboratories for a thorough examination."

Charley held her breath as stone continued to move, widening the gap.

"Enough. Stop there," Kincaid commanded.

Reaching for Charley's hand, he squeezed it and drew in a hissing breath.

Leila crowded close, breathing hard, animosity obviously forgotten in her excitement.

Charley held her breath for as long as she could and peered into the sarcophagus. She had expected a foul odour, but only the faint mustiness of air long sealed in a tightly confined space leaked out. Her first impression was of gold and jewels – turquoise, coral, jade, obsidian, mother-of-pearl. Then she realized the priceless jewellery adorned the bones of a skeleton. The skull gazed back at her with unseeing eyeholes. A turquoise and gold multi-strand necklace with a large pendant of the same material, incised with a jaguar hanging from it, rested on the breastbone. Circular earrings and an intricate headdress lay beside the head. Gold bracelets and jewel-studded armbands encircled the arms from wrist to shoulder.

Charley sucked in a shuddering breath. A silver and turquoise ring, an exact replica of the one she wore, adorned the middle finger of the skeleton's right hand.

Charley forced herself to detach from the sight of Zanazca's body. This had once been a real person. Had anyone mourned her passing? Whose hands had prepared this body for burial? Scalding tears prickled the back of her eyelids, and she willed them away.

"The flesh decomposed millennia ago," said Kincaid. "But this body wasn't wrapped in the usual reddish putty, which has a fairly high acid content. Also, the stone floor and granite sarcophagus acting as barriers to the soil's natural acidity have preserved the body all this time."

A babble of noise filled the cave as everybody started talking at once. Kincaid kissed Charley exuberantly, ignoring Leila's malevolent glare, and he announced: "These are the first intact Olmec remains ever discovered. Imagine what we can learn. They'll be able to reconstruct facial features from the skull."

"Congratulations, Kincaid. I'm so happy for you," Charley said, feigning joy through a growing knot in her throat.

"It means so much more to me than I thought possible with you by my side, lass," he whispered in her ear so quietly, no one else could hear.

Her chest tightened with grief. Her betrayal would soon cloud the joy of his discovery.

Chapter 33

Kincaid shivered in the biting night wind that whistled around the top of the pyramid and morosely reviewed his afternoon. Concern over Charley's inexplicably grumpy attitude had dampened his jubilation over his historical discovery. He didn't know what the hell he had done to upset her, but she definitely had her knickers in a twist about something.

Women were a never-ending mystery.

On their return to camp, she had barely spoken two words to him, answering only in curt monosyllables. Then, at the exact moment he finally established a faint, static-laden connection with the Director of the Regional Museum of Oaxaca to discuss shipping arrangements, she wanted to discuss the embargo on her article.

Kincaid's irritation grew. Why did women always need to talk at the worst possible times? The chat would simply have to wait until he had a spare fifteen minutes.

As if that wasn't enough to take the edge off his excitement, he'd spent the remainder of the day entangled in unavoidable bureaucratic bullshit. His afternoon consisted of filling out forms, making telephone calls, using the satellite up-link to send e-mails, and dealing with the NIC watchdog who'd insisted he file a bilingual report. Unfortunately, Kincaid had no choice but to comply. The NIC could halt the dig at any time.

After dinner, Kincaid had announced: "There'll be a wee change in the security patrol, folks. I'll do the overnight shift in the cave until reinforcements arrive on the next plane. Our two guards will continue to patrol the camp and ancient city." When Charley had insisted on accompanying him, he'd asserted his authority by saying: "Definitely not. Much too dangerous." The glint of mutiny in her eyes had heralded another argument, so in an act of supreme self-sacrifice, he'd stalked away before she could coax him into changing his mind.

Oh, crap. There'll be hell to pay tomorrow. He sighed and dragged his attention back to his surroundings.

Dark silence filled the temple. Tree frogs croaked out a raucous chorus in the brush below. He rubbed his hands together to warm them before taking a sip of hot, sweet coffee from his thermos. Although the days were sweltering, nights got chilly at this altitude. Even wrapped in a sleeping bag and sitting in the mouth of the tunnel, partially sheltered from the wind, he shivered.

Periodically, he lowered the sleeping bag to listen for potential thieves, then, satisfied that all was quiet, pulled it up again around his shoulders and ears, grateful for its warmth. The down filling protected him from the cold night air. Unfortunately, it muffled all night noises better than a pair of earmuffs. Great for sleeping, terrible for surveillance.

Leila slipped into the back entrance to the caves, well aware of Kincaid, holed up in the tunnel behind the temple.

Time was running out and she had much to accomplish before daylight. She smiled to herself. By dawn, the discovery would belong to her, and her alone. After Kincaid and his whore were dead, no one in camp would challenge her authority.

Her tinkle of soft laughter bounced off rocky walls and echoed back, magnified.

She removed her boots to ensure the scuff of leather on stone wouldn't alert Kincaid to her presence and switched on her penlight. Padding silently as a cat, she skirted the bottomless chasm, which had swallowed Felipe's body, and gave a mocking salute with a whispered parting: "You'll soon have plenty of company."

Tonight, she would deliver another meal to the Master of Darkness.

Once in the cavern, she lit the wall torches, the fire, and the incense, then quickly stripped off every article of clothing she wore. Clothes were a useless encumbrance for the task ahead. She shook out a loose ceremonial cape, a gift from Felipe, from her backpack and donned it, more for warmth than for modesty.

Naked, except for the cape, she sank to the floor of the cavern and opened the leather pouch. As the peyote buttons fell into her open hand, her heart beat faster. *My passport to power.*

One by one, she chewed them and swallowed, welcoming the bitter taste, the dryness in her mouth. When she had eaten the last button, she closed her eyes. Tonight, she would succeed in achieving *bè ta mè*, fusion with the jaguar spirit dwelling within her heart.

As incense filled the cavern with its sweet, acrid scent, Leila allowed the swelling power of her *nagual* to rise and fill her body. For now, she wished only to borrow the animal's stealth, speed and strength for her immediate mission – immobilizing Kincaid. Only later, for the final ceremony, would she complete the shift.

She remained motionless, deep in the self-induced trance, feeling her body vibrate with nerve-tingling energy pulses as the animal tried to escape. She had to interrupt the complete transition to the beast, and the task was more difficult than she'd anticipated.

Sweat trickled into her eyes as she felt the razor-sharp claws start to erupt from the tips of her fingers. Her entire body itched and burned. With a conscious effort, she exerted her will and suppressed all but the most essential elements of the jaguar.

In response to her intention, the lethal claws retracted reluctantly and the rippling movement under her skin ceased.

After several minutes, she arose, flexing her muscles and stretching. She flicked her tongue, tasting the salty sweat on her upper lip. The pungent stench of incense almost overwhelmed the more subtle odour of wood smoke. She cursed as the acrid combination of pungent scents tickled her nose and made her want to sneeze. The crackle of the fire as it consumed dry twigs seemed almost deafening.

The victory marked a milestone. She had suppressed full physical transformation, yet still manifested the beast's characteristics – the strength, the stealth, the acute senses.

She was now a creature of the night.

Balancing on the balls of her feet, she glided, jaguar-like, out of the cavern and into the black tunnel where she halted, sensing the air. She waited patiently until her pupils dilated fully before heading down the passageway to the mouth of the tunnel.

Leila's nostrils flared. The odour of coffee and Kincaid's distinctive masculine scent hinting of moors and heather alerted her to her prey's presence even before she rounded the bend.

A three-foot chunk of wood abandoned by the work team caught her eye. She hefted it in her hand as easily as if it were a plastic toy. *Yes, it should do the job.* She wanted Kincaid unconscious, not dead.

At least, not yet.

She crept along the passageway until she could discern his form silhouetted against the night sky.

She watched him settle the thermos on the ground and pull the sleeping bag more snugly around his head.

Soundlessly, she bared her teeth. The sleeping bag would cushion his head from serious damage. He would regain consciousness in time to understand the significance of his own sacrifice.

With every fibre of her being, she concentrated on stealth, raising one foot at a time and placing it deliberately and soundlessly on the ground, much like the jaguar. Slowly, silently, she glided closer, grasping the board tighter in both fists. She raised it above her head and struck.

Kincaid slumped to the ground without a sound.

She reached down and turned off the lantern. He wouldn't need it where he was going.

Grunting softly, she slipped her hands under his armpits and started to drag the inert form down the passageway towards the cavern and the waiting altar.

Chapter 34

Kincaid's bed seemed huge and very empty without his large, long-limbed body hogging three quarters of the mattress. Charley missed the heavy warmth of his leg over her thigh, his sleepy voice whispering Gaelic sweet talk in her ear. Even Horrie's rasping purr didn't come close to filling the void.

"I can't sleep," she muttered aloud.

In two days, she would fly home to San Francisco and her life would resume its old humdrum path. "Not true," she corrected herself aloud, as if Horrie understood. "My life will never be the same again without Kincaid."

Regret swirled into a cyclone of longing she must ignore. The unpleasant revelations about her past life had left her with a cold and numbing certainty about her next move. In a previous lifetime, Zanazca had betrayed the people she'd loved in her relentless quest for power. Charley's present lifetime granted a golden opportunity to make better choices this time around – selfless choices that would rectify the mistakes she'd made many centuries ago.

She stroked Horrie, feeling the silky fur and loose skin slide over his knobby vertebrae. "You understand, don't you? If I let Mom continue on her downhill path of self-destruction and booze, I'd be condemning another person I love to certain death."

Her heart twisted as she considered the impossible dilemma. In order to help her mother, she had to betray Kincaid. Despite her growing feelings for him, she couldn't turn her back on her mother. She sighed. No matter what the cost to her happiness, she would publish her article the minute she returned home.

A cold wave of self-loathing washed over Charley. She had never broken her word to anyone before. A promise had always represented a sacred trust. *Until now*. The grief she felt nearly undid her. Earlier today, she'd made one frantic final effort to convince Kincaid to lift the embargo on her article, but all she got from him was an impatient wave of his hand and an abstracted grunt before he resumed his endless phone conversations.

The clock was ticking a countdown to the zero hour.

Taking care not to crush the cat, Charley rolled over and buried her head in Kincaid's pillow, sniffing the familiar scent clinging to the fabric, trying to memorize the distinctive combination of soap and heather-scented aftershave.

"Pretty soon, he's going to hate me, Horrie."

Although she wouldn't blame Kincaid if he never wanted to see her again, the thought of his loathing caused scalding tears to prickle behind her eyelids. *Enough wallowing*. She choked back the tears. If she allowed herself to continue the downward spiral, she'd disintegrate into a sloppy mess of tears, tissues and gritty eyes. Weeping would only cause her sinuses to swell until her nasal passages were blocked tighter than a submarine's airlock. Besides, once the floodgates opened, she doubted she'd be able to close them before morning.

Huffing out a sigh, she sat up in bed and turned on the light, renouncing any pretence of sleep. Horrie climbed into her lap and flopped down. He stuck his left leg in the air in the double-jointed way only cats can accomplish, and started licking.

The prospect of breaking her word to Kincaid wasn't the only reason for the endless night of insomnia. Her mind kept returning with reluctant fascination to her past life as an Olmec High Priestess, then darting away again, like a tongue prodding an abscessed tooth. The unpleasant sensation didn't prevent her from reliving the days leading up to Zanazca's death over and over, certain she had overlooked a vital clue. The more Charley struggled to remember, the more frustrated she became.

"The only way I'll ever remember is if I revisit the cave," she announced to Horrie. "I need to see the burial chamber again, and no matter how overbearing Kincaid is, he can't stop me."

Horrie eyed her quizzically.

She cut to the chase. "Okay. If I can catch him alone, maybe I can convince him to lift the embargo."

Before her resolve faded, she hopped out of bed and donned a pair of ancient frayed jeans and a warm shirt. Remembering the painful footwear fiasco, she pulled on thick socks and the borrowed boots. She completed her ensemble with a dab of lavender-scented essential oil that not only promoted peace of mind, but also repelled mosquitoes. "A lady should never leave the house without a dab of her favourite scent," her mother always said. Charley made a wry face. Funny, the things that stuck with you.

The trip to the ancient city would seem endless without a weapon.

A chill slid down her spine. Dammit, Kincaid must have taken the shotgun and machete. Her gaze slid to the Smith and Wesson handgun hanging over the back of the chair. Gingerly, she removed the weapon from its holster and examined it carefully. Hallelujah, she knew how this one worked. Thank God she'd spent a couple of weeks at a dude ranch last summer and learned the basics of shooting a handgun.

She stuffed the weapon in her belt, flicked on the flashlight and set off for the cave.

Charley called out softly as she approached the top of the pyramid. She didn't want Kincaid to mistake her for a thief and blast her head off.

There was no answer.

When she arrived at the summit, a chill of dread crept down her spine on stealthy feet. There was no sign of life, but Kincaid had obviously been there.

Her blood ran cold as she surveyed the scene in the mouth of the tunnel. Why had the lantern been turned off? A folding camp chair lay discarded, overturned, and a thermos of coffee stood open next to a rumpled sleeping bag.

Where the hell was Kincaid? Something terrible had happened to him. She knew it.

Her heart pounded in her ears as she contemplated the

dire possibilities – Felipe had killed him and dragged the body away, he'd gone after the jaguar and was lying, horribly mutilated, somewhere in the bushes, he'd triggered an ancient curse when he'd opened the sarcophagus.

She shook herself. Hysteria would only make the situation worse.

She bent down to check the coffee with trembling hands. Still warm. He hadn't been gone long. He must be nearby.

A faint, echoing cry caused her to flinch violently. She wasn't sure where it had come from, and it was impossible to tell if it was a man or a woman.

Charley held her breath and listened intently, her hands like blocks of ice. The deafening silence stretched out until she thought she'd jump out of her skin.

Another muted shout that died abruptly shattered the stillness.

The call had come from the tunnel to the caves. Someone was in trouble, and Charley was afraid it was Kincaid.

Running for help was out of the question. There was no time to lose. Fear for Kincaid's life bolstered her courage. She drew the pistol from her belt and held it in front of her with one hand while grasping the flashlight firmly with the other.

She stepped into the tunnel, hugging the wall. Her legs quivered with tension as she crept down the empty passageway. It hadn't seemed nearly as long this afternoon amidst excited chatter and speculation.

When she reached the bend in the tunnel, she switched off the flashlight and allowed her eyes to adjust to the sudden darkness. Sure enough, a faint, flickering light in the distance pinpointed the large cavern.

She pushed down the apprehension that threatened to swamp her. The darkness of the tunnel would mask her approach, and she doubted anyone expected company.

Holding the pistol outstretched, Charley crept towards the cavern and peered through the opening. For one split second, she stared, uncomprehending. She had no idea what she'd expected, but never in a million years, could she have conjured up the sight that greeted her. Her rational mind rejected the unspeakable pageant. Things like that simply didn't happen.

As the full horror of the scene registered, small details began to coalesce. Charley's disbelieving gaze darted to the naked body bound on top of the altar, the chest exposed. A sacrificial victim.

She shook her head. This couldn't be happening. There were no sacrifices in the modern day and age. It was too primitive. Too horrific.

She felt the bile rise in her throat as she recognized the body. The tall, muscular frame and shaggy head of dark hair could belong to only one person. *Kincaid.*

A sixth sense warned Charley to remain motionless. Breathing hard, she flattened her back against the wall and waited, nerves stretched to breaking point.

Kincaid moaned and moved his head.

Charley's heart rocketed around in her chest. Thank God. He was still alive.

She took one silent step towards him but flicker of movement in the darkness surrounding the altar stopped her in her tracks. In soundless haste, she sank back against the wall and strained her eyes to probe the gloom. Nothing moved. It must have been a shadow cast by the guttering torches.

Her imagination was running away. She waited anyway.

There it was again – another furtive movement. She shook her head and blinked. No, it wasn't her imagination. A darker shape that hadn't been there a second ago crept across the floor.

As Charley watched in frozen disbelief, the head and neck of a jaguar emerged from the gloom. Slowly, the entire animal became visible. Creeping stealthily, its belly almost touching the ground, the creature stalked towards its prey. Step by step, the animal glided closer to the altar.

When the terrible truth registered, Charley wanted to dismiss the evidence of her own eyes. A jaguar, here, in the cave, was impossible.

The predator crouched low to the ground, tensed to spring, every muscle of its lithe body as still as a rock. The cat's yellow eyes reflected the torchlight and glowed with a near-human intelligence, hot with hatred. With supple grace, the jaguar leaped on top of the altar and crouched beside the recumbent body that writhed and strained at the bonds.

A silent sob caught in Charley's throat. Kincaid would be dead in seconds if she didn't do something. She wouldn't allow herself to panic. A cold, preternatural calm descended over her and steadied her hand. She wouldn't miss.

The animal reached out a paw and raked it down Kincaid's chest in a deliberately cruel motion. Blood oozed, black and oily in the dimness of the cave, and trickled down his skin.

Kincaid spat out a defiant curse.

Charley raised the weapon and took careful aim.

Chapter 35

The ear-splitting crack of Charley's two gunshots reverberated off the walls, echoed, then died away, leaving behind a vibrating hush that hung in the air, as if alive.

Reflexively, Charley blinked her eyes shut. When she opened them again, the jaguar had disappeared.

Unable to move her feet, she froze to the spot, praying one of her shots had hit the jaguar before it could execute the killing slash. Her entire body shook in a delayed reaction to Kincaid's narrow escape from death. If she had hesitated for one split second longer, she was sure he'd be dead, mangled under the animal's wicked claws.

Charley refused to contemplate how she would feel if she had missed.

This was no time to fall apart, she chided herself. The animal might still be alive and furious. Although powerful tremors still shuddered through her body, the thought of a repeat attack broke the spell that held her immobile. She stiffened her spine and forced one foot ahead of the other. Pistol held at waist level, she crept across the cavern to peer on all sides of the altar, searching for the creature.

A trail of droplets, gleaming dark in the torchlight, led towards the far recesses of the cave.

She smiled in grim satisfaction. Her marksmanship might not have earned her any prizes at the dude ranch, but she'd hit the target this time, when it really counted.

Kincaid lay on the stone slab following her every movement with pain-darkened eyes, his face as white as a sheet – a brutal contrast to the scarlet claw marks trailing across his chest.

Cold knots of apprehension tightened Charley's heart as she leaped up the steps to the altar. Deliberately, she placed the handgun on the platform beside her feet and stroked his face.

He tried to sit up, forgetting his bonds, then slumped back. "Charley." His weak grin transformed into a dark scowl. "What the hell are you doing here? I thought I told you to stay in camp."

An incredulous laugh bubbled in the back of her throat in spite of the horror of the situation. How typically Kincaid. He was lecturing her about disobeying his orders while still strapped to the altar, trussed up like a turkey. She bit back a sob of relief. "You can thank your lucky stars I don't react at all well to direct orders."

"Damn, but you're a stubborn woman."

She laid a gentle hand on his arm, savouring the living warmth pulsing beneath her fingertips. "If you'll stop squirming for a moment, I'll untie you. The jaguar's still alive, and it might return at any moment to finish the job." Her hands fumbled with the bonds, but Kincaid's struggles had tightened the leather thongs until they bit cruelly into his flesh. "Dammit. They're too tight. I need something sharp to cut them," she muttered. Tears of frustration stung her eyelids. She looked over her shoulder, scanning the corners of the cave for signs of movement in the shadows, expecting the cat to return at any moment.

"There's a ceremonial knife somewhere around here. Try looking in the jaguar's mouth up there." He jerked his chin at the stone carving above his head.

Charley gaped at him in surprise.

"Hurry." He twisted with impatience. "I'll explain later."

She stood on tiptoe and thrust her shaking hand inside the open maw, groping blindly and straining to reach the bottom. Her fingers met with the gritty emptiness of chiselled rock. "Nothing," she muttered in despair, aware of the precious seconds flying by with alarming speed. Hoisting herself up on the altar to kneel beside his head, she stretched her arm deeper into the cavity, as far back as she could reach. With an exclamation of triumph, she wrapped trembling fingers around a smooth handled knife and hopped down onto the platform with a soft grunt.

"Good work." He smiled encouragingly. "Steady now.

Take your time."

Charley took a deep breath and willed her hand to stop shaking. She sawed frantically. Several nerve-wracking seconds later, the cord binding Kincaid's right wrist parted with an audible snap. She heaved a sigh of relief and turned her attention to the other arm, then his feet.

He groaned and rubbed his wrists to restore circulation.

"Can you sit up?" Charley asked anxiously.

"Aye, I think so."

She placed her arm around his shoulders to support him as he swayed dizzily before he swung his legs over the side.

She licked her lips impatiently and voiced her deepest fear. "I think we're running out of time. Let's get out of here before the jaguar returns."

As if in answer, a coughing growl from the shadows at the back of the cave announced the animal's presence. The small hairs on her arms stood on end.

"Too late," he whispered. "Stay calm. No sudden movements."

She whirled around to face one of the most feared and respected predators staring at them across the space of the cavern. It looked a lot larger at close range – over a hundred pounds of sleek, steel-muscled killing machine.

Charley's blood ran cold as she locked gazes with the animal, magnificent in its lethal glory. She knew it could go from stalking to killing in the space of a heartbeat. The gunshot wound had left a dark streak of drying blood on its left haunch, marring the intricate pattern of black rosettes covering the sleek, golden pelt.

Hatred radiated from the unblinking, golden stare as it limped closer, favouring its wounded leg. The cat snarled, exposing wicked canines.

Charley knew in her heart this was no ordinary animal.

Kincaid reached for the ceremonial knife and stood upright, leaning heavily against the altar for balance. "Back up." He hefted the knife to a striking position. "Slowly. Whatever you do, don't run. We'll put the altar between the cat and ourselves."

"The pistol," she whispered. "I left the pistol on the other side of the altar."

They edged along the platform, Kincaid urging Charley ahead of him.

The jaguar swung its massive head around and gazed at Kincaid, then turned the full, mesmerizing force of its golden eyes on Charley again. She understood the animal's wordless message. It would deal with her later, after it was finished with Kincaid.

When they reached the far side of the altar, Charley watched in frozen terror as the animal's powerful haunches rippled and bunched beneath it. "Watch out. It's going to spring," she warned under her breath.

"Down the stairs," Kincaid barked.

Charley placed her arm around Kincaid's waist and supported him as they stumbled down the stairs and backed away towards the tunnel's exit. Unable to drag her gaze away, she watched helplessly as the creature propelled itself through the air in a single bound to land on top of the altar. It poised there, muscles coiled, ready to spring.

Kincaid must have sensed the animal's next move. Startling Charley with an adrenaline-fuelled strength, he yanked her from the path of imminent danger. With a strong shove, he pushed her towards the wall a split second before the jaguar launched itself from its perch and sailed through the air towards them.

Charley stumbled and sprawled on the ground, barely registering the sharp pain of elbows and knees connecting with the rocky floor of the cave. All of her attention was focused on the deadly drama unfolding in front of her eyes.

Kincaid leaped away from the deadly predator, but not quickly enough.

Paralyzed and powerless to help, Charley raised herself to her knees and watched in horror as the jaguar's claws raked a path down the firm flesh of his thigh. He cursed and rolled away. Crimson blood trickled from the wound.

The jaguar's momentum carried it to the middle of the cave where it skidded to a halt and turned towards Kincaid again, golden eyes fixed on its prey. A trail of saliva dripped from open jaws. Its tawny hide gleamed in the torchlight, unspeakably beautiful, as it inched towards Kincaid again, belly low to the ground, slinking closer, as if it knew it had all the time in the world to play a leisurely game of cat-and-mouse.

Charley's blood froze. Fighting down the crippling panic, she backed away until she felt the wall behind her. Fear for Kincaid's life pierced Charley. Heart thundering in her ears, she searched for a rock, anything to buy him some time. A sob tore loose from the depths of her soul.

The animal circled Kincaid, toying with him, prolonging the game.

It's enjoying itself. The animal's killer instinct surpassed all natural laws.

Her brain pirouetted in a mad dance. She could smell the hot, feral stench of the jaguar mixed with the sharper tang of fear – her own fear. A wail lodged in her throat, straining for release, but she swallowed the knot of panic. Losing her head guaranteed certain death for Kincaid, then herself.

Kincaid's knife glinted, weaving an intricate pattern in the air, as if trying to intimidate the animal. "Get the hell out of here and get some help. I'll distract the animal long enough for you to escape."

A ceremonial knife was scant protection against a full-grown jaguar that had tasted blood. The sheer nobility and hollow futility of his act caused her heart to twist in her chest. For one breathless moment, time stood still.

After that, everything seemed to happen in slow motion, although in reality, she realized only scant seconds had elapsed.

Her vision dimmed, then darkened. A humming grew in intensity until she thought her eardrums would rupture. She braced herself against the inevitable wave of nausea churning through her body. Almost certain she would black out, she managed to cling to a shred of conscious thought and hang on grimly.

Glimpses of impossible and powerful forces tantalized her with their promises. This time, she refused to let go of the present and retreat into the past. Kincaid needed her *now*.

The fog that clouded her senses parted, allowing the long-forgotten knowledge of ancient arts to coalesce and solidify. She, and she alone, possessed the ability to save Kincaid, possessed the ability to tap into her past life and perform the alchemy of changing evil into a blessing.

Unflinching, Charley stared into the darkest recesses of her soul. Straining to latch onto elusive memory fragments, she summoned up the mystical gifts from her past – gifts so awe-inspiring, yet so familiar, they felt, at first, like old friends.

The change began. Heat coiled inside her body, gathering in intensity until she thought she would explode into a million pieces. She bit her lip to suppress the scream lodged in her throat. The bright, coppery taste of blood flooded her mouth. How could she have forgotten the pain? Her skin started to itch and throb. Deep inside her body, a dangerous energy coursed through her veins with irrevocable power, and she watched in horror, caught in a primal urge to run and hide, as her skin rippled and bulged.

Struck by a sudden and unpleasant thought, she ran trembling hands over her face and neck, and promptly wished she hadn't. Rough patches of fur had replaced smooth skin. Wiry whiskers sprouted from her cheeks and forehead. Gasping for breath, she strained to fill her lungs with air, telling herself over and over: *It isn't too late to stop this madness.*

But a quick, panicky glance over her shoulder at the man she loved, now pinned against the wall by the menacing jaguar, warned her there was no turning back. She had run out of time. With a conscious effort, she stopped hyperventilating and forced herself to encourage the animal to emerge, trusting she could send it back when its time was over.

Muscles stretched and her clothes were suddenly unbearably tight. Impatient, she ripped at the buttons and tore at the fabric with fingers that were suddenly clumsy, until her blouse fell away from her body. Seconds later, jeans, boots and socks followed.

Knifing pain shot through every bone, tendon and ligament. Her body writhed and contorted, and she was unable to prevent tears of agony from streaming down her cheeks. When the torture subsided, untamed strength, a gift from the past, rippled through her body.

Off-balance and no longer able to stand erect, Charley dropped to the ground on all fours and glanced at what used to be her hands and arms. Black, furry legs ended in paws tipped with lethal talons, thick, curved and dangerous. She flexed and unflexed the claws, gouging the rocky floor in front of her with deep scratch marks.

Dimly, she comprehended that she had shifted many times before. She remembered everything, and a fierce, protective longing filled her with fury. She would shield Kincaid from the evil forces that threatened to destroy him.

A hoarse, coughing growl lodged in her throat.

Kincaid stared in disbelief as the ebony jaguar materialized from behind the altar. He looked around frantically, searching for Charley, but she had disappeared, hopefully looking for the pistol. Favouring his wounded leg, he dragged himself away from the two animals.

The newcomer, larger and more powerful than the first, stalked towards its opponent, tail twitching from side to side.

In slow motion, the black jaguar raised its head and roared. It crouched low and took two tentative steps towards the smaller animal, lips drawn back from razor-sharp fangs in a harsh snarl, obviously the aggressor. When it halted, it locked gazes with the smaller animal and roared again, sending out a clear challenge.

It seemed to Kincaid as if the smaller beast weighed the odds of success before breaking eye contact and backing off, as if the animal had actually decided the chances of success were slim.

Impossible. Animals can't reason like humans.

For the space of a heartbeat, the spotted cat swivelled its tawny head from the black jaguar to stare at Kincaid, its yellow eyes glinting. It uttered a low, throaty growl he swore sounded like unadulterated hatred and frustration.

He must be losing his grip on reality.

The smaller cat whirled and bounded towards the dimness at the back of the cavern where the tunnel led into the depths of the mountain. The black jaguar followed at its heels, as if to prevent the other animal from changing its mind.

As if to protect him.

Dimly, Charley heard Kincaid calling her name. Torn, she slowed her headlong rush and looked over her shoulder. The part of her that was still human reached into the recesses of her brain for the love and tenderness she felt for Kincaid. The man she loved lay on the floor, torn and bloody. He needed her.

She felt the change begin.

The call started in the core of her being, commanding the animal to return to its place of oblivion. Her lungs burned, as if a huge vacuum had sucked all the air from her body. A moment later, she cried out in pain as her muscles contorted and her shape reverted to human form.

Kneeling awkwardly on the cavern floor, Charley bit her lip in frustration. Letting the animal escape was infuriating, but she couldn't leave Kincaid untended a moment longer. Wearily, she heaved herself to her feet. Man, this shifting thing took a lot more energy than she could have believed possible.

She stared at the spot where she had last seen the jaguar, expecting to see only empty darkness, and locked startled gazes with the animal.

Everything inside her went still and her legs wanted to fold. She couldn't freak out. Not now. If she didn't summon the energy to shift again, and quickly, she was finished. And so was Kincaid.

Again, the pain started to slam through her body when, out of the corner of her eye, she caught a subtle change in the motionless jaguar. Never taking her gaze off her adversary, she dragged herself back from the brink.

The jaguar's feline form blurred and softened, as if a giant hand rearranged its composition with gleeful disregard for anatomical accuracy. Particles around the edges whirled, tearing apart and reassembling. The dark shape dropped to the ground where it writhed and twisted before lying still. Seconds later, a taller, slimmer figure scrambled to its feet, snarling, its body a pale blur against the blackness of the tunnel entrance.

Charley recoiled from waves of palpable rage emanating

from the feminine figure who spat out a string of curses in an unmistakable voice, before whirling and disappearing from sight. It didn't occur to Charley to be surprised. Deep down inside, she had recognized her enemy right from the beginning.

"Come back, Leila. I know it's you," she shouted. "We have some unfinished business."

But the figure had faded into the darkness.

Chapter 36

Gripping the string that passed as a curtain rod, Charley drew the parrot print curtain aside and peered out the cabin window. White-hot sun blazed down from a cloudless sky. Not a breath of air stirred the palm fronds overhead, and the lagoon was as still as a millpond, reflecting the intense blue of the afternoon sky. A pair of scarlet-breasted birds chirped and chattered in the trees, then darted away into the green world of enchantment.

In spite of the breathtaking beauty, her last day in camp promised to be distressing. The only good news was Kincaid's wounds weren't as bad as she had feared and Leila was probably long gone by now.

"Another shitty day in paradise," she muttered under her breath, letting the curtain fall from limp fingers. She flicked a glance at Kincaid. He slept on, his chest rising and falling under the light sheet.

She gave herself a mental whack on the side of the head. Why had she been so idiotic as to believe she could relegate the archaeologist to a neat compartment labelled Quick Fling, then erase him from her mind? Although her dismal track record with men was legendary, she had outdone herself this time. She'd gone and fallen in love with the man she had lied to, the man she would betray....

The man who would hate her guts as soon as he found out she'd released the article without permission.

Doesn't it ever rain around here? A storm would have been more in keeping with her black mood. She aimed a vicious kick at the wicker trash basket. It sailed across the room, spilling its contents across the floor in a gratifying spray of papers and debris. She contemplated punching out the screen window next, except a high-pitched whine reminded her of the fleet of mosquitoes hovering hungrily outside, waiting to chow down on fresh meat.

Perhaps, it was time to rethink her approach to stress reduction.

As her therapist often preached, a little positive thinking might alleviate her gloomy outlook. She tried it for a couple of minutes and hit on an idea that perked her up. She could extend her stay in camp a couple of extra days – if only her mother could manage to keep out of trouble a little longer.

A light snore indicated that Kincaid was still in a drugged slumber. Figuring she'd better make a dutiful daughter-to-mother check-in call before waking the poor man to check for a concussion, she coated herself with bug spray and tiptoed outside onto the porch. The phone's blank window stared at her, mocking, daring her to make the call. She took a deep breath and punched in her mother's number. After four rings, her mother's frosty voice came on the line.

"Yes?"

"Hi, Mom, it's me – Charley." In case there was any doubt.

"I know. Hello, Charlotte. How kind of you to call."

Was it only her imagination or were her mother's words slightly slurred? "I've been busy."

"You're always busy. I was beginning to wonder if you had dropped off the face of the Earth."

Ah, guilt. Her mother could lay it on with a few well-placed words. "Sorry," Charley said through clenched teeth. "We had a little trouble here last night, but everything's fine now. There's nothing to worry about. Really." *Please ask me if I'm okay, Mom.*

"Excuse me? I can hardly hear you, Charlotte. You really must learn to enunciate clearly."

Obediently, Charley raised her voice and enunciated clearly. "I'm fine. Thanks for asking." She waited for the caustic reply.

Sure enough, her mother never failed to deliver. "I don't think I like your tone of voice or your attitude."

Deficiency of tone, attitude and deportment in general were rat-holes Charley didn't want to go down, so she changed the subject. "What's up, Mom? Sounds like another party."

There was a pause filled with the buzz of animated conversation. Charley knew, just knew, her mother had taken a quick gulp of the drink she was clutching.

"Speak up, dear. I'm just wrapping up a celebration luncheon with a friend. If you'll recall, I am receiving an award at the annual fundraiser the day after tomorrow. I distinctly remember telling you about it four months ago."

Her mother's voice sounded a little too bright, a little too animated, a little too strident, as she enunciated each word with intoxicated precision. Charley's tiny wisp of foolish hope puffed out. She tried to keep the surge of anger out of her voice as she shouted into the mouthpiece: "Sounds like you're celebrating."

"You forgot about the award, didn't you?"

Absolutely. "Of course not."

"You promised you'd be home in time to accompany me. I'm relying on you to keep your word."

Charley didn't remember promising anything of the sort, and she hated being manipulated. "I thought I might take a couple of extra days to kick back and relax before I return home."

"Surely you don't need to fritter away more of your life than you already have. You have abandoned me for several months now, and it's time to think about someone other than yourself. I trust I can still count on you to join me at the head table."

Charley's patience, already strained to the limit, finally snapped. "In case you pass out again?" Her shout must have startled a heron, for it burst out of the reeds and flapped away.

"Really, Charlotte, nasty remarks are uncalled for. Last year, I was simply tired after all the excitement of the silent auction. I may have nodded off for a few moments in the ladies' lounge, but I certainly did not pass out."

Charley counted to ten. It didn't work. "You could have fooled me. It took two of us to haul you out to the car and stuff you into the back seat."

"Ridiculous. I have absolutely no memory of anything of the sort. You must have dreamed up that silly story."

"Certainly not."

"Excuse me?"

She had to bellow to make herself heard. "You blacked out. Then, I had to hold your gown aside while you stood in the front hall and puked onto your new Via Spiga pumps."

Her mother didn't dignify the accusation with an answer. Over the background noise, Charley heard the distinct ring of fine crystal against teeth, and shouted: "Are you drunk now? It's only three o'clock and you sound drunk already."

Her mother's voice took on a defensive edge. "How dare you imply I'm inebriated? I only had two teeny martinis before lunch and a glass of wine with my salad."

More like a bottle. "Mom, listen. You need help."

Her mother notched up the volume to match her daughter's. "The only help I need is for my daughter to care enough about her mother to drive her home after the fundraiser."

Roaring into the mouthpiece, Charley made her final pitch, hoping her mother had magically transformed from an active alcoholic into a woman who recognized the supreme value of sobriety and Twelve Step Programs. "I'll get you into the Betty Ford Center. I've heard great things about the place. They can make you better."

"I would rather fry in hell, thank you."

Charley wanted to smash something, preferably over her mother's rock-hard head. "Keep on drinking and you may get your wish."

Her mother must have remembered there were other people within earshot because she lowered her voice to a whisper. "You don't need to yell. I can hear you perfectly well. I'll have you know I can quit any time I want."

Charley had heard that argument many times, and never had a snappy comeback.

Her mother must have thought she was losing control of the argument, because she changed tactics and softened her voice. "Charlotte, darling. I'm sorry for all the things I said earlier. Please come home." Then, she played her trump card. "You're all I have. I need my daughter."

Anger and resentment bubbled in Charley's throat, but she tried to swallow it. What the hell difference did it make?

She had to go home sooner or later, and it would never get any easier. Resigned, she said: "Right, Mom. I'll be there. That way, I will not only try to prevent you from making a fool of yourself, but also see you home safely and pour you into your bed."

"I didn't bring you up to be disrespectful. Furthermore—"

Charley pressed the off button before she said something else she would regret.

Stupid, stupid, stupid. Why had she phoned her mother, hoping this time things would be different? She must be a glutton for punishment. Without her faithful watchdog to keep her in line, her mother had slipped further downhill. In the past, she'd tried to pace herself during the afternoon, allowing the truly heavy drinking to start along with dinner. Today, she was flat out drunk during lunch.

Charley had forfeited her chance at a couple of extra days of happiness with Kincaid. What other choice did a good daughter have? Obviously, Mom needed a steadying presence to help her confront the unpalatable truth of her alcoholism, and that's exactly what she would get. Dammit, sometimes life sucked.

Idly, Charley swatted at a mosquito and tried to focus. All day long, a nagging sense had plagued her that she'd forgotten something vital, something that might help her make sense out of everything – last night's events, her love, even her life. Her thoughts drifted to the cave and lingered, trying to figure out what was so important. After a few minutes, she gave up in frustration.

The brilliant afternoon loomed ahead, dismal, empty and interminable. If she didn't find a distraction, her thoughts would drive her crazy. Pocketing her phone, she rose to her feet and grasped the door handle. "I have to pack," she muttered under her breath.

"Over my dead body," Kincaid's disembodied voice replied through the screen.

Kincaid winced when Charley slammed the door, causing the entire cabin to shake on its foundation. *Imigh sa diabhal,* but his head pounded, and his left thigh burned like hell under its thick layer of surgical dressings. The scratches on his chest had turned out to be shallow, but the damned jaguar had done a number on his thigh. Otherwise, he was on the mend.

Charley's eyes crackled blue fire. She stood over him, hips slanted, hands fisted. "Don't mess with me right now, Kincaid. I'm warning you."

"Displaced anger is so unfair."

"You're supposed to be asleep."

"It's hard to get a decent sleep around here, especially when the head nurse engages in a screaming match with her mother right outside the window. I think I'll complain to the management."

She shot him an exasperated look. "You were playing possum, eavesdropping on my private conversation."

She was adorable when she was pissed. "My, my. Eavesdropping. Sounds familiar," he drawled.

She had the grace to blush.

"Any chance of getting something to drink?" he asked. His voice felt rusty, as if he hadn't used it in over a week.

In fulminating silence, she poured a glass of water and shoved it in his face. "Here, drink this."

"Thanks." He tossed it down obediently. The water slid around his parched mouth, washing the dryness away. He cleared his throat. "It occurs to me you're the sadist who kept waking me up every couple of hours."

"It was for your own good. You might have a concussion."

That explained the herd of elephants stomping through his skull. "My head is too hard for a concussion."

"No argument there. Colin claimed the pain killers would knock you out for a week." She stormed towards the alcove that served as a closet and bent over, giving him a perfect view of her rounded ass – an ass that begged to be squeezed – as she rummaged in the furthest corner.

He addressed the denim-encased cheeks. "Pills sometimes have the opposite effect on people, rev them up instead of sedate the hell out of them. Maybe I'm one of those people." Pocketing the last handful of pills instead of swallowing them had probably helped, too. He hated taking medication.

Maureen Fisher

A loud bumping and scraping emanated from the tiny alcove.

Kincaid struggled to sit up. A stab of pain shot down his thigh. "What the hell are you doing?"

She backed out, dragging her backpack and duffel bag with her. "What does it look like I'm doing?"

Feeling at a distinct disadvantage, Kincaid swung his legs over the side of the bed and stood up gingerly, testing his bad leg while she watched. When everything proved to be more-or-less functional, he limped across the room and pulled on the pair of shorts he'd left dangling over the chair.

"Going commando today, are we?" she asked sweetly.

"No clean underwear. Where's my shirt?"

She tossed him a purple and green aloha shirt patterned with huge, crimson flowers, then heaved the duffel bag onto the bed.

Kincaid released a gusty sigh and resigned himself to a long, hard battle. Now that the confrontation was imminent, he felt calm, almost confident. Gone were the panic and despair he'd felt when he realized Charley intended to walk out of his life. He was a man on a mission, focused, ruthless. Untidy emotions were a distraction he could ill afford. Somehow, he would find the words to convince her to stay.

She avoided looking at him and shook the wrinkles out of her turquoise blouse. After buttoning it meticulously, she spread it flat on the bed, folded it, but then jammed it into the duffel bag anyway.

To Kincaid, this was a very bad sign. His throat tightened at the thought that after tomorrow, he might never see her again. He wanted to touch the fine spray of freckles on her nose, but figured this wasn't the time or the place. Striving to appear unconcerned, he stretched his lips into the biggest shit-eating grin he could muster.

She ignored him and snatched up his favourite nightie, the pale pink one that left nothing to the imagination.

His next words surprised the hell out of him. "Were you planning to tell me you were leaving, or were you just going to sneak off while I was sleeping?"

Good God, I sound pathetic and girly.

"Dammit, Kincaid. You *knew* I was leaving tomorrow. We

314

agreed up front this was nothing more than a quick fling."

"I guess after everything that has happened between us, I assumed you had changed your mind." He tried to pull a lacy bra out of her grip, but she held on.

"Let go of my bra. I can't do anything to help my mother while I'm so far away."

He searched for inspiration and found it. "You can't help your mother." *Shit, that didn't come out right.* Frantically, he back-pedalled and tried to soften his words. "At least, not the way you're going at it."

She stared at him as if he'd lost his mind, but at least she'd stopped flinging underwear into her bag. "Someone has to keep an eye on her."

Dear God, he was dealing with a woman who didn't understand the rudiments of dealing with an alcoholic. He wanted to shake her until she understood, but managed to restrain himself by picking up a red thong and dangling it on one finger. "Damn, but this thing looks uncomfortable."

"Not your colour." She snatched the thong, wadded it together with a handful of panties and tossed the lingerie on top of the nightie.

When she turned her back, he stooped and removed the red thong, stuffing the wisp of fabric into his pocket. "You can't force your mother to stop drinking."

Her voice sharpened. "You sound just like my therapist, and I'll tell you the same thing I tell him. *I CAN TRY.*"

"But...."

"At least I won't blame myself later. No one will be able to say: 'Her daughter didn't try hard enough to make her stop drinking.' I can take her to movies where there's no booze, or at least try to convince her to drink more slowly. If she lands in trouble, I can bail her out. If she's broke, I can lend her money. Whenever she isn't watching, I can pour her wine down the sink. Then, she'll have to stop drinking ... at least briefly."

He wanted to erase the pain from her eyes. Instead, he tried to swamp her with his confidence. "This is not your battle to fight."

Charley made a wry face and bundled a pair of jeans into the duffel bag. "Of course it is."

Sweat dribbled down his back. He could see he was making a fine mess of his calm and systematic approach. "You can't live your mother's life for her. She's making her own choices, even if you don't like them. Only she can decide to stop drinking, but I guarantee she won't as long as you make life easy for her." He hadn't meant to shout, but she just wasn't getting the message.

The look in her eyes could melt steel. "If I don't help her, I don't know who will. Eventually, she'll kill herself."

Damn, but the woman exhibited dismaying signs of mulish obstinacy. He forced himself to speak calmly. "It's not your choice to make. Hard as it is, you must allow your mother to follow her own path."

Annoyance tightened her voice. "How can you be so heartless? What kind of daughter would I be if I sat back and let her poison herself?"

"A wise and caring daughter. You're not helping with your fussing and enabling."

Eyes snapping, her face flushed with anger, she stomped to the alcove and returned with an armful of blouses, which she dumped onto the bed. "What do you know about it anyway, Kincaid?"

Bloody hell. She wasn't buying the logical approach. Clearly, his well-reasoned arguments weren't working. Calm resignation filled him with fatalistic gloom. To hell with it. He saw no other choice but to implement his backup plan. Charley deserved the unvarnished truth. She needed to hear the whole sordid story of his struggle with booze and drugs. She needed to understand that an alcoholic usually has to hit rock bottom before deciding recovery was a better choice.

He had to give it his best shot, even if he ended up driving her away.

Chapter 37

A bead of sweat trickled down the neck of Kincaid's shirt, soaking the dressing on his chest and releasing a pungent, medical odour, compliments of the industrial strength antibacterial ointment on his wounds. The cabin smelled like the hospital where the ambulance had taken his sister after she committed suicide. Hospitals still made him nervous. That explained why his mouth had dried up.

He poured another glass of water and took a quick sip, watching Charley methodically folding blouses until he couldn't take it one minute longer. "Would you stop packing, Charley, and listen to me for a few minutes?" When she continued to stuff blouses into the duffel bag, he injected a note of urgency into his voice. "Please. I want to tell you a story very few people on this planet have heard."

His vehemence must have sunk in, because she perched on the edge of a chair, clutching the blouse to her chest and favouring him with a glare. "I'm not sure I want to listen to any story."

"This one might interest you. It's about a fascinating subject – me."

She refused to bite. "And you would be relevant to my mother's situation – how?"

He took a deep breath. "This story's about an alcoholic and drug addict. From the addict's perspective."

That caught her attention. She stared at him, her eyes round with surprise.

He would have laughed if a knife wasn't slicing a hole in his gut. "Surely, you guessed. You know I don't touch anything stronger than ginger ale."

"You could have mentioned it earlier, before...." She swallowed the rest of her sentence and looked uncomfortable.

He understood only too well what she meant – before she seduced him, before they made mad, passionate love beside the lagoon....

Before he fell in love.

Time stood still. The roaring inside Kincaid's head made it difficult to concentrate. It was true! No wonder he felt nauseated about Charley's imminent departure. Without realizing it, he had fallen head over heels in love. How had he not seen this coming? He felt like he'd been blindsided, sucker punched and hog-tied.

Conflicting feelings of fear and elation left him reeling. He wanted to grab her, kiss her silly, get down on bended knee and profess his undying love, but he stopped himself in the nick of time. He couldn't make a spur-of-the-moment decision of this magnitude. *Mo Dhia*, there was too much to absorb, too much to think about, too much to process. He needed more time.

Right now, he had a goal to accomplish – convince Charley to stick around in his life. So far, he was doing a piss-poor job of it.

She looked pretty much ready to bolt.

He cast his mind around for a logical solution and hit on a brilliant tactic. In the classroom, authority had always served him well. Students listened to the professor. No reason it wouldn't work now. Testing his theory, he addressed the student. "Okay, listen up...." He narrowly avoided addressing Charley as 'class' and cleared his throat to mask his close call. "This is hard for me, so I only want to say it once. Please don't interrupt, and if you have any questions, I would ask you to save them until I'm finished."

She crossed her legs and folded her arms across her chest, a blouse tail protruding from her fist. "I wouldn't dream of interrupting. You have my undivided attention."

He stalked across an imaginary podium, so focused on the logical case he wanted to build, he hardly noticed his aches and pains. "I believe I mentioned that after my sister's suicide, my mum became an alcoholic. What I didn't tell you was that I, too, turned to the bottle. I truly believed I should have been able to prevent Mairie's death."

"I already told you it wasn't your fault. You couldn't have known."

He shot a glare at the student who looked dismayingly unrepentant. "That's an interruption. To continue my story, if I might, when my mum started hitting the bottle, she didn't hide her booze well enough. I used to pour myself a couple of stiff ones and drink them in my room. It helped alleviate the guilt. Soon, I needed more, so I found a bootlegger who kept me well supplied. By the tender age of sixteen, I was a full-fledged drunk."

"But you were only a kid."

He stopped pacing and met her gaze, anticipating revulsion. He found only an impassive expression he didn't dare decipher. "Unfortunately, the younger you are, the quicker it happens."

"How did you get the money?"

"I was big for my age. I talked myself into a job at the corner shop. I cut lawns. I stole from my mum's purse when she was too drunk to care. Now, where was I before you interrupted?"

"You were a full-fledged drunk at sixteen."

"Right." A dribble of sweat trickled down his cheek and he dug into his pocket for a handkerchief. He had already mopped his forehead before the flash of red caught his eye. *Shit.* He had just wiped his face with her underwear. Hoping she hadn't noticed his momentary lapse, he balled up the fabric in his fist, and retraced his steps across the cabin floor. "Pretty soon, I fell in with a rough crowd. We partied, we drank, we cut classes, and some of us used drugs – cocaine and even heroin. The hard stuff was easy to get if you knew the right people. Before I knew it, I was hooked."

Kincaid didn't look at Charley. Her disgust would destroy him, and he wanted to get the rest of the story out before he fell apart. "For a long time, my parents and I pretended nothing was wrong. If I was puking ill with a hangover, my mum made my excuses to the school or lied to my boss. If I passed out on the weekend, she pretended I was tired and overworked. When I had a car accident, she pleaded with the police to be lenient."

"What was your father doing all this time?"

He risked a glance and lost his focus. She had stopped her pretence of folding the blouse and sat perfectly still. "Huh? Oh, my dad. He was too busy raising my sisters and trying to cope with my mum's drinking. For a long time, he didn't know I had a problem. By the time he figured out what was going on, it was too late. I was an alcoholic and an addict.

"Drugs and drinking became my entire life, but we never talked about it. I flunked my year. My girlfriend dumped me. My parents told everybody I was suffering emotional distress over my sister's death. They insisted I get help, but I refused to admit I had a problem. The more they nagged, the more resentful I became. How could I give up the very substances that filled my life with meaning and excitement? Finally, my dad ordered me to leave home unless I stopped drinking. I chose to live on the street for the rest of the summer and damn near broke my parents' hearts." He stopped pacing and faced Charley, gauging her reaction.

"That's a terrible story. Are you suggesting I desert my mother the way your parents deserted you?" Her eyes had turned dark and stormy.

She wasn't getting the point. He answered in his best professorial voice: "Excellent question. But perhaps I can convince you that my parents gave me the greatest gift of my life by kicking me out of the house. You see, as long as they were making it possible for me to drink and buy drugs, I had no reason to quit. After I left, I was a mess. My world collapsed and my parents wrote me off. Fast forward three months, I woke up one morning lying on a Glasgow sidewalk in a puddle of my own vomit, barefoot because somebody had stolen my shoes during the night."

"Oh, my God," she whispered.

He let the interruption ride, doing his best to ignore the contempt she was surely feeling. "I knew I had arrived at a crossroad. I had to make a choice. I could either finish the job of killing myself, or I could dry out. I chose to live. Choosing recovery over booze was the hardest decision I ever made, but I knew I'd be dead inside six months if I didn't pull my life together. I called my parents and they placed me in a rehabilitation centre where I sobered up and got clean."

Drained of energy, he sank into a chair. The squawk of a parrot outside the cabin emphasized the heavy silence inside. He figured she could hear the thunk of his heart as it landed on the floor.

Finally, Charley cleared her throat and said: "It's a touching story and I'm glad of the outcome, but what has it to do with my mother and me?"

Bloody hell. Obviously, the teacher hadn't conveyed the salient point to his student. "Because I want you to understand the dynamics of addiction from the alcoholic's point of view. And I want you to forgive yourself for your inability to convince your mother to stop drinking."

She shook her head. "Don't you get it? If I could only find exactly the right words to use, the right way to make her see what she's doing to herself, she would understand and quit."

"Can't be done," Kincaid said gently. "Nothing you say or do will force her to stop. She'll only accept the help she needs when she faces the problem head-on. Alcoholism is a terrible disease."

She raised her eyebrows. "Oh, man. I have a hard time buying into that disease theory."

"Full-blown alcoholism is a physical craving. You have absolutely no control over your mother's drinking any more than you'd have over, say, diabetes or cancer, but you've shouldered the impossible task anyway. You aren't helping her with your meddling."

Charley stiffened. "*Meddling*? How dare you accuse me of meddling when all I'm doing is trying to save her life."

Kincaid took his time collecting his thoughts. He wanted to plead and grovel, beg her not to leave, but she had to make her choice freely. After a few seconds, he hit on another logical argument. "As long as you protect her from the consequences of her actions, she will have no reason to quit drinking."

Charley turned and gazed out the window, leaving Kincaid staring at her back. She was quiet for so long, he knew he had put his foot in it. His head throbbed like crazy, and vicious little devils drove pitchforks into his thigh. Drained of energy, he flopped back onto the bed and said: "Take all the time you need. It's a lot to absorb in one swallow. Takes most people months or years, if ever, to come to terms with the fact that we are helpless to control another human being's actions or thoughts."

The irony of his advice caused a small bitter smile to play around his mouth. Without actually saying the words, he had spent the previous hour of his life trying his damndest to convince Charley to stay.

Charley stared blindly out the window, her stomach a mass of knots. She scarcely noticed the sunshine slanting through the trees, painting a dappled pattern on the grass outside the cabin.

A small bubble of hope, so ephemeral she was afraid to trust it, flared in her chest. Until today, she had never allowed herself to believe she had a choice. Oh, sure, her therapist had pretty much told her the same thing, but she hadn't been ready to listen.

Today was different. The phone call with her mother had pushed her to the brink, but Kincaid's story had sent her freefalling over the edge. His words had opened up the possibility that she had the power to reclaim her life. She could simply slip off the noose she had placed around her neck and tightened voluntarily, until it was choking off her life.

Still, the idea took some getting used to.

She felt Kincaid's presence behind her and heard the bed springs squeak. Warmth spread throughout her body as she contemplated the gamble he'd taken. He'd risked her condemnation and cared enough to reach out and tell her the story of his life. The least she could do was to keep an open mind and consider his advice, as impossible as it might sound.

When she turned around, she saw that Kincaid had thrown one arm over his eyes. The red thong lay neatly folded on the pillow beside him. She drew up a chair and sat beside him. "I've thought about everything you said."

He lowered his arm and sat up. "Oh, aye?" he drawled, his eyes shuttered, deep lines dragging his mouth down at the corners.

"If I understand you correctly, you're telling me I should

butt out and stop trying to force my mother to quit drinking."

Some of the tension around his mouth relaxed. "That about sums it up."

"And if I leave my mother alone, I'll be doing her a favour and saving my own sanity at the same time."

"True."

"You sounded a lot like my therapist."

"He's a very perceptive man. You should listen to him."

"It can't be that simple."

"It is. But you'll find it's far from easy."

"I honestly don't know if I can let go."

"The best thing you can do for your mother is to stop picking up the pieces. Allow her to make her own mistakes. I know it may seem counter-intuitive, but every time you rescue your mother, you betray her."

The word 'betray' pierced her wall of denial. She went very still.

Her intuition warned her that her own spirit would never survive the trauma if she committed another betrayal. She thought of all the unfaithfulness, all the deceptions, and all the desertions that had blighted her lives, past and present. The silken thread of betrayal wove an ever-present pattern in the tapestry of her life. Was it possible to end the cycle here and now? To find a path that did not involve betraying either her mother or Kincaid?

She raised her gaze and studied his face, seeing the compassion brimming in his eyes. She sighed in acceptance. "I never looked at it that way. I would never knowingly betray my mother."

"I know, Charley. But enabling her is not the answer."

Something hard and unyielding inside of her cracked. The full impact of the freedom within her grasp sank in, and tears trickled down her face, slowly at first, but soon they gushed out in a salty torrent.

"Come here, *Mhuirnin*."

With an incoherent cry, she flung herself into his arms and let go, welcoming the healing flood. Tears exploded in a downpour and washed away the despair that had gripped her ever since she could remember. Long-buried and highly toxic emotions bubbled from her inner core and shook her body. A tidal wave of release washed over her as the hopelessness, guilt and fear streamed away. She sobbed until there were no more tears left inside her. When the hurricane subsided at last, she raised her head, feeling a bone-deep peace.

"There, now. Everything will be okay." He held out a box of tissues.

"I don't know how to thank you enough," she mumbled through a fistful of tissues.

He smiled, and for the first time that afternoon, she sensed his grin was genuine. "They're only tissues."

"Not for the tissues, you idiot. For caring enough to tell me your story. For opening my eyes to possibilities."

His next words caught her unaware. "I hope that means you'll stay."

She stiffened and pulled away, unable to give him the answer he wanted to hear, unwilling to lie. "I don't know, Kincaid. This is all so sudden...."

He ran a thumb over her cheek. "At least give us a chance."

Pain started deep inside and spread. Yesterday, all things being equal, she would have eaten worms to hear those words. Today, they caused nothing but pain. Man of Science wouldn't look at her the same way after she'd made her fateful confession. Past life flashbacks were one thing; shapeshifting was quite another.

She squirmed away from him and gave him a saddened look. "My head is still spinning, Kincaid. It's too soon. I need to go for a walk and take a little time alone to adjust."

He looked surprised and a little hurt. "Of course. I have a few things I need to think about, too." When she tried to sidle away, he put a hand on her arm and detained her headlong flight. "Later though, I'll need to talk to you about last night. I have a few questions."

I'll just bet you do. And when you hear my answers, you'll find you can't hustle me onto the plane fast enough. How could she possibly tell him the truth? Did she really expect him to believe she was a reincarnated Olmec high priestess who had merrily shapeshifted into a jaguar to save his life? She scarcely believed it herself.

"No problem." She chirped, avoiding eye contact. "I'll tell

you everything I remember. And after that, I'll have to finish my packing." She picked up the red thong and placed it in the duffel bag along with the rest of her underwear.

His eyebrows slammed together. "I don't believe it. You can't still be thinking of going home."

Sometimes safe was better than sorry. "Only until I decide what I need to do with the rest of my life. I thought I might try my luck in Manhattan." Her throat wanted to fall out.

He ground out the words. "Bloody hell. It's because I'm a recovering alcoholic, isn't it?"

She could only gape at him, at his abysmal misunderstanding, then she quickly recovered. "No, no. It's nothing like that."

He narrowed his eyes. "Then prove it. Stay here. I know you have feelings for me."

She shook her head, but her heart gave a treacherous little flutter. Torn between a desperate hunger to stay with the man she loved and fear that another rejection would destroy her bruised heart beyond recognition, the fear won. She couldn't take the chance. She managed a brilliant smile. "Hey, I'm saving us both a lot of heartache. All I wanted was a quick fling. I got it, now it's over, end of story."

He gripped her shoulders, and stared into her eyes, her heart, her soul. She tried not to squirm. After a moment that lasted a lifetime, he nodded, as if he had seen what he was looking for. "Cut the crap, Charley. You're not that great an actress. Your eyes give you away every time. If I didn't know better, I'd say you were a coward."

She straightened until she was almost nose-to-nose with Kincaid, feeling the flush spread over her face. "Bull. You take that back."

"Not a hope in hell, beautiful. If you give up without a fight, you're a damn coward."

Those were fighting words.

Suddenly, the air around her head throbbed and pulsed with an energy that created a mild tingling all over the surface of her body. Her joints starting to pop and tighten. Refusing to give in to the panic, she ordered herself to concentrate. Finally, she succeeded in pushing the jaguar back inside where it belonged. She sucked in a shaky sigh of relief.

That's all she needed right now – to sprout fangs, whiskers and a black furry coat.

When she'd pulled herself together, she realized Kincaid was staring at her, disbelief and shock written on his face. "For a moment there, I could swear I saw … " He massaged his temples. "It was your eyes. They turned yellow. Reminded me, somehow, of Horrie…."

Dammit, that was a close call. She had to get this shapeshifting thing under control. "Must be the whack on the head, Kincaid. Hallucinations are a dangerous sign. You should go to bed."

"Only if you join me." His heavy-lidded eyes promised unlimited afternoon delight.

She bit her lip to suppress a smile. "Really, really bad idea. Think of your concussion. Besides, there's something I have to do." *But what was it?*

Suddenly, she realized the near-transformation had blasted away a barrier in her mind. The nagging sensation that she had unfinished business to take care of had blossomed into certainty. She knew now what she had to do.

"You're not running out on me, are you?"

"Don't worry. I'll be back later to tell you about last night."

Chapter 38

Kincaid limped into the kitchen and sniffed the air. Steamy odours of *Frijoles Borrachos* and *Mixiotes de Carne* filled the air with their heady perfume. Colin stood in front of the stove, stirring a pan of sizzling onions. He tossed in a handful of chopped garlic, releasing a symphony of fragrant steam. Kincaid's mouth watered.

Colin looked up and grinned. "I wondered how long it would take you to get here."

"What made you think I was awake?"

Colin set a plate of muffins on the table. "Charley dropped in a few minutes ago for a wee snack. You just missed her."

Kincaid wolfed down a muffin in two chomps, enjoying the buttery sweetness. "The woman has the appetite of a grizzly bear. Did she say where she was going?" he inquired around a mouthful of muffin.

"She didn't seem exactly sure, but just as she was walking out the door, she mentioned the cave."

Kincaid spun on Colin. "You let her go to the cave alone after what happened last night?"

"Have you ever tried to prevent Charley from doing something she's set her heart on?"

The two men shared a look of deep commiseration.

Kincaid shook his head in perplexed frustration. "Why is she hell-bent on going to the cave?"

Colin shrugged. "Some nonsense about unfinished business. Don't worry about Charley. She can take care of herself. Besides, you posted a guard at the entrance of the cave."

Kincaid dropped into a chair and brooded for a few minutes, watching Colin puttering. Finally, he blurted: "She's

327

leaving for San Francisco tomorrow."

"So she said." Colin cast an accusing glare at Kincaid. "Well, what did you expect? You haven't told the lass how you feel, have you?"

"How the hell would you know how I feel?"

"Och, it's written all over your face, clear as a bell. Every time she walks into the room, you light up and melt into a blob of warm goo, just like one of those newfangled lava lamps."

"Oh, bloody hell," Kincaid said. "I'm not sure I want romantic complications in my life right now, especially after Leila. Besides, I have no idea how Charley feels about me. She claimed all she wanted was a quick fling, but I'm pretty sure she has feelings for me." He cracked his knuckles, pondering the incomprehensibility of women. "Strong feelings. I'm certain she's lying for some reason."

"Then what are you waiting for?" Colin smacked Kincaid's hand. "And stop that knuckle cracking. You'll develop rheumatism when you're my age."

Kincaid gave his left hand a final satisfying pop while he considered Colin's question. "I need time to consider all aspects of the situation, make sure I'm doing the right thing."

Colin shook his head in mock despair. "You great, hulking gowk. If you analyze your feelings to death, you'll lose her. Luckily, you still have the rest of today to change her mind before the plane arrives." He stopped and scowled at his friend. "I assume we're both talking about your telling Charley how you love her madly, desperately, and with all of your dry, shrivelled up, wee heart."

Kincaid shot Colin a baleful glare. "Aye, I suppose we are. I can't stop replaying the moment when I saw Felipe crouched over her, his hands clamped around her neck .... " His voice faded as he contemplated the unthinkable. If she had died on the mountainside, he would have spent the rest of his days going through the empty motions of living without the woman he loved by his side.

"Then stop wasting time. You'd better go put the lass out of her misery."

"You're right. I have to talk to her."

"You shouldn't walk too far on that leg. As soon as you put away a decent meal, I'll drive you as far as the ancient city. That way, you'll both arrive at about the same time."

"I want some real food," Kincaid growled. "Steak and chips."

"Dry toast and sliced banana," Colin countered.

Kincaid groaned. "A man needs meat to recover his strength."

"Well, maybe a nice, wee poached egg with your toast."

"Three eggs, six sausages and a stack of pancakes."

"Two eggs, two sausages, toast, some fruit and a large glass of milk," said Colin firmly.

Realizing he had lost the battle, Kincaid changed the subject. "Has anyone seen Leila since last night?"

"Not a trace," said Colin. "But we found footprints on the hillside behind the cave. She's probably holed up somewhere."

"You've notified the police?" asked Kincaid.

"Aye. I reported everything that has happened around here as soon as I stitched you up – Felipe's abduction of Charley, Leila's attack on you, and their disappearance."

A hint of satisfaction touched Kincaid's smile. "She won't get far without food and transportation."

"Exactly what I told the police. They'll keep an eye out for her, but she'll probably take to the hills." Colin put a plate in front of Kincaid.

"What about Felipe?"

Colin fished the poached eggs out of boiling water and placed them onto the plate beside two lonely sausages. He grinned, a glint of gold proclaiming the extent of his glee. "Ah, yes. Felipe. You'll never believe this."

Kincaid felt like throttling his friend. "Spit it out, man. Don't keep me in suspense."

Colin sauntered over to the counter bearing a steaming mug of coffee and sat down. He took a huge, leisurely, slurp before he spoke. "Turns out, the police have been keeping an eye on Felipe for over a year."

"Impossible. He's been working with me the entire time."

"One of your workers is an undercover agent."

"A cop? Here in camp?" Kincaid was unable to mask his surprise.

"Aye. One of the best. As you know, there have been

suspicious fires and explosions on several digs over the last ten years. The police were finally able to link them to Felipe and now he's disappeared again. It was difficult because he changed his name and appearance several times. And you'll never guess where he worked several years ago." Colin paused dramatically, then caught Kincaid's glare. "With us," he said hastily. "On our first dig together. His name used to be Pedro Silviero."

Kincaid hissed in a breath. "Isn't he the Mexican lad Leila used to spend time with?"

Colin nodded. "One and the same."

"He deliberately hid his identity from me. I wonder why."

Colin shrugged. "Probably because he knew you couldn't stand the sight of him thirteen years ago. Do you think Leila recognized him?"

"They may be hiding out together." Kincaid swallowed the last bite and threw down his napkin. "We've wasted enough time here. It's time for me to tell Charley how I feel about her."

Chapter 39

Charley had yielded to her growing compulsion to climb the pyramid, but now that the answers were within reach, she was having second thoughts. After last night's events, the very thought of entering the cave made her blood run cold.

Conceding momentary defeat, she lowered herself onto the slab of rock that had once served as a throne – her throne. It wasn't that she was a coward, exactly. She simply wasn't quite ready to open herself up again to the cave's energy.

The fitful breeze tossed her hair around her shoulders. Bright, golden peace settled like a balm over her uneasy spirit. A tiny gecko darted away between her feet and Charley followed its path with her gaze until it disappeared into a crevice.

Except for the guard posted at the tunnel entrance, she had thought herself alone until a deep voice rumbled in her ear. "You shouldn't be here alone."

She catapulted from the bench and faced the intruder. Dark stubble covered the lower half of Kincaid's face giving him a dark, dangerous look. "Dammit, Kincaid. One of these days, I won't survive the shock of your stealth attacks." She reflexively gripped the strap of her backpack. Her heartbeat escalated to a frenzied drum roll and her legs quivered as if she'd run the twenty-six-mile San Francisco Marathon.

His mouth tightened and his eyes glittered with a strong emotion held on a short leash. He pried the mesh shoulder strap out of her nervous grip. Long fingers enveloped her hand. "I won't let you walk out of my life without putting up a fight."

Pain sliced through her heart. As soon as she told him the truth about her past life escapades, she would kill any chance they might have of a future together.

When he stroked her quivering palm with his thumb, she shivered, remembering those clever hands. How could her body have a mind of its own while her brain screamed out a warning? Charley pulled her hand away. "Please don't do that. You don't understand." She backed away until she felt the rocky wall at her back, aware of a dull ache in her chest. She'd just have to get used to it.

Kincaid's face was set in rigid lines with furrows cut deep from nose to mouth. Only someone who knew him well would discern that pain, not anger, lay behind his eyes. He limped towards her and placed his hands on her shoulders. "I know you're afraid of getting hurt again, but I'm asking you to trust me."

Charley drew in a trembling breath. "It's safer not to feel anything."

He shook his head slowly, as if to deny her words. "No. You're cutting yourself off from the best things life has to offer – love and trust. That fair terrifies me. I'm afraid you will never let yourself trust another man again. How can I convince you to take one more chance?"

She hunched her shoulders and let out her breath in a long sigh. "You'll be stuffing me into the plane tomorrow after I explain to you everything that happened in the cavern."

Kincaid brought one hand to her face and cupped her cheek while he stroked her quivering lips with the other. "Charley, nothing you say will make me change my mind. I must have been mad to think I could keep you at arm's length. If you leave me now, then all of this," he waved his arm in the air to encompass the entire dig site, "won't mean a damn."

She wanted nothing more than to lean into his warmth, but she forced herself to remain rigid and unresponsive. "I have to tell you the truth. I don't want any secrets between us. Then, we'll see if you've changed your mind."

He frowned. "This sounds serious. What dark skeletons are you hiding?"

An unfortunate choice of words, given the gruesome crimes Zanazca had committed. "Before I tell you my tale, I want to know what you remember about last night."

Kincaid's smile had a bitter edge. "Let's sit down for this." He pulled her down onto the bench beside him and draped an arm over her shoulders, as if confirming they were both still alive.

An undercurrent of sensual awareness hummed along her nerves. She leaned into him, enjoying the solid warmth of his body next to hers.

"It's all kind of fuzzy," he said slowly. "I was guarding the entrance, freezing and thinking about you. Someone stole up behind me and whacked me over the head. I didn't hear a thing."

"Leila."

"I know that now. When I regained consciousness, I discovered someone had tied me to the altar. Next thing I knew, Leila was standing over me, waving a knife in my face and shrieking about revenge."

"Then what?" Charley prompted.

His voice roughened. "I could see in her eyes she wanted to kill me. She disappeared for a few moments then the first jaguar appeared." He paused reflectively. "But I have the distinct impression of two animals." He raised an eyebrow, inviting a response.

Charley made a non-committal noise intended to sooth and divert.

"After that, everything's a bit of a blur, between gunshots and your popping up out of nowhere, then black jaguars, spotted jaguars, fighting jaguars. I'm not too clear on the details." His gaze raked her face. "But I could swear you wandered into the cave, stark naked, and then I must have blacked out again because—"

"The whack on the head must have affected your vision," she interrupted, changing the subject. There was no easy way to explain her distressing lack of clothes.

"There are some things in life a man can never forget, and your strolling around the cave naked would be one of them." He narrowed his eyes as if sensing her evasion. "I'm beginning to think you know more about what happened last night than I do."

Charley felt her face grow hot. She had no wish to lie to him again, but he'd never believe the truth. Shapeshifting was

333

too farfetched for even the most liberal freethinker to swallow, let alone a scientist with an analytical turn of mind. She sighed. "This is very difficult for me, Kincaid. You're going to think I've lost my marbles, and I don't blame you. Even I can't wrap my mind around what happened."

He cut off her words by laying a large hand over hers. "Stop procrastinating, Charley. How can I understand if you don't tell me?"

She chewed her bottom lip. How could she find the correct words to explain the inexplicable? All morning, she had rehearsed several variations in her head and rejected every one of them in despair. How could she possibly expect Kincaid to believe she had spontaneously shapeshifted into a jaguar? Without concrete proof, his scientific mind would reject her story.

She twisted her ring nervously. If ever she needed the healing power of a turquoise, now was the moment.

Just as she began to resign herself to facing Kincaid's inevitable scorn and disbelief, a blaze of clarity burned away the paralyzing confusion. The reason she had felt herself inexplicably drawn to the cave was now abundantly clear. How could she not have seen it sooner?

She jumped to her feet.

"Come with me!" she exclaimed, her voice filled with renewed energy and excitement. "Tell the guard to stay outside. I have something to show you."

The flashlight wavered in Charley's trembling hand as she led Kincaid into the tunnel. What if she was wrong?

Kincaid's voice echoed behind her. "Where are you taking me?"

"You'll see."

They entered the cavern and Charley took Kincaid's hand, feeling its warmth close around her own. "There's something I have to do and I need some space. I want you to sit on the steps to the altar."

"Are you sure you know what you're doing?"

No. "Yes." She could not suppress a sudden shiver. If this didn't work, nothing would convince Kincaid that she wasn't insane. "Here, take the flashlight."

For once, he didn't argue, but took the flashlight from her hand.

Charley reached up and ran her fingers over his cheek, enjoying the rasp of stubble. "This shouldn't take long."

Favouring his bad leg, he limped towards the altar and looked at her over his shoulder, his voice doubtful. "I don't know what you have in mind, but be careful."

"Don't worry. I'll be fine," she said, injecting a note of certainty into her voice.

Charley started circling the perimeter of the cavern, searching for something she didn't understand, knowing only that the cave held the key to her future. She tried to clear her mind of everything, sinking into herself, deeper and deeper. Fragments of memories flickered at the edge of her consciousness, but she was unable to hold on to them before they faded.

Stop trying so hard. She paused and heaved a breath.

Stretching out one hand, she trailed her fingertips across the stone wall, feeling the slick smoothness of impervious rock. She closed her eyes and welcomed the velvet obscurity, hoping it would impart a message she could decipher.

She circled the cave slowly, letting her hands roam freely over the surface. She had no idea what she was looking for. All she knew was she'd recognize it when she found it. The thud of her pounding heart filled her head and she bit down on her lip hard, to subdue the whimper of frustration. Time after time, her questing fingers met with only rocky walls, depressingly unmarred by any cracks or knobs. "I know I can find it, dammit," she muttered.

The rumble of a deep voice in her left ear startled her from the trance. "Might I ask what you are trying to find?" Kincaid had crept up on her once again and was sounding mildly amused. "You don't need to do this alone. I want to help." He directed the flashlight on the wall ahead of her.

"Dammit, Kincaid," she burst out, glaring at him in exasperation. "I asked you to stay back. Now look. You broke my concentration." Her hand moved jerkily against the wall.

"You have no idea what you're looking for, do you? Let's get out of here."

She refused to admit defeat, not when the answer was so close. "It's around here somewhere, I know it. Shine the light higher."

She held her breath and stretched her arm upward in a wide arc until her fingers brushed against a rocky protuberance. She froze. A bolt of energy shot from the rock and resolved itself into the frantic humming noise that was music to her ears. She relaxed and gave herself up to the torrent of memories that poured over her in waves, dimly aware of Kincaid's voice fading into the distance.

Zanazca sensed her allotted time on this earthly plane was nearing an end. She had seen the mouth of the underworld gaping open to welcome her home and understood that strong forces would soon snip the fragile thread of her life. A sense of urgency gripped her. She must complete the chronicle of her life before she died.

Day after day, she had hunched over the rough wooden table set into a niche in the wall of the sacred cave, incising stone tablets using fragments of the magic rock that had fallen from the sky. The ancient symbols and glyphs handed down by her ancestors would reveal her story to future generations. Only then would her tortured soul find the peace that eluded her in this world.

She had recorded everything with stark accuracy, sparing nothing – her hopes and fears, loves and hates, joys and sorrows, deeds of goodness and evil.

And regrets.

Most of all, she had recorded her regrets.

The chisel almost slipped from tired fingers and she closed her eyes. Her most beloved acolyte, her successor, would betray her soon, possibly tonight. She rubbed her eyes wearily. Would she be able to gather the strength and will to fight the treachery, or would she merely accept it as her just punishment for the depraved life she had lived?

She did not know the answer.

When Zanazca etched the last character of her signature, she lay down her tools and sighed, dispirited to the core. One last time, she reread her final entry – a curse, a prophecy, and a promise – an explanation to future generations for the inevitable fall of her people, should death overtake her tonight.

She ran her fingers over the words she had carved, feeling their roughness under her fingertips: "When I die, my enemies will destroy the city. Walls will crumble, forgotten, as if they never existed. Death and destruction are the legacy I leave. When the time is right, I will return to tell my story and break this chain of evil. Thus will I redeem my soul."

She picked up the heavy stone slab and carried it to the secret spot. When she pressed her palm against the rock, the stone slab swung away with a low, grating reverberation that set her teeth on edge. This might be the last time a human hand opened the portal for a timeless measure of cycles.

Charley regained her senses to find herself locked in Kincaid's arms. He stared at her as if she had two heads, terrible comprehension dawning in his eyes.

"Don't ever do that to me again," he growled and squeezed her so hard, she thought he would crack a rib or two.

Damn, he was strong. She pushed against his chest to loosen his grip. "Easy, Kincaid. You're crushing me." She gasped, trying to catch her breath. "This is it. Do you understand? I found it," she said, twisting away.

She grasped the knob of rock and jiggled it while Kincaid watched in disbelief.

Nothing happened. Her heart sank into her stomach with a thud. She had been so certain. In desperation, she pressed harder, then twisted.

A faint grinding sound was audible in the heavy silence of the cave, and she could have sworn the rock moved an inch.

There had to be a trick. She closed her eyes and let her hands remember. One of them grasped the knob and twisted, while the other placed pressure on the wall, slightly to the left.

The rock swung back in a soundless motion to reveal a black cavity.

Chapter 40

Charley let Kincaid precede her, enjoying the inarticulate noise he made as he shone the light into the hole, illuminating the smaller cave.

"How did you know it was here, Charley?" He gazed at her, a stunned expression in his eyes. "If I hadn't seen you open the door using the wee hidden mechanism, I would never have believed it."

He doesn't know the half of it yet. A sense of nervous anticipation overwhelmed Charley.

He tested the air by sniffing deeply. Apparently finding it breathable, he stood in the middle of the chamber and turned slowly in a full circle, as if trying to grasp the magnitude of the discovery.

She hung back in the entrance, simply enjoying his gratifying reaction. He opened his mouth and snapped it shut several times. The sight must have rendered him speechless, she noted in surprise – a rare affliction for Kincaid.

The chamber was exactly the way she remembered it. The round cavity measured approximately ten feet in diameter. Stone shelves encircled the walls at two-foot intervals, each divided into niches containing three stone tablets stacked one upon the other. Only a few of the shelves had collapsed under their own weight.

He planted an exuberant kiss on her lips, swung her around, and found his voice at last. "This may be the biggest discovery of the century, even bigger than the sarcophagi. Here. Hold the flashlight." His eyes gleamed with an archaeological fervour as he reached out and selected a stone tablet at random. "It seems to be written by a high priestess called Zanazca. That's the same name that appears on the sarcophagus."

338

He replaced the tablet and selected another. "I think it's her life story. Listen to this." Kincaid spoke haltingly, tracing the characters with his fingers as he read. "*I have reached the pinnacle of my ... power. It is time for me to train another ... to take my place. I will speak to her ... this day.*"

Sudden goose bumps popped up on Charley's forearms. Zanazca had loved Uxatle, the young acolyte, like a daughter.

He placed the tablet back in its spot and turned slowly to face her. He cleared his throat, as if searching to find the right words. "I'm almost afraid to ask, but how did you know this hiding place was here? How could you possibly have known how to open the door to this secret cave?"

"You won't believe me if I tell you," she hedged.

"Try me."

"Let me show you something first. Pick another tablet and set it down over here where I can see it."

He selected one at random and placed it gently on the floor. "Now what?" he said, running his fingers across the surface.

She squatted beside him and directed the beam onto the tablet. While he looked over her shoulder, she traced the glyphs incised in the stone with her finger and read the ancient writing aloud in a confident voice.

When she stopped speaking, he didn't move. "Dear God, you can read the script more fluently than I can, and I've had years of training."

"So have I."

She could feel the weight of his gaze in the heavy silence following her words.

"Let's try this again," he said abruptly.

Three more times, he presented a new tablet, and three more times, she translated the glyphs flawlessly.

Kincaid made a very Gaelic sounding oath and grunted, "Impossible. You're a reporter, not an archaeologist."

"Investigative journalist," she said calmly and reached for the tablet she knew contained Zanazca's last journal entry. "Now I'm going to recite the exact words carved on this rock without reading them. When I'm finished, you can tell me if I'm correct."

"You can't possibly know what's written there."

"Ah, but you're wrong. This is Zanazca's last entry – a curse and a promise. Listen to this." Charley closed her eyes and recited from memory. "*I have seen the future and I have not long to live. When I die, my enemies will destroy the city. Walls will crumble, forgotten, as if they never existed. Death and destruction are the legacy I leave. When the time is right, I will return to tell my story and break this chain of evil. Thus will I redeem my soul.*"

As the impact of what she had recited hit home, Charley rubbed arms that were covered in sudden goose bumps. If she truly believed Zanazca's life was real, then she had just proved that the soul truly was immortal.

He raised his head and stared. "*Mo Dhia*! You knew."

"And every word of it has come true."

"Aye." He paused, collecting thoughts. "The city crumbled into ruin and remained hidden until one of my men stumbled over it."

She shivered. "Get your walking stick and let's go. This place still gives me the creeps."

Before she could take a step, the sound of tinkling laughter from behind the altar riveted her to the spot. She shielded her eyes from the sudden beam of light slicing the darkness.

A slim figure glided towards them. The pistol in the outstretched hand glinted a dangerous message.

"Stop right there or I'll shoot." Leila's stance and aimed weapon belied her conversational tone.

Chapter 41

The pistol felt good to Leila. Its grip nestled in her palm, cold and solid. With her left hand, she skewered Alistair and his whore with her penlight's concentrated beam. The sight of the pair, frozen into terrified silence by the sight of a tiny handgun, was beyond hilarious. It was hysterical. Leila giggled, feeling the peyote pulsing through her body and vanquishing the pain of the gunshot wound in her thigh. She swung the pistol towards Alistair, then back at his slut, resisting the urge to pull the trigger.

She knew a better spot to kill them, a spot where tons of stone would muffle any screams or gunshots. True, killing both of them at once would be complicated, but she could handle it. The trick would be to find a way to control the pair for the next few minutes.

The Master of Darkness was impatient for his next meal.

Killing was the ultimate rush. Goose bumps popped out on Leila's arms as she recalled Felipe's death. She could pinpoint the exact moment when his soul left his body and she'd inhaled his life force, augmenting her special powers with his strength. Now, she was damned near invincible, but that wasn't enough. Not yet. The last two people on her hit list cowered before her – her own dearly beloved husband, the man who had promised to love, honour and cherish, and then kicked her to the curb like unwanted trash, and his fancy little whore, the slut who had bewitched him with her black magic and sneaky tricks.

The Master of Darkness had promised Leila the gift of immortality if she killed them.

She sniffed the air, enjoying the combination of suppressed rage, fear and hatred. "Place the flashlight on the ground and step away from it."

When Alistair complied, she picked it up and shone the beam into Charley's eyes. "Well, well, bitch," she drawled. "We meet again."

Charley shielded her eyes and squinted into the glare. "Cut the crap, Leila. And get the damned light out of my eyes."

Anger built in Leila's chest, but she held the beam steady. "It's about time you obeyed my summons. I've been calling you here all afternoon."

Charley went rigid and a growl rumbled in her throat. "Don't be ridiculous," she said in a choked voice. But her eyes clearly telegraphed stark understanding of Leila's superiority.

Power pumped through Leila's veins. "You're here, aren't you?" she gloated, savouring the feeling of control unlike anything she'd ever experienced. "I hardly expected Alistair, though, wounds and all. This is even better – two for the price of one."

Alistair took a slow step forward, impotent fury written all over his face. "You can't—"

Leila pointed the handgun at him, cutting him off in mid-sentence. "Stay right where you are, darling. I'm calling the shots today. And thanks for leaving me the pistol yesterday."

He took another step. "You're high on something, aren't you?"

"Step back or I'll shoot your whore." Leila squinted and aimed the handgun square at Charley's stomach. She softened her voice to a conversational caress. "Don't do anything foolish. Did you know a gut shot takes hours to kill its victim?"

"*Shit.*" He gave her a long stormy stare, scowling his frustration, then sighed, defeated. "You'll never get away with this."

"Don't be naive. Of course I will. The Master of Darkness protects me."

Charley spoke up, her voice cold and brittle. "Bullshit! You don't believe that Master of Darkness crap."

Leila gestured with the pistol. "Don't mock matters you can't begin to understand."

"I understand you've lost your grip on reality. You've been hanging out with Felipe too long."

Leila heard the resentment in Charley's voice and laughed. "So, you guessed where I spent my nights."

Alistair interrupted in his usual overbearing manner. "Speaking of Felipe, where is he? My guess is the bastard's hiding out in the tunnels."

Leila shrieked with laughter, thinking about Felipe's body lying crumpled at the bottom of the sinkhole. She pulled herself together. "He's here somewhere. You'll see him soon enough." Another bubble of laughter escaped her lips and she let the weapon drop to her side.

"What do you want from us?" Her ex drew his eyebrows together in a ferocious scowl, no doubt intended to intimidate.

"Truth be told, I would love it if you gave me an excuse to use the pistol, but right now, I prefer to keep both of you alive. I need a couple of hostages." *Until we get to the killing place.*

Charley shrugged away from Alistair's grip and took a step towards Leila. "Man, I thought I had taught you a lesson yesterday."

Leila's tongue flickered around her lips. She pointed the light at Charley.

Molten gold cat's eyes stared back, unblinking, glinting defiance.

Dear God, Charley was starting to shift. Leila hoisted the handgun and aimed at her adversary's chest. "Don't even *think* about it."

Charley started a slow stalk, undoing her belt with fingers that had curved into lethal claws.

An uneasy sensation crawled through Leila, and she backed away. "Stay back."

Charley took another step closer and taunted under her breath, "We both know a small calibre bullet won't stop a charging jaguar."

With an effort of will, Leila forced conviction into her voice and pointed the pistol a couple of inches lower. "I'll put a bullet through your belly."

Always the hero, Alistair started to move forward, but Leila stopped him short by barking out an ultimatum. "One more step and I shoot your whore."

Normally, Leila would have snickered at the way he

froze, rooted to the spot, but she was in no mood for laughter. She needed to find a way to prevent Charley from shifting.

"Go ahead." Charley hissed through lengthening fangs, her thinning lips curled back in a snarl. "Make my day. Even if you manage to hit me, I'll still bring you down and Kincaid will finish the job."

Leila's throat ached. Her dream couldn't end this way. In a burst of inspiration, she swung the pistol around to point the muzzle at Alistair's gut. "Stop, or he dies a slow, painful death."

A flicker of fear crossed the feline features.

Leila cocked the hammer. "Say good-bye."

Charley halted, her entire body quivering. Leila could almost feel her weighing the odds. Seconds ticked by, and, imperceptibly, the whore's features resumed their normal appearance, fangs disappearing, claws retracting.

Leila released the breath she'd been holding. "Wise choice."

Charley fastened her jeans and groped for her belt with fingers that shook as if she was having a seizure. When she spoke, her voice was husky, almost a growl. "Okay, Leila. You win."

Damn, but this was better than sex. They're scared shitless, compliant as robots. Who would have thought the fools could feel so strongly about one another, they'd be willing to sacrifice themselves for a fleeting hormone rush called love? She brandished the pistol, satisfied she had found the perfect formula to control her hostages. "Let's go. We're wasting time."

Alistair's voice tightened. "Why do you need both of us? Wouldn't one be enough?"

She shrugged. "Call it insurance. If one of you misbehaves, then the other dies."

He nodded, trying to placate her, but Leila wasn't fooled. This man was as dangerous as a snake. "Don't do anything to make me angry, Alistair."

"Not bloody likely when you're holding a gun. What do you want from us, anyway?"

"I want to get the hell out of here and I need you to get me some wheels."

Alistair looked desperate. "Sure. Anything. You can take the truck. For God's sake, Leila, have a heart. At least release Charley."

Leila pretended to think, then tossed him a crumb. "Well … if you behave, I'll go you one better. When we get far enough away, I'll release you both. In the morning, you can make it back to safety."

Alistair and Charley exchanged a furtive glance.

Leila could *feel* their frantic hope. What better way to ensure cooperation than to plant a seed of optimism? She needed to keep them docile for a few more minutes, long enough to march them to the chasm, *el hoyo oscuro*, where they would join Felipe at the bottom, far from the prying eyes of the police.

Alistair's throat bobbed as he swallowed. "Aye, you win. We'll help you."

Leila allowed her smile to widen. "We'll go through the tunnels. You didn't know there was another entrance to the cave, did you?"

Alistair raised an eyebrow. "I knew the tunnel must lead somewhere. Locals claim the entire hillside is a labyrinth."

Laughter bubbled in her throat at his look of surprise. "The slut will lead the way, and I won't have to worry about her. If she decides to make a break for it or do anything else that's, um, shifty, she knows I'll shoot you."

"I can't lead the way without a light."

What harm could it do? Leila tossed Charley the penlight and let the laughter consume her. The Master of Darkness had selected her as High Priestess at his altar of death, and she couldn't wait to do his bidding.

The narrow beam of light reflected off the tunnel ceiling in time for Charley to avoid crushing her skull on a jutting rock. Behind her, Kincaid muttered inventive curses under his breath. Goddammit, she had to make her move soon, before it was too late.

Although reluctant to relinquish the perfect opportunity to shift, she struggled to control the transformation, never forgetting Leila had a pistol pointed at Kincaid's back. On the other hand, if they didn't escape soon, she and Kincaid would never see the light of day again.

The tunnel walls pressed in on Charley, suffocating her with their tantalizing familiarity. In a previous lifetime, she had travelled this dark path countless times, a path she preferred to forget.

She was almost relieved when Leila's muffled voice barked out an order. "Stop here, whore, and wait for us."

If she calls me 'whore' one more time, I'll chew off her arm and feed it to her as an appetizer. Nevertheless, Charley halted, plastering her back against the wall. She shone the penlight around her, already knowing what she would see. The tunnel veered to the left, its glassy walls reflecting the beam. The dark abyss she remembered so well sank away on the right.

Kincaid staggered to a halt, his mouth twisted with pain. "How much further is it?"

Leila's teeth flashed in the darkness. "Oh, you've reached the end of the road, darling. Nobody can hear you now."

Charley put her hand on his arm trying to telegraph a message. *Stay calm. Don't provoke her.*

Leila tilted her head. "Alistair, you were inquiring about Felipe."

"Aye. What about him?" Charley couldn't see his expression, but he sounded suspicious.

"You're about to join him."

Kincaid grunted his confusion, but Charley knew what the chilling statement meant. Dread curled like smoke in her stomach. "You killed Felipe and dumped the body in the chasm, didn't you?"

"I think he would appreciate some company, don't you?" Leila's shriek of laughter spiralled up and bounced off the walls.

Silhouetted in the light, a dark form fluttered up from the gaping maw of the sinkhole.

Leila bit off her laughter and backed away slowly. "What was that?" Her voice quavered.

Kincaid dismissed Leila's panic with an airy wave of his hand. "It's only a harmless wee bat. You probably woke it up."

Omigod. The descendants of the ancient bat colony still roosted in the crevasse.

Another bat joined the first, squeaking its apparent displeasure at the intruders.

Leila shrank against the wall, moaning: "Shit. I hate those things."

The bats circled their heads, then flapped away to hunt for bugs, or fruit, or human blood or whatever they ate for dinner. Leila recovered her equanimity enough to push away from the wall and level the pistol at Kincaid's chest.

Charley didn't like the glitter in their captor's eyes. She needed some time to flesh out the plan taking shape in her mind. If she could find a way to stir up the bats, Leila's phobia might kick in long enough to distract her from pulling the trigger. She had to keep Leila talking.

"Where will you go?" Charley asked.

Leila's voice still sounded pretty shaky. "You mean after I kill you?"

Charley felt a quick hitch in her belly, but she managed to keep her voice steady. "Right."

Kincaid released a low growl in the back of his throat and Charley elbowed him sharply in the ribs, hoping he'd get the message and shut up. As long as she kept Leila talking, they were safe.

Leila hefted the gun a little higher. "I'll head across country on foot. I feel quite at home in the jungle these days. But that's not the best part."

Charley nodded politely, drawing her out. "And that would be?"

Leila gestured with the handgun. "Here's the thing. Felipe wired the cave and tunnel with explosives."

Kincaid nudged Charley and hissed: "I knew the bastard was up to something."

Leila ignored the interruption. "When I'm far enough away, I'll use my satellite phone to detonate the explosives." She patted her pocket. "Felipe programmed the numbers on speed dial."

Charley felt Kincaid go rigid, probably more with indignation at the destruction of priceless artefacts than at the thought of their impending deaths. Confirming her suspicions, he blurted: "Jesus Christ, Leila. You wouldn't. You're too good a scientist."

Leila shrugged and a slow, sinister smile twisted her mouth. "Sure, I would. I don't need archaeology any more." She lowered her voice to a confidential whisper. "Yesterday, the Master of Darkness showed me something better."

Yeah, Charley got the picture. A chill of dread shot down her spine. She scanned the ground, looking for a piece of wood, a rock, *anything* to toss into the crevasse to stir up the bats. "You'll never get away with this, Leila," she said.

Leila's teeth glinted in her shadowed face. "Oh, I'll get away with it, all right. The entire mountain will come crashing down, burying your bodies, along with your precious Olmec sarcophagi."

"The police will hunt you down like a rabid dog."

Leila's gurgle of laughter sounded disconcertingly normal. "I doubt it. They'll think I died in the explosion, too."

Time was running out. Charley edged closer to the lip of the crevasse, trying to appear casual. "How deep is this thing, anyway?" she asked, shining the tiny penlight into the darkness, trying to rouse the sleepy bats.

A dry whisper of sound from the depths indicated that the natives were getting restless.

Leila's voice sharpened. "Get the light away from the pit." She waved the pistol, herding them away from the edge. "Move against the wall, both of you. I want to get this over with so I can get the hell out of here."

When neither of them moved, she pointed the handgun at Charley.

Conceding defeat, Kincaid limped backwards and slumped against the wall, but Charley hesitated.

As fast as a cat, Leila darted towards Charley. "I said *move your ass*, whore," she shrieked, and swung the heavy flashlight.

Charley saw the blow coming and twisted away, but not fast enough. The flashlight glanced off her shoulder and she fell to the ground, struggling to catch her breath. Pain radiated from shoulder to fingertips in a fiery burst of exquisite agony, but she had the presence of mind to hang onto the penlight.

"*Move it.*"

Holding Leila's hate-filled gaze, Charley struggled to her knees and flexed her shoulder. It was bruised, but not broken. She had to make her move now or lose the opportunity forever. Gritting her teeth against the pain, she tossed the penlight into the air, praying it would land in the abyss.

While Leila was distracted by the unexpected move, Charley heaved herself upright and ran towards Kincaid.

It was all over in a second. The beam of light arced through the darkness, marking the missile's flight across the tunnel. When the miniature flashlight hit the ceiling, it dropped to the floor with a clink, rolled a few wobbly inches and disappeared over the edge. Metal crunched against rock and ended in the distant tinkle of shattered glass. The faint light from inside the abyss snapped off, leaving the tunnel cloaked in a deep gloom, illuminated only by Leila's flashlight.

The scrunched parchment rustling sound Charley had heard earlier increased in volume. Three heads turned in unison towards the abyss in time to see the first of the bats flit out of the chasm. No doubt, they were properly pissed by the unexpected light interrupting their afternoon slumber, and in no mood to negotiate a truce.

Leila shrieked and backed away, shining the light around the tunnel and illuminating the winged attackers.

A cloud of tiny mammals emerged from the pit, filling the air with a darting, flapping maelstrom of swishing wings and grasping claws. Tiny, high-pitched squeaks mingled with Leila's shrill screams.

Elated by the unqualified success of her scheme, Charley prepared to implement the next phase of her plan. She focused her attention inward, letting go of the pain, determined to find her centre in short order. If ever she needed a jaguar, this was the time.

Before the change began, Kincaid's shouting dislodged Charley from her trance.

"Bloody hell, you wee idiot. Get down on the ground or the bats will be all over you, too."

"Relax."

He made a Scottish sounding oath in the back of his throat and clamped his hand on her arm. God, he was strong.

She tried to dislodge his iron grip, but found herself dragged down and spread eagled on the floor. "Ouch. Dammit Kincaid. You're breaking my good arm."

"Sorry," he said, but he didn't relent. Before Charley knew it, the hard length of his body blanketed every square inch of her frame with smothering efficiency, sending sparks of pain down her arm.

Talk about bad timing. Kincaid's misguided chivalry was spoiling her brilliant plan. How could she concentrate on shifting with a shoulder that hurt like hell and over two hundred pounds of male flesh squeezing the breath out of her?

"Bats have radar," she hissed, trying to squirm away. "They won't hurt me half as much as you are right now. Let me up."

He leaned more heavily. "Don't start in with the arguing again."

Charley gave up struggling and raised her head, bumping his chin in the process. "Sorry," she said, straining to see what was happening through the chaos. From the little she could see, Leila had all but disappeared, lost in the darkness of a thousand whirring wings.

Amidst a series of incoherent screams interspersed with frantic incantations, a shot rang out. The bullet ricocheted off the ceiling, then the floor beside them.

A large hand plastered her head to the ground and held it there. Charley could feel his heart pounding against her back. "Keep down," said Kincaid. "She's shooting the bats," he added, quite unnecessarily in her opinion.

Two more shots caused Charley to cringe.

"We're safe now, I think," Kincaid muttered, raising himself slightly. "She's out of ammunition. A Smith and Wesson only holds five rounds, and you used up two." He tensed and flattened himself again. "Holy crap. I think she's going to pitch the handgun."

A metallic *thunk* followed his warning.

He propped himself up on his elbows again and peered. "All clear," he announced.

Charley sucked in a full breath of air for the first time in several minutes. "Oomph. You're heavy. Get off me. Leila's still more dangerous than you can ever know."

He rolled aside and Charley kneeled, straining to see her enemy through the moving, swirling cloud of bats. Wild power rolled through her body, begging for release, but she fought off the transformation to assess the situation.

The bats dispersed rapidly, probably more interested in their dinner than the strangers invading their turf. Charley got her first clear view of the battle ground littered with the corpses of those unlucky bats that had come too close to Leila. In the centre of the tunnel, one persistent creature still circled Leila's head. Step by step, she backed away, brandishing the heavy flashlight as if it were a club.

"She's forgotten the abyss," Kincaid whispered.

Leila squealed and took another powerful swing at the bat, oblivious to the looming danger behind her. "Die, you bastard," she hissed, her features contorted with terror. She stepped closer to the lip of the sinkhole.

Something inside Charley rebelled and she scrambled to her feet, shouting: "Oh, no you don't, you stupid bitch. Watch out behind you."

Forgetting about the bats, Leila turned to face the new threat.

Charley stalked towards her foe, her breath a sibilant hiss in her ears. "A quick death is too easy for you. I'll see to it you rot behind bars for the rest of your natural life."

Behind her, Charley sensed Kincaid heaving himself to his feet and waved him away impatiently. "Stay back, Kincaid. I want to take care of this myself."

Leila stared at Charley. She took a panicky step backward, but Charley was faster, and whipped out her hand to dig her fingers into the soft flesh of the woman's upper arm.

Leila howled her rage and spat in Charley's face.

Ignoring the foulness oozing down her cheek, Charley let her claws emerge to pierce the surface of her quarry's skin. Proud of her restraint, she used a controlled motion, barely drawing blood.

"You're coming with us."

"Not as long as I have a breath left in my body." Leila drew back and slammed a fist into Charley's bruised shoulder.

A wave of fresh agony arrowed throughout Charley's body. She responded by lengthening her claws, fixing Leila more firmly in her grip. "You'll be sorry you did that," she spat.

Heedless of the deep lacerations, Leila twisted away, snarling an incoherent message of hatred. Her arm dripping dark streams of blood, she cast a triumphant glance over her shoulder, and sprinted along the edge of the chasm towards freedom.

Cursing under her breath, Charley clutched her shoulder, willing her legs to move. Before she could react, Leila skidded on something, probably a dead bat, which had crawled away to die.

A look of utter horror and belated understanding spread over Leila's face as she lost her balance, teetering on the edge. The wavering light threw her once-lovely features into harsh relief as they twisted, broadened and elongated, transforming into a snarling mask of fear. Clothes ripped, revealing patches of black-splotched golden fur, and the hand holding the flashlight sprouted claws. As the creature slipped, it tried to twist its sinuous body in an attempt to regain a foothold and failed. One front paw scrabbled on the lip of the chasm before the nightmare apparition, half human, half animal, disappeared into the depths, carrying with it the only source of light.

A jaguar's roar filled the cave before it died, leaving Charley's ears ringing in the sudden silence. She wished she could feel triumph, but all she felt was emptiness.

The inky darkness was absolute. It pressed down on her eyeballs, a tangible presence.

Charley and Kincaid froze in shock. Only a few faint squeaks and rustles from the remaining bats broke the profound silence.

"Kincaid? Kincaid? This wasn't part of the plan."

They groped for one another in the darkness, and grasping his hand, Charley pulled Kincaid to his feet.

"What happened to Leila?" whispered Kincaid. He sounded shaken.

Charley turned in the direction of his voice. "I'll explain everything once we're out of here."

His voice rose in agitation. "Tell me you saw the jaguar, too. It was the same one—"

She didn't want to get into long-winded explanations now. "I told you, I'll explain later."

"Why do I think this is going to be one helluva story?"

Dammit, but he was persistent. She said the first thing she could think of to settle him down. "Right now, I have to concentrate on getting us out of here."

"How? We can't see a damned thing."

At one time, she could have manoeuvred this tunnel blindfolded. She hoped she had retained the memory. "I know the way back to the cave."

The silence stretched out too long and Charley felt Kincaid's gaze bore into her face. After what seemed like an eternity, he said: "Not possible. You don't know this tunnel any better than I do."

"You are so, so wrong. Let's go."

For once, he didn't give her a hard time.

Chapter 42

Favouring his bad leg and breathing heavily, Kincaid staggered out of the cave and into the sun-drenched warmth of the temple courtyard. His thigh throbbed like a son-of-a-bitch and his shoulder wasn't much better, but he didn't care. He could see the sky and breathe in huge gulps of fresh air.

The sinking feeling in his gut warned him Charley's story would turn his neat, scientific world upside down. Even if he'd hallucinated the jaguar, and he sincerely hoped he had, he couldn't deny that somehow, some way, she had led them safely through the impossible darkness of the tunnel without faltering, seemingly following some mysterious internal compass.

He turned his head and studied her, hoping his apprehension wasn't too obvious. "I think it's time you told me everything. You're hiding something, and I want to be prepared before we notify the police."

She met his gaze. He held his breath, waiting for the smart-mouthed retort he knew was coming. He didn't have long to wait.

"If you'll cast your mind back, Kincaid, I tried to tell you the other night in the kitchen, but you didn't want to listen. If you hadn't been so mule-headed and superior—"

Amusement edged out apprehension, and he made a 'time-out' sign to cut off her tirade. "I'm ready to listen now. My narrow wee mind is as open as it gets, so let's start at the beginning."

She glared, then relented. "Maybe you'd better sit down for this."

He shot her a long look. "Aye, probably," he muttered and limped to the edge of the pyramid where he lowered himself to the top step and stretched out his throbbing leg.

She settled beside him, close, but not touching.

Five months ago," she began, "I started experiencing what the doctors tactfully called 'panic attacks'. The episodes began when I was writing an article about illegal aliens entering the U.S. from Mexico. One of the men I interviewed was from a village near the Olmec centre of La Venta. He was the first to mention the curse of the Olmecs. The next day, I experienced my first full-blown panic attack. Soon, they were occurring twice a week."

His stomach made several somersaults. After a long pause, he said: "I supposed you're going to tell me you believe the attacks were tied to the curse of the Olmecs."

Her reply unsettled him even more. "Yes, I am. I don't believe in coincidences. Anyway, one of the attacks nearly cost me my life along with that of a colleague. I was driving back from an interview with the Mexicans when I freaked out. We'd both have been killed if my passenger hadn't grabbed the wheel."

Kincaid sat up straight, feeling cold all over in spite of the sun's sultry warmth. "I know. I read about it. Then what?"

Her gaze met his. "The shrink diagnosed panic attacks compounded by delusional disorder. The newspaper ordered me to take extended stress leave, so I spent the next couple of months recuperating at a friend's villa in Puerto Escondido. The episodes had nearly disappeared. I thought I was better until I talked to the worker you fired and decided to visit your dig."

"And the attacks returned." It wasn't a question.

She nodded. "Worse than ever. You saw what happened when I touched the colossal head." Her voice shook. "At first, I felt as if the hallucinations were happening to someone else, a person called Zanazca." She paused and looked him straight in the eye, flinging out the challenge he had feared was coming. "Now I know they were my own memories. I was the High Priestess, Zanazca."

Kincaid could tell Charley believed every word of her story. He massaged his forehead, trying to ward off a massive headache, then scrambled to his feet, leaving her sitting on the step looking apprehensive.

Ignoring the shooting pain in his thigh, he paced the

courtyard, limping back and forth several times, trying to collect his thoughts. He needed to keep an open mind, he reminded himself, but *reincarnation*? The possibility of past lives flew in the face of everything he believed in – rational thinking, logical theories, scientific proof. Mysticism did not fit into the nicely organized and intellectual ideology he had clung to all his life. There had to be another rational explanation.

When he had finished pacing, he sat down beside her again and apologized. "Sorry. The idea of reincarnation takes some getting used to. I'm working on it."

"Work harder."

With a little effort, he stretched his lips in a reassuring smile and nodded "Go on. Tell me the rest of the story."

During the half-hour it took her to describe her past life as an Olmec High Priestess, Kincaid felt a muscle in his jaw flicker as he clamped his mouth shut to prevent a series of incredulous interruptions from popping out. He knew he was in danger of losing his eyebrows in his hairline, but he had lost all control over his facial features. When she finished her recital, he was grateful she didn't press him for his reaction. She allowed him to sit in silence and digest her story.

His stomach felt as if he'd swallowed a few cockroach clusters, alive, instead of poached eggs. He groped for words and couldn't find any. Past lives and reincarnation – that sort of mystical nonsense simply didn't happen in real life. There was no scientific justification for any of it. And yet, he reminded himself for the twentieth time, the evidence was indisputable. He'd seen it with his own eyes and he'd stake his reputation on the authenticity of the stone tablets.

Charley directed her gaze towards her hands, clasping and unclasping them in her lap. At last, she looked directly into his eyes, her face troubled. "Don't just sit there like a sphinx, Kincaid. For God's sake, say something."

His brain refused to function properly. "You believe you were this Zanazca woman in a past life," he parroted.

Charley's face paled. "It's not a question of believing. I *know* I was."

He knew he was digging his grave deeper and wider, but he couldn't seem to stop himself. "And you remember uttering the prophecy about the city crumbling and falling, forgotten until you returned to tell the story."

"You make it sound trite and foolish. But, yes, I suppose that's the gist of it." Her voice dripped icicles. "And you may not have noticed, but that's exactly what I'm doing."

His hands were cold and he felt slightly nauseated. "Please be patient. I'm trying to understand, but I'm almost afraid to ask the next question."

When Charley spoke, she sounded defeated, resigned. "Go for it, Kincaid. Don't pull your punches. We might as well get it all out in the open."

"What about the jaguars and Leila? How do they fit into the picture?" He steeled himself for the answer.

"Leila learned how to shapeshift," she said bluntly. "You saw it for yourself in the tunnel."

Kincaid processed this information in silence. He couldn't deny what he had seen, but he still wasn't ready to admit it. The silence stretched out until Charley finally said: "If you don't say something, Kincaid, I'm going to have to break something hard and heavy over your thick skull."

"Do you have anything a wee bit more concrete to substantiate this ... er, assumption that Leila could shapeshift?"

"Other than being an eye witness? Yes, I do." Charley's blue gaze was defiant and she held her ground. "You know the jaguar last night? The one attacking you in the cave? Well, that was Leila, too. I saw her revert to human form when she was running away."

He processed this information, liking the implications less and less. "But how did she learn?" The question was purely rhetorical. Kincaid already knew what her answer would be.

"Felipe taught her."

"And how did you come to this conclusion?"

Kincaid watched in fascination as her hands curled into fists, but amazingly, her voice showed no signs of her inner agitation. "I'm a writer. I track down the truth. As I told you earlier in the week, Leila was out of the tent every night until dawn, and she admitted today she was with Felipe. She was his acolyte. I think she transformed into the snake that attacked me, then graduated to the jaguar."

"It's a long leap from spending time together to shapeshifting."

"Felipe believed that he was a descendant of the Olmecs, didn't he?"

"True enough," he admitted.

"Then is it such a stretch to think he might have inherited some of their powers?" That he might want to train a gifted acolyte? Leila was Mexican. She could have had traces of Olmec blood in her veins as well."

Kincaid tried to hide his scepticism. "Okay, so for argument's sake, let's say Felipe taught Leila to shapeshift and she turned on him." He paused, formulating his next question. "Then who leaped onto the scene as the second jaguar to prevent jaguar number one from making a meal of me?"

She simply looked at him and he saw the truth in her eyes.

Every fibre in his body tightened and he drew away. "Oh, no, Charley. That's too much to swallow. You're not trying to tell me *you* shapeshifted into a jaguar as well."

He watched her throat move as she swallowed. "You asked me if I was naked in the cave. The answer is yes. When the change started, I had to get rid of my clothes."

His light, invalid-friendly breakfast threatened to make a quick reappearance. "It's not possible. No one can actually shapeshift. Not for real."

"The Olmecs could."

"You're not an Olmec," he pointed out in his most reasonable tone.

Her voice sharpened. "Haven't you been listening to anything I said? I've been trying to explain. I used to be an Olmec high priestess. Once, long ago, I knew how to shapeshift. In the cave, when there was no other way of stopping Leila from killing you, something deep inside of me remembered how to do it. I felt my body change. Even if I'd wanted to, I couldn't have prevented it. When I looked down, I found I had shifted into a jaguar, and I damn near did it again today. The only thing stopping me was the sight of Leila's pistol pointed at your stomach."

His mouth dropped and he simply gawked at her. He knew he must look foolish, but he was too startled to move.

"Don't look at me like that, Kincaid. I'm perfectly sane. There are names for this kind of phenomenon. In Leila and Felipe's cases, it's called 'cellular memory', where every cell of the body retains ancestral information from our genetic heritage. In my case, it's called 'karmic memory'. Every cell of my body contains memories of my past life as an Olmec priestess."

At last, Kincaid's voice sparked to life again. "Sweet Jesus, you've got to be kidding!" he blurted, then wished he could retract his answer. "Sorry. Brain not engaged. Let me try again."

With a sinking heart, he watched her eyes narrow to a dangerous blue glint and felt her body stiffen before she shifted away. Her voice crackled with frost. "Please do."

Oh, crap. He had to make things right, but his easy gift of the gab had deserted him, just when he needed it most. Charley's story made no sense whatsoever. It flew in the face of all rational thinking, but he sensed that unless he could reassure her he believed every word, she would slip through his fingers. The least he could do was to grant her the courtesy of conducting a thorough assessment of the situation. Thinking was what he did best.

"Give me a few minutes to process this, ah, new information."

Out of the corner of his eye, he caught her staring anxiously, but he turned his attention inward in order to focus on his analysis.

Minutes ticked by. Still nothing made sense. Sweat dribbled down his back at the thought of a life without Charley. In that moment of desperation, the admonition of his favourite professor returned. "*Always keep an open mind, lad. There are more things in Heaven and Earth than are dreamt of in your philosophy.*"

Figuring he had nothing to lose, Kincaid suspended, just for a wee moment, his disbelief in reincarnation. Damn, he must love Charley a lot if he was willing to entertain the notion of past lives. Like a giant puzzle, the pieces meshed, one inescapable conclusion leading to another. Charged with crackling energy, he ticked off each fact mentally, and every one of them fit. All his doubts and reservations fell away to be replaced with unshakeable certainty.

He opened his mouth to share his findings, but Charley beat him to the punch. She smiled brightly and said in a brittle voice: "It's okay, Kincaid. I know how I must sound. I'm sure you must believe—"

He placed his finger on her lips, silencing her voice. How he had been such a blind, narrow-minded fool? "I'll be the one to tell you what I believe."

Her gaze dropped. "Sorry."

"Let me summarize. Centuries ago, a psychopath called Zanazca started, for lack of a better word, a chain of evil by killing her master, her lover and God knows who else, all in the name of power. We also know her acolyte followed her example. My best guess is the killing continued until the present day, ending with Leila and Felipe. I'll bet if we dug hard enough, we'd discover Felipe had murdered his own mentor."

Her mouth opened and closed, but, remarkably, no sound emerged.

"No need to look so surprised. Once I accepted the theory of reincarnation as a valid premise, everything else fell into place. I can now formulate a hypothesis based on sound logic and reasoning."

She stared at him as if he'd lost his mind. "You can?"

Oh, hell. She didn't look convinced of his sincerity. He had to make her understand.

"Aye. For example, I can rationalize your uncanny knowledge of the tunnel today, even though you had no more memory of it than I did, based on present day experiences."

"Karmic memory. Makes sense."

That was better. He was making headway. Logic always worked. He continued: "I can even tie my postulation to the last part of the prophecy, you know, the bit about breaking the chain of evil and redeeming your soul. That's what today was all about."

She shook her head. "I must be missing something."

"Zanazca forged the first link in the chain by killing her master." The more he talked, the more his excitement grew.

"Listen. This is incredible. Only a reincarnation of the high priestess herself would be powerful enough to halt the carnage." He gripped her hand. "You broke the chain today, Charley."

"How do you figure that?"

"You woke the bats, triggering a chain of events that resulted in Leila's death. She was the last of the links. Without a successor, the chain is broken." He let his words sink in.

"And you believe I've paid off my karmic debt?"

He nodded. "Paid it off with interest." Her lower lip quivered.

Crap. She was going to cry. His stomach lurched. He would never understand women. What had he said to cause the waterworks? He truly thought he'd explained his position clearly, but somewhere, somehow, he must have missed the boat.

"What's wrong?" he asked. "Did I say anything offensive?"

Bluebell eyes brimming, she sniffled a little. "Yes. No. All along, I've been so afraid I might repeat Zanazca's mistakes, and when you called me – I mean her – a psychopath, I thought you probably...."

Bloody hell. He'd screwed up royally. Kincaid wrinkled his brow, trying to choose the words to rectify his mistake. "Don't you see? You're not anything like Zanazca. You got it right this time around. You even tried to save Leila."

"Then why are you frowning?"

He swallowed and tightened his grip on her hand, needing the reassurance that she couldn't bolt. "I'm trying to figure out how to tell a high priestess and jaguar-woman that I'm desperately in love with her."

Charley stared at Kincaid, scarcely believing her ears, then glanced away, overwhelmed by the emotions tumbling around in her chest. The incredible view in front the pyramid wavered and swam. She blinked back the ridiculous tears that prickled her eyelids as the ice surrounding her heart started to melt.

He pressed his lips to her unresisting hand, leaving behind a trail of heat. "*Mhuirnín*, I want you more than life itself."

She had dreamed he would say these words to her, but had never thought she would live to hear them. She opened and closed her mouth, unable to speak. Only a thin, almost inaudible squeak emerged.

He gave her a long, hard look, undoubtedly interpreting her silence as disbelief. "I won't let you leave tomorrow."

She gave an exaggerated sigh. "Still giving orders, I see."

He gave her a look of incredulity. "For God's sake, Charley, I'm being serious. I've never felt so miserable in my entire thirty-six years. I can't think of anything except you. I can't concentrate. I can't sleep." He must have noticed her look of scepticism because he amended hastily: "Well, okay, I can sleep, but only because of those pills you and Colin have been forcing down my throat, but the rest of it's true. I've been tearing my hair out at the thought of your leaving tomorrow." He bent his head and parted his hair with both hands to display the crown of his head. "See? I think I must have created a wee bald patch."

Charley searched those dark eyes, brimming with love and hope. "Still looks like a full head of hair any man would envy."

In the characteristic gesture that betrayed his discomfort, Kincaid raked his fingers through his hair, leaving it mussed. "If this is what love feels like, then I'm head over heels in love with you."

Her heart pumped a little harder. "How long have you known how you felt?"

His lips twitched and Charley knew he was trying to suppress a laugh. He gave up the pretence and grinned. "I think I was a goner when I first saw you flopped across the path, waving your legs in the air and making wisecracks to divert my attention from your camera."

When she spoke, her voice shook a little. "Are you trying to tell me what we have is more than just a quick fling for you?"

"Aye. Much more. Commitment and white picket fences

are suddenly looking like the best thing in the world." His voice dropped to a whisper as he touched her hair, then her face and neck. "I don't know what I'll do if you run away. Say you'll stay here. I can't face the thought of losing the best thing that's ever happened to me."

Charley felt the last barrier tumble away. She threw her head back and pealed out a laugh, causing several students to turn their heads.

"I'll assume that's a 'yes'."

She reached up and smoothed down a tuft of hair. "Yes. Yes. I'll stay. I want to spend the rest of my life showing you how much I love you."

He pulled her to her feet and swung her around in his arms, his eyes soft with love. "If that was a marriage proposal, Horrie and I accept."

Charley blinked. "It was? You do?" She was silent for a moment, breathing in the distinctive, mouth-watering scent of him. Sliding her body against his, she twined her arms around his neck and said: "Okay then, everything is settled. My mother will be so pleased."

He brushed the hair back from her face. "I just have one question."

Alerted by his tone, she sniffed suspiciously. "What's that?"

"What about our children?" he inquired casually.

Her voice was cautious. "What about them?"

"Aye, weel." He cleared his throat delicately. "Do you think they will have black, silky fur, just like their mother?"

Charley stared at him for a heartbeat, uncomprehending, then started to giggle, harder and harder, unable to stop. "No, silly," she gasped between snorts, "I don't think karmic memory is inherited."

"That's a relief. Now it's my turn to ask. How long have you known?"

"I think I fell in love when I was lying on the path at your feet, drooling up at you, fantasizing about ripping off your clothes, and you started feeling up my leg, pretending you were checking for broken bones."

She felt the rumble of laughter against her chest before he said: "And there I was, thinking I was being ever-so-subtle.

You might have had the decency to let me know how you felt a lot sooner."

His hands were on her then, warming her skin, gathering her close, demanding everything. Heat pulsed between them. All conscious thought disappeared and sensual power rippled through her body. She sighed once and gave herself up to the kiss that swept away every vestige of doubt and fear.

About the Author:

Born in Scotland, Maureen immigrated to Canada at the age of seven. A University of Toronto graduate, she convinced the federal government to hire a Fine Arts specialist as a computer programmer. Three years later, Maureen graduated again, this time to full-time homemaker and mom, raising two wonderful sons. Plunging back into the business world, she and her second husband started a management consulting company. This marriage survived because she and her husband pledged never to work on the same project again. Ever.

After a century in the consulting world, Maureen grew weary of wearing snappy power suits, squeezing into panty hose, and fighting rush hour traffic. She made a life-changing decision. She wanted to write books. Not dry, boring, technical treatises, but fresh, funny romantic suspense novels.

Between exotic trips, Maureen and her husband live in Ottawa where she volunteers for an addiction family program, plays bridge, and slaves over her computer to improve her writing skills.

Other titles being released

I WILL RISE (written by Michael Louis Calvillo)

THE HUMAN VIRUS MUST BE DESTROYED!

I WILL RISE is an apocalyptic love story about faithlessness in humanity, personal insecurity and destructive choice in a world where symmetry rules and contentment within one's own skin is nearly impossible. Funky, grotesque and ferocious, I Will Rise is a rollercoaster ride of literary horror that will infiltrate your senses and alter your perceptions forever.

IN TWENTY-FOUR HOURS ...

Upon death, a bitter, societal outcast named Charles is given the ability to annihilate the human race. Risen and relishing the opportunity to make the world suffer, he embraces his bloody destiny, but as his killing touch spreads death and destruction, his new status affords unexpected human interaction. Second thoughts surmount as he falls for Annabelle, a fiery redhead tasked with guiding Charles and orchestrating mayhem. As feelings deepen, Charles wonders: Has he been excluded by society or is his lonely existence a product of his own narrow ignorance? As realization flowers and regrets begin to surface a choice must be made between the legion of the dead and the pleas of the living.

... EVERYONE YOU KNOW WILL BE DEAD.

Does all of humanity really deserve to perish at his hands? Is it too late for Charles to defy death, escape meat cleaver wielding pro-human maniacs, prevent zombie hordes from rising and stop the cataclysmic forces raging inside his body? Is it too late to discover purpose and rejoin the ranks of the living? Unfortunately, Charles is already dead. Unfortunately, even if Charles could find a way to throw his deathly state in to reverse, Annabelle isn't having it. Driven by anti-human rhetoric, red herrings and forces unbeknownst to Charles, she wants to see the world suffer and die so badly her insides jitterbug madly when she envisions the infinite end.

Echoes of Terror (an anthology by well renown, award-winning authors)

Terror on its own can send chills up your spine, make your heart race uncontrollably, chill your blood, and turn your mind insane. But when it turns into Echoes of Terror ... BEWARE! The ricocheting effects are DEADLY!

Out of Darkness (written by Vanessa deHart)

On a darkened street in the Old Quebec City quarter, a car swerves, cutting Genny Lynn down. The driver momentarily stops to enjoy his handiwork then drives off leaving her for dead. Lost in the darkness of her mind, Genny Lynn wakes, her disoriented gaze capturing that of a handsome stranger staring ominously at her from the foot of a hospital bed.

For three years, Luc Savard has fought his wife's terror tactics – wrestling for control of his family's fortune. He has longed for freedom from her evil presence. Until now.

Could a cease-fire be possible, when she looks at him with such vulnerable and seemingly innocent eyes and asks: "Who am I?" Would he dare risk his fortune, and his heart, on the off-chance that this lighter and whimsical version of his wife would stay? Could love shed light on the truth and drive out the darkness that has shadowed their marriage for so long?

Printed in the United States
71926LV00001B/76-123